A HARLOT AT THE HIGHLAND COURT

CELESTE BARCLAY

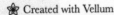 Created with Vellum

When one door closes, another will open. Sometimes you find a hidden blessing when you're closest to despair.

Happy reading, y'all,
Celeste

SUBSCRIBE TO CELESTE'S NEWSLETTER

Subscribe to Celeste's bimonthly newsletter to receive exclusive insider perks.

Have you read *Leif, Viking Glory Book One*? This **FREE** first in series is available to all new subscribers to Celeste's monthly newsletter. Subscribe on her website.
Subscribe Now

Have you chatted with Celeste's hunky heroes? Are you new to Celeste's books or want insider exclusives before anyone else? Subscribe for free to chat with the men of Celeste's *The Highland Ladies* series.
Chat Now

THE HIGHLAND LADIES

A Spinster at the Highland Court
A Spy at the Highland Court
A Wallflower at the Highland Court
A Rogue at the Highland Court
A Rake at the Highland Court
An Enemy at the Highland Court
A Saint at the Highland Court
A Beauty at the Highland Court
A Sinner at the Highland Court
A Hellion at the Highland Court
An Angel at the Highland Court
A Harlot at the Highland Court
A Friend at the Highland Court
An Outsider at the Highland Court
A Devil at the Highland Court

PROLOGUE

Emelie Dunbar glanced over her shoulder as she closed her chamber door behind her; her sister Blythe's light snores were trapped within as Emelie scanned either side of the passageway. With no one in sight and nothing stirring, Emelie gathered her skirts in both hands to ensure she made no sound as she picked her way down the corridor. She wound her way through the dark passageways of Stirling Castle, familiar with nearly every nook and cranny after almost seven years in service as a lady-in-waiting to Queen Elizabeth de Burgh.

Emelie shivered as she entered the northern wing of the stone castle. Despite the warm summer air during the day, the nights grew chilly, and the northern castle bricks never insulated the passageways well. She pulled her cloak's cowl higher around her neck and adjusted her hood, both to keep herself warm and to maintain her disguise. It didn't take her long to reach the chamber she sought. She rapped softly on the door and counted to ten before pressing down on the handle. The staff kept the door's hinges well oiled, so they didn't make a sound as Emelie slipped inside the solar.

It only took a moment for Emelie to spot the

ghostly outline standing just beyond the low-burning fire's glow. She turned the key in the lock behind her and dashed across the chamber, pushing her hood back as she went. Long arms wound around her waist and pulled her in for a passionate embrace, the kiss stealing her breath away.

"Henry," Emelie murmured.

"I began to fear you'd changed your mind again," Henry Pringle whispered, the note of censure seeming loud in the quiet chamber. Emelie tensed before easing away from the Clan Pringle heir.

"I didn't change my mind. I was using an abundance of caution since we've come so close to being caught twice already. Until you hear from Father, you know we must be careful. *You've* warned me to be careful," Emelie reminded him.

"I've just missed you so. It's my impatience. Forgive me, dove?" Henry offered her a repentant smile that made her own lips twitch. The man standing before her was dashing and charismatic. While he wasn't as tall or broad as the Highlanders many of her friends had married, he *was* handsome. Blond, wavy hair fell to his shoulders in a way Emelie always suspected was far from as natural as he meant it to look. Light brown eyes twinkled at her. Always dressed fashionably, Henry had drawn Emelie's attention the first time she saw him arrive at court nearly six months earlier.

"I missed you, too. This trip seemed particularly long. I wondered if you were ever coming back," Emelie pouted coyly.

"How could I stay away?" Henry winked. But Emelie's mind rebelled at the question. It sounded too smug, and they both knew Henry had to return to the royal court, not to see her, but as his father's delegate. She couldn't pinpoint why his tone rankled,

2

as though he were giving her a subtle reminder that he would attend court regardless of whether she was there. Sensing her shift in emotions, Henry pulled her in for another passionate kiss. "Come now, dove. I told you I missed you. We haven't much time. Let me show you just how happy I am to return."

Without hesitation, Henry's hands roamed over Emelie's body, already familiar with each dip and peak. His left hand slid to her breast, cupping and kneading it before his fingers slipped beneath her neckline. His right arm pinned her against him. His lips blazed along her neck until he reached her earlobe, which he nipped. Emelie turned her head toward him, her mouth seeking his. Henry backed her toward the wall and pressed her against it. As Emelie's fingers tangled in his hair, she felt a breeze around her legs. Moving with more speed than she anticipated, Emelie found her skirts around her waist just as Henry lifted her from her feet as though she were a doll. Their bodies joined before Emelie had a moment to consider what was happening. She glanced down between them as Henry drove into her. She hadn't felt him untie the laces to his breeks, so she realized Henry had prepared for this well before she entered the chamber.

"Henry," Emelie hissed.

"I know. It feels so blessedly good."

"No. Yes. I mean, it does. So good. But we agreed. We shouldn't have the first time. We can't. Put me down. This is wrong." Emelie gripped his shoulders as temptation and sensation threatened to overcome her common sense. Again. She moaned with each surge as she clung to him.

"Do you really wish me to stop, Emelie? Or do you wish to moan and scratch my back like you did the last time?" Henry taunted as he thrust over and over.

3

"You must pull out," Emelie insisted, but as she spoke, Henry's hands gripped her hips as he plunged into her once more and stilled. She felt him twitch within her and knew her request came too late. Or rather, Henry came far too soon. His body collapsed against hers, and he lowered his head to her shoulder as he panted. Unsure of what to do and unable to move, Emelie looked around the room as she stroked the back of his head. She was left unsatisfied—again —and fearful. They'd coupled once before, and while she expected they would do so again many times throughout their marriage, she'd been unprepared to do so again so soon. No priest had even read the banns.

"Emelie, you make me lose control. You feel divine; I can't help myself," Henry mumbled before pulling free and lowering her to the floor.

"But we agreed we would wait until you heard from my father, and the banns were at least posted."

"I had to have you. I couldn't stop myself," Henry protested. He appeared so contrite that Emelie forgave him.

"I can't say that I didn't want to do the same thing," Emelie confessed. "I hope Father responds soon, so we can inform the king."

Henry appeared distracted as he nodded. Emelie's stomach knotted as she cupped Henry's jaw. She pressed until he met her gaze. Her stomach cramped painfully. "You have written to my father, haven't you?"

"I had to rush home so suddenly that I haven't had the chance. But I will do so now that I've returned."

"But it could be nearly a moon before we have a response. Then another three sennights until a priest can wed us, assuming the king agrees and informs the church immediately."

"All will be fine, my dove. Worry not."

"But—"

"Emelie," Henry barked. "I said not to worry."

Emelie blinked thrice before nodding her head, surprised at Henry's tone. She attributed it to his fatigue and whatever caused his unexpected return home. She stretched onto her toes and kissed him. He responded immediately, his tongue diving into her mouth. He moved to pull her skirts up again, but Emelie pushed him away and stepped out of his reach.

"You know I want to. There is so much you've promised to teach me. But we can't be so reckless, my love." Emelie watched Henry flinch at the endearment. She'd tried it twice before and gotten the same reaction. While Henry promised his adoration and devotion, the speaking of the word "love" always made him withdraw. She reasoned he was a man and not given to saying aloud such a deep emotion.

"I must leave again tomorrow."

"What?" Emelie spluttered. "You just returned."

"I know, my dove. But my father needs me to return. I am his tánaiste, after all, and I've spent a great deal of time here of late. I may be his trusted representative, but I have duties there."

"But how will you court me if you're all the way at Hoppringle?" Emelie demanded. Her tone brought a glare to Henry's face, and she had a moment of trepidation.

"The same way I have for the past moon."

"But I didn't hear from you at all during that time," Emelie countered.

"But I returned, didn't I? I'm here with you, aren't I?"

"Aye, but—"

"Enough." The finality in Henry's tone warned

her not to press any further. She nodded as she adjusted her gown and pulled up her hood.

"I should return before Blythe wakes and finds me gone. Will you please write to me when you hear from my father? Will we marry here or at Hoppringle?"

"I don't know yet. And yes, I'll let you know." Henry's tone softened as he pulled her back into a gentle embrace. Emelie relaxed against him, the man she was familiar with having returned. She rested her head against his chest and sighed. Henry kissed her on the head before tipping her head back and brushing a kiss on her lips. "Hurry now before your sister discovers you're gone. I will miss you once more, my little dove."

Emelie nodded as she pressed a last kiss to Henry's cheek before she hurried to the door. She looked back to find Henry adjusting himself and pulling the laces to his breeks tied. She grinned as her eyes darted to the wall where they'd just coupled. She was looking forward to being a wife.

ONE

One Moon Later

Emelie swallowed the bile in the back of her throat as her stomach churned once again. The smell of incense made her want to heave as she kneeled beside Blythe during morning Mass. The aroma had never bothered her until a sennight ago. Now every scent seemed to send her belly into turmoil. She glanced sideways at Blythe, who watched her closely. Emelie offered her younger sister a wan smile before bowing her head once more.

Emelie had felt ill mostly in the mornings, but for the past two days, she'd barely been able to look at food without wanting to run from the Great Hall. The nausea persisted, hour after hour, until she was fairly certain of her malady. As she kneeled before the holy crucifix suspended above the altar, she prayed her suspicions were wrong. She prayed she hadn't made the gravest error a young, unmarried woman could make. She made her last sign of the cross and mumbled "Amen" as the service ended.

"Emelie?" Blythe whispered.

"Aye. I don't know why the incense burns my nose and eyes these days. I seem to be developing an

7

aversion to it." Emelie hoped her preemptive explanation would placate her sister. Blythe said nothing more, but Emelie knew her sister as well as she knew herself. They were barely a year apart in age, so Emelie had no memory of a time without Blythe. While they were several years younger than their older sister, Isabella, they were practically twins. Their white-blonde hair and blue hazel eyes were mirror images. Their hair was only faintly darker than Isabella's. The only way many people could tell Emelie and Blythe apart from a distance was Emelie's petite stature. She was so short that many confused her for a child until they saw her face.

Emelie breathed deeply as they left the castle's chapel and progressed along with the other ladies-in-waiting to the Great Hall. Emelie forced herself to choke down the morning meal, feeling somewhat better once her stomach was full. She wanted nothing more than to climb back into bed, exhaustion nipping at her in alternating waves with the nausea.

"You really don't look well," Blythe whispered, trying once more to gain her sister's attention. "Should I summon the healer?"

"No. I feel a little poorly, but I don't think there's much to do aboot it. It will pass as easily as it came." Emelie assumed she was telling the truth.

"Perhaps you should retire. I will make your excuses. I'll say your courses have come," Blythe offered.

If only they would. Then I wouldn't be in this mess. "I would appreciate that. I'm certain more rest is all I need." Emelie squeezed her sister's hand before slipping off their bench and turning to look at the queen, who sat beside King Robert the Bruce on the dais. Emelie wound her way through the crowd of people leaving after breaking their fast. She hurried

8

to her chamber, where she waited half an hour to ensure no one came to check on her. She donned her cloak and hurried away from the keep and into town.

Keeping her head down, Emelie made her way to an apothecary she'd long ago heard of. The midwife there kept secrets and had assisted more than one woman from court who discovered herself with child. Attempting to draw as little attention as she could, she entered the small structure and passed her gaze over the array of bottles and powders. The midwife's husband ran the apothecary, which was most convenient. Emelie spotted a woman she guessed was the midwife, but she was already talking to someone.

Emelie peered at the woman and twirled on her heel. The last thing she needed was Margaret Hay recognizing her. While neither would ever mention finding the other visiting a midwife, Emelie didn't need Margaret knowing her secret. Margaret told her sister, Sarah Anne, everything; and in turn, Sarah Anne was merciless to the other ladies-in-waiting. There had been no courtier as vindictive as Sarah Anne since her distant cousin Mary Kerr set her sights on fellow lady-in-waiting Deirdre Fraser, who was now a Sinclair. Even Madeline MacLeod had seemed mild-mannered compared to Sarah Anne. When Emelie heard the door shut behind Margaret, she peeked over her shoulder at the woman who approached.

"Good morn, my lady," the midwife greeted her. "What are you in need of today?"

"Good morn, Goody Thomas," Emelie nodded with deference. "I am in need—I need—could you—"

"Ah. Come with me." Goodwife Thomas motioned toward a staircase tucked away in the corner. She led Emelie in silence to a chamber and pointed toward a freshly made bed. Emelie looked around before approaching it. She stared at the furniture before taking a deep and fortifying breath. She toed off her slippers and reclined. Without speaking, the midwife eased Emelie's skirts above her waist. She was efficient and gentle, setting Emelie at ease. The middle-aged woman palpated Emelie's abdomen with her lips pressed into a thin line. "How far along do you think you are?"

"A moon or two," Emelie murmured. She hadn't had her courses since before Henry's first departure from court, but she'd been due for them just after his return. She couldn't know whether their first or second interlude resulted in pregnancy.

"I would have you use the chamber pot," Goodwife Thomas stated. Emelie rose and made her way to it. There was no screen for her to step behind, but she figured any modesty dissolved the moment the midwife raised her skirts. When she finished—her cheeks heated to a cherry red—she stepped away and watched the woman pour the chamber pot's contents into a bowl of wine. The midwife swirled the bowl and waited. Emelie fought not to fidget. "It's so early that I cannot be completely certain, my lady. There is one other test that has been definitive since ancient times."

Goodwife Thomas beckoned Emelie to follow her. As they left the chamber, Emelie glanced back, unsettled by how quickly the examination ended. She took the stairs back to the ground floor, moving just behind the midwife until the older woman stopped at a counter. She picked up a cluster of wheat and a cluster of barley. Emelie's brow furrowed as she took what the midwife offered.

"If you can go again now, then I would have you do so over these. I can keep them for a few days, then you can return, or you can take them with you. If you can't go now, then take them back to the castle."

"And do what with them?" Emelie wondered.

"The ancients believed if a woman's pish made the wheat bloom, she was having a son. If the barley blooms, she's having a lass. Either way, if one blooms, you ken you're with child."

Emelie stared down at the plants in her hands and nodded mutely. Her mind seemed to both race and be blank at the same time. She couldn't pull forth a coherent thought. She already suspected she was with child, and she'd come to the midwife hoping for a conclusive answer. But holding the barley and wheat, knowing she either needed to return or watch for blooms while in her chamber, she feared she would be ill all over the woman's clean floors.

"If you are, my lady, there are options," Goodwife Thomas's kind voice was soft and lilting. Emelie still couldn't speak, so she nodded once more. She closed her eyes against the tears that threatened to fall. She wished she'd thought of those options before she coupled with Henry either time. But both occasions had happened so spontaneously that she hadn't prepared. Though, as she considered their last tryst at the castle, she knew she should have expected Henry to act as he did. He'd cajoled her many times before until she relented one night. And upon his last return, he'd clearly already decided, since he'd untied his breeks before Emelie arrived. She should have known he would assume they would couple again once they'd done it the first time. "Were you forced?"

Emelie's head jerked up. "No. Not at all. I can't claim that as an excuse. I was just wretchedly foolish." Emelie closed her eyes and shuddered as Goodwife Thomas laid a gentle hand on her arm.

"Do you wish me to keep these until you can come back to learn of the results? You could decide then what you will do."

"I don't know how easily I can slip away again." Emelie worried her bottom lip, knowing she took an extreme risk leaving the keep without guards, telling no one where she went, and with no one discovering her whereabouts. She reached into her pocket for her coins, and her voice was a hoarse whisper. "Thank you."

"Nay, my lady. You know you've erred. You're not here because of recklessness or convenience. I think you will have much to consider soon. All I ask for is you return if you need me."

What could it be if not recklessness? It was the very definition of recklessness, and now it has likely come home to roost.

"Thank you, Goody Thomas. I won't forget your kindness." Emelie forced a smile. She tucked the wheat and barley into the folds of her cloak before ducking out of the shop. She hurried back to her chamber, grateful that it was still empty. The Mistress of the Bedchamber didn't always allow sisters to share chambers, but Emelie and Blythe had been one of the fortunate pairs. While Emelie wasn't ready to confess, not even to Blythe, it didn't terrify her if Blythe discovered her secret.

Emelie poured a mug of fresh water and gulped it down before pacing the chamber, hoping movement would hurry the water's descent. When she was certain she could use the harvested plants, she laid them over the chamber pot and closed her eyes. When she finished, she stared at the plants, wondering how long it would take. She hadn't thought to ask where she should store them. She prayed wrapping them in a drying linen and keeping them in her chest would be fine. She tucked them away before climbing into bed. Her tears soaked her pillow.

TWO

Emelie's hands shook as she read the missive for at least the seventh time. Her legs gave out as she approached the bench tucked away in the royal garden. She missed her target and landed hard on the ground without caring. She stared into space, seeing nothing but the words in her father's missive in her mind's eye.

Daughter,

I have received no missive from Henry Pringle asking for your hand in marriage or otherwise. I could not, since the man married more than a moon ago. He wed Laird Kenneth Elliot's third daughter. You may recall Alice is your former peer's sister. Of course, Allyson is no longer an Elliot, but now a Gordon.

I do not know why you would think to ask on Pringle's behalf, but it is obvious that I cannot grant you permission to marry a man already married. If you are so eager to wed, I will make arrangements. You are of an age. I shall look into matches for you and your sister. But your mother and I had hoped you and Blythe would find husbands much as Isabella did. We wish you and Blythe the same happiness that Isabella found with Dedric.

I will send word when I've secured a betrothal.

Faithfully,

Father

Emelie couldn't cease shaking. She didn't sob; she didn't even cry. She merely trembled to the point where she knew she must appear like she convulsed. Her heart hurt to such an extreme that she wished it would stop beating. Her ears rang as she heard her father's voice reading the missive to her once more. As the words faded from her mind, her mother's devastated face replaced the image of the missive. It was her mother who she saw sobbing, not herself. She was entirely numb.

Just that morning, she'd checked the wheat and barley once again. It had been three days since she visited the apothecary and the midwife gave her the harvested plants. She'd managed not to look for two days, but her fear and anticipation demanded she check that morning. The wheat had clear blooms while there was no change in the barley. She'd pretended to pull a pair of stockings from her chest while their maid helped Blythe with her hair. She'd nearly dropped the lid. Through shallow breaths that made her lightheaded, she prepared for Mass and even endured the service. She'd been on her way to the Great Hall when a page sought her.

The young boy handed her a folded sheaf of parchment, and she immediately recognized her father's insignia in the wax. Blythe knew Emelie believed she would marry Henry Pringle. That wasn't a secret, since many had witnessed him pay court. She'd even confided in her sister that she'd written to their father to learn why she hadn't received his approval. As she sat on the damp grass, she now knew why.

Dominic Campbell watched the young woman wander into the garden. She appeared distracted; upon first glance, he'd thought she was a lost child.

He'd followed, thinking she had become separated from her parents. But he caught sight of the parchment dangling from her fingers. When he noticed her gown, there was no longer any doubt of her position. The ornate stitching and lavish material signified she was a lady-in-waiting. When Dominic watched the woman miss the bench entirely and land ungracefully on the ground, he rushed to her. Even from his distance he could see that she shook. The parchment drifted to the ground, but she didn't appear to notice.

"My lady?" Dominic said as he neared. It surprised him when she didn't turn toward his voice. She didn't appear to even register his presence. He tried again. "My lady."

Emelie heard a fuzzy noise beside her, and part of her mind recognized it as a man's voice. But she couldn't collect herself enough to look toward its owner. It wasn't until an enormous hand gripped her elbow that she looked toward the towering Highlander. He pulled upward with caution, but she didn't budge.

"My lady, should I fetch someone? Are you unwell?" Dominic didn't know what to do. The young lady didn't respond to his words, nor had she accepted his help. He didn't want to manhandle a stranger, but he knew he couldn't leave her on the ground. He wasn't certain he could even leave her side. He glanced at the missive that now laid beside her. He caught the words "daughter" and "father" before he flipped it over, recognizing the Dunbar crest. Dominic looked at the woman once more. She was ghostly pale and still trembling. Resolved to seat her on the bench, he prayed she wouldn't fall off.

Dominic looked around to ensure no one watched them. When he was assured that they were alone in the garden, he wrapped his hands around her waist. While he'd noticed her diminutive height, she didn't feel as fragile as he expected. He lifted her onto the bench and sat down beside her. She turned unseeing eyes toward him and wilted against his shoulder. Unsure what to do, he wrapped his arm around the strange woman's shoulders. He heard her inhale—or sniff—before she curled into him and burst into tears. Sobs wracked her body as her tears dampened Dominic's doublet. Baffled but sympathetic, he tightened his hold on her. She burrowed closer, as though he could somehow solve her unknown crisis.

"My lady, what can I do to help you? Can you tell me what's wrong?" Dominic tried again. She shook her head as she continued to cry, but the sobs subsided. It was just a steady onslaught of tears. The longer he held her, the more she calmed. Absentmindedly, he stroked her arm, just as he had done countless times when his wife, Colina, grew overwrought about one thing or another. Thoughts of his dead wife soured Dominic to his soul. He grimaced as he forced himself to ignore any reminder of the treacherous woman. Instead, he focused on the one in his arms.

"I'm—so—sorry," Emelie stuttered as she fumbled to wipe tears from her face. She was utterly humiliated. First by the contents of her father's missive, then being found mute in the garden before bursting into hysterics, and finally realizing she'd practically crawled onto this strange man's lap. She couldn't reason out why his scent had suddenly felt like a sanctuary. His sturdy presence and brawny arm felt like a shield from reality. And he'd merely held her. He hadn't shunned her or even demanded she answer him.

"Is there aught I can do? Someone I should fetch?" Dominic offered. Emelie shook her head as she sat up and wiped the last of her tears. She glanced down and saw the missive in the man's hand. Her eyes widened as she stared up at him in fear, then anger. "I didn't read it, my lady. I only glanced and noticed Laird Dunbar sent it. I assume he's your father, since you have the missive."

"You didn't read it?" Emelie asked, stunned.

"Of course not. Laird Dunbar didn't address it to me, nor did you offer it to me," Dominic answered indignantly.

"You found a lone woman in hysterics, and you didn't read the missive to learn why," Emelia stated, incredulous that he hadn't been nosy.

"Whatever caused you such upset is none of my business. I was more concerned that you were safe and would recover. And you were not in hysterics." Dominic was emphatic about his last statement. He'd spent three years married to a woman given to histrionics. The woman beside him didn't remind him of Colina in the least.

"That is kind of you to say. Most men wouldn't agree with you—" Emelie snapped her mouth shut. She was certain no one had ever introduced her to the man, but she had a sound idea who he was. "Are you Laird Campbell's kin?"

"I am. I'm his younger brother and tánaiste. I'm Dominic. How did you ken?" A twinge of his Highland burr slipped out.

"You and Laird Campbell bear a striking resemblance in your face. My friend Laurel is now Lady Campbell. I suppose that makes her your sister-by-marriage."

"Aye. Laurel is my sister." Dominic's smile was genuine, and Emelie didn't miss that he added no qualifier. The man was fond of the woman his brother married. Her eye twitched, and Dominic chuckled. "I know she wasn't popular at court, but

17

she's the kindest and most generous woman I know. That isn't to say she doesn't have strong opinions, nor does she fear sharing them with me or my brother. But she's not the ogre her reputation made her out to be."

"She isn't. She was a woman misunderstood and unappreciated."

"You were her friend."

Emelie nodded. There didn't seem to be much more to say on the matter since they agreed. She reached for the parchment Dominic held and folded it before tucking it into a hidden pocket. She attempted a smile, but she knew it was unconvincing.

"Thank you for your kindness, Dominic." Emelie liked the sound of the braw Highlander's name. This time her smile was genuine until she realized she'd been even ruder than she thought. "I apologize. I didn't introduce myself. Actually, I apologize for several things, but I should have said my name is Emelie Dunbar."

Dominic grinned. "Laurel has mentioned you. I wondered if you were Emelie or Blythe." At Emelie's furrowed brow, he pointed to where the missive hid in her pocket. "I saw the insignia. I just didn't know which sister you were."

A breeze rustled the leaves surrounding them, and it made Emelie look around, noticing for the first time just how secluded their spot was. She didn't fear Dominic in the least. But she knew it would destroy her reputation, and they'd find themselves betrothed, if anyone found them alone together.

"Should I accompany you to the edge of the garden?" Dominic offered, sensing what caused her unease.

"Thank you, but I need some more time alone." Emelie hoped she didn't sound ungracious after the comfort he offered when she feared she would fracture into shards.

"Is it safe to be alone out here? I confused you for a lost child." Dominic slammed his mouth shut as he realized the insult he'd just unintentionally doled out.

"Fear not. You are hardly the first and certainly not the last." Emelie attempted to infuse mirth into her tone, but she heard it fall flat.

"I'm sorry. I did not say that well. I wouldn't want anyone to intrude, believing you needed returning to someone." Dominic grimaced. "Bluidy hell. That didn't sound any better. I didn't mean to say you were a pet or a horse. *Christ.*" Dominic winced at his curse. He glanced up at heaven before looking at Emelie, who playfully leaned away.

"I hope the lightning only strikes you," Emelie teased. "And I understood what you meant from the beginning. You've been exceedingly kind to me. Thank you." Emelie hoped sharing her appreciation would signal an end to their conversation. Dominic nodded before standing. He reached for her hand and bent over it.

"I am glad I could help, little that I did."

"Dominic—" Emelie waited for him to turn back to her as he stepped away. She blushed at the informality. "You did far more than you realize. Please know that I appreciate it."

"I do, my lady. Good day." Dominic turned away and made his way to a hedge he'd passed as he hurried to Emelie's side. He stepped around it but went no further. He'd mis-stepped several times with his words, so he hadn't pressed her about being an unchaperoned young woman alone in the garden. It was hardly safe, and she was fortunate that he'd stumbled upon her and not someone who would have taken advantage of her. He hid behind the bush, a self-appointed sentry.

Emelie knew Dominic hid out of her sight but remained nearby. She wanted to tell him that his protection was unneeded, but she also recognized his wisdom. She'd been oblivious to his approach, and she hadn't considered the danger she'd risked by being alone so far into the garden. She appreciated the privacy, but she wondered what manner of man would be so considerate to a stranger and then waste his time milling around while that stranger sat on a bench.

Mayhap it's because he's a Highlander. They're different from Lowlanders for certain. Strong and silent isn't an exaggeration. And he's sinfully handsome. I even noticed that despite being a watering pot. I've never felt such strength. I mean, I know I could stand to gain a stone or three, so it was no struggle for him to lift me.

Bluidy hell!! He had to lift me onto the bench. One more thing to add to my humiliation. But it wasn't that. It was the strength I felt in his arm and his chest. He could crush me, yet you would think he was holding a bairn the way he was so gentle with me.

He's a mountain of a mon. He couldn't be more different from Henry. I thought Henry was so debonair. He's hardly going to pot, but he definitely isn't as sturdy as Dominic. I don't know that I'd ever feel so protected by Henry if he merely wrapped an arm around me. Not that any of that matters now.

Bluidy bleeding hell with the Devil on a cross! The bastard is married. And a moon ago. He was telling me he would marry me. He coupled with me. He was already bluidy well married. Ugh. I'm naught more than a harlot. I helped him commit adultery.

Though…I suddenly have an overwhelming sense that I'm not the only one who's done that. I even doubt I'm the first woman he tupped who wasn't his wife. Bastard.

What the devil am I going to do?

Emelie inhaled deeply as she rose. She patted her pocket, checking that the missive hadn't somehow disappeared. She shook out her skirts, smoothed back her hair, and squared her shoulders. She moved toward the path, expecting to find Dominic where she suspected he hid. She experienced a pang of disappointment when he wasn't there. But she spied him standing off to the side with his back to her as she entered the bailey. A slight twist at the waist and a turn of his head allowed one eye to glance at her. He made no other gesture to acknowledge her, but she read something in that mere single-eyed stare. She wasn't certain what it was, but she felt safe once more. It disconcerted her how much she appreciated knowing someone was looking out for her, looking after her. She tilted her head an inch as she continued walking. She steered herself across the bailey, forcing herself not to look back.

Dominic stared across the bailey to the left of where Emelie walked, but he was aware of every step she took until she entered the keep. She was something of an enigma, but more than that, she seemed so vulnerable while she sat beside him. But it was a resolute and self-assured woman who left the gardens and made her way into the castle. The contradiction was staggering. Had he not just felt her trembling against his side, he would never guess she'd been sobbing not twenty minutes earlier.

Dominic had barely dismounted his horse when he saw Emelie entering the gardens. He'd dismissed his guards, telling them to find their bunks in the barracks. He wouldn't need them again that day. He'd intended to seek the Campbell suites that were always at the ready, but he'd followed the mysterious

Emelie instead. Now he ambled across the bailey until he reached the same door Emelie passed through. He wound his way through the castle until he came to his chamber. He dropped his saddlebags beside the bed and toed off his boots. He'd relinquished his sword at the gates as a formality.

As the brother of Laird Brodie Campbell, one of the most powerful lairds in the country, Dominic knew he could have demanded to keep his sword, and the guards would have obliged. But with dominance and influence came great resentment. The Campbells had been ever loyal to the Bruce's cause, and the king had rewarded them generously. Not everyone in the realm appreciated the clan's wealth and power.

It was the ongoing conflict with the MacArthurs that brought Dominic to court. Their rivals continued to encroach upon Campbell territory, attempting to reclaim land that hadn't been theirs in generations. Once the more powerful lineage with a shared progenitor, the MacArthurs had yet to accept the rise and supremacy of Clan Campbell. With delegates from Clan MacArthur also at court, more than one threat lurked within Stirling Castle. If Dominic sensed even a hint of trouble, he would claim his sword from the armory. But for now, the empty scabbard stood beside the foot of his bed.

Dominic poked his nose into the passageway and called to a page standing at the ready. He requested a bath, wanting to rid himself of the dirt from days on the road. He hadn't considered how filthy he must be while he was comforting Emelie. However, as he waited for the tub and steaming water, he sniffed. He didn't smell as foul as he expected. He'd felt Emelie smell him as she leaned against him, and she hadn't recoiled in disgust. But he was hardly as clean as he preferred. His eagerness grew when servants arrived.

"Would you like help, my lord?" A saucy brunette maid offered, leaning forward and offering a view of her cleavage. "Your back is so broad. It must be hard to reach." The woman's cooing grated on Dominic's suddenly exhausted nerves.

"With a broad back comes long arms. I can reach by myself, lass. But I thank you." Dominic offered a coin to each of the servants who hauled the tub and buckets to his chamber. His encounter with Emelie unsettled him more than he realized, and he wanted privacy and a long soak to consider what happened.

As Dominic lowered himself into the wood and copper tub, regret that he didn't read the missive nipped at him. He chided himself for even considering violating a stranger's privacy. He felt worse still once he reminded himself that he'd spoken to Emelie and held her against his side. But he wondered what could cause her such distress. He could only imagine that someone's death would cause her to be so bereft, but she likely would have volunteered that as an explanation. She'd offered none, and he hadn't pressed her. However, curiosity ignited his thoughts as he tried to reason out what led Emelie to seek solace in the garden, and what could have caused gut-wrenching sobs.

The more Dominic attempted to figure out the cause of her pain, the more wild and unlikely his guesses became. Eventually, he shook his head and chuckled. He abandoned his guessing game, dunked his head beneath the water, then scrubbed himself clean. As he dried himself, he eyed the bed, considering whether he could catch a nap before the midday meal. He was certain King Robert would already know of his arrival, but the monarch hadn't summoned Dominic to the Privy Council chamber. Dominic assumed that meant the Bruce was in no rush to see him. Rather than wait in the sultry pas-

23

sageway with every other petitioner just to have the chamberlain send him away, Dominic gave into his wish. He climbed into bed and was soon slumbering. A blonde garden nymph tiptoed through his dreams, one after another. When Dominic awoke, he couldn't remember the last time he'd slept so well.

Do I tell Henry? Don't I owe it to him to tell him he'll be a father? If he would claim the bairn, is that what I want? He or she will be a bastard, regardless. Would it be better or worse for Henry to acknowledge them? What have I done?

Emelie sat at the table in her chamber. It was still predawn, and Blythe had yet to stir. A tallow candle sat on the table beside Emelie's left arm, a sheaf of parchment before her. Her right hand grasped a quill, but she had yet to dip it into the ink. She was torn yet again.

Emelie had made discreet inquiries over the past few days, trying to learn when Henry would return. But no one she asked had an answer. She'd vaguely hinted about it to Queen Elizabeth, but she was cautious, since she was certain the queen knew Henry was now married. The pitying expression she received told Emelie definitively that not only did the queen know about Henry's marriage, she knew that he wouldn't return to court soon. Emelie had no choice but to nod and excuse herself.

Now Emelie sat in her dimly lit chamber, trying to decide what to do. Henry had abandoned her. She didn't know whether he would even care that she was pregnant. The glimpse of a temper she'd witnessed the last time they were together made her fear his reaction, but she felt obligated to tell him. Her morals may have flown away twice already, but they demanded that she be honest. She dipped her quill and considered her wording.

H,

Circumstances have changed for us both. I am aware of yours, but I thought you should know of mine. Fear not that I'll be alone. You've ensured that I won't be. I'll likely travel to Druchtag Motte within the next two moons. I won't be able to wait much longer.

E

"I wonder when Henry will be back," Blythe teased Emelie at the evening meal, pressing her shoulder against her sister. Blythe worried about Emelie, watching her retreat further each day. She didn't want Emelie to pine for a man who wouldn't follow through on his flirtations. She hoped that lightening the mood would help Emelie relax, but her comment had the opposite effect. Emelie flinched and looked around.

"I don't know. He was supposed to be back already, but as he told me, he is his father's tánaiste. He has duties at home." *And a wife he's likely bedding every night and promising the world to now that he isn't doing that with me. At least the promising part. I will cut off his cock if he ever brings it near me again.*

"I know how you must miss him. Surely he will return as soon as he has Father's blessing."

Emelie looked at her sister and debated confessing everything to her. She'd never kept secrets from Blythe until she met Henry Pringle. Now everything about her life felt like a secret. Her eyes traveled from table to table as diners finished their evening meal. It had been three days since she received her father's message and embarrassed herself in front of Dominic Campbell. She'd caught sight of him several times since their chance meeting. He'd smiled and nodded, always polite, but they hadn't spoken except for the mildest banalities when they partnered during dances.

"Come outside with me," Emelie whispered. The pair eased away from their table, appearing to mingle until they could wander out to the terrace. Emelie drew Blythe into the shadows and kept her voice low. "I doubt Henry is coming back. Blythe, he's married."

"What?" Blythe hissed.

"Shh." Emelie's eyes darted around, but they were alone on the terrace and too far from anyone inside to overhear. "I grew impatient and sent a missive to Father. I heard back. Henry married Alice Elliot a moon ago."

"A moon ago? Alice? Alice, as in Allyson's sister?" Blythe watched as Emelie nodded. Neither woman had ever met the former Alice Elliot, but they knew from their friend and former lady-in-waiting, Allyson, that her next-oldest sister was hardly a woman of high moral standards. Allyson hadn't said as much, but the Dunbar sisters easily deduced Alice was loose. They learned how Alice and Allyson's other sisters attempted to seduce Ewan Gordon while he and Allyson were only betrothed. Anyone who met the couple would see how ridiculous the notion was that Ewan would ever choose someone over Allyson. They'd been married a few years and had children, but the man was still as besotted as a new bridegroom. "Wait. He was married the last time he was here."

"I know that now."

"But you sneaked out to see him."

Emelie gasped. "You knew aboot that?"

"Of course. We share a chamber, Emelie. We

26

both know any time one of us comes or goes. I just didn't say aught because it wasn't my business."

"But you're my sister," Emelie blurted.

"But I'm not your keeper." Blythe pulled Emelie in for an embrace. "I thought he was making you happy. We've both been here so long. I thought you'd finally found your chance to have what Father and Mother have, what Isa and Ric have. Mother and Father aren't very warm in front of others—not like how Isa and Ric still can't keep their hands off one another—but we all know they love one another. Even if things were more like our parents than our sister, I thought Henry loved you."

"I thought so, too."

"It was likely an arranged marriage. He must be heartsore that he couldn't marry the woman he wanted."

"Hardly," Emelie sneered. "He let me think he was going to ask for my hand. He let me think he was coming back for me. I was clear aboot my impressions for our future. But now that I think back, he was evasive. He said just enough to placate me. I'm such a fool."

"Oh, Emmy." Blythe fell back on her childhood name for her sister. "There will be other men. Men far more worthy than that prick. I bet his cock isn't that big." Blythe sniggered. Emelie pretended to be shocked, but she already knew exactly what Henry offered. She just had no basis for comparison. She assumed it was average.

"We will see." Emelie peered around her sister and strained to see into the crowded Great Hall. The summer sun still hadn't set, despite the evening meal's completion. She'd contemplated what she would do now that marrying Henry was an impossibility. She'd procrastinated in visiting the midwife again, but she had to decide. Looking back at Blythe, she infused warmth into her smile. "Let's dance. I don't want to think aboot him anymore."

Feeling a slight reprieve from her guilt after admitting one of her many secrets, Emelie walked arm-in-arm with Blythe as they reentered the Great Hall. The musical set changed, and the women took places among the other ladies. Emelie grinned at Blythe, but it slipped an inch when she faced forward and found Dominic standing before her. Her cheeks heated, just as they did every time they partnered. Fortunately, every dance they'd shared required changing partners, so they never stayed together long. But this set would keep them together for its entirety.

"Lady Emelie," Dominic said as he bowed. It disconcerted him to see Emelie's unease. She'd blushed prettily each time they came together during a dance, but this was the first time she looked as though she wished to flee. As their hands joined, they both glanced down before their gazes met. There was something unidentifiable, but almost tangible, that passed between them. Emelie twisted toward Dominic as his other hand came to rest on her waist. They stepped together, but neither hurried to step away, causing them both to miss a beat.

"Dominic," Emelie whispered, unsure what she should say.

"I'm enjoying our dance, but I'm afraid I have to pay close attention to the music. I don't practice often."

Emelie smiled gratefully, appreciative that he let her off the hook from conversation. They both knew what he said was a falsehood; Emelie had already noticed he was an accomplished partner to any woman he twirled about the floor. He might not perform courtly dances often at home, but he was at ease in the royal Great Hall. They moved together in silence.

The quiet between them wasn't uncomfortable, but it made them both more aware of one another. When the music ended, they were slow to release each other.

"Thank you." Emelie lingered when she knew she should step away, but Dominic didn't seem in a hurry, either. She hoped he understood she meant her gratitude was for more than the dance. She had almost forgotten her situation while they moved together, and she'd relished the reprieve of being in Dominic's arms again.

"I hope we can share such a set again," Dominic said as he bowed. It could have been a perfunctory comment, but Dominic realized he was sincere. His curiosity about the events in the garden had abated, but the lady-in-waiting herself intrigued him in a way he'd never been before, not even when he met Colina. He clenched his teeth and forced away the sneer that tickled his nose and lip. He'd noticed he loathed thinking about Emelie and Colina in the same moment.

"I would like that." Emelie curtsied before inching toward a set of doors. Her insignificant height made it easy for her to maneuver through crowds unnoticed. She knew Blythe would assume she merely couldn't see Emelie, and thus wouldn't worry. This happened every night. Emelie rushed to her chamber and snatched her cloak from the peg upon which it hung. She knew it was unlikely she would pass anyone but servants in the passageways. Nonetheless, she kept her head lowered whenever she was near someone until she stepped into the bailey. She pulled her hood up, as her hair was far too distinct for anyone not to recognize it.

When Emelie and Blythe used to walk on each side of Laurel, the three women always stood out. Laurel's strawberry-blonde mane was as unique and identifiable as the Dunbar sisters' white-blonde hair. Only Arabella Johnstone's deep red hair had been as eye-catching as the hue Emelie shared with Blythe and Isabella.

With her hair tucked into the shadows of her hood, Emelie hurried through town until she reached Goodwife Thomas's door. She knocked without trying the door. The hour was too late for the apothecary to be open, but Emelie prayed that the woman would see her. It was the woman's husband who opened the door, but the midwife stood just behind him. She nodded and waved Emelie inside as she told her husband to let Emelie pass.

"Was it the wheat or the barley?"

"The wheat," Emelie replied.

"It didn't take long," Goodwife Thomas mused.

"It didn't, and I don't think I have much longer to decide what I should do." Emelie pursed her lips before pressing them flat. "I already know what I should have done."

"The past is the past, my lady. But you have a choice."

"I'm not sure I can go through with it." Emelie felt her gorge rise as she fought to keep her tears at bay. The matronly woman patted her shoulders, careful not to overstep the bounds of propriety while still offering comfort. Emelie was hardly the first young woman to visit her in the same predicament. Goodwife Thomas went to the stack of narrow drawers and pulled one open. She scooped out something Emelie could not see and dumped it into a sachet.

"In that case, take this pennyroyal with you. If you decide to use it, boil it into a tea and drink it three times a day until it brings on your courses." The midwife handed Emelie the sachet, which was filled with petals. It was what Emelie knew she should have purchased before her first encounter with Henry. She knew other women used pennyroyal to prevent pregnancy, and she suspected it was what Margaret purchased the morning Emelie first came in.

"Thank you." This time, Emelie pressed coins into the woman's hands, but not just because the midwife's husband glared at her with narrowed eyes. He'd obviously learned his wife hadn't charged Emelie the first time. She wanted to pay the woman for her discretion and lack of judgment.

"Come back to me if ever you need me."

"I will." But Emelie prayed it would never come to that. She clutched the pouch in her hand as she made her way directly back to the castle. The sun had now set, and it grew dark quickly. Emelie had underestimated how long it would take her to visit the midwife, and she feared being outside the gates when they closed. She was also nervous about who she might encounter while she was alone. Her free hand drew the dirk she kept at her waist. She wasn't overly skilled with it, but it was long and sharp. As long as an attacker didn't turn it on her, she figured it would do enough damage to buy her time to get away. She didn't breathe easy until she pulled the castle's side door closed behind her.

THREE

Emelie drew open the pouch she carried and peered inside. It wasn't heavy, but it surprised her to find how full it was. Goodwife Thomas told her to drink the tea three times a day until her courses came, but she didn't know how many petals she needed to use each time. She didn't know if she needed to ration them because it could take several days, or if she should make it strong and assume it would induce her monthly cycle sooner. She wasn't even certain she could go through with it.

Emelie had never considered what other women experienced when they found themselves in her position. She'd never judged others for their choice to use pennyroyal as a contraceptive or a means to terminate a pregnancy. She never thought it her business, but now that she faced a monumental decision, she felt sympathetic to the faceless and nameless women.

Can I do this? Of course, you can. But do you want to? Are you willing to? You have what you need. Whether it takes a day or ten, Goody Thomas gave you what she knew you needed. Even if it weren't a sin—which I hadn't even thought aboot till now—is this right? Plenty of other women do it. But I'm not other women.

I might not have qualms aboot other women doing it. But I can —

Emelie cried out as she slammed into a wall, or at least what she assumed was a wall. But the set of bricks that surely knocked her backwards had firm hands that grasped her upper arms. As she fought to keep her balance, Emelie dropped the pouch and watched in horror as the pennyroyal spilled on the wood floor. She glanced up to see who she'd collided with and froze with mortification.

"Lady Emelie, are you all right? I beg your pardon," Dominic said. "I wasn't paying attention."

"It—it was my fault. I wasn't looking—" Emelie's heart pounded such a rapid staccato that she struggled to speak. She hurried to bend down and collect the medicinal, now strewn across the floor. Dominic stooped too but froze when he picked up the first leaf.

"Pennyroyal."

Emelie locked eyes with Dominic, shocked that he recognized the flower. She couldn't think of any other man besides the apothecary, and perhaps the king's physician, who would know what Dominic held. She reached for the petal, but he closed his hand around it. He stared at her, having not moved except to keep her from taking the pennyroyal. Dominic watched Emelie's face first drain of all color, then grow an even deeper shade of red than when they danced together. He'd recognized the plant with ease. He'd found a pouch like Emelie's among his dead wife's belongings. It was the clan's healer who explained what it was. The woman confessed that Colina had been using it since she arrived at Kilchurn. It had kept not only Dominic, but Colina's lover, from impregnating her during his three-year marriage.

"Please, may I have it," Emelie whispered, desperate to flee. She could only imagine what Dominic thought of her. It was obvious the Highlander knew the plant's use. She didn't want to face his scorn. She wanted to flee to her chamber. Dominic nodded. His stunned expression said it all. It shocked him to discover Emelie was loose, and it was clear she disappointed him.

"Emelie—" Dominic didn't know what else to say. The pennyroyal didn't sit right with him. Nothing about Emelie spoke of a woman who offered her favors freely. There was an innocence and naivete that gave Dominic the impression that she didn't have much experience with men, inside or outside a bedchamber. "Is someone pressuring you?"

"What?"

"Is a mon pressuring you? Is that why you have this?"

Emelie opened and closed her mouth like a trout. He was far too close to the truth. She couldn't imagine how he would react if he knew what had already come to pass. "No. No one is pressuring me to do aught."

Dominic studied Emelie before his eyes darted to her midriff. He straightened to his full height, towering over Emelie by more than a foot. Despite his erect posture, there was nothing imposing about him; at least, Emelie didn't find him threatening. He remained silent, waiting. As they stood staring at one another, Emelie resigned herself to Dominic being able to last longer than she could. He wouldn't budge until he had some type of answer. She sighed as she attempted to collect her courage. But he spoke before she did.

"Is that what upset you in the garden? Did he upset you?"

"Sort of." Emelie looked around. The passageway was the least private place to have this conversation, short of standing on a table in the Great Hall. She whispered, "Come with me."

Emelie led Dominic through the doors she'd entered only minutes ago. The temperature had dropped, but it wasn't unbearable. As it grew chillier, it would give her a reason to escape the conversation. She licked her lips as she turned back to face Dominic once they stood in a recessed portion of the wall.

"The missive from my father informed me that someone else already married the mon I thought was courting me." Dominic grimaced but said nothing, waiting for Emelie to continue. "He didn't force me, but even though I knew I was foolish, I let him guide me astray."

"Guide you astray?" Dominic whispered. His piercing gray eyes bore into Emelie, making her want to fidget.

"I mean, it was my choice. My exceedingly poor and reckless choice. But in my defense—my only defense—I trusted him. I didn't think there was a reason not to. It was only twice, but as my mother warned me, it only takes once." Emelie tucked her chin and looked at their shoes. She was unprepared for the soft touch that eased her chin up.

"I wasn't blaming you, Emelie. How auld are you? How auld is he?"

"I'm three-and-twenty. He's mayhap thirty. I'm not sure."

"Och, Emelie. Ye're but a lass. He is a mon full grown, who kenned the risks he was taking. He didna do right by ye." Dominic's brogue flowed freely, and it wrapped around Emelie like the honey in treats she enjoyed at fairs. He shook his head as he gazed into Emelie's blue-hazel eyes. She hadn't noticed how translucent his gray eyes were until the rising moon shone upon them. "Does he ken?"

35

"I sent a missive. He was unmarried the first time. I—I didn't know he was the second time. I never would have. It was just over so soon." Emelie's brow furrowed at Dominic's chuckles.

"Then ye've likely saved yerself from a lifetime of disappointment." Dominic grinned but sobered when he recalled the pennyroyal they'd left on the floor where they collided. "He's left ye with someone to remember him by, hasnae he, lass?"

Emelie nodded as tears prickled her eyelids. She bit her bottom lip until it stung, but it distracted her from the tears that wanted to flow. She inhaled sharply, unprepared for Dominic to pull her into his embrace. Hesitant, she raised her hands until she reached his waist. He didn't wear the doublet she was accustomed to seeing him in. Instead, he wore breeks and a Highland leine. She leaned against him until she relaxed.

"Why do I feel safe with you?" Emelie wondered.

"Because ye are. I willna hurt ye. This mon has already done enough of that. Ye deserve some kindness."

"But why do you care?"

"I dinna ken."

Emelie was unprepared for Dominic's blunt answer. But she appreciated his honesty to some flowery explanation neither would believe.

"Whatever your reason, I'm grateful. Your wife is truly fortunate." Emelie had assumed Dominic was married given his age; she estimated him to be older than Henry. His gentleness when he first met her, and his initial belief that she was a child, made him seem paternal. But as Emelie stood with him, nothing felt paternal about their embrace. It took her a moment to realize Dominic's body language drastically shifted. She leaned back to look at him. "I hope she won't think that you're being untoward. I didn't take it as such."

"Ma wife is dead." It shocked Dominic that he blurted out his widower status without thinking. He'd had to admit to his wife's death to only a handful of people, since everyone at Kilchurn Castle knew the circumstances.

"I'm so sorry for your loss, Dominic." Emelie canted her head, and her shoulders sank. "It was recent."

"Aye." Dominic felt the usual anger, guilt, and re-crimination surge from his gut into his chest before it threatened to strangle him. His nose flared as he fought to keep from plowing his fist into the stone wall. He'd just come from an infuriating meeting with King Robert, where he'd had to recount details he knew Brodie and Laurel explained the last time they were at court, shortly after Colina's death.

It relieved Emelie that they were no longer speaking about her situation, but it pained her to see the raw grief in Dominic's eyes. She moved without thinking as she stepped back into his embrace and soothed her hands over his back. Surprised by her offer of comfort, Dominic was slow to wrap his arms around Emelie again, but when he did, he thought he might never want to release her. As they stood to-gether, he could feel Emelie's body pressed against his, and there was nothing childlike about it. She may have been short, but there was nothing con-fusing about the full bosom and flared hips resting against him. For the first time in months, arousal sparked, and Dominic felt his cock stir. He pulled away abruptly. Without his plaid and sporran on, there was little to hide his swelling rod. The Lowland breeks he wore while at court left little to the imagi-nation. He didn't want to terrify Emelie, nor did he want her to think he would take advantage of her.

"We should go back inside," Dominic croaked before he cleared his throat. He led them back to where they'd met. Both came to an abrupt stop when they found the mess they'd left behind. Once again, Emelie bent to collect the pennyroyal petals scattered on the floor. Dominic helped, but it brought back all the unresolved questions. He didn't know why it mattered to him, but it did. "What're you going to do?"

Dominic had collected himself enough to rid himself of his burr and to adopt his courtly speech once more. Emelie hadn't seemed to notice his Highland brogue, but most Lowlanders looked at Highlanders with disdain even before they spoke. Most Lowlanders at court believed the Highlands' accent was as uncouth as its owners.

"I thought I knew. But I can't do it. I can't go through with it, even though I went to the apothecary tonight. Having the medicinal now makes me realize I'm just not someone who can go through with it. I still haven't fully come to terms that I will be a mother, but I guess I want to be one more than I don't want to be one. Even if the situation isn't ideal."

"How far along are you?" Dominic felt a seed of an idea taking root. He knew it would be impetuous, but he also sensed it would be the right thing to do. A chance for redemption seemed within reach.

"I'm uncertain. But no more than two moons," Emelie answered.

"What will you do?" Dominic asked again.

"Retire to my clan's home in shame. Bear the child there and pray my parents don't turn me out."

"Do you think they would?"

"No. But I don't know that my father would ever forgive me or accept the bairn."

"And the father? Would he acknowledge his child?"

"I wrote to him. I truly don't know. But either way, he's married, and this child is illegitimate."

"Do you wish to marry?" Dominic pressed a little more.

"I did. I thought myself in love, and I thought I'd be marrying Henry." Emelie snapped her mouth shut, not having intended to give away anything about her unborn child's father.

"My wife's name was Colina." Dominic struggled not to hiss the woman's name, but he felt he owed the admission to Emelie, since he knew she hadn't intended to tell him her former lover's name. He took a deep breath before continuing. "If you wish to marry and you wish for a home where no one will know the circumstances around your child's paternity, then mayhap you'd consider marrying me."

"What?" Emelie barked before she glanced around. She tugged Dominic's sleeve until they slipped into an alcove. She couldn't believe their good fortune that no one had stumbled upon them yet, but she didn't intend to press their luck.

"Mayhap you'd marry me. Emelie, I don't care that you're not a virgin. And I'm not doing this out of pity, before you accuse me of that. You're a young woman in a tenuous position, but naught aboot you makes me think you're without morals."

"But what if this bairn is a son? You would claim another mon's son as your own?" Emelie shook her head. "I know Laurel is with child too, but no one will know if it's a lad or lass until the bairn arrives. Until she bears your brother a son, you're his heir. That would make any son I bear your heir. Eventually, the Campbell laird might not be a Campbell. Is that something you'd risk? I don't know any mon who would."

Dominic's mind had already whirled through that possibility. He knew he wouldn't keep such a secret from Brodie, which meant not keeping it from Laurel. "Blood is but blood. It is red regardless the body from which it pours. If I raise the bairn as my own, then he or she is mine. I don't think I will ever lead Clan Campbell. The way Brodie and Laurel are together, they're likely to have an entire army of children within a decade. But if, somehow, I became laird, and this child is a lad, then he would be my heir, just as much as any son born of my seed."

"And if you should have a son of your own one day?"

"One day? My own? Wouldn't it be our son? You make it sound as though I would have a wife other than you."

Emelie shrugged. Things were moving too quickly for her. "Would this be a marriage in name only?"

"Is that what you wish?" Dominic countered.

"I don't know what I wish. Five minutes ago, I had no prospects and no idea what to do."

Dominic cupped Emelie's jaw. "This is impetuous, and I know that. I'm not generally an impetuous mon, but I just have a feeling that I can't ignore. But if marriage is overwhelming to you, if you doubt I can be a loyal father to your bairn, then handfast with me. It would give you time to have your bairn. The child would bear my name, so he or she would be legitimate. But if you don't wish to remain married to me, then you can repudiate it at any time or let it run its course after a year and a day."

"Then what would I do?"

"You could return to your clan with no disgrace. I would accept fault for the handfast ending and your wish to leave."

"You would do that? You'd let people think I left you? What if you wish for a proper wife one day?"

"Mayhap we get through deciding whether you

40

wish to handfast, then we can get through a year. After that, we'll see." His thumb swept over her cheek, each pass more soothing than the last.

"It cannot be that simple." Emelie shook her head as she closed her eyes. Her head spun as she considered what Dominic offered. It was the most outlandish—most ideal—thing she'd ever heard. "I don't know," she said lamely.

"I'll be here at least another fortnight. You don't have to decide tonight, but you will have to decide soon. If we go through with this, we can't delay; otherwise, people will talk when your healthy bairn arrives too soon."

"Wait. What if I am already two moons along, not one?"

"I've been away from Kilchurn for nearly three moons already. I've come and gone from court during that time, but I didn't socialize. Few people knew I was here, but it's reasonable to say we handfasted during any of my trips here. It doesn't require a priest."

"But people knew Henry was courting me."

"Aye. But he hasn't been here in some time. And if you were successful sneaking around to see him, why can't we say it was me you sneaked off to find?" Dominic reasoned.

Emelie licked her dry lips, and Dominic's gaze followed the tip of her tongue. He had a sudden desire to taste her lip, and he wished it were his tongue gliding along her flesh. When he shifted his gaze, he found Emelie watching him. The interest in her eyes matched his own. He cupped her jaw with his other hand and slowly brought his mouth down to hers. It was a soft brushing of their lips before they met halfway, each adding pressure until their lips pressed together. Emelie opened to Dominic as he slid his tongue past her teeth.

The feel of Dominic's tongue reminded Emelie of crushed velvet. She felt the tension, the lust that sparked between them, but Dominic kept it contained. Her hands fisted his leine as she swayed into him. His massive hands that contained such strength were light on her waist, letting her grow accustomed to their feel before he lifted her off her feet. She wrapped her arms around his neck and hung from him. The difference in their height likely looked ridiculous, and it made it difficult to kiss, but Emelie reveled in the feel of Dominic holding her.

Dominic thought to offer a tender kiss to show Emelie that he desired her as a man should a wife and that he would be gentle with her. He didn't expect the inferno she ignited as his tongue swept the satiny insides of her mouth. He wished to wrap her legs around his waist and press her against the wall. He hadn't wanted a woman since Colina. He hadn't been sure he would ever want one again. He'd been devoted to her, but discovering her betrayal with Graham, his and Brodie's illegitimate older brother, made him want nothing to do with women. At least until now.

As his cock stirred yet again, Dominic lowered Emelie back to the floor. He didn't want his lengthening arousal to scare her. He knew she was no virgin, but he didn't want her to fear he would make assumptions. He didn't want a marriage or a handfast in name only, but he would follow Emelie's lead. He wouldn't presume anything.

"Can I think aboot it and give you my answer in a day or so?" Emelie whispered.

"Of course, lass." Dominic kissed her forehead, and Emelie once more had a feeling that it was a paternal gesture. But it was so contrary to the desire they'd just shared. As she watched Dominic, she was rapidly coming to understand that while he was enormous and his size clearly came from hours upon hours of swinging a sword, there was a gentleness that belied his size. A moment of envy and guilt sparked in her chest. She was lusting after a man who still grieved his wife, but she sensed he'd been a loving husband. Emelie wished she'd had a chance for the affection and devotion that she suspected Dominic felt for Colina. When she forced herself to think of Henry, she felt nothing. There was no love like she'd believed she'd once felt. There wasn't even anger or hurt; there was only antipathy. He may have sired the child growing within her, but having discovered his true character, Emelie realized she didn't feel she was missing anything.

"I will find you when I decide. I feel like I keep saying this, but thank you. You are offering me something I never imagined. Dominic, if you change your mind—if you wish to rescind—I won't hold it against you." Emelie slipped out of the alcove before Dominic could argue. He watched her go. As she moved further along the corridor, he knew he wouldn't rescind. If anything, he would urge her to agree. There was something about Emelie Dunbar that was already getting into his blood.

43

FOUR

Dominic fought to keep a rein on his temper as he stood across from King Robert and to the far left of the MacArthur delegate. He'd listened to the man spend ten minutes spewing lies about Clan Campbell and asserting his clan's dominion over the very land the Bruce had granted Clan Campbell after the Battle of Bannockburn. Brodie kept the king alive on that battlefield, and Dominic had come the closest he'd ever been to dying. He'd been gravely wounded, and few people besides Brodie believed he would survive. It galled him to stand and listen to any MacArthur attempt to steal land Dominic and his brother nearly died protecting.

Dominic knew the king would side with the Campbells, but it further infuriated him that the king let the Campbells' enemy drone on, slighting Dominic's clan and, specifically, his brother and laird. King Robert must have realized Dominic was coming to the end of his tether when he glanced down and noted Dominic's white-knuckle hold on the edge of the table. The last thing the king needed was blood splattering over the important documents strewn across the table.

"Enough, Alfred," King Robert intoned as he

raised his hand to silence the man. "I have let you vent your spleen. Now I shall tell you what will happen. You and your men will return home. You will tell your uncle that not a single Campbell will see hide nor hair of your clan. And if they do, they have the right to run any of you through on sight. I will not fault them for it. Your memory must be incredibly short if you don't recall my family connection to the Campbells. You never met my sister Mary, but she is a Campbell now."

Dominic kept his eyes forward despite the consuming desire to gloat. It even tempted him to stick his tongue out at Alfred MacArthur, but he controlled himself. Barely. Dominic waited for King Robert to turn to him, unsure of what would happen next. He couldn't fathom what else should happen. He'd been back and forth to Stirling several times after riding throughout Campbell territory, securing their borders from the MacArthurs and their friends the MacGregors. The Campbells and MacGregors would likely never come to a truce. It was their land the king gave the Campbells. Dominic and Brodie's father, and now Brodie, had pushed the MacGregors further out of Glencoe, defeating the MacGregors during every standoff. Dominic, as tánaiste, had enough worries, since he was the one who led the Campbell patrols. He didn't need more.

"Dom," King Robert started. Dominic knew the familiarity of the diminutive was for Alfred's sake, not his. "Inform Brodie that the MacArthurs will cease their incursion and will remain far from Kilchurn. Under no circumstances will they cross the River Orchy again."

"Thank you, Your Majesty."

King Robert's eyebrows rose, expecting Dominic to say more, but Dominic felt there was little more to say. He'd presented his case, then waited for the king's judgment. He wouldn't defend himself against Alfred, nor would he beg. He'd gotten what he came for, and he'd expressed his gratitude. Succinctly.

"Very well. Alfred, you may leave. Dominic remains."

Now Dominic wanted to groan. He suspected what else King Robert wanted to discuss, and he was in no mood for it. He fought the scowl that wanted to take hold of his visage. He listened to the door to the Privy Council chamber close behind Alfred and watched as the king motioned his other advisors away from the table.

"Sit."

While Dominic followed the king's command, he didn't appreciate it making him feel like a dog. The Campbells were hardly the Bruce's lapdogs. They'd been instrumental in Robert the Bruce's rise to power. But King Robert had tested Brodie's loyalty a little too far the last time he and Laurel were at court. Thinking to tease Brodie, even prove a point that Laurel was a better woman than many believed, he'd insulted her. Brodie had warned the king, but as sovereign, he'd pressed on. Brodie hadn't forgiven the king yet, and that was largely why Dominic represented their clan right now.

"Is your brother still in a fit over the wager?"

"Aye." Dominic once more kept his answer brief. He was insulted on Laurel's behalf, and didn't appreciate the king's role in betting that Laurel would shock everyone and be more obedient to Brodie than other women were to their suitors or male relatives. She'd proved her naysayers wrong despite her past as a hellion. Once known as the "Shrew of Stirling," Laurel had come into her own when she met Brodie. They complemented one another in a way Dominic had never seen in another couple. Even during his most blissful days with Colina, he'd never felt he and his wife had what he saw between his brother and sister-by-marriage.

"It's just as well that you came instead of your brother. It's time you remarried."

"What?" Dominic blurted. "I haven't been widowed for even a year, and you're already negotiating my next marriage. And I'm a second son. What does my marriage matter? You didn't arrange my betrothal to Colina."

"I didn't have to. You were a besotted pup trailing after her until Brodie agreed to your marriage. But it was a convenient tie to the MacLeans."

"A bluidy load of good it did. She was never loyal to the Campbells. She was naught more than a spy."

"I see you haven't put the past behind you yet."

"It's barely been six months. No, my anger hasn't subsided. Talking aboot her does little to help."

"Tread carefully, Dom," King Robert warned. Dominic opened his mouth with another rejoinder, but thought better of it. "A marriage to Laird Mac-Arthur's sister would end these troubles, and it would align the two clans once more. You share a common heritage."

"We don't need to align ourselves with them. You just solved that problem, Your Majesty. And at the moment, I am not at liberty to commit myself to someone."

"Oh? Has the grieving widower already found someone else? In less than a year?" King Robert taunted, but there was a bite to his tone.

"I have. The lady is considering my offer." Dominic remained tight-lipped about Emelie, not wanting to name her as his intended in case she declined. He wouldn't share the circumstances of his offer, either.

"Do you believe Lady Emelie will accept?" King Robert chuckled at Dominic's struggle to keep the surprise from his face.. "Come now. Do you think aught goes on here that I don't know aboot?"

Dominic thought there was plenty that went on that the king didn't know about, but he wouldn't point that out. His surprise stemmed from King Robert's interest in Emelie and him. They'd danced together at least twice each night for the past four days. He'd accompanied her on walks each morning when the queen went for her morning constitutional. They hadn't spent a great deal of time together, but they'd had an opportunity to get to know one another better, and Dominic suspected she would agree to at least the handfast. The more time he spent in her company, the more he hoped she would.

"If you know of my interest, why suggest someone else? Is it because the Dunbars are Lowlanders and too far away to do much good along Campbell borders?"

"Err—no. Henry Pringle recently courted the young lady. Everyone believed he would ask for her hand, but I knew his father was arranging a marriage to Laird Elliot's daughter."

"And no one knew to warn Lady Emelie?" Dominic cocked an eyebrow. He was certain the queen knew and could have spoken up. They'd allowed Pringle to play Emelie for a fool, and now she was dealing with the consequences alone. At least until she and Dominic married, as he hoped.

"Naught was said," King Robert hedged. "I believe it was more of a dalliance than a courtship." King Robert's eyebrow rose to match Dominic's. The latter understood the implications.

"I'm aware of all of the circumstances of that brief courtship."

"And it does not bother you that Lady Emelie is un—"

"Your Majesty," Dominic warned. He glanced at

48

those who might hear their conversation. "I have asked her to consider a handfast, if not a marriage. If she agrees, she will be my wife. A wife I will defend."

"Settle, Dom. I'm not impugning her. I'm merely ensuring you are aware of what you're getting yourself into. Your first wife was a virgin when you wed. I assumed you wished for the same again."

"What I wish for and what Lady Emelie is or isnae is nay one's business but our own. Nay one's neb needs pushing into our marriage if there is one." Dominic kept his voice low, his brogue heavy, and the censure to his king clear. He risked much being defiant to the monarch, but he wouldn't accept anyone implying Emelie was less than worthy of marriage.

"Very well. And I thought Brodie was the hot-tempered one of the two of you."

"We've always been as alike as two peas in a pod." Dominic grinned as King Robert grunted. They'd been stubborn children, haranguing their mother to no end. But what appeared as recalcitrance to some was the determination that kept them alive during one battle after another, and it was what made Brodie an irrefutable leader.

"Do you think Lady Emelie will agree to your offer?"

"I hope so. I am giving her time to decide without pressure."

"You make a handsome couple, though you look like Goliath to her David." King Robert grinned at his jest. Dominic pursed his lips, but there was mirth in his eyes. He saw nothing wrong with Emelie's petite height. He rather liked it. Colina had been tall and willowy; Emelie couldn't be more her opposite.

As strongly as he'd been attracted to Colina, Dominic's desire for Emelie made any past lust pale in comparison. At first, he suspected it was merely the deluge after the drought. But now he knew his desire for Emelie came from far more than a dry spell. He forced himself to temper that lust whenever he was near her, not wanting her to fear he would use her as Henry had. Fear plagued him that if they married and consummated their union, it might be harmful to her. It was the only aspect where her diminutive size worried him. He feared crushing her even if she wasn't pregnant, but it terrified him that he would injure her or the babe.

But when Dominic was alone in his chamber each night, his memory inevitably floated back to the feel of her in his arms as they danced only hours earlier. It was the sound of her laughter and the twinkle in her blue-hazel eyes as the sun shone on them during their walks. Those plagued him until he eased his longing with his own hand. The same maid who'd helped prepare his first bath upon his return came back each evening. She continued to make the same offer, and he was sorely tempted to accept, merely to ease his aching bollocks in a way far more satisfying than he could offer himself. But he would look at her, and it was Emelie he longed for. He declined each time and groaned as he entered the warm water. The bath eased not only his aching muscles from training in the lists but his aching need to explore Emelie's body.

"Ahem," King Robert cleared his throat. "Mayhap you could remember where you are and with whom you sit rather than thinking aboot your lady-in-waiting. Mayhap the more appropriate title would be mon-in-waiting."

This time Dominic let his scowl play across his face, and his eyes held no humor. He hoped King Robert would be discreet and not mention the situation to anyone else at court. He suspected the king and queen had already discussed it, or they would after this conversation. But he didn't want it to be common knowledge beyond what people already observed.

"Since you seem aware of the situation, you might accept that if she agrees, we will say we hand-fasted during one of my previous visits."

"Is that necessary?" King Robert examined Dominic's expression, seeking any hint of whether his suspicions were true.

"Nay. But I would prefer people not to think Lady Emelie impetuous and flighty. It's been some time since Pringle has been here. During that absence, people have seen me come and go. It stands to reason that I replaced him as her suitor, but we were discreet in our interest." Dominic interpreted the word necessary as he saw fit. He wouldn't confirm that Emelie was with child, even though he was certain the king now believed that.

"Very well. If the lady agrees to your offer, I will say naught aboot when and where the handfast took place. I shall act as pleasantly surprised as I was today."

"Your Majesty, you do know that pleasure and dread aren't the same, don't you?" Dominic asked with a devilish grin, but the king took his point and nodded.

"I shall do my best." With that, King Robert dismissed Dominic, and he was only too happy to escape the Privy Council chamber. He wound his way through the keep, headed to the lists. He'd already been for a walk with Emelie that morning, then met with the king. He looked forward to sparring with his men to burn off much of the tension and frustration that made knots upon knots form during his time with King Robert.

As he descended the stairs to the ground floor, Dominic heard women's voices before he caught sight of the cluster walking together, their skirts swishing around them. His eyes gravitated to Emelie, who happened to look up at the stairs as she passed. She whispered something to a woman who was clearly her sister, Blythe, but no one had formally introduced them yet. Emelie hung back from the group and slipped into an alcove.

Emelie hoped Dominic would follow her into the private nook. They hadn't spoken alone since the last time they ducked into the recessed area with a tapestry hanging as its door. It meant they hadn't shared another kiss since then, and Emelie found herself thinking about it constantly. She chided herself for being a harlot when she wanted to explore her desire while she carried another man's child. A man she never should have coupled with since he wasn't her husband. Recrimination and lust warred within her while she was awake, but it was Dominic who filled her dreams. They weren't all explicit in nature. Many of her dreams painted scenes of them walking hand-in-hand along a river. Many showed Dominic carrying a little boy while he wrapped his arm around Emelie's shoulders, much like it had been when they met. That dream always ended with them facing one another and Dominic's hand on her swollen belly.

Emelie told herself that she couldn't—shouldn't —base her decision on the whimsy of her dreams. But it wasn't a flight of fancy that drove her. There was bone-deep certainty that there was no better man for her than Dominic. His stoic presence during their walks gave her a confidence she hadn't experienced before. She felt comfortable talking to him about her childhood and her experiences as court. He was attentive and serious, where Henry had seemed indulgent and patronizing now that she could compare the two men.

Dominic was jovial when they danced each night, twirling her extra times to make her giggle. Their obvious difference in build drew stares, and Emelie saw the envy on other women's faces, but they never lingered at the end of a set. She'd overheard women talking, and most assumed they merely enjoyed partnering. She didn't think there were any suspicions or rumors. At least, not yet.

"Lady Emelie," Dominic whispered as he came to stand in front of her, the tapestry dropping back into place.

"I'd like you to call me Emelie." Emelie smiled but looked away, embarrassed at her forthrightness without offering him a greeting.

"I'd like you to call me Dom," Dominic offered in return. He was happy to oblige and do away with the formality of her honorific, but he wasn't ready to confess that he already thought of her as Em. He didn't know when the pet name came to mind, but it was what he thought whenever she did, which was altogether too frequently.

Emelie bit her top lip, debating whether she should engage in pleasantries before saying what she wanted. She opted to be forthright. "I accept and would like to handfast."

Dominic smiled, and it transformed his face from striking to dazzlingly handsome. Emelie swallowed as her breasts tightened and her sheath ached. She held her breath as she waited for him to respond.

"When?" Dominic breathed.

"Now? Could we do it now? I don't know too much aboot the Highland custom beyond what you already told me."

"And you'd agree to it based on just that?"

53

"I agree based on me trusting you. I pray it's not misplaced, but I don't think it is."

"I will never do aught intentionally to betray your trust, Em. I put too much credence in my honor as a mon, a Highlander, and my clan's tánaiste. I don't lie." Dominic didn't notice that the first chance he had to use Emelie's name, he let the pet name slip.

"Em?" A bashful smile flashed across Emelie's face. She whispered, "I like that."

Dominic slipped his arm around Emelie's waist, and she stepped into his embrace without hesitation. With one massive arm wrapped around her, he tucked a piece of hair behind her ear, then cupped her cheek.

"If you decide even before the year and a day is over that you no longer want to remain with me, I will take you wherever you wish. I never, ever want you to feel trapped. I made my offer because I found a brave young woman in need who already seemed to feel trapped. But I've been praying you would accept because I'm growing fonder of you by the day. I will strive to be the best husband I can to you, Em. But if it isn't enough, tell me. I will try to make amends. If it still isn't enough, I will take the fault and ensure you are safe wherever you choose."

"I offer the same. If I am not a wife you wish to keep, even if only for a year, I will not contest your decision for us to part. I never imagined such a self-less and considerate mon would enter my life when I most needed support. You are a blessing in more ways than one, and I grow fonder of you by the day. I will strive to be the wife you want, and I will honor you always. I know you didn't come here intending to find a bride. I know you weren't ready, which makes me appreciate your offer even more. I don't feel trapped, Dom. I feel free."

Dominic tilted Emelie's head back, catching a particular phrase that troubled him. "I am ready, Em. More so than I thought. I want to be your husband. Don't doubt that, please."

Emelie saw such earnestness in Dominic's gaze that she could almost forget the grief she witnessed any time his first wife was mentioned. She wanted to believe that the widower who stood before her was ready to move on, but she would respect that he might not be as able as he believed. If nothing else, she gained a friend and a confidant. She might have to live with the memory of a dead woman in her marriage, but Dominic offered too many other blessings for her to turn him away.

"What do we say to handfast?" Emelie asked.

"Truly, what we just pledged is enough. There are no specific vows to recite. A handfast is an agreement to a trial marriage, and that can happen merely by the mon and woman saying they wish it. Some couples exchange more traditional blessings, but it isn't a requirement. I rather liked what we just promised, rather than flowery phrases."

Dominic fought to push aside the memory of the vows he'd sworn to Colina on the steps of the Mac-Leans' kirk. They'd been the same that every couple recited to make a marriage binding before God and the law. He'd been heartfelt and reverent when he pledged himself to Colina, and was devoted to her in all ways. But the simplicity of his promises to Emelie felt even more authentic than saying the same words thousands of other people had.

"There is one more thing I wish to promise you, Em. No matter what happens in the next year, I will always be faithful to you. This may be a handfast and not binding before the law, but I will never dishonor you or humiliate you by straying."

Dominic's last pledge struck Emelie silent. She

hadn't expected it. She assumed he would do as he pleased. Even a widower had desires. She hadn't thought about whether she would arrive at Kilchurn to find a leman waiting for him. She would never be so brazen as to ask a husband if he had a mistress. She understood she had no right to expect fidelity. It was the woman who became chattel, not the other way around. She felt a wave of certainty that Henry would have kept a mistress, even if they married. She never got that sense with Dominic.

"I believe you," Emelie confessed. "I don't know yet if it's just you or the way of Highlanders, but I believe you when you make a promise. I can sense your honor is at the core of who you are. It's why I trust you."

Dominic gazed into the blue-hazel eyes he was coming to know so well. Emelie's expression was open and honest, and he prayed he would be worthy of the bride who stood before him. But her mention of honor was a like a stab to his chest. It was the sense of honor that made him feel so disgraced and wretched after bringing Colina into his clan. She'd betrayed not only him by having an affair with his half-brother, but she'd betrayed the entire clan by sharing secrets with her clan of birth, the MacLeans, and the Lamonts. They'd used the information Graham smuggled on Colina's behalf, and they'd plotted against the Campbells. It cost Brodie his first bride, a woman barely more than a girl who Brodie married for an alliance.

It was, in part, redemption that Dominic sought. He prayed helping Emelie would redeem him in God's eyes and his own. He prayed that bringing her home to Kilchurn would redeem him to his clan. While they would deceive his clansmen and women by making them believe Emelie's child was his, he had a certainty that Emelie would be a beneficial addition to the clan. He'd never considered Colina's role in his clan when he courted her. He assumed she would help around the keep and do what most women did. He never considered her worth until it was too late. The only bone of contention they ever had was that Colina took no interest in running the keep after Dominic's mother died.

At first, Dominic and Brodie believed it was Colina's grief that kept her from taking on the chatelaine's duties. She'd appeared the ideal wife and helpmate when she arrived at Kilchurn on Dominic's arm. But Dominic's mother soon grew ill, and Colina became her nursemaid. It was the first grave error Dominic made besides marrying the woman in the first place. Colina killed his mother.

"Dom?" Emelie's voice broke through his thoughts.

"I was just thinking how fortunate I am, and how fortunate my clan is. I ken there is much we must still learn aboot one another, but I wouldn't have offered for you if I didn't feel you would be good for my people too."

"I hope I never disappoint you."

"Stay as you are, and you won't," Dominic whispered before the steely band wrapped around her middle lifted her off her feet. Their kiss combusted the moment their mouths fused together. Emelie's fingers tangled in Dominic's rich chestnut hair as she angled her head to allow Dominic's tongue to brush the back of her mouth. She moaned as she felt his rod harden along her belly. She pressed her hips forward, aching for more contact. She wondered if they would have a wedding night.

Dominic's hand glided along her ribs until it cupped her backside. He groaned as soft flesh filled his palm. He squeezed as he felt the urge to thrust his hips into her. He wanted nothing more than to retire to his chamber, strip her bare, and explore every inch of her lush body. But when his hand pressed against her breast and her moan was one of pain, he nearly dropped her as he set her back on her feet and jumped back.

"I'm sorry," Dominic swore.

"You did naught wrong, Dom. They're just tender these days. I—I still liked it." Emelie covered her face with her hands, embarrassed by her admission. "You must think me such a whore."

"What? Never." Dominic fought Emelie's grip and pried her hands away. "Please look at me, Em. I have never thought that. Not when I discovered you with the pennyroyal. Not when you told me your situation. And certainly not now. Aye, you have experience most brides don't. But I'd rather know you're attracted to me than fear I repulse you."

"Repulse me? I'm quite certain you have never repulsed any woman in your life."

Dominic once would have agreed with Emelie, but after Colina, he wasn't so sure. He'd believed his wife loved him, just as he loved her. But after discovering her perfidy, he didn't know if she merely tolerated him in her attempt to grasp the title of Lady Campbell, or if she'd ever had genuine feelings for him.

"I don't hold your past against you. If I did, I wouldn't have asked you to join your life with mine. And it doesn't make any woman a whore to enjoy a mon's touch. If the Lord didn't intend for men and women to enjoy intimacy, He wouldn't have made our bodies able to."

"But I did so without being married," Emelie mumbled.

"You trusted the wrong mon. He made promises he likely never intended to keep. You're young. You have admitted to your error in judgment, and you're

58

taking responsibility for it. Never have I heard you blame him. But he shoulders as much culpability as you, if not more. I never thought you would go from one mon to another. I don't fear you being unfaithful. You don't strike me as having taken a coin from him, nor would you take it from a mon in the future. You are not a whore. Don't call yourself that. Ever."

"I won't," Emelie whispered, pressed into agreement by the sternness in Dominic's voice. "But what if people find out? What if they call me that?"

"They would be fools to ever let me find out. I will defend you to my last breath. If anyone slights you over your past, it will be the last mistake they ever make."

"You can't kill someone just because they aren't nice to me," Emelie countered.

"That isn't what I meant. If they slight you, if they impugn your honor, then they put your life and the bairn's at risk. I won't accept that."

Emelie swallowed as she realized the gravity of what Dominic meant. She'd begun to think about the babe growing within her as a part of her. She discovered a protectiveness she hadn't imagined before. Any threat to her child tore at her, creating a visceral reaction to defend him or her to the death.

"I will always protect you, Em. Not just because you're a woman. Not just because you're mine. But because you deserve it in your own right. I don't want you to live in fear of people finding out. What goes on behind closed doors is our business, not anyone else's. I cannot keep this from Brodie, which means Laurel will know. But no one else. And I will tell Brodie as my brother, not as my laird. We've never kept secrets from one another."

Emelie nodded as she pulled her lips into a flat line. She swallowed as her gorge rose. "I haven't told Blythe aught. It's felt too scary."

"Naught?"

Emelie shook her head. "I didn't tell her that I sneaked out to tryst with Henry, even though I learned she knew I sneaked out. She doesn't know we coupled, and she doesn't know I'm with child. It terrifies me to tell her, but I don't want to keep these secrets any longer. I've never kept secrets from her or Isa until I met Henry. Then it seemed to be one after another. At first, it felt exciting and illicit. Then it felt necessary. Now it feels horrid."

"Would you like me to be with you?"

"You'd do that?"

"Emelie, I know you've never married before. But a husband and wife should support one another in all things. If you wish for a marriage in name only, I accept that. But that won't make me treat you any differently than if we wed in truth."

Emelie opened her mouth to contradict Dominic. She didn't know why he thought she wanted an unconsummated handfast. But noise outside their alcove made them both fall silent until it passed.

"We shouldn't linger. Do you wish me to be with you when you talk to Blythe?" Dominic asked softly, and Emelie nodded. "Do you wish people to know we handfasted?"

"I do. I feel immense pride in the idea that people know we handfasted. It's not because you're the handsomest mon at court. It's because you're the most admirable." Emelie didn't realize what she confessed until Dominic's mien adopted a wolfish grin. He lifted her off the ground and kissed her soundly. She didn't understand how any man who kissed her with such passion and accepted her response in equal measure thought she didn't want him to bed her. Dominic turned to push the tapestry aside, but Emelie realized there was something she didn't know about her husband.

"How auld are you?"

Dominic turned back and smiled. "I'm three-and-thirty."

"Doesn't that make you a lot younger than your brother?"

"Aye. Five years."

"And ten years my senior," Emelie mused.

Dominic paused. "Does that bother you?"

"Oh, no. It was just an observation. I would worry more that you think me too young. You've pointed it out before."

"You haven't had as much life experience as Henry or me. He played upon that to his advantage and abused that knowledge. That's what I take issue with. I don't think you're too young to know your own mind, or to understand the consequences of your decisions, be it having a bairn or marrying me." Dominic brushed a petal-soft kiss on Emelie's cheek. "Would you like to find Blythe now?"

"Aye." Emelie said before Dominic moved the tapestry aside, and they slipped out of the alcove. As they moved through the passageway, Dominic slid his hand in Emelie's, a silent statement to all they passed.

FIVE

Blythe looked back in shock as Emelie and Dominic entered the sisters' chamber. She hadn't noticed that they arrived only moments after her. She looked at the couple holding hands before she squinted at Dominic.

"You can cease, Blythe," Emelie said.

"He can't be here," Blythe interrupted.

"He can. He's my husband."

Blythe's mouth dropped open, the hurt clear in her expression. "You married without telling me, without me there?"

Emelie released Dominic's hand and crossed the chamber to embrace her sister, but Blythe turned away. Emelie glanced back at Dominic, but he took an unobtrusive stance beside the door. She grasped her sister's hand and tugged her toward Emelie's bed.

"Blythe, there is so much for me to tell you, and so much for me to apologize for. You will never know how much I regret keeping any of this from you. It may be an even greater regret than what I'm aboot to say." Emelie braced herself for her sister's anger. Blythe peered around her to glare at Dominic before turning back to her sister, her expression closed off.

"You only know part of what happened with Henry."

"I knew you sneaked off with him during the day and at night. I ventured a guess what you were doing. Is that what this is aboot?"

Emelie's breath whistled as she inhaled. "Only part of it." She scrubbed her hands over her face. "It happened twice. The first time—" She paused to look at Dominic, not having told him the details of either of her sexual encounters with Henry. He nodded with encouragement, but she could tell he wasn't excited to hear the details. "The first time was in the scullery storeroom."

"It was where?" Dominic demanded as he pushed away from the wall and crossed the chamber. He squatted beside Emelie and took her hand. "Och, Em. I'm so sorry. I wish it could have been different. That wasna right."

The distress in Dominic's voice surprised her; he looked genuinely upset. She knew he was because his burr returned. She noticed he hid it when he was around any Lowlanders. She squeezed his hand and smiled. "We didn't know each other then. You aren't responsible for my choices or his. It didn't seem so bad at the time, it was even exciting. Now I realize how unromantic and tawdry it was. I thought we were just going to kiss like we had before, but it progressed quickly. He promised I would be his wife soon, and that it was unbearable for him to wait. He made it sound as though he wished to worship me, not degrade me."

Emelie turned back to Blythe before she continued. Her sister's hurt hadn't diminished. Instead, it seemed to have only grown worse as she learned the details of Emelie's deceit. But Emelie knew her sister. She knew the hurt was no longer about being left out. It was hurt for Emelie and her plight.

"I told him we couldn't do that again, that it was foolish. And we didn't. We went back to kissing and holding one another. But it was always just as rushed as it was in the storeroom."

Dominic listened to Emelie's description, and he wanted to ride to Hoppringle and wring Henry's neck. It was clear there was much the despicable man had denied Emelie. He doubted Henry took his time introducing Emelie to the various ways a man and woman could share their bodies and their affection. He feared Emelie's first time had likely been confusing and painful rather than cherishing.

"The second time was when he returned the last time. The night you told me you knew I sneaked out. I met him in the north wing in one of the solars. He seemed so eager to see me and happy that we reunited. Before I knew what he intended, we were coupling. He didn't force me either time, but neither did he give me much time to think. It was over before I could remind him not to finish in me."

Emelie closed her eyes and dipped her chin, too humiliated to look at Dominic or Blythe. She felt her sister squeeze her hand as Dominic pulled her against his chest and buried her face against it. She clung to Dominic and Blythe, needing their support as she spoke aloud her deepest shame. When she felt able to proceed, she pulled away from Dominic but not before she kissed his cheek. She knew Blythe watched everything, but she didn't want to miss the opportunity to offer Dominic a moment of affection after he had been there for her.

"I realized aboot a sennight and a half ago that I was likely with child. That is why the incense bothered me, and I looked poorly. I went to a midwife in town, and she confirmed it."

"But I don't understand what he has to do with all of this," Blythe interrupted.

"Blythe," Emelie hissed before she inhaled again. "Dominic ran into me when I returned from my second trip to the midwife. I dropped the medicinals Goody Thomas gave me, and he recognized the pennyroyal. He deduced my situation and offered me a solution that didn't involve ridding my body of the bairn."

Blythe looked scathingly at Dominic. "And why would you know what pennyroyal is or what it does?"

Dominic glanced at Emelie before looking squarely at Blythe. If secrets were coming out, then he would have to tell some of his. "I was a widower until half an hour ago. My first wife was a deceptive woman who I gravely mistook for a loving partner. After her death, I discovered pennyroyal in her belongings. My clan's healer admitted my wife used it to keep from bearing my child or my illegitimate, aulder half-brother's, who was her lover."

Both women gasped. He hadn't told Emelie the details of why he recognized the plant. He hadn't intentionally hidden it from her. Their conversation had drifted away from it, and they'd never revisited it. He couldn't recall if he'd told Emelie about Colina's faithlessness. The pity in her gaze rankled, but he knew she had good intentions. He took over explaining his arrangement with Emelie.

"I offered your sister the chance to marry me or handfast, if she preferred. Your sister is a good woman who made an awful choice. She doesn't deserve to live a life in shame." Neither woman missed the edge of warning in Dominic's tone as he locked eyes with Blythe, almost daring her to speak out against her sister. "I know we don't know each other well, but I offered her the chance to have a home and to make her bairn legitimate. She accepted my offer of a handfast, knowing I will take her back to your clan or anywhere else if she wishes to end it before the year and a day is up, or when the handfast expires."

"She is a wonderful woman, but I don't understand why you would help her. Why would you take a woman carrying another mon's bairn into your home and among your people? Can you not sire your own?"

"Blythe," Emelie hissed again.

"As far as I know I can, even if I never have. I have no bastards, and as I've just told you, my wife took precautions never to get with child. But I have no reason to think I can't. No bairn controls who they are born to. My father despised my mother and would have rather married my half-brother's mother. Had he done so, my half-brother might be alive and laird right now," Dominic shrugged. "I didn't ask for a mon who was cruel and ill-tempered to my mother to sire me. I didn't ask for a mother who my father cowed. We get who the Lord gives us. In this case, I think he's giving me a chance to be a father and giving this bairn a father who will honor and protect him or her."

"But it won't be yours," Blythe pressed.

"It will be," Dominic said with finality. Blythe opened her mouth, then frowned. She nodded her head before she looked at Emelie. She rose and pulled her sister's hand. Dominic had to move to allow Emelie space to stand. Blythe shot him a warning glare before she led Emelie to a corner.

"Is this really what you want?" Blythe whispered. "We could tell Father that you eloped, but there was an accident. We could say you're a widow."

"Father knows I was interested in Henry. It won't take much for him to deduce what really happened. I won't be married, but Henry would be dead."

"Does Henry even know?"

"I sent a missive several days ago. I don't know

what to expect. But Dominic is a good mon. Despite his wife's deceit, he loved her and he grieves for her. I believe he was a good husband to her, and I think he will be a good husband to me. He's sworn that he will take the blame if I wish to leave, and I trust him. I can't explain it, but I just know. I thought I loved Henry, but at best I was enamored. I think I loved the idea of being loved, of being courted and desired, of becoming a wife. I'm not even angry at him. I'm just naught. But Dominic—" Emelie peeked at him. "He makes me feel different. He makes me feel safe. He has never once looked down at me, reviled me, or admonished me for the situation. I never imagined a more understanding and accepting mon existed."

"Are you sure aboot this, Emmy? I'm scared for you."

"I know. I'm nervous too. But it's not aboot being with Dom. I'm nervous that people will discover the truth, and I'm nervous his people won't accept me."

"What will you do when your bairn arrives too soon?"

"Dom has already said we will tell people we handfasted during one of his earlier trips here. He's been away from home for nearly three moons. It would make it plausible."

Blythe wrapped her arms around her older sister and held on, just as they had since they were children. Emelie returned the embrace, realizing for the first time that she would soon leave Blythe at court. She might even leave Blythe that night if Dominic expected her to share his chamber.

"Will you be all right here alone?" Emelie asked. "I haven't considered the position this places you in."

"We've always known one of us would likely be here alone. It just happens to be me."

Emelie pulled back, remembering something

from their father's missive. "Father said he is going to look into betrothals for us. We must send word to him immediately aboot my handfast. But you should prepare for a groom sooner rather than later. I know you wished for—"

"Don't say his name," Blythe mouthed, tears welling in her eyes. Emelie nodded as she embraced Blythe once more. When both women felt composed enough to step apart, they turned toward Dominic, who had returned to his place against the wall. "I owe you and my sister my felicitations."

"Thank you, Lady Blythe," Dominic responded with a nod.

"You are my brother-by-marriage now. I think you can call me just Blythe."

"I appreciate that, Blythe." Dominic offered a warm smile as he moved to stand beside Emelie. Without thought, he wrapped his arm around her shoulders. He glanced down, realizing he wished she were tall enough to wrap his arm around her waist. But he was happy to have her at his side. She returned his smile, and he felt her lean against him. Blythe watched the couple, their unintentional body language telling her more than either of their explanations. She'd never seen Henry offer such silent surety as she saw from Dominic. Her doubts and worries eased.

"Would you like me to help you pack?" Blythe asked Emelie.

Emelie's stomach sucked in. She and Dominic hadn't even broached the subject of a living arrangement at court or at Kilchurn. She didn't even know when they would depart. She glanced up at Dominic once more.

"Em, what do you wish?" Dominic knew Blythe heard his question, but she was discreet and moved to her side of the chamber as if she looked for some-

68

thing. "If you wish to remain with your sister until we leave, I understand."

"Are you merely offering to give me more time, or do you not wish to share a chamber with me?"

"Just more time, Em."

"Won't people think it odd if they learn we hand-fasted—supposedly sennights ago—but I remain in a ladies'-in-waiting chamber with my sister?"

"Probably. But many husbands and wives do not share chambers." Dominic wanted to ask Emelie if she would like to share a chamber once they were home, but he didn't dare bring that up when he knew Blythe could hear. This conversation was bad enough. He hoped she would come with him that night, but he feared rejection.

"Mayhap I can put off the packing, but I—I—" Emelie's cheeks grew hot, and for the millionth time in her life, she cursed her fair coloring. She was certain she looked like a tomato.

"I'd planned to leave the day after tomorrow. If you don't wish for anyone to know that we hand-fasted, we could leave without even telling anyone other than Blythe."

Emelie shook her head as her eyes darted to her sister, who sat on her bed with her back to them while she sewed. "There will be a barrage of questions that I'm leaving Blythe to answer. I don't want to make it worse. People should know, otherwise they'll claim I left in haste and disgrace. It won't save my reputation or Blythe's. She'll suffer."

"Then dine with me this eve and retire with me," Dominic suggested. He held his breath, suddenly more nervous than when he waited for Colina to answer him after he asked her to marry him. His throat went dry, and he told himself to make no assumptions if she shared his chamber that night and the next. Emelie nodded as she rested her hands on his chest, which he covered with his massive ones. He thought they looked like bear paws compared to her dainty fingers and palms.

"I'd like that." Emelie stood on her toes, and Dominic bent down to receive a quick kiss before she spoke to her sister. "We can pack tomorrow. I'm going to dine with Dominic and his clansmen tonight, but I will break my fast and share the midday meal with you. The queen hasn't dismissed me from her service yet. I have one more day with you, Blythe."

Both sisters looked at one another with solemnity and finality. As Dominic watched, he knew he would insist Emelie spend all the next day with Blythe. He would even sneak her back to this chamber if they wished for one more night together. Dominic promised to return later to escort the sisters to the evening meal. He needed to inform the king that he and Emelie were moving forward with the handfast, and to prepare his men to travel with his new wife. He knew there would be speculation and confusion, but none of the men would speak against Emelie. Many of them had been in Stirling during Brodie and Laurel's whirlwind courtship. He supposed there wasn't much he could do that would surprise the men after what he heard about Brodie and Laurel.

As he left the sisters' chamber, the gravity of his new circumstances hit him. He had a new wife. He would share his chamber with another woman, something he hadn't considered until he met Emelie. He found he looked forward to it until he reminded himself that she might not wish for the same intimacy as he did. And his fear for her health remained. He swore he wouldn't rush Emelie, and he would respect her wishes at all times. With a lighter heart than a moment ago, he headed toward the Privy Council chamber for a second time that day.

Emelie kept her eyes forward as she entered the Great Hall on Dominic's arm. She heard tittering and whispers, but she avoided most of the confused and envious stares. Word had spread throughout court that Dominic was a widower, and it made him one of the most eligible and sought-after men in Stirling. There was more than one nose out of joint to see him enter the Great Hall with a woman. As Dominic guided Emelie through the crowd, she struggled to remain calm, praying her fair coloring wouldn't grow mottled and red from all the attention. No man had ever escorted her into the evening meal. As they neared the table where the Campbell guards sat, Dominic shifted and wrapped his arm around Emelie's shoulders to guide her forward. His thumb grazed the bare skin at the top of her shoulder in reassurance. He hadn't considered what he was doing, but it caused an even greater stir.

King Robert rose from his seat before the diners took theirs. He raised his chalice and waited for the crowd to fall silent. The monarch's eyes scanned the crowd before he turned his attention to Emelie and Dominic. She wanted to sink through the wooden floor. Clearing his throat, King Robert announced, "My felicitations to Dominic and Lady Emelie Campbell."

The king waited for the buzz to settle before he continued. Emelie knew her face was ablaze. Mortified, she still stood proudly next to Dominic, whose arm tightened around her, and his thumb continued to sweep her exposed skin. She focused on the sensation and calmed. It surprised her how soothing it was.

"Dominic and Lady Emelie handfasted during one of his many visits here over the past few moons,

71

and I learned of it recently. It is my wish to acknowledge them as husband and wife before they depart court. My best wishes to the happy couple." King Robert raised his chalice to them and smiled. Dominic nodded, and Emelie dipped into a shallow curtsy.

The couple settled onto the bench at their table as a servant placed one trencher before them. It was another first for Emelie. She'd never shared the hardened bread platter with a man. She chanced a glance at Dominic, who lifted a piece of quail from the servant's tray and placed it on Emelie's side of the trencher before taking one for himself.

"What else would you like?" Dominic asked. He recalled Emelie mentioned during one of their walks that she enjoyed the poultry, but he wasn't certain what else she preferred.

"I don't mind. Whatever the servants bring. I'm not picky," Emelie murmured. Her brow furrowed as she considered her first wifely duty. "Shouldn't I serve you?"

Dominic glanced down at her as he accepted pieces of roast lamb. "Mayhap, but today is special. I'd like to do this for you."

Emelie grew quiet as she considered what Dominic said. She wasn't sure if he considered it their wedding day or merely a day that was out of the ordinary for him. When his hand covered hers on the bench between them, she opened it and accepted his fingers slipping along her palm. As the meal progressed, Emelie studiously watched what Dominic favored, tucking the information away for later. She signaled passing servants to refill their chalice whenever it dipped below half full. Dominic squeezed her hand and smiled at her when he realized her attentiveness.

"I'd like to do this for you," Emelie whispered, a

72

twinkle in her eye as she returned his smile. Dominic had a sudden flash of what he would like Emelie to do for him, and it had nothing to do with the evening meal. His cock stirred for the hundredth time around her, and he forced his eyes back to the food before him. They hadn't spoken again about Emelie sharing his chamber, and he still intended to offer her a chance to spend their last two nights with Blythe. He couldn't imagine leaving Brodie's side permanently.

As brothers, it had never been a consideration. Five years his senior, Brodie went away to foster and returned before he and Dominic were of ages with mutual interests. Even when Colina's behavior caused a wedge to develop between them when Brodie arrived home with Laurel, he'd never considered Brodie as anything less than his best friend. While Graham had been Brodie's second-in-command among the warriors, it was with Dominic that Brodie made his decisions.

As newlyweds, Dominic and Emelie could spend most of the night dancing together without causing any more rumors than their entrance and unexpected handfast had caused. They enjoyed the time together, Dominic once more twirling Emelie until she giggled. The only moment of unease came when Emelie spied a member of Clan Pringle, who appeared to be making a beeline for her.

"Dom," Emelie whispered. "I don't want to dance with that mon. He's a Pringle."

"You never have to dance with anyone you don't wish to. You're a married woman now. You can assert yourself and decline." Dominic realized his assurance did little to ease Emelie's discomfort. He maneuvered them through the mingling dancers until they reached a side door. Dominic held it open as they stepped into the passageway. He figured it was as good a time as any to make his offer. "Em, I know things are moving faster than you likely imagined. I know it upsets you to leave Blythe behind, especially when you didn't know you only had one more day with her. If you wish to spend the night with your sister, I can take you back to your chamber. I will come back before the servants stir, so no one sees you there."

Emelie stood stunned at Dominic's offer. Excitement and rejection warred within her. She wished to spend more time with Blythe, and the knowledge that they must part made her heart ache. But she didn't know if Dominic made the offer because he wanted her to have the time with her sister or if he didn't want her to share his bed. She didn't even know if they had to consummate a handfast for people to consider it real.

Dominic watched the emotions flicker across Emelie's pretty face. He spotted the rejection and feared he'd erred in his offer. He tilted her chin back and pressed a soft kiss to her lips, keeping himself under control when all he wanted was to maul his bonnie little bride. "Em, I'm not sending you away. I thought aboot how hard it would be for me to say goodbye to Brodie. As a mon, I will never have to do that. I don't want to shortchange you time with your family. I can't promise when you might see any of them again."

"Thank you, Dom." Emelie smiled ruefully. "I feel like I spend most of our time together thanking you, but I do mean it. I've never met a mon so considerate of anyone's feelings, let alone a woman's."

"You're a brave woman to accept a handfast with a mon you barely know. There are risks to any woman marrying a mon she doesn't know, but you're placing your trust in me. I want to honor that. Your life is aboot to change in myriad ways. I would give you a few more moments of what you're used to."

Emelie tilted her head as a soft smile played across her lips. "Are you like this because you're so auld?" She teased.

Dominic's chuckle rumbled in the quiet passageway. "Mayhap I've had time to mature with age. Do you know, Laurel asks Brodie the same question? He's eleven years her senior."

Emelie attempted to stifle her giggle but failed. When Dominic cocked an eyebrow, she shook her head. Once she could speak, she explained, "I recently heard *The Merchant's Tale*. It's part of Geoffrey Chaucer's recent work, *The Canterbury Tales*. In that story, a mon name Januarie is quite auld when he finally marries. He's sixty, and his bride named May is barely twenty." Emelie's smile dropped as she remembered the rest of the story.

"What happens?" Dominic prompted. He watched as Emelie swallowed and shifted uncomfortably. He waited for her to answer, but she couldn't meet his eye.

"She's unfaithful to him," Emelie whispered. She closed her eyes before continuing. "I didn't think aboot that part before I began speaking. I just thought of the difference in age since you're aulder than me. I didn't mean that I would be unfaithful."

"Em, look at me," Dominic murmured, his voice growing thick as he tried to ease Emelie's chagrin. "I didna think that. And I already kenned. I've heard the tales, too. I wasna trying to trick ye. I just wanted to hear how ye would retell the story. There are some vera amusing parts." He didn't want to see Emelie distressed after hearing her lighthearted laughter. There would be plenty of time for seriousness ahead of them, when he arrived with a wife on his arm and Emelie found her place among his clan. "Would ye like to go back to yer chamber?"

"Yes, please."

They walked together in silence until they arrived at Emelie's door. She unlocked it, and they stepped inside. When Emelie turned around, she found her nose in Dominic's chest. His hands rested lightly on her waist.

"Rather than I wake ye early," Dominic's brogue persisted now that he didn't think about it. "We can always say ye returned here early because ye needed to dress for the day. I must meet with a mon tomorrow. Brodie is still smoothing things over with the MacMillans after the laird's daughter died only days after marrying Brodie. The Lamonts attacked their entourage as Brodie rode to Kilchurn with her."

Emelie's brow furrowed as she learned details of her friend Laurel's marriage that she'd never heard before. She supposed matters concerning Clan Campbell now concerned her. "He was a widower too?"

"Brodie never consummated the marriage because he couldnae stomach the idea of bedding his young bride. He said she was young enough to be his daughter. He'd returned the dowry in full. But the MacMillans still blame the Campbells rather than placing the blame where it belongs, with the Lamonts."

"Why did he marry her if she was so young?" Emelie cut in. She'd said many prayers of thanksgiving that she hadn't been a child bride.

"For the alliance. The MacMillans' territory lies between two portions of Campbell land. It would have secured our access to a waterway. Brodie intended to wait at least two years before he even considered touching her. The only reason anyone called it a marriage was because they swore their vows on the kirk steps. It was more of a betrothal. We also needed a chatelaine."

"What aboot—" Emelie snapped her mouth

shut, recalling Brodie already said Colina hadn't taken to the role. She didn't want to remind him of something that brought him pain.

"It's all right." Dominic squeezed her waist. "Anyway, I must meet with the MacMillan delegate and see if I can calm them enough to keep us on good terms. That will probably take most of the afternoon, and I can spend the morning in the lists. That will give ye the day with yer sister."

Emelie was torn once more. She was grateful for the time to say goodbye to Blythe, but she enjoyed their morning walks. She looked forward to it. "Would you attend Mass with me?" Emelie asked.

"Of course. I look forward to sitting beside ye. Em, I am nae shunning ye. I hope ye ken that."

"I do. I just fear what people will think if they don't see us together the day after we supposedly handfasted."

"King Robert never said when the handfast took place. It could have been yesterday or a fortnight ago. People have seen us together every day since I returned. If anyone asks, ye've spent every night with me, but we chose discretion rather than flaunting our relationship. We made it known because of our imminent departure together."

"You have an answer to everything."

"I've considered this several times. We owe nay one the full story—whatever we decide that is—so dinna feel pressured into telling more than ye need to."

Emelie's laugh was hollow. "You have spent little time at court after all. Every lady-in-waiting feels pressure in one way or another. It's not an unusual feeling."

"That doesnae mean it has to continue now that ye're married," Dominic reasoned. He brushed the back of his fingers over her cheek before pressing a light kiss to her lips. They hadn't had a passionate kiss since their interlude in the alcove earlier that day. Emelie was growing frustrated at the sudden distance Dominic put between them. She feared he regretted his impetuous decision and missed his actual wife. She nodded before pressing her own kiss to his mouth. She tried to deepen it, and Dominic groaned. He crushed her against him as he opened his mouth to her tongue. But it was all over sooner than Emelie expected. Dominic took a step back. "I should go now before the ladies retire and someone sees me here."

"Goodnight, Dom."

"Goodnight, Em. I will find ye before Mass. I promise." With one more quick peck to her nose, Dominic was gone.

SIX

Dominic met Emelie for Mass the morning following the announcement of their handfast. He accompanied her to the morning meal, where she sat among Dominic and his men. She joined him for the midday and evening meal as well, but she spent the time in between with Blythe. She realized how fortunate she was that Dominic offered her this opportunity. Saying goodbye proved even more challenging than she expected. He took her back to her old chamber for their last night in Stirling, where she drafted a missive to her parents with Blythe's help. Blythe promised to send it with a messenger in the morning. Just as they had the night before, the sisters climbed into bed together. They reminisced about their childhood and time spent at court. They also discussed the challenges they expected Emelie to face, both as a mother and as someone with a grave secret.

Blythe admitted she stared at Emelie and Dominic every time they were together, and her new brother-by-marriage impressed her. She had no reason to doubt his sincerity, since she noticed slight gestures he made that likely no one else noticed. Blythe was confident they were genuine and not for show. It eased her worry as yet another older sister left for the unknown. Isabella and her husband, Dedric, had returned to Dunbar land shortly after they married. But as politics shifted they took the opportunity to move to the northern Highlands, far from the border. They now lived among the Sinclairs, and Dedric was one of Laird Sinclair's senior guardsmen and a close friend to the four Sinclair brothers.

As they stood together in the bailey, the Campbell guards surrounding them with stomping horses, Blythe engulfed Emelie in her embrace. She'd often teased Emelie that she was the big sister, since she was nearly half a head taller than her next-older sister. Emelie returned the hug and whispered, "If you ever need to leave court for any reason and you can't go home, come to me. If I need to, I'll get you to Isa and Ric. Don't think twice. Send for Dom or find a way to Kilchurn. I hate leaving you behind."

"I'll manage," Blythe murmured against Emelie's ear. "Isa survived plenty of years alone here. We didn't arrive until after she left. If she could do it, so can I. But if you need to leave Dominic or the Campbells, come here. I will get you to Mother and Father, or I'll get you to Isa and Ric. Don't stay if it isn't safe. Don't stay if you're unhappy."

"If unhappiness were a reason to leave any place, you and I would never have spent more than a moon at court. No one is promised happiness in this lifetime. But as long as I'm safe with Dom, Brodie, and Laurel, I think I can find happiness. I didn't plan to become a mother under these circumstances, but I am happy that I will be."

The sisters squeezed one another once more before stepping apart. Dominic kept his distance, giving the sisters their private moment. When Emelie looked back at him and smiled, he approached. On the pretense of giving her brother-by-marriage a peck on the cheek, Blythe whispered so only Dominic could hear. "If you make her unhappy, if you cannot protect her, I will cut off your cods and feed them to a goat. Then I will cut off your cock and shove it up a ram's arse. Hurt her, and I will kill you."

"Lady Blythe, I take your warning seriously, just as I do my duty as your sister's husband." Dominic glanced at Emelie before leaning forward to speak so only Blythe could hear him. "She is a woman any mon would fall in love with and keep beside him until his last breath."

Dominic straightened and gave Blythe a pointed look, to which she nodded and offered a hesitant smile. He turned to Emelie and offered her his hand before lifting her into the saddle. He mounted his own steed, and then they were off. Emelie looked back and waved to Blythe as they passed under the Stirling Castle gates and began their trek into the Highlands.

"It will be a four- or five-day journey," Dominic explained as they left the town limits. "If the weather holds, it should only be four days. I'm afraid there are few inns along our route, so we will sleep under the stars."

"That wouldn't be a first. It takes several days to travel from Dunbar land to Stirling, and I've been on summer progress with the queen," Emelie pointed out, but she frowned when Dominic looked no more reassured.

"You likely had a tent when you traveled, at least with the queen. Since I didn't expect to have—didn't expect to travel with you, I don't have one."

Emelie knew he was about to say he hadn't expected to have a wife. She thought she even noticed a faint blush rising in Dominic's cheeks, and she caught his gaze shifting to his men. She steered her horse a step closer to Dominic's and kept her voice low.

"If I can have a moment or two of privacy each night, that's all I need."

"I will do whatever I can to make sure you have everything you need. Em, I can already see you're an experienced rider, but I doubt you often spend the long days in the saddle that we will. There will be hilly terrain that will test your endurance. Don't be embarrassed to admit when you need a rest. I don't like that you're riding, but I don't have a wagon either. And walking is obviously out of the question."

"You don't like me riding?"

"Aye." Dominic glanced at her middle. "A horse can throw even the most experienced rider."

Emelie didn't know what to say to Dominic's last comment. She hadn't thought about how riding might endanger her babe. Dominic surprised her once again by his astute observation and consideration. She wondered how he even thought about it, and it made her wonder how often he thought about her condition. As if he read her mind, he smiled.

"Brodie had a fit the first time Laurel tried to go riding once he knew she was carrying. He wanted to make her switch her gelding for a plow horse. I expected Laurel to chew his ear off for giving her orders and stifling her daily rides. It shocked me to my roots that she just nodded and embraced him. Later, when I asked why she relented without argument, she explained she hadn't even thought aboot the risk. She didn't want to cause Brodie undue panic after what she'd already survived. And she admitted he was right."

"Already survived?" Emelie asked.

"I assumed you'd talked to Laurel the last time they were at court."

Emelie blushed. "I wasn't a particularly good

friend to Laurel just before she married your brother. She overheard several of us discussing the wager Nelson MacDougall orchestrated. I rudely pointed out what most of us thought: Brodie only paid attention to her to win the bet. Blythe defended her, but even that was tepid. We were among Laurel's few friends by the time she married, and I failed her by talking aboot her behind her back. Or as it turns out, right in front of her face."

"And you resolved naught during her last visit?" Dominic pressed.

"Not really. She avoided Blythe and me, even though we apologized. I don't think she was angry. It was worse. I think she was still deeply hurt." Emelie bit her bottom lip as she met Dominic's gaze. "Do you think she'll forgive me and welcome me into her home?"

"It's now your home as much as it is hers, and aye, I think she'll forgive you. From what Brodie and Laurel have told me, she's an entirely different person now that she's away from court and back in the Highlands. She never wanted to leave Ross land or be a lady-in-waiting. I think she will surprise you when you see her again, and I'm certain it will be for the better. Apologize and be a sincere friend." Dominic shrugged. Emelie hoped it were so simple, but she suspected female relationships were more complex than most male ones.

Dominic brought them back to what they'd originally been talking about. "When Brodie traveled with Laurel once she was carrying, they went slower than they usually would. If I had birlinns, I would have us sail. If we're going too fast for you, there is no shame in speaking up."

Emelie swept her eyes over the men in front of her. She didn't think they would agree. No matter what they told anyone at Kilchurn, Dominic's men likely knew that they hadn't handfasted weeks ago, and they would question how she got with child so quickly. It was the first prickle of fear that her secret would destroy her arrival. She didn't believe any of the men would lie for her, and she didn't want them to lie on Dominic's behalf. She squeaked when she suddenly found herself lifted out of her saddle and placed in front of Dominic on his. He wrapped his powerful arm around her middle and held her in place as he deftly managed his horse and tied her reins to his saddle.

"No one needs to hear our conversation but you. We appear the happy newlyweds," Dominic spoke quietly. "My men aren't privy to what I do within the keep. They fight hard and serve my clan loyally, but they are not my advisors nor my confidants. I have been a widower for six months. It's not beyond reason that I would remarry, even if it is within my year of mourning. They understand why I would want my privacy in this matter, so I don't want you to worry that they will tell anyone that we only handfasted two days ago. As far as they know, it could have been two days ago or nearly three moons ago."

"If it was that long ago, wouldn't they think it odd that we never sat together for meals, that we never went riding together, and that it's only been within the last fortnight that you've publicly paid attention to me?"

"I told them the queen hadn't released you from service until I knew we'd be leaving for good. All the ladies-in-waiting sit together. Half the matrons at court don't sit with their husbands. Hell, most of them don't even talk to their husbands. It wouldn't seem that implausible. They know I have bedded no tavern wenches or whores, so they won't believe me unfaithful. But who I bedded while I was in the keep is naught they would know."

Emelie stiffened as she wondered who he had bedded during his visits to Stirling. Once again, he seemed to read her mind. Or perhaps he felt how rigid she went because his hand stroked her back as that arm tugged her closer.

"I told you, I have no mistress. I haven't even thought aboot touching a woman since my first wife died. There has been no one else."

Emelie wasn't certain whether that reassured her or made her feel worse. It was a stark reminder that Dominic still grieved his wife's passing. Her heart ached for the sorrow she was certain he still felt, and it made her sympathetic to why he might not have been ready to share his chamber with her after all. It had hurt to think he might not be attracted to her as she was to him, but she couldn't begrudge him his grief.

"I don't want you to worry aboot the men gossiping or questioning us," Dominic said as he broke into her thoughts. He kissed her temple, and she relaxed against him. Even if Emelie had to accept that theirs was going to be a more platonic relationship, she still took comfort in his nearness. She rested her head against his chest and soon grew sleepy. "Sleep, little dove."

Emelie jerked away so quickly that her head slammed into the underside of Dominic's jaw and made him bite his tongue. "Don't call me that. Ever." Emelie hissed. "He called me that. I never want to hear it again."

"Wheesht. I'm sorry," Dominic soothed. Emelie eased back against his chest and released a shuddering breath as the sudden surge of rage dissipated. "I think *mo sparradh beag* fits better anyway."

"I don't speak Gaelic," Emelie confessed, confused by the phrase she didn't understand. She thought he called her a sparrow. Why did men keep calling her birds?

"It means my wee sparrow," Dominic interpreted. "You are hardy, even if you are tiny." Dominic tickled her ribs, and Emelie rewarded him with one of her coveted giggles. The sound shot heat to his groin every time he heard it. He forced himself not to shift in the saddle, but he feared he'd erred when he felt his cock twitch. He prayed she didn't feel it, but Emelie's quick glance before resting against him again told him she had. He barely moved until he felt Emelie's breathing grow slower and deeper as she fell asleep.

Dominic hadn't pointed out what he'd observed as a child who loved climbing trees. Sparrows also mated for life. As he glanced down at Emelie, he hoped they would discover they suited well enough to marry in earnest. It still surprised him how easily he accepted the idea of raising another man's child. It hadn't fazed him at all. Perhaps it was because he didn't know the man, nor had he any claim over Emelie before she got pregnant. He was certain he would have felt the visceral opposite and refused to raise any child Graham had sired with Colina. Just as always happened when he thought of the lovers, anger filled his chest to near busting. He wanted to roar and throw something, anything, as he pictured the woman he'd devoted himself to in bed with Graham, his own half-brother.

When Emelie shifted, and her full breast brushed against his forearm, he reminded himself that Colina was his past and, hopefully, Emelie was his future. He didn't want to think about that conniving woman while he held Emelie. He imagined all the ways he could introduce Emelie to passion, but he reminded himself that he might have many moons to wait before he could. He still didn't know if it would be safe for a man his size to couple with a woman as petite as Emelie while she was pregnant. Laurel's condition never slowed her or Brodie, but she was tall and sturdy. His brother treated his wife as the most precious thing in the world, but Dominic never saw Brodie treat her as fragile, which was just how he thought of Emelie while she was expecting. He would protect Emelie from any danger, including his own lust.

If asked, Emelie couldn't recount much of the journey to Kilchurn. She began each morning on her horse with the sun shining on her face as they moved ever closer to a mountain range. The rugged landscape impressed her, and she found the fresh air suited her. But it also made her incredibly sleepy before midmorning. Dominic kept a close eye on her and lifted her onto his horse when she drooped. Then she would sleep away the rest of the first half of the day. He would rouse her for the midday meal, which she often had to refuse when her stomach recoiled at the dried beef. She dozed in the afternoon, once more riding with Brodie. She didn't sleep as deeply as she did earlier in the day. She was ravenous by the time they made camp each night.

Dominic quietly slipped her most of his share of the rabbits and squirrels they caught and roasted. Emelie objected at first, horrified that her colossal husband ate so little while she scarfed down everything within reach. A little teasing and a passionate kiss tucked away behind a giant oak tree convinced Emelie to accept Dominic's offers graciously.

When they bedded down each night, Emelie burrowed against the warmth of Dominic's larger body. She wished he would initiate something intimate, and she even convinced herself that she would try. But she always she fell asleep before anything happened. She awoke each morning sprawled across Brodie's chest with one of her legs between his, and his morning arousal poked her mons. The urge to press her mound against him made her body ache until she fell asleep for her morning nap.

Dominic was in agony. He'd never experienced such dreadful pain in his bollocks in all his life. His mind was split between keeping his raging cock from growing anytime Emelie was in reach, paying attention to any hidden danger, and ensuring Emelie didn't fall from a horse when she drifted off. His need to relieve his ever-constant arousal tempted him to ease the ache during his nightly watch, but he would never risk being distracted. Not only did his men count on him to lead by example and to do his duty, now he had someone who needed his protection. He kept his back turned whenever he took Emelie near a loch or stream to bathe. He knew if he caught even a peek, he would likely throw himself at her. His only relief came when he could have his turn to bathe. He spent more time with his hand wrapped around his cock than he did scrubbing himself clean.

It was early afternoon on their fifth day of travel when they spotted Kilchurn in the distance. They traveled along the banks of the River Orchy, so Dominic roused Emelie and offered her a chance to refresh herself before they arrived. He knew the men were eager to arrive home, and they had traveled slower because of Emelie. But he was set on giving Emelie the chance to make herself more presentable. He could sense her worry increased each day they rode closer to home. She'd admitted she feared making a poor impression on her new clan members.

What she didn't admit was she feared she would disappoint them compared to Colina. She knew the woman hadn't been helpful around the keep and that she'd been unfaithful to Dominic, but she reasoned there must have been many excellent qualities about her if Dominic continued to grieve. She and Dominic shared a handful of passionate kisses when they shared their bedrolls at night and when they woke. They even caught brief moments alone, but there was almost no privacy, and Emelie slept most of the time. She wondered if things would change, but she was too nervous to ask Dominic.

The bells rang as Dominic, Emelie, and their entourage approached Kilchurn's massive gates. As they passed under the portcullis, Emelie spotted Brodie and Laurel. Her former peer was noticeably pregnant, and even waddled a little as they descended the steps with Brodie's arm wrapped around her waist. Halfway down, he lifted her off her feet and carried her down pinned to his side. Emelie watched as Laurel good-naturedly scolded him, but she watched the moment Laurel recognized her. Shock replaced the indulgent grin she'd offered her husband.

"Emelie?" Laurel called as she hurried toward them. Emelie had insisted that she ride her own horse into the bailey, but Dominic had merely shaken his head and hoisted her onto his. He'd explained that he wanted everyone to know he was glad to have her as his wife and that theirs hadn't been an arranged marriage. It would make it easier for people to believe she'd gotten with child so quickly. Emelie had only nodded her head, realizing once and for all that Dominic viewed their arrangement as a marriage of convenience—one that was only convenient for her.

"Laurel," Emelie greeted her friend hesitantly.

The air whooshed from Emelie when Laurel's arms squeezed around her. It was an awkward embrace with Laurel's belly in the way, but Emelie felt the sincerity in Laurel's welcome.

"What are you doing here?" Laurel bubbled. Emelie had never heard Laurel sound so effervescent. She relaxed when Dominic wrapped his arm around her shoulders. She dared for the first time to wrap her arm around his waist. She felt him still for a moment before his hold tightened, and he practically crushed her against him.

"Laurel, don't think to monopolize all of my wife's time," Dominic teased. He couldn't think of a better way to make the introduction, since he knew his announcement would stun everyone. He'd sworn never to marry again.

"We handfasted at court." Emelie kept her voice low as Laurel and Brodie stared at her, then simultaneously swung questioning gazes to Dominic.

"It's been a long five days, and I think we're both starved. Perhaps we could eat and get settled before I launch into the story," Dominic suggested. When Laurel's eyes narrowed, he realized he'd excluded Emelie from the upcoming conversation. He hadn't thought beyond knowing Emelie would likely need to sleep. As he considered that, he knew they would have to tell Laurel and Brodie their circumstances sooner rather than later, or Laurel would guess. He recalled she'd spent a sennight early in her pregnancy barely able to remain awake for more than two hours at a time.

"Mayhap we could talk first," Emelie said as she looked at Dominic. He knew she'd come to the same conclusion as he had.

"We can go to our solar, and I'll have a servant bring up a couple of trays," Laurel suggested. Her astute gaze told Dominic that she was already piecing things together, but there was an accusatory edge that Dominic wanted to blunt. He wouldn't let his sister-by-marriage believe he'd wronged Emelie.

Emelie felt people staring as she walked beside Dominic and followed Brodie and Laurel to a chamber abovestairs. It surprised her to discover that what should have been the lady's chamber was a solar that Laurel and Brodie shared. There were two desks that faced one another, along with a padded window seat. Three chairs sat before the fire, and Emelie realized Dominic must have often spent time in there. He guided her to the window seat, and despite it being a squeeze, he sat beside her. No one spoke until servants brought food and drink, then closed the door behind them.

Emelie licked her dry lips as she watched Laurel ease into a chair near the fireplace. Brodie pulled a chair beside Laurel's and took his wife's hand as he sat. The weary travelers ate in silence. When Emelie could manage no more, she knew she couldn't delay the inevitable any longer. Two expectant faces watched as Emelie gathered her thoughts. She sighed when Dominic took the lead.

"Emelie and I handfasted two days before we left Stirling," Dominic began. "I know what I've sworn in the past, but I changed my mind." Dominic wished that would be enough of an explanation, but he wasn't foolish enough to believe it was. When a gentle hand rested on his leg, he glanced down at Emelie. He watched her muster her courage, so he squeezed her waist in encouragement. He realized it was the first time he'd been able to sit with his arm resting there. He found he preferred it immensely to any other position in which they could sit, short of her being on his lap. He didn't think they'd reached that stage yet.

"I believed Henry Pringle, heir to his clan, was

courting me. He promised me things," Emelie confessed. "And I was too naive to understand he was playing me for a fool. He never forced me, but he coerced me into making the same mistake twice. It didn't seem like a mistake at the time. I thought we loved one another. I thought we were going to get married."

Emelie watched Brodie and Laurel as she spoke. She watched shock, then anger register on Brodie's face. She feared he directed it toward her. Laurel didn't look surprised. Emelie couldn't decide if Laurel had deduced everything already, or if she expected little more from Emelie. She desperately wanted it to be the former, and it wasn't implausible since Laurel was the most quick-witted person she knew.

"Stop scowling, Brodie," Laurel admonished before she smiled at Emelie. "He's angry on your behalf, not at you. Would you like me to save you from having to say it aloud?" Laurel's voice softened with her question, and Emelie nearly burst into tears when she witnessed the genuine sympathy in Laurel's eyes. She'd braced herself for scorn and ridicule. The kindness nearly overwhelmed her.

"I think we all understand," Brodie replied. "I'm not angry with you, Lady Emelie. And I can already guess why my brother handfasted with you. I'd just like to know how it came to pass."

"Dominic found me in the far end of the gardens just after I read a missive from my father. I'd grown concerned when Henry didn't send word that my father approved his request to marry me. My father bluntly told me Henry couldn't because he married Allyson's aulder sister Alice."

"Does he know?" Laurel asked.

"I sent word, but we left before a messenger returned."

"Do you think he'll want to acknowledge the bairn? Even claim it?" Brodie asked. "I take it you're planning to claim the bairn is yours, Dom."

"I will. We are handfasted now, so as far as it concerns anyone else, this bairn is mine. I promised Emelie that she can repudiate the handfast or let it expire. Either way, I will take the fault and help her settle wherever she wishes. Even if the handfast ends, if the child is born while we are together, it will bear my name and be deemed legitimate." Dominic's tone bordered on defiant at the end, almost challenging Brodie to argue that the child could not be a Campbell.

"What color hair does Henry have?" Laurel asked. Three sets of eyes turned to her. "As long as it isn't reddish like mine or black, then it will be believable that Dominic sired the child. If the bairn doesn't look like either of you, we claim the bairn looks like one of Emelie's family members." Laurel shrugged as the others continued to stare at her. With one brief idea and quick explanation, Laurel welcomed Emelie into their family.

"Laurel, I'm sorry," Emelie blurted. A sudden urge to sob swelled in her chest. She regretted how she acted toward Laurel, but the strength of her emotions alarmed her.

"Wheesht," Laurel said as she flapped her hand. "Dinna fash." At Emelie's confused expression, Laurel chuckled. "It means, don't worry. I can't blame anyone for their suspicions, even if they were hurtful. And considering how I acted only moments after you spoke, I would say your comment made sense. And don't be scared by those sudden changes in emotions. I was a watering pot for most of the first three moons of this pregnancy. I still am at times. It's Dom who should look out. You'll be happy as a bumblebee in summer one moment, then spring a leak, only to roar like a thundercloud the next. They say the worse it is, the more likely you're having a lad."

Emelie's mind flashed to the memory of finding the blossoming wheat. If the legends were true, then she already knew she was having a son. While she would be happy with a son or a daughter, forcing Dominic to accept an heir that wasn't his still made her uneasy. She didn't know what she would do in seven or eight months, but she told herself the right thing to do would be to set Dominic free.

"Whatever you're whittling aboot can be sorted out," Dominic whispered. Emelie nodded before she attempted to stifle a yawn. Between the travel and the emotional rollercoaster of their brief conversation, she wanted nothing more than to sleep. He helped her to her feet and slid his hand into hers. "I remember how sleepy you were at first, Laurel. Em is going through the same thing."

Laurel nodded, noting the diminutive Dominic used for his bride. She wondered where their relationship stood. There was a distance between them, or rather an awkwardness, she corrected herself. She mused silently that they wanted the same thing, but neither wanted to admit it.

"I'll get Emelie settled," Dominic offered as the two couples walked to the door.

"I know we're not the same height," Laurel said as they neared Dominic's chamber. "But even if all your belongings come from court, you won't be able to wear them much longer. I have several gowns I altered to fit as my waist expanded. I can alter them to suit you." Emelie knew Laurel was an adept seamstress. She'd hidden her talent for years, but the former lady-in-waiting possessed a gift with a needle and thread.

They came to a stop outside Dominic's chamber. He opened the door and stepped inside, memories slamming into him. Everywhere he looked, there was a reminder of Colina. He hadn't been inside the chamber for months and forgot that nothing had been packed away or changed. He heard Emelie's gasp. Still holding her hand, he spun on his heel and practically dragged her down the passageway until he reached a chamber he knew wasn't in use. He threw open the door and breathed easier.

"I'm sorry," Laurel stammered. "I—I didn't know to—I didn't remember when you arrived that…"

"It's all right, Laurel," Emelie smiled. She wondered if Laurel and Colina had grown close. From Laurel's ashen appearance, she assumed being reminded of Colina's death brought back her friend's grief, just as it had Dominic's.

"I'll have a maid come up and air out the chamber. The linens are fresh." Laurel looked back and forth between Dominic and Emelie, waiting for Dominic to speak up, to say anything. When her brother-by-marriage remained silent, tension radiating from him, Laurel suggested, "Perhaps the maid can wait. You might want to rest first."

"I would," Emelie nodded. Laurel and Brodie disappeared, leaving Emelie looking at Dominic. She couldn't read his expression, and it worried her. She stepped in front of him and placed her hands on his ridged belly. "It's all right. I understand."

Dominic looked down at Emelie. He knew he should explain his reaction, but he couldn't. He couldn't form any thoughts beyond anger and a need to escape. He covered her hands with his and forced a smile before stepping away.

"I know the journey exhausted you. I'll let you get some rest." He made to turn around, but thought better of it and dropped a kiss on her right temple. Then he spun around much like he had in his chamber and disappeared through the doorway. Emelie stood watching him, then stared into the empty passageway. She had no idea what to make of Dominic's behavior, but she felt bad for him. The few times she'd tried to broach the subject of his married life, Dominic had abruptly changed the subject. She didn't want to cause him undue upset, so she'd abandoned trying to learn what type of husband he'd been. Now she didn't know what to think. But Colina's ghost felt so present that it tempted Emelie to talk to the dead woman.

SEVEN

Dominic had to escape. He had to escape the keep. He had to escape Emelie. And he had to escape his memories. His desire to get away was so strong he considered saddling his horse and riding out to join a patrol. That was how he'd avoided his chamber and his memories before he went to court. He'd gone through a handful of Colina's belongings the day she died, but he'd been too irrational to remain in the chamber. He'd broken several of her perfume vials before Laurel shooed him away. He'd slammed the door behind him and hadn't been back inside since.

Dominic hadn't remembered what would greet him until he opened the door. His thoughts had been to get Emelie comfortable, so she could nap. It was a suffocating reality that wrapped around him, and he couldn't bring himself to let Emelie anywhere near the evil that lurked within the chamber he'd shared for three years. He didn't think he'd ever be able to enter the room again, let alone share it with Emelie.

As Dominic hurried down the steps and across the bailey, he heard swords clanging in the lists. He swerved toward the training field and drew his weapon as he approached his fellow warriors. Many called out greetings that he barely acknowledged. He was terse as he picked out three partners to spar against. Wielding his sword was the reprieve he needed. He concentrated on keeping his arms and legs attached rather than remembering the past or worrying about the future.

"Ye wouldnae ken ye've been on the road for days," Stanley mused. The warrior was younger than Dominic by a few years, but he was strong and held his own.

"I saw that bonnie bride ye rode in with," Jacob grinned, and Dominic wanted to smash the leer off the man's face. They were the same age, but they hadn't gotten along as children and didn't care for each other much as adults. But he was a good sparring partner, so Dominic tolerated him. "I would think ye'd be helping her settle in. Mayhap showing her around yer chamber."

"Mayhap he's already worn her out," Stanley teased. Dominic drove his fist into Stanley's nose before wrapping his hand around the man's throat.

"Lady Emelie is ma wife, nae one of the slattern whores ye prefer. Speak aboot her like that again, and I will challenge ye, then I will kill ye." Dominic shook Stanley before pushing him away. He turned toward Jacob, raising his sword. Jacob shook his head.

"We didna mean aught by it, Dom," Jacob swore.

"Would you say the like to Brodie aboot Lady Campbell?" Dominic regained control of his temper and evened his speech. They all knew the answer to that question. "The past is the past. If you want to insult me for my mistakes, then do so. But if you bring my wife into it, Brodie will look like a pup compared to me. Test me and find out."

Disgusted with himself and his men, Dominic abandoned the lists and slipped through the postern gate. He made his way to the natural bay the River Orchy formed just outside the retaining wall. He considered going for a swim, but he couldn't muster the energy, so he sat on a boulder and skipped stones. He wasn't sure how long he loitered until Laurel nudged him out of the way and took his spot.

"You haven't told her, have you?" Laurel asked without preamble.

"She knows Colina was unfaithful."

"And that's it?" Laurel sighed. "No wonder she thinks you're grieving for her."

"What?" Dominic glanced at Laurel before skipping another stone. "Why would a mon grieve a cheating wife?"

"Because she believes you still love Colina. She thought it was grief, not anger when you saw your chamber. She thinks you couldn't go in there because the memories were too painful. She's right, of course. But she thinks it's because you miss Colina, not because you despise her. Why haven't you told her?"

"Did you spill all your secrets to Brodie within days of meeting him?"

"I did." Laurel's answer was succinct and practical. Dominic turned to look at his sister-by-marriage and realized she wasn't exaggerating. Her blunt answer matched the truth. "Are you too angry to even speak of her?"

"No. I mean, I can contain my anger most of the time. I know I overreacted, but I didn't want Emelie anywhere near the evil Colina possessed. You know Em. She's naive, but she's not cruel or deceptive."

"No, she is not. That's why she deserves the truth," Laurel pointed out.

"What am I supposed to say? 'Hello, new wife. My auld wife only married me to become Lady Campbell. She killed my mother and tried to kill Laurel. She plotted to have Brodie's first bride murdered. And she was lazy to boot.' That's a fine welcome to her new home."

"I don't see why not. That's what happened. Colina was evil. She played you and Graham for fools. You saw in her what she wanted you to see. She did the exact same thing to Graham. The difference is, you chose honor and duty when Graham chose envy and malice." Laurel slid off the boulder and stood before Dominic. She smiled as she considered how similar the brothers appeared. But she'd never been attracted to Dominic, and she could already tell that the only Campbell brother who held any appeal to Emelie was Dominic. "No one saw Colina for who she really was. If I hadn't come along, it's likely no one would have. Her pride led her to boast and made it easy for me to deduce what she did. But you were a good husband to her. I saw it, and I've heard how you were. It wasn't your fault."

"Nae ma fault!" Dominic exploded. He registered the shock on Laurel's face, but she didn't step back. "How the hell was it nae ma fault? I brought that bitch into our home, made her part of ma family and ma clan. I coddled her and defended her to everyone. I chose her over duty. I even ran from a bluidy battlefield to see her and ease her fears rather than stay with Brodie and help with our dead and wounded. She cuckolded me, and there isnae a member of this clan that doesnae ken that. She betrayed us all. She betrayed me." Dominic's voice was a raspy whisper by the time he finished.

"Dom, let yourself grieve." Laurel's voice was soothing, but it grated on Dominic's frayed nerves. "You might not be grieving Colina, but you have a right to grieve the death of your dreams, of what you believed your life would be. Take if from someone who bottled up that same grief for years on end. It doesn't make you a pretty person. It drives everyone around you away. Is that what you want with Emelie? Is that why you brought her here? To abandon her?"

"I would never abandon her," Dominic growled.

"Your body might be here, but your heart won't be. That's the most painful kind of abandonment. It's the cruelest." Dominic listened to the pain in Laurel's voice. She'd reconciled with her older brother, Montgomery, but little had changed between her and her parents or her other sisters. They refused to accept that she wasn't the shrew people had called her, nor did any of them admit that sending Laurel to court was the wrong choice. "Dom, I'm her friend, but I'm not her husband. I will help her adjust, and I'll make sure she has aught she needs for her and the bairn. But there are some things only you can provide."

"I ken." Dominic sighed, tossing the last of his pebbles in the water, before scrubbing his hands over his face. "I never want her to regret coming here. I want her to have a place to call home, even if she only accepts it for a year."

"Do you want her to stay longer? Do you really want to be her child's father?"

"Yes, to both. The bairn is ours, not hers, as far as I'm concerned."

"Then you'd better tell her. And sooner rather than later. She won't appreciate you keeping secrets when she's trusted you with hers."

"I ken, and I will. I promise." Dominic accepted Laurel's embrace. They walked back to the keep as the bells chimed for the evening meal.

Dominic ducked into the barracks and rushed to run a soapy linen over his neck and chest before changing out of the breeks he'd worn while at court and traveling. He breathed a sigh of relief when he wrapped his plaid around him and donned his sporran. He felt normal once more. He'd been sleeping in the barracks whenever he was home, so he still had a set of clothes waiting for him. He couldn't fathom why Lowlanders preferred the ridiculous breeks to the freedom of a plaid. The single piece of clothing was more useful than an entire Lowland wardrobe put together.

Settled into his regular attire and looking once more like a proper Highlander, Dominic entered the Great Hall just as Emelie descended the stairs. He could tell she'd bathed because the long platinum braid that hung over her shoulder was still damp. She had on a subdued gown compared to what she would have worn at court, but she looked stunning. The kirtle fit her perfectly, accentuating all the right angles. But Dominic immediately noticed that it was snug across the bust. He caught her surreptitious glances down at it and when she tried to adjust the neckline inconspicuously. As he crossed the floor to meet her at the bottom of the stairs, he noticed she was nearly spilling out of the top. When she spotted him, her cheeks flamed red.

"It was the only one that even came close to being presentable. I'm so sorry." At Dominic's confused stare, she explained. "My breasts have swelled. None of my gowns fit properly. The two I traveled in were meant for the journey and kept me more covered. I need to find Laurel. I'll embarrass you and me both if I go around like this. Mayhap she has a shawl I can borrow."

As though she had a sixth sense, Laurel approached with two pieces of fabric in her hands. She handed a plaid and a brooch Emelie hadn't noticed to Dominic. She kept a white triangular linen that Emelie didn't recognize. "Go in Brodie's solar,"

Laurel instructed. She cocked an eyebrow at Dominic, but Emelie didn't understand. Dominic led her into a chamber that felt far more masculine than the solar upstairs. Books, maps, and ledgers lined the walls. An enormous oblong table sat in the center, and Emelie knew this was where Brodie met with the clan council.

"Em," Dominic said as he closed the door. He turned her toward him and gazed into the blue-hazel eyes that drew him like a moth to the flame. "I would have presented this to you on our wedding day, or even at our handfast if I'd had it. This sash is made with the Campbell laird's family pattern. When you wear it along with this brooch, people will know you're the clan tánaiste's wife."

Dominic tentatively draped the plaid sash over Emelie's left shoulder and pinned it in place. His heart stuttered to see her in his clan's plaid. He didn't know where Laurel found the brooch, because it wasn't the one he'd given Colina; he assumed the sash was one of hers and not his dead wife's. The deep blue complimented Emelie's eyes and made them sparkle. He'd never seen a more lovely sight than his bride standing before him, and he felt a sense of pride that had been missing for longer than he realized. It had burned low while Colina was alive, and the shame he lived with snuffed it out.

"You're beautiful," Dominic murmured before lowering his head to kiss Emelie. She wrapped her arms around his neck and sighed when their lips met. The soft, warm puff of air snapped Dominic's control. He lifted her off her feet and brought her to the edge of the table. He wasn't certain who guided who, but Emelie reclined while he brought his body over hers. The kiss shared their combined hunger for more contact. Emelie's knees bracketed Dominic's hips as his hands roamed over her ribs, shoulders, and neck. He was careful not to trap her tender breasts between them. When he recalled why he was being cautious, he jerked away.

Dominic stared at Emelie as she propped herself on her elbows, looking hurt and confused. But she still looked delectable and ravishing. He wanted to dive in for a second helping of her kisses. But he also noticed that he'd nearly coupled with her for the first time, and it would have been on a table in his brother's solar. It felt as wrong as knowing her first time with Henry had been in a scullery storeroom.

"I didn't lock the door," Dominic said gruffly. "I don't want Laurel or Brodie to walk in and embarrass you." Emelie nodded as he helped her off the table. Her eyes still looked dazed as he led her to the door. He paused before they entered the passageway and tilted her head back. "You are so beautiful, Em. You deserve to be cherished."

Before Emelie could reply, Dominic wrapped her arm around his and guided her toward the dais. She wanted to ask if he would ever be the man to cherish her. With each day that she spent with Dominic and each moment that she got to know him better, her longing for him to reciprocate her growing feelings only grew stronger. Losing Henry pained her because of the consequences of their actions. Losing Dominic would crush her because she knew she was learning what it really meant to fall in love.

Emelie noticed two women standing beside Laurel as she and Dominic approached the dais. The women were older, beyond her own mother's age, and wore kindly smiles as they looked toward her. Dominic leaned over to whisper.

"The woman on the left is Aggie, our house-keeper. Berta, our cook, is on the right."

Emelie couldn't imagine why the two women would stand on the dais when servants were about to bring out the evening meal. It was one of the busiest times of the day for both women. Emelie climbed the steps and expected Dominic to guide her toward her chair. His hip bumped hers as he steered her toward the three women. She glanced toward him with panic as he released her and moved toward a chair, leaving her standing with Laurel and the two strangers before the entire clan. It felt as though hundreds of eyes stared at her. She supposed she wasn't far off in her estimation, since the Campbell clan was huge, and the Great Hall was enormous.

"Lady Emelie," Laurel greeted her with a loud voice that all in the Great Hall heard. With her first words, the diners settled. "In the Highlands, we have a tradition for newly married women. A woman's mother and sisters would usually present a bride with her first kertch. I hope you will accept my wedding gift to you. Aggie and Berta asked to help me with the kertching ceremony."

Emelie nodded, not understanding what a kertch was or what type of ceremony she found herself in the midst of. When Laurel gestured for her to stand facing the crowd, Emelie turned. With so many people watching her, she was grateful Laurel had given her the sash. She couldn't imagine the entire clan living at Kilchurn staring at her while her breasts were on such shameful display. The plaid was wide enough to cover her cleavage.

Emelie twisted to watch Aggie take her place behind her, then she looked to her left, where Berta stood. Each woman held a corner of the white triangle. She turned to look at Laurel as she began the blessing once she, Aggie, and Berta held the kertch above her head.

"If there is righteousness in the heart, there will be beauty in the character," Laurel said as reverent silence filled the Great Hall.

"If there is beauty in the character, there will be harmony in the home," Aggie recited.

"If there is harmony in the home, there will be order in the clan," Berta finished.

"If there is order in the clan, there will be peace in the land." The women spoke together.

The clan cheered, "So let it be!" as the three women placed the kertch over Emelie's head, and Aggie tied it. Emelie jumped at the boisterous endorsement. She fought the urge to lift her hand to her head and feel the strange new head covering. Despite the buzz of the crowd as the ceremony ended, Emelie was certain she heard Brodie.

"Wretched things, aren't they?" Brodie leaned toward Dominic, who sat to the laird's right. Dominic had given little thought to the piece of fabric women wore. He'd listened to the same blessing given when Colina received hers, but he hadn't considered it once she wore it. He hadn't cared that she wore it. Now he couldn't agree more with Brodie. He disliked seeing the voluminous cloth cover Emelie's platinum locks. She didn't look any less lovely than she had just minutes ago, but he found he missed looking at her unique hair color. He understood why Brodie felt that way about not seeing Laurel's strawberry-blonde hair when she wore it. He also realized that was likely why Laurel took it off whenever they were in their family quarters.

Emelie welcomed Laurel's embrace, finding comfort in the confusion that plagued her since arriving at Kilchurn. "Welcome to our clan, and welcome to the Highlands," Laurel murmured. Berta and Aggie dipped curtsies before giving Emelie brief embraces. The two women rushed from the dais, and Laurel led Emelie around the table. Dominic was quick to rise and pull out Emelie's chair, which was to his right. Brodie harrumphed as he stood to pull out Laurel's chair, not to be outdone by his younger brother. Laurel gingerly lowered herself into the seat to Brodie's left with a smirk.

Much like the evening King Robert announced their handfast, Dominic chose dishes he believed Emelie would enjoy and served her half of their trencher first. They hadn't shared one since they left Stirling, since they'd been on the road and eaten meat directly from the spit. Emelie sat quietly as she let the meal begin around her. She jumped once again when Dominic's hand patted her thigh. It was a moment of encouragement, but it helped set her mind at ease.

Dominic sensed as much as felt when Emelie relaxed. He'd noticed her rigid posture during the kertching, and he regretted not explaining the ceremony while they were in the solar. But he hadn't thought of it, even though he'd seen Laurel holding the kertch. He knew it was a tradition that few Lowlanders shared, but he hadn't imagined how uncomfortable it must have been for Emelie to stand before the clan without an introduction from him.

Dominic looked at his fellow clan members, and when he was certain the servants were finished passing around the platters, he pushed back his chair. He raised the chalice he shared with Emelie and cleared his throat. Once again, the crowd fell quiet as their tánaiste waited for their attention.

"Thank you, Lady Campbell, for welcoming Lady Emelie as a newly married woman and to our clan. I would like to introduce my wife, Lady Emelie Campbell." Dominic offered Emelie his hand. She rose gracefully as he watched. She had a serene expression on her face that belied her nervousness. He recognized it as one she'd worn at court the evening of their handfast. It signified unease, the very opposite of how Emelie appeared. "Lady Emelie and I handfasted during one of my many visits to court while I've been away. I believe you will find Lady Emelie is kind, patient, and giving. I am truly proud to call her my wife."

Dominic waited for the inevitable buzz as people finally commented on what they must have been curious about during the ceremony. He feared someone would speak of Colina and embarrass Emelie, especially since he hadn't explained the entire circumstances of Colina's death. He plowed on.

"I am certain this comes as a surprise to many, but I could not ignore Lady Emelie once we met. It is my sincere belief that you will find her to the perfect helpmate to Lady Campbell and the partner I wished for." Dominic caught his use of the past tense, but he didn't want to draw attention to it by correcting himself. "I look forward to everyone welcoming Lady Emelie and getting to know her for the enchanting and endearing lady I know her to be."

Dominic prayed that was enough for people to understand they should judge Emelie on her own merit and not by their jaded memory of his first wife. He raised his cup higher as his hand released hers and came to rest at her waist. "Welcome, wife," he toasted.

Rather than taking a sip or passing the chalice to Emelie, Dominic pulled her in for a kiss. He'd done it to ensure the clan understood theirs wasn't an arranged marriage or one of convenience, despite how it began. What he meant to be a kiss merely to prove a point soon heated into more as Emelie opened to him. When the crowd roared and a few randy suggestions made it to the couple's ears, they pulled apart and sat, both in embarrassed silence.

"I should have made the introduction first," Dominic confessed in a whisper to Emelie, once he composed his thoughts. "I didn't realize Laurel would give you the kertch before I welcomed you into our family. I'm sorry it made you uncomfortable. I'm sorry my toast did, too. I just want the clan to know that you are a welcome and wanted addition to our family."

"That's why you kissed me," Emelie mumbled. Her heart ached at the idea that the kiss had been for show.

"What that kiss proved doesn't negate what I felt."

Brodie stole Dominic's attention before Emelie asked Dominic what those feelings were. Seated three chairs down from Laurel and knowing none of the men seated at the high table, Emelie remained quiet. The maid who helped her with her kirtle after her bath had laced her too tightly, and Emelie grew increasingly uncomfortable the longer she sat. She picked at her meal, since she feared she'd be ill if she filled her belly. She felt out of place and lonely despite the people filling the massive chamber.

Dominic sensed Emelie grew tense once he turned his attention toward Brodie, but he couldn't ignore his brother. As laird and tánaiste, they had much to discuss. Dominic summarized his meetings with the Bruce and relayed what he discovered along their borders. But as Brodie asked for more details, his sense of urgency to return his focus to Emelie grew. Eventually, he'd had enough.

"Brodie, this is Em's first meal here, and I'm ignoring her. Can't we discuss this after she retires or in the morning?" Dominic whispered. Brodie offered him an inscrutable look before nodding his head. With a sigh of relief, he turned back to Emelie. His heart ached for her, since he was certain she felt abandoned during the meal. He had a sudden understanding of what Laurel meant when they spoke at the loch. As his gaze rested on her, he admired her composure and bravery. The more he discovered of his bride's character, the more enamored he grew. He promised himself that he would spend time getting her settled in her new home over the coming weeks, even if he didn't do more than share kisses with her.

"Is there aught else you'd like, Em?" Dominic said softly. "You've barely eaten. I'm sorry."

"You keep apologizing," Emelie noted.

"Because I've failed you this evening. I haven't done my duty by you as my wife."

Duty. That's all I am. More fool am I for thinking I meant something more personal to him. He kissed me to prove a point. Is that what all the kisses have been? Points I should have understood. He would make sure I, along with everyone else, believe I'm his wife. But he wants naught more than what's for show. Better I realize that now, only a few days into this coming year. Guard your heart, Emelie, lest you're made a fool again.

"Fear not, Dominic. I haven't taken offense." Emelie's cool tone made Dominic's stomach sink to his boots. His inattentiveness had offended her, and he wasn't certain how to rescue the evening. He offered her more wine and nudged food back toward her, but it wound up being left in the middle. As the meal progressed, and more courses arrived, he grew concerned by Emelie's lack of appetite. She'd been ravenous by the evening meal each night they traveled. They'd ridden for most of the day. He assumed she would be hungry again.

"Does this meal not suit you? Would you prefer

something else, perhaps not so rich?" Dominic inquired. Emelie looked at him, surprised to find concern etching deep lines between his brows. It appeared so genuine.

"The maid tied my kirtle too snug," Emelie confessed.

"Do you wish to go to Brodie's solar? I can retie the laces. Are you in pain?" Dominic felt like the worst cad. He hadn't considered Emelie's discomfort might be physical.

"People will wonder why we're leaving in the middle of the meal and then why we return."

"They'll think I'm showing you where you might have a moment of privacy," Dominic suggested.

"Your clan will think I can't manage to go to a chamber pot on my own. I've done that since I was a wean. If that's what I needed, I would ask a maid. At best, they will think me a clinging simpleton. At worst, they will think me a whore because they will assume we dashed off for a tryst. Once we slaked our lust, we returned. I'd rather not create either of those impressions."

Emelie's brusqueness and detachment took Dominic aback. He didn't understand why she was being so cold, but he supposed he deserved it after ignoring her for half the meal, and he couldn't fault her if she didn't feel well.

"When you wish to retire, you have only to let me know, and I will take you abovestairs," Dominic offered. Emelie not only saw Dominick's worry lines grow deeper, she heard the despair in his voice. She knew he was doing his best, and she was growing testy the longer she remained uncomfortable and as she grew more tired. She glanced down at their trencher before nodding.

"I think I'd like to go now. I'm sorry to take you away from the meal. I know you haven't seen your family or your people in months. I can find my own way." Emelie hadn't finished speaking before Dominic was pushing his chair away from the table. He rose and adjusted Emelie's chair, so she could step around it. With a smile to Laurel and Brodie, Emelie controlled the urge to run down the steps of the dais and bolt up the stairs to the family chambers. She and Dominic walked in silence until he opened the door.

"Do you need help to remove your gown?" Dominic asked. Emelie felt a spark of hope that they might finally consummate their handfast, but it fizzled when Dominic spoke again. "I can summon a maid to help you."

"No. There's no need to interrupt someone else's meal. If you could pull the laces loose, I can manage."

Dominic swallowed as he stepped behind Emelie. He tugged at the tie, then pulled the laces free of the eyelets. He spied the creamy skin beneath her chemise, and his fingers itched to touch it, to run them along her spine. The curve of where her shoulder met her neck tempted him, beckoning him to rain down kisses over the bare flesh. His hands rested on Emelie's waist as he inhaled her fresh scent. It was a combination, but he couldn't identify the individual parts. His cock ached and demanded relief only Emelie could provide. His desire for the woman standing before him surpassed anything he'd ever felt. Not when he was a young man discovering lust and bedding his first woman. Not when he met Colina, and he'd believed then that there could never be a more desirable woman. Not on his wedding night when he finally had Colina alone and stripped her bare. Not during any of the years he'd pledged himself only unto his first wife.

It was only remembering that she'd been uncomfortable, and he supposed exhausted, that made her wish to retire. He chastised himself for lusting over her when what she needed was rest. He stepped away from her and moved to the bed. Intending to turn down the bed covers for her, Dominic missed Emelie's speculative glance. If he'd seen it, he would have recognized that Emelie's lust matched his own.

"If you need aught, you have only to summon a maid. Would you like Berta to send up a tray?"

Emelie stared blankly at Dominic, not understanding why she would ask for a maid in the middle of the night when he would be there. He came to stand before her, placing his hands on her upper arms. He kissed her forehead before dropping an all-too-brief kiss to her lips. He stared at her, and she realized he was waiting for an answer.

"No, thank you. Berta need not go to any extra trouble."

"Very well. I will let you retire." Dominic lingered for a moment before he nodded. He walked to the door where he turned back to see Emelie's confused and rejected expression. He walked back to her and embraced her. "I know you don't feel your best, and I'm certain you must be weary after so many days of sleeping on the ground. I don't want you falling ill, Em."

Emelie nodded against his chest. She didn't understand how coupling, or even sharing a bed, might put her at greater risk of getting sick. She appreciated his consideration, but it wasn't what she wanted. She wanted her husband. She wanted to be his wife in truth, not just in name. But she didn't dare say a word. Had she been a typical bride, she would know nothing about how pleasurable coupling could be. She should still be a virgin, so she couldn't bring herself to admit she desired Dominic and longed to feel his touch. She'd already felt like a harlot when she

113

admitted her situation to Dominic. She didn't want to confirm it by begging him to take her to bed.

"I'll see you in the morning. I'd like to take you for a walk if you feel up to it. I doubt you wish to be on horseback again soon, and I really don't like the idea of you riding. But I'd like to show you the village, the bay, and the river."

"I'd like that very much, but aren't you supposed to go to the lists in the morning? I imagine Brodie expects you to meet with him," Emelie pointed out.

"Neither the lists nor Brodie are going anywhere," Dominic replied.

"Neither am I." Emelie kept herself from muttering her response, but just barely. "Tend to your other duties, Dom. I'll be ready if you still wish to go in the afternoon."

Dominic hesitated, unsure what Emelie meant by "other duties." He feared she thought he considered her one. By the time he realized what he said during the meal had given her the wrong impression, the moment passed. She stepped away from him and offered a weary smile.

"Sleep as long as you can. No one will fault you for needing your rest after an arduous journey."

"Arduous? It's not like we traveled to the far-flung corners of Scotland. People will wonder why a healthy, young woman needs to sleep. They will think me lazy. I—I don't want them to think you chose poorly. Unless—" Emelie bit her bottom lip. "Do you intend to tell people aboot my condition?"

"Do you wish me to?" Dominic asked.

"I don't know."

"Mayhap you could see our healer and describe how you felt on our journey. Tired and queasy, then famished. She'll tell you what we already know, but she'll be the first to know outside our family. That might be easier for you than saying you've known all along. People might be less likely to ask how far along you are."

"You wish for me to spin even more tales than we'll already have to. You want me to start my first full day here lying to your healer. If anyone would know I'm not telling the truth, it would be a woman who's spent her life delivering bairns."

"I just want you to be at ease," Dominic insisted. Emelie opened her mouth to say she would feel better if he stopped putting distance between them, but he spoke first. "I'll let you get your rest, and I will see you when we break our fast."

Emelie's shoulders slumped as she watched Dominic leave her chamber. The room she'd thought—hoped—she would share with him. There didn't seem to be anything else to do than strip off her kirtle and climb into bed. She felt herself drifting off quickly, and she supposed Dominic hadn't been wrong. She needed sleep more than she needed her husband bedding her. But not by much.

EIGHT

Dominic didn't know what to do with himself. He knew with certainty he would not spend the night in his old chamber. He wouldn't humiliate Emelie by returning to the barracks or sleeping in the Great Hall. He debated whether it would be a safer bet to sleep in Brodie's solar than to sleep in a guest chamber, even if he didn't request any bedding. In the end, he settled for attempting to sleep on the window seat in the upstairs solar. It only took a couple minutes to accept that he was far too large to attempt that. He stoked the fire, pulled the extra length of his plaid over his head, and fell asleep beside the hearth.

Images of Emelie filled dream after dream. They began as she looked now, no hint of the child she carried. He could see them walking hand-in-hand along the river. They planned for when their babe arrived, talking about names for a lad or a lass. As the dreams progressed, the events seemed more mundane but comfortable. He pictured them lying in bed beside one another discussing their day. Just before the sun rose, he dreamed of them in the chamber Emelie now occupied. But there were four slumbering children wrapped around them.

"Dom?" A woman's voice roused him from a lurid dream he was having, and when he cracked his eye open to find Laurel standing over him, he was grateful that his sporran hid the outcome of the vivid dream of making love to Emelie in the bay's warm summer water.

"Aye. I'm awake," Dominic rasped.

"What the devil are you doing sleeping in here? What did you say to Emelie?" Laurel demanded.

"I said naught. I—"

"Well, there's the bluidy problem," Laurel interrupted. "Get up and go meet your wife. She's already belowstairs."

"What?" Dominic scrambled to his feet and looked toward the door. He straightened his sporran when he realized Laurel would have a view of his morning arousal. He recalled shifting several times in his sleep because he'd been unable to get comfortable with a raging cockstand. "I told her to sleep in."

"On her first day here? She would never!" Laurel exclaimed. "Why are you in here?"

"I wanted to make sure she slept well last night."

"Slept well? Alone in a strange new place. You are a henwit. Go see to her. She's now alone in the Great Hall."

"Why aren't you with her?" Dominic felt his defensiveness rising.

"Because I was searching for you. When I passed her in the passageway, she said she didn't know where you went. At least I knew you had the sense not to go to the barracks or the Great Hall last night." Laurel huffed as she shooed Dominic toward the door. He hurried down the stairs, but Brodie waylaid him before he reached the dais. He peered over Brodie's shoulder to where Emelie sat alone as people filled the gathering hall.

"I need to see you this morning. I would like to

117

hear your last update on the MacArthurs and Mac-
Gregors' camps near our borders," Brodie explained.

"They would be more than a moon auld. You
should ask the men who patrol there." Dominic
made to step around Brodie, but his older brother
shifted.

"I want to hear it from you."

"And I want to greet my wife, who is sitting
alone," Dominic snapped.

"This again," Brodie barked. Dominic narrowed
his eyes and fisted his hands by his side.

"That was uncalled for," Laurel hissed from behind Dominic. "Take it back."

"I will not. I knew naught of this handfast until
he shows up with a stranger. Now he's coddling her
just like he did the last bitch he married."

A gasp made Brodie whirl around as Dominic
lunged past him. Emelie took a step back and shook
her head. She put her hands up to ward Dominic
away. With more composure than Dominic could
have mustered, she walked up the stairs to her
chamber.

"You're an arse. She's naught like Colina," Dominic snapped.

"You thought the sun shone out of Colina's arse.
How can I be sure you don't think the same about
this one? You will not shirk your duties anymore."

"*This one?* Emelie is my wife. Never refer to her
like that again, Brodie. She doesn't deserve it, and I
will defend her. And you owe her an apology. You
made it sound like you hold her in the same low es-
teem as Colina. You don't even know her."

"And you do? After a sennight. Hardly," Brodie
scoffed.

"Keep your voice down," Laurel snapped. "Both
of you. You wanted to marry me within a sennight.

Don't you dare hold your brother to a different standard. Dom may not know Emelie well, but I do. I'll vouch for her. I'm happy Dom found her and married her."

"Handfasted," Brodie corrected. "And Dom will not shirk his duties."

"I never said I would. I didn't refuse to meet with you. I just didn't think this was the time to begin our discussion aboot something I couldn't give you accurate information aboot, anyway. You're an arse."

Dominic didn't wait for Brodie or Laurel to say anything more. He took the stairs two at a time until he reached the landing, bolting toward Emelie's door. He knocked once before he burst through the portal. He nearly skidded as he stopped. Emelie stood in front of the window embrasure, her shoulders shaking from crying. Spurred into action once more, Dominic crossed the chamber in five long strides. He attempted to turn Emelie toward him, but she wouldn't budge. Rather than force her, he wrapped his arms around her. When she didn't pull away, he eased in between her and the window. She sank against his chest and sobbed.

Emelie regretted every moment of her life from the past three months. She regretted every decision she made, including handfasting with Dominic and coming to Kilchurn. She should have taken her chances with her own family. She even considered the falsehood Blythe suggested she tell about being a widow. But despite the heartache, she couldn't deny the immediate comfort she drew from Dominic. However, the longer she remained in his arms, the worse she felt. The memory of him leaving her the night before to go God knows where burned in her mind. He said he didn't have a leman, but she questioned whether he'd told the truth. Whose bed had he sought? She knew he hadn't gone to his former chamber. She'd knocked on the door that morning. Her knocking brought Laurel out of her chamber.

Emelie stepped back and wiped her eyes. She raised her chin and took a deep breath. She could feel the muscles in her neck straining as she fought to regain control. When she was certain she could speak without bursting into tears again, she nodded at Dominic. "Thank you. I am well now. I overreacted."

"You did not," Dominic argued. He hated seeing her shoulder the blame for Brodie's—and his, if he were honest—insensitive behavior. "He didn't like her."

Emelie frowned. "I gathered as much. That must have been awfully hard for you. I can't imagine how conflicted you must have been." Emelie tentatively patted Dominic's chest before pulling her hand away. But he captured it and held it over his heart.

"He disliked her toward the end, only after we learned of her affair with Graham. But aye, there were times when it was difficult to choose between them. Sometimes I made the wrong choice."

"You picked him," Emelie surmised, but her brow furrowed when Dominic flinched.

"No. I picked her." Dominic tucked a stray hair beneath Emelie's kertch, then thought better of it. He pulled the dreadful thing from her hair. She reached back to catch it, but Dominic flung it onto the bed. "Your hair is too beautiful to cover with that ugly piece of cloth."

"But I'm married now, or at least handfasted," Emelie corrected. She'd heard Brodie the entire time she climbed the stairs. She'd prayed the rest of the clan hadn't. "It would be disrespectful to you and your traditions if I didn't wear it."

"Then don't wear it when we're together," Dominic commanded. His authoritative tone made

Emelie shy away. When he felt as much as saw Emelie retreat, he brushed the backs of his fingers against her cheeks. "I've made a mess of this morning. I didn't mean to snap at you. I'm frustrated with Brodie, not you. Would you take that walk with me now?"

Emelie shook her head. "I won't come between you and your brother. See to your other duties. I will find out what Laurel expects of me. If there's time, we can always go this afternoon."

"This is the second time you've said 'other duties' as though I see you as one of them. I never have."

"That's not what you said last eve," Emelie countered.

"When?"

"You said you hadn't done your duty by me as your wife. You feel obligated to deal with me."

"That is not what I meant." Dominic was emphatic, and Emelie wanted to believe him. "I may have a duty to protect you and ensure others respect you. But I do not see you as a duty or an obligation. If I've given you the impression that I do, then I'm sorry. I was trying to do right by you and be a good husband."

Emelie's heart softened, and she stepped back into Dominic's arms. This time, as she rested her head against his chest, she found only the comfort she craved. She'd slept poorly all night, tossing and turning, saddened every time she rolled into the empty spot she'd hoped Dominic would fill. She missed sleeping beside him after getting used to it on their journey. Her eyes drooped closed as she listened to Dominic's heart, and his heat seeped into her. Dominic felt her relax and realized she was nearly asleep. He carried her to the bed, laying her down and covering her with a blanket. He straightened, but she reached out to him with her eyes closed.

121

"Please don't go." Emelie was groggy, but she knew what she was saying. "I didn't sleep well without you."

"Em, I don't want you to fear being here. This is your home."

Emelie yawned. "Not afraid. Missed you." She was nearly asleep as she mumbled now, not aware of what she said. Dominic toed off his boots and eased onto the bed beside her. She curled against him, and he didn't fight the temptation to hold her. She sighed as he slid his arm beneath her neck and drew her closer with the other. It wasn't long before he was asleep, too.

※

Emelie stirred and found a warm cocoon wrapped around her. She didn't have to open her eyes to know Dominic lay beside her. She sighed with contentment. She felt the soft kisses pressed to her crown just as she realized she draped her arm over his waist. She tilted her head back and looked into his gray eyes. They reminded her of storm clouds just before a torrent of rain. But they mesmerized her rather than making her want to dash for cover. His breath wafted across her face, and his lips parted. She took it as an invitation, even if it wasn't. She strained her neck and brought their mouths closer. Dominic didn't hesitate. He cupped her jaw and pressed a passionate kiss to her, as though he was starving. As the kiss deepened, a groan rumbled through Dominic's chest.

Emelie reveled in the sound Dominic made, her desire and relief matching his. She rolled onto her back, urging Dominic to follow her. He held himself above her on his forearms as the kiss carried on. His hand drifted down to her thigh, and she felt air

122

rather than material. His calloused palm slid to her backside, massaging the lush flesh. He groaned once more, eager to feel the ample globe in his hand. He'd never felt a bottom so soft. He trailed his hand over her hip until his fingers reached the juncture of her thighs.

This canna be dangerous for the bairn. This should be all right. God, how I pray it's all right. I dinna ken if I can walk away right now without touching her. Ma desire is driving me to madness.

Dominic's fingers slid along Emelie's seam, dipping within her entrance when he felt the dew that coated her petals. When her grip on his shoulder tightened, he pressed into her sheath, stroking the silky skin within her. Her legs widened in invitation, but Dominic refused to rush. He stroked her over and over, heightening her arousal as they continued to kiss. Her breath hitched when his thumb brushed against her sensitive bud. He rubbed circles, increasing the pressure by slow increments. Emelie's hip rocked to meet his rhythm.

Emelie couldn't believe the sensations Dominic's touch elicited. It was unlike anything she'd ever felt. Henry had never touched her as Dominic was touching her now. She hadn't imagined mere fingers could drive her arousal far beyond what she'd felt when she coupled with her former lover. Her sheath ached, a needy burn that grew to near discomfort as she longed for Dominic to lift his plaid and thrust into her. The longer he tortured her with his fingers, the more her belly tightened until a wave of pleasure washed through her. Her sheath felt as if it hummed as the sensations peaked.

Dominic watched Emelie climax, the need to enter her and spill within her almost overpowering his resolve. He'd seen other women in the throes of passion, since he hadn't been a virgin when he married Colina. But he'd never seen a more expressive face. For a moment, he wondered if Colina had been pretending. His dead wife's reactions seemed embellished as he watched the genuine wonder and enjoyment cross Emelie's visage.

"What was that?" Emelie breathed.

Dominic paused, understanding dawning on him. As he suspected, Henry Pringle was the cad he believed. The man had taken advantage of Emelie in the worst way and hadn't satisfied her to boot. "That was a climax, Em. Didn't you feel that with Henry?" He needed to be sure before he said anything else.

"No." Emelie shook her head.

"Not when he touched you or when you coupled?" Dominic feared Emelie's response since he'd already guessed, but he wanted to be certain he didn't jump to any conclusions. How he would proceed depended on it.

"He never touched me like that. No one has," Emelie assured him.

"I didn't think anyone had, not even Henry." Dominic kissed Emelie's swollen lips. His stubble had rubbed her skin around her mouth, leaving evidence of their tryst. "He should have. He should have pleasured you rather than thinking aboot himself. I can only imagine how painful each time must have been."

"There was some pain the first time, but it wasn't unbearable. The second time was a bit uncomfortable and over before I understood what was happening."

Dominic pulled his lips in to contain his laughter. He doubted Emelie would appreciate it, even if the jab was at Henry's expense. Tentatively, he drew Emelie's hand beneath her skirts. When she didn't resist, he pressed her fingers along her seam.

"Em, do you feel how you are now? That would

have made joining with him much easier and more pleasant, though I can't say that he would have ever taken the time to ensure your pleasure. There shouldn't have been any discomfort after he broke your maidenhead, only pleasure."

"I suspected as much. But he made it seem like he couldn't contain his eagerness to be with me. I suppose he couldn't contain his eagerness for release." Emelie glanced down at her belly. "That's how I got myself in this predicament."

The mention of Emelie's pregnancy was a bucket of cold water on Dominic. He eased his hand away as he remembered why he kept putting a halt to their amorous encounters. He still wasn't convinced that coupling with Emelie wouldn't harm her. He straightened Emelie's skirts and longed to adjust himself. His cock demanded relief, but he wouldn't ask Emelie. He wanted her to enjoy the moments when he tended to her and expected nothing in return.

"Are you up for that walk?" Dominic prayed a stroll along the river would distract his swollen rod as much as he hoped it would distract his mind. All he wanted was to strip them both bare after locking them into the chamber. He wanted to hide away with Emelie for a month of Sundays. Emelie stared at him for a long moment before she nodded her head. Her brow creased, but she rolled to the edge of the bed and stood up. She retrieved the kertch from where it still lay at the foot of the bed. She stepped before the looking glass and adjusted the head covering.

"I'll never like that," Dominic muttered.

"You must be used to it though," Emelie smiled, sympathy in her eyes. Dominic thought he would be sick. He reached out his hand, and Emelie took it without hesitation. He led them through the Great Hall and out to the bailey. He spotted three guardsmen he'd known his entire life and trusted. He whistled and nodded toward the postern gate. The men fell in behind them at a respectful distance. He would never leave the walls with Emelie without men to help keep her safe. He wouldn't take any risks with her life or their bairn's.

NINE

Dominic and Emelie walked in silence, but she didn't mind. Her gaze swept over the landscape as they walked to the bay, then along the river. With the keep still in sight but nearly half a mile away, Dominic stopped them. He glanced at the guards, and they scattered to create a perimeter that afforded the couple a chance to speak in private. Dominic unpinned the extra length of his plaid draped over his shoulder. He settled on the grass along the bank and hastened to spread the wool on the ground as Emelie made to sit, embarrassed that she would think he had no manners by sitting first.

"I don't want your skirts to get dirty or damp," Dominic explained. He wrapped Emelie's arm around his. Emelie glanced up at Dominic and found him smiling at her. It was a soft expression that felt intensely intimate, and she supposed it was after what they shared. She leaned her head against his shoulder. Without a second thought, he pulled his arm loose and wrapped it around her. She shifted so that her head rested against his chest. They sat watching the current drive a few fallen leaves and snapped twigs. "Em?"

"Hmm," Emelie replied with a sigh.

"There is a great deal I need to tell you because I think—*I know*—I've led you to a false impression of how I feel. I don't want you to think I've been keeping secrets from you. I just couldn't bring myself to discuss it with you."

"If it's aboot your wife, you don't need to talk aboot it. I understand."

"She was my wife. But you speak as though she still is. You're my wife, Em. You're the woman I see my future with."

Emelie sat up as she took in the earnestness in Dominic's expression. She got the feeling that he meant far longer than a year. But she couldn't understand how he saw a future with them if he were going to grow more distant. Though she had to admit he hadn't been distant when he pleasured her. But he had made no move to let her reciprocate. It had hurt and confused her further.

"I met Colina aboot four years ago at a Highland Gathering. The Campbells and MacLeans weren't on good terms, but I was infatuated with her. I was certain that it was love at first sight, at least for me. I trailed after her for a fortnight, surely falling more and more in love by the day. I hounded Brodie into arranging a betrothal when Colina said she wanted to marry me."

Emelie sat as still as a statue, not sure that she wanted to listen to her husband describe how much he loved another woman. As uncomfortable as listening was, she appreciated that Dominic was finally sharing more about him.

"We married at the MacLeans' keep and returned here. Colina seemed like the perfect bride. She eagerly helped my mother with her duties as chatelaine, but within weeks of Colina's arrival, my mother fell ill. Colina became her constant companion. Whenever Brodie and I came to visit, she would give us time with our mother. We couldn't understand why she grew so agitated when Colina left. We assumed she missed her but could no longer communicate with us. It was Laurel who deduced that our mother was trying to tell us how badly Colina mistreated her. Colina killed my mother."

Emelie's eyes widened to saucers as she swallowed her gasp. She didn't realize how her fingernails bit into Dominic's thighs until he eased her hand from his leg. The declaration stunned her.

"Brodie and I thought it was grief that made Colina lose interest in the chatelaine's duties," Dominic continued. "Aggie and Berta took on those duties for three years until Brodie arranged a marriage with Eliza MacMillan. The girl was auld enough to become a chatelaine, even if she was still young. Brodie intended to leave her a virgin until she was at least six-and-ten, but we would have someone to manage the household."

"She refused? Did she not know how?" Emelie whispered.

"She knew how. But the longer she procrastinated, claiming grief, the more the household adapted to not having a chatelaine. I didn't push her into it because she seemed so distraught at first. Then, I suppose, I gave up. Keeping her happy was more important to me than arguing over who kept count of the candles."

"Is that really all you think a chatelaine does?" Emelie was aghast that Dominic could be that flippant or misinformed about the weight a chatelaine shouldered.

"No. I saw Mother do far more than that. But Aggie and Berta made it look simple, so neither Brodie nor I gave it much thought after a while."

"But Brodie must have if he thought Eliza would make a suitable chatelaine."

"The alliance was what mattered to Brodie and to me. It would give us access to a waterway to connect us to another portion of Campbell territory. The best way to secure the alliance was marriage, and that meant a wife who could be chatelaine." Dominic inhaled deeply and released it slowly. "As time went on, Colina manipulated me. At the time, I thought it was endearing that she needed me. I thought it meant she loved me. I wanted to take care of her, and I thought, as my wife, I owed her my loyalty."

Dominic stared into the distance as memories flashed before his eyes. Emelie sat silent as she waited for him to collect his thoughts.

"Toward the end, she made me choose between my loyalty to her and to our clan. I will forever regret leaving Brodie and the others to sort through the dead and wounded when I rode away from this very place to check on Colina. She threatened she would be distraught throughout the battle and would be ill if she didn't know whether I survived."

Dominic's memory flashed to that horrible day. He knew he was doing the wrong thing even as he rode through the gates and into the bailey. When he found Colina without a hair out of place while he heard how exhausted and frazzled Laurel was, he knew she had played him for a fool. But he was too stubborn to admit it, to accept the humiliation that came from coddling a woman who clearly didn't need it or appreciate it.

"That was a mistake and a regret I will live with. She didn't need me. She did it because she needed to know whether she was any closer to being Lady Campbell."

"Lady Campbell? That's Laurel. How would she ever be Lady Campbell unless she married Brodie?"

"It was far more complicated than it seemed. But

it all unraveled when she tried to kill Laurel. My sister-by-marriage is the smartest person I've ever met. She nearly died more than once at Colina's hand, but when she poisoned a waterskin, she erred. She assumed Laurel would be the one who needed a drink after her ride with Brodie. Instead, it was my brother who drank from it. The dose would likely have killed Laurel, but it only made Brodie ill. We learned it was Graham who'd filled it and did naught to warn us."

"Graham? You said that Colina had an affair with him."

"She did, until their deaths."

"Their? I suppose I never wondered what happened to him. I figured I would meet him eventually."

Dominic sighed as he looked up at the sky. "I found them together. I found them kissing. Graham ran to warn Colina that Brodie was the one to drink the water, but that he would likely live. I went after Graham when Laurel told me he filled the waterskin. Brodie and Laurel heard us in the Great Hall. I'd guided them there at the end of my sword. Brodie and Laurel arrived to discover Graham had his arm wrapped around Colina, and I was pointing a sword at them both. I would have killed them right there and stepped over their bodies without a second thought had Laurel not stopped me. I suppose it was just as well that she did. Colina confessed to a far more sordid tale than any of us could guess."

"Oh, Dom. I'm so sorry. It must be so hard to both love and regret someone," Emelie said as she rested her hand on his thigh again.

"Emelie, that's what I'm trying to get at. I don't love Colina. And my only regret is that I married her. My grief isn't for her. It's for my lost pride and for what I thought I had. I don't miss her, Em. It sur-

131

prises me that I don't, but then she was pure evil. She married me, thinking it was just her first step in rising to be a powerful woman."

Dominic gazed down at Emelie, hoping he could convey his feelings and put her misunderstanding to rest.

"The Campbells hold sway throughout the country and at court. She wanted a part of that. Her aunt married David Lamont, their clan's former laird. She used Graham to feed information to the Lamonts and the MacDougalls. She told them when Brodie would return with Eliza. She facilitated the raid that killed Eliza, so she wouldn't have competition. She would have killed Brodie and me given enough time. She tried to kill Laurel to keep my sister from figuring out what happened and to get her out of the way."

Emelie noticed that, once again, Dominic didn't qualify Laurel as his sister-by-marriage. It was clear he accepted her as close family, and Emelie was glad for it as she learned what Laurel faced upon her arrival. It made Emelie's hurt feelings pale in comparison.

"She killed your mother, arranged for someone to kill Eliza, tried to kill Laurel, and would have killed you and Brodie. All for what? More work she didn't do?" The tale Dominic told astounded Emelie. If she didn't trust him, it would seem too outlandish to believe.

"She wanted the title and what she thought it would bring her. She didn't want the work or responsibility. She wanted the notoriety. She thought Graham would become laird when Brodie and I died. She wanted me to return to the keep after the battle only to learn if she still needed to do away with me."

Emelie shook her head unable to believe such a

tale. But she knew Dominic wasn't a liar. And she knew he wouldn't tell a tale that Laurel or Brodie could easily refute. She suspected things were worse than what Dominic described. She bit her bottom lip before asking, "How did she die?"

"I drowned her." Dominic said without emotion. "The clan council sentenced both her and Graham to death for treason against Brodie as their laird. They confessed before half the clan, who saw everything in the Great Hall. He hanged from the gallows, but the usual punishment for women is drowning. They say it's more merciful than hanging, but I will never forget the experience. I didn't feel merciful, and it didn't look merciful. Brodie offered to carry out the sentence, but I had to. I had to be the one to purge our clan of the evil I brought in. It was my fault so many suffered and died. It may as well have been me who poisoned my mother or lopped off Eliza's head."

"Is that how Eliza died?" Emelie rasped. She wrapped her hand around her own throat.

"Aye. David Lamont killed her, and Brodie couldn't protect her. It's why I will always have men with us, Em. You are never to leave the walls without at least three guards. Things are quiet now with the Lamonts, but people begrudge us for what we have, what we've fought for, and what we've earned. There will always be threats, always people wishing to lay us low." Dominic shook his head as he looked at Emelie's ashen face. "I should have warned you of that before offering marriage. I should have made you aware of what you were accepting. I just didn't think aboot it. I wanted so much for you to say yes."

"You're a fixer."

"I'm a what?" Emelie's declaration confused him.

"You want to make things better. You wanted to fix things between you and Colina, so you catered to her whims. You wanted to fix things between you and your clan, so you carried out her sentence. You wanted to fix me, so you offered to marry me."

"I don't want to fix you. You're perfect as you are," Dominic argued.

"I wouldn't go that far. But you wanted to make things better for me, to take care of me. You're a mon with an enormous heart who cares aboot others and wants to see the best in them. I find no fault in that, Dom. You believe it's your duty."

"Roundabout as it is, you're back to calling yourself my duty. I wanted—want—to help you. I don't feel obligated, and I never did."

"Mayhap. But you wanted to rescue me." Emelie bit her bottom lip again. "Why?"

"Because you were naive and alone. I saw the opportunity to help you."

"But why did you even feel compelled to help me?"

"I don't know. I thought I could—" Dominic broke off. Emelie's eyes locked with his, and he feared she felt everything he thought. He knew what he felt, but he didn't want to say it aloud, to admit that his motives had been selfish.

"You thought you had a second chance. A second chance that would redeem yourself. You'd feel better by taking me in and rescuing me, and you thought your clan would approve of me after what Colina did." Emelie stood up, and Dominic followed. "Regardless of whether you grieve your dead wife, you want me as a substitute."

"I do not," Dominic hissed as he grabbed Emelie's arms.

"Ow," Emelie whimpered.

"Dear God. I'm sorry, Emelie. I didn't mean to be rough with you, I swear. I didn't realize." Dominic took a broad step back, and Emelie could see the shame written across his face. It crushed him to think he'd done her any harm. As she looked at Dominic, she realized that he was a man in pain. A pain soul deep, and eating him alive. She took a step toward him, and she feared he would be the one crying. She took another, tentative as if she approached a wounded animal.

"I know you didn't, Dom. You never would do it on purpose. You're a wee stronger than me, and a good deal bigger. You didn't realize it," Emelie soothed as she ran her hands over Dominic's chest.

"I just didn't want you to walk away. I will never imprison you and use my size against you. I truly am sorry. I acted without thinking."

"Dom, it's all right. You've given me much to think aboot and much to digest. It's a wee overwhelming to know the truth."

"Emelie, I need you to know something else."

Emelie braced herself for whatever was coming. She doubted she would appreciate whatever it was. "What else?"

"Yesterday, I couldn't take you in my auld chamber because it reminded me of Colina. But not because I miss her. It felt as though her evil lurked within. I want you nowhere near that. You are too pure of heart to be dirtied by aught that was hers. I will never use that chamber again."

Emelie was certain her lip would crack from how often she bit down on it during this conversation. She released the tortured skin before gaining her courage to ask, "What chamber will you use?"

Dominic didn't have an answer. It wasn't uncommon for married couples not to share a chamber, but he had with Colina. He didn't want anyone to think he shunned Emelie, nor did he want people gossiping that she barred him from her bed. But he wanted to respect Emelie's space.

"Where did you sleep last night, Dom?"

Dominic heard no accusation in Emelie's tone, but there was doubt. He would disabuse her of any fear that he'd made his bed beside another woman. "On the floor before the hearth in Brodie and Laurel's solar."

"The floor? Dom, really?"

"I won't embarrass you by going to the barracks or sleeping in the Great Hall."

Emelie felt tears stinging the back of her lids, and a lump swelled in her throat. "You would rather sleep on the floor than share a chamber with me. You said it was so I could have more time with Blythe. You just didn't want to be near me. Are you disgusted by the idea of sharing a bed with an unchaste woman?"

"Disgust me?" Dominic cupped Emelie's jaw and swooped in for a kiss. Emelie didn't hesitate to reciprocate in full measure. He wrapped his arms around her waist and lifted her off the ground. If there weren't guards with them, she would have wrapped her legs around him and clung to him like a bear climbing a tree. "You do not disgust me, Em. You never have. Far from it."

"I just don't understand."

"I told you the truth, Em," Dominic said as he lowered her to the ground. "I can't imagine not living in the same keep as Brodie. You've been with Blythe your entire life. I didn't want to rob you of your last few chances to be together when I couldn't imagine how hard it would be for you. I don't think I could have left Brodie behind."

Emelie nodded. Her lips thinned and turned down, but she believed him. "But what aboot now?"

"I don't want to intrude on your privacy or your chance to sleep. I fear disrupting you when you need rest."

Emelie looked at the ground, too embarrassed to

admit how she really felt. She closed her eyes, hoping shutting out the world—even Dominic—would make it easier to tell him the truth. "I didn't sleep well last night because I missed you."

"You missed me?" Dominic nudged her chin until their eyes met.

"When you were beside me, I slept better than I imagined I could, even on the ground. I fell into a deep sleep this morning with you beside me. It's not that I'm scared to be in my chamber alone, but I feel much better when you are near." Emelie felt the heat rising in her cheeks. As she repeated her words to herself, her chest tightened and her belly sucked in. "I shouldn't have said that. That sounds horrible after what you told me."

"It's my turn not to understand."

"You said she manipulated you into coddling her. It sounded like she was clingy and needy to get you to do her bidding. That wasn't my intent."

Dominic tucked Emelie against his chest and pulled the kertch from her hair for a second time. He stroked the white-blonde locks that hung to her waist. "Em, that's not what I thought. The idea never crossed my mind. There have been plenty of chances for you to wheedle me into doing your bidding, and you never have. I think you're extremely uncomfortable admitting that you might need me. You are not she. I wouldn't let Brodie make that comparison, and I won't let you either. Naught aboot you reminds me of her. She is part of my past, not my present or my future."

"But you loved her."

"Em, I loved who I thought she was. I loved being needed. It made me feel like even more of a mon than any battle. I loved the marriage I thought I had. But none of it was real. I loved a woman who didn't exist. That is what upsets me. Anger, regret, and remorse, not grief. If she were alive, I never would have met you. She would never have allowed me to be away so long, so I likely wouldn't have been at court. If she were alive, I never could have offered you my protection or my name. If she were alive, I wouldn't be holding you right now. And there is nowhere else I want to be right now than with you."

Emelie sighed and breathed easier. The conviction in Dominic's voice soothed her just as much as his hand running over her back did. "Will you stay with me tonight? I don't want you sleeping on the floor somewhere."

"Aye. I'd like that, Em."

"If you didn't use your auld chamber, where did you sleep after—everything?"

"The barracks when I wasn't on patrol. I volunteered to be away from the keep every chance I got."

"Is it painful to be back here then? Do you wish you can leave again? I'll be fine."

"I don't want to go anywhere anymore, Em. This is my home, and I won't let ghosts chase me away anymore. There is too much here to appreciate. And I will not abandon you among strangers. I know you know Laurel, but that's not enough."

"I don't want you to fear leaving me behind. I won't keep you from your responsibilities."

"I know you won't, *mo sparradh beag.*"

"Why did you call me a sparrow again? Why do I remind men of birds?"

Dominic chuckled. "Calling a woman dove is rather —common." Dominic grimaced admitting that since he'd attempted to call Emelie that. "But you remind me of a sparrow. They are small and appear fragile, but they are hardy. They survive even in the harshest climes in the Highlands. And I think they're pretty."

"They're brown."

Dominic chuckled again. "True. But I like the way they look." He shrugged. "You're pretty and small, too."

"Thank you," Emelie replied ruefully. Dominic tickled her side, and she giggled. The sound shot straight to Dominic's groin, and his cock responded of its own volition. He stooped to kiss her neck and cheek, wanting to devour her as his rod twitched. "I'm also short."

Dominic nodded as he continued to kiss her neck, but he had to admit the position was awkward. He felt like he bent in half to reach. With a cluck of annoyance, he straightened and repinned his plaid. Their hands clasped together as they walked further upstream. Dominic pointed out landmarks along the way and showed Emelie where he and Brodie used to swim.

"I never learned how," Emelie admitted.

"You never learned? Would you like to?" Dominic asked.

"Aye. We're practically surrounded by water. I suppose I should know how."

"Do you fear someone throwing you in?" Dominic's question wasn't entirely in jest.

"No. But I should hate to tumble in."

"I can start teaching you tomorrow. We can go to a calm section of the bay."

"Won't more people see us?"

"Nay. There's a place Brodie takes Laurel."

"She knows how to swim?" It surprised Emelie to hear this.

"Like a bluidy fish, apparently. Terrifies him how long she can hold her breath and how far out she swims. She claims the loch is like bathwater after learning to swim in the North Sea. From what Monty told us, she was a hellion even as a child.

She'd climb the crags along the beach. She's both a squirrel and a selkie."

Emelie grinned. "Perhaps she should teach me."

And let me miss the chance to see ye in a wet chemise clinging to ye. Nae on yer life, mo sparradh beag.

"I'm a more patient teacher than she is."

"If you say so."

Emelie and Dominic turned back toward the keep, chatting about what a typical day was like for Dominic. He noticed Emelie asked insightful questions about which of Laurel's duties were becoming more challenging for her as her pregnancy progressed. She asked whether he believed Laurel would accept her help. She even asked his advice on how to approach Laurel. When he pointed out that Emelie had known Laurel far longer than he had, she reminded him that Laurel at Kilchurn differed greatly from the bitter and shrewish Laurel at Stirling. By the time they returned to the bailey, they were both cheery and looking forward to the midday meal.

TEN

E melie entered the chamber she would now share with Dominic and looked back at him as he stood in the doorway. His unease was obvious as he shifted his weight. They'd enjoyed a better meal than the evening before. When they returned from their walk, Emelie sought Laurel while Dominic met with Brodie. Dominic explained while they ate the evening meal that he'd spent the time discussing patrols and securing their borders from encroachment by the Lamonts and the MacArthurs. She appreciated that he shared the information with her after what she learned Colina did with the same knowledge. She'd shared the responsibilities she offered to take on to ease Laurel's days as her pregnancy progressed. Now they were retiring as a newly married couple, and Dominic appeared the antsy virgin.

"I will give you a moment to get settled," Dominic offered before he ducked back into the passageway.

"Dom," Emelie called. When he poked his head back into the chamber, Emelie turned her back to him and pointed to her laces. "I need help, please."

Emelie looked over her shoulder as Dominic hesitated, then made his way to her. He pulled the laces loose, just as he had the night before. And just like the night before, his hands came to rest on her waist. She leaned back against his broad chest, wishing his hands would slip around her waist. Or better yet, up to her breasts. She longed to feel him touch her again as he had that morning. She thought they'd made progress. However, Dominic released Emelie and strode to the door, which he closed softly behind him. Emelie looked around the chamber and sighed. She couldn't understand why he ran hot and cold each time they were near one another.

Dominic had been cautious when they'd kissed in Stirling and even on the journey, but he hadn't retreated as he did now. It felt as though the greater the passion grew between them, the further he ran when he remembered who he was kissing. She wondered if things would be different once they lay together in bed. She hurried to slip off her gown and hung it on a peg. She'd just pulled the covers up when a knock came at the door.

"Enter," Emelie called. Dominic eased the door open and appeared relieved that she was already in bed. He looked around the chamber much like she had done only moments earlier. But Emelie feared he would take a place beside the hearth. She watched as he toed off his boots and approached the bed. She knew he wore a fresh leine and plaid, since his rich brown hair had been damp when he arrived at the dais for the meal. Dominic appeared at a loss as he glanced at the bed before he sat down. "Aren't you going to at least remove your belt? That must be uncomfortable to sleep in."

Dominic opened his mouth to explain that if he removed his belt, his plaid would unravel while he slept. He shook his head and laid down on top of the covers. Emelie wanted to ask him why he wouldn't make himself comfortable, but she feared the possible rejection that could come with his answer. He kissed her cheek and adjusted the blanket around her shoulders. She once more had the brief thought that his actions felt paternal, as they sometimes had in Stirling. But there was nothing paternal about the way he kissed her when he allowed himself to indulge.

"Goodnight, Em. Wake me if you need aught." Dominic kissed Emelie's cheek again before rolling away from her. He gritted his teeth and scrunched his face as he forced himself not to sweep her into his arms before ravishing her. He knew she stared at him for a long while before she rolled away. He lay awake for what felt like hours as he listened to Emelie's deep breathing. He finally eased onto his other side and slipped his arm around her waist. He was asleep within minutes.

Emelie controlled her breathing, appearing as though she slept, but silent tears cascaded from her eyes. She felt lonelier than she ever had in her life. Dominic turning his back to her wasn't how she envisioned him sharing her bed. Even if he wouldn't couple with her, she'd thought he might hold her as he had each night they traveled. She thought he was asleep, but she was certain he was very much awake when he rolled over and wrapped himself around her. With a shuddering sigh, she closed her eyes. She basked in the feeling of him for a few minutes before sleep overtook her.

Emelie and Dominic's days and nights followed nearly the same pattern for the next sennight. After everyone broke their fast, Emelie and Laurel planned how they would divide the day's chores. Laurel appreciated Emelie's initiative, especially for the tasks

143

that would have kept her on her feet for hours. While they worked within the keep, Dominic trained in the lists with Brodie and the other warriors. The men returned for the midday meal most days, but on a couple occasions, Dominic and Brodie entrenched themselves in Brodie's solar with the clan council.

The highlight of Emelie's days were the afternoons. Dominic refused to allow anyone to dissuade him from spending the time with Emelie. He took her on walks along the river, pointing out more places he and Brodie had played as children. He told her stories of how their mother used to take them riding when they were children, and that it was she who taught both men to ride when they were still young. He pointed out the mountains in the distance, regaling Emelie with stories of dares he and Brodie swapped as they learned to survive among the peaks. He spoke of his father's stern manner, and how the man browbeat his mother but had made Brodie and him into warriors. As Dominic told her that particular story, Emelie realized why Dominic had been so attuned to Colina's wishes and how that made him easy to manipulate. He'd wanted to treat his own wife the opposite of how his father treated his mother. Silent pieces fell into place as they spent time together.

It was the nights that plagued Emelie. Just as the first night passed when Dominic agreed to share a chamber, he remained in the passageway until she slipped into bed. Then he kicked off his boots and climbed onto the bed. Emelie would pretend to fall asleep as soon as her head hit her pillow, then Dominic would roll over and embrace her. She knew Dominic woke before her because he was back to his own side of the bed. As soon as she stirred, he would rise and rush to put his boots back on. He would kiss her forehead and cheek, then wait for her outside.

By their ninth night in their chamber, Emelie had moved past frustrated and hurt to blazing anger. As Dominic opened the door to the chamber and stood aside, Emelie stood within the doorway. She narrowed her eyes at Dominic. She knew it was unreasonable to expect him to understand why she was upset, but she assessed him as though he failed to read her mind.

"Em?"

"Why don't you want me?" Emelie blurted. Dominic's face flamed red, and it was the first time Emelie witnessed him blush. He guided them into the chamber and closed the door behind him. Emelie stared at him, her silence demanding he speak.

"I do want you," Dominic whispered. "More than I should."

"Then why do you retreat? Why do you kiss me, then push me away?" Emelie closed her eyes, unable to look at him. "It hurts, and it's confusing."

She gasped when his brawny arms engulfed her. She hadn't heard him move nor sensed him standing before her. His mouth crashed down to hers as he tugged at the laces to her gown. He ripped them from the gown before pushing it down her arms. It soon pooled around Emelie's ankles. She reached for the pin at his shoulder but had to pull away lest she stab him with it. As Dominic unfastened the brooch, Emelie tugged at his belt, releasing the prongs. As it dropped away, she discovered it was heavier than she imagined.

"How can it be comfortable to sleep in this night after night?" Emelie wondered.

"It isn't particularly."

"Then why? Why do you insist upon coming to bed fully dressed? Why do you wait until you believe I'm asleep to touch me? Why do you roll away from me before I wake? Why, Dom?" Emelie shot one question after another at Dominic. He allowed his plaid to fall to the floor beside Emelie's kirtle. He tugged her against his body, his arousal pressing against her belly.

"That's why. Because if I touch you while I believe you're awake, I won't let go. I don't want to let go."

"Have I done something to make you think I don't want you to touch me, to couple with me?"

"No." Dominic tilted his head back and looked at the ceiling as he exhaled, his breath whistling in the otherwise silent chamber. "I'm so much bigger than you, Em."

"So?" Emelie was baffled by his response.

"Ye're with child, Em." Emotion filled Dominic's voice, making his speech slip back into his burr. Emelie shivered, the rolling sounds nearly as arousing as the feel of his cock against her. "I dinna want to hurt either of ye. I'm so much bigger that I fear harming ye."

"If you think you'd be too heavy…" It was Emelie's turn to blush. She was embarrassed to admit what she knew. But there was no point in pretending either of them were virgins. "You don't have to be on top of me."

"I ken. But, Em, all of me is large." At Emelie's speculative glance at his rod, Dominic thought he'd spill without touching her. "I dinna want to injure ye if I force ma way into ye. Ye're so tiny."

Emelie pulled her lips in as she attempted—and failed—to hide her smile. She covered her mouth to stifle her giggle. She ceased when she saw how her laughter hurt Dominic. "I don't mean to laugh at your concern. But do you fear you'll poke the bairn?"

Dominic's ears were surely afire. He wished he could stick his head in the river and cool off. "I dinna think I can. I dinna think that is how a woman's body is made, but I can also see how narrow yer hips are."

"Didn't you say that if my body was ready, there would be no discomfort, only pleasure?"

"Aye. But I've never..." Dominic groaned. He didn't want to talk to his bride about his past sexual congress with other women.

"Never coupled with an expectant woman?" Emelie supplied.

"Aye."

"Are you really that fearful?"

"I never want to do aught that might hurt ye, Em. I only want to protect ye, and that may mean from me."

"I don't need protecting from you, Dom."

"I dinna trust maself nae to lose what little control I have around ye. Em, ye drive me to distraction. I canna think of much else but how badly I want to be with ye."

"You seem fine when we go walking. You don't seem distracted at all."

"Then I'm even better at hiding how I feel than I thought."

"What do we do?" Emelie asked, her voice hushed since she wasn't certain she would like his answer.

"I tried to see our healer, Honoria, but she's away from the village. A woman recently gave birth on one of our more remote farms. She nearly died birthing her son, so Nora went to care for her."

"Oh, Dom. That couldn't have made you feel any better aboot this."

"It didna. I wanted to ask her advice aboot whether it's safe."

"It must be. I know Laurel and Brodie certainly aren't abstaining, and she's further along than I am."

147

"But she's also tall and sturdy," Dominic countered.

"I'm not exactly going to blow away in the wind. You make me sound like a child. I'm short, but I'm an adult. You will not break me, and I have a mind of my own. I don't need you making decisions for me."

"But—"

"No. You're trying to rescue me again, fix me. You decided how things were going to be without considering what I want. I want my husband to touch me. I want to not feel rejected every time you kiss me, then push me away. Mayhap you won't couple with me, but at least you've admitted that you want to."

Emelie clenched her jaw as she fought not to cry or scream. Dominic watched her, uncertain what to say or do next.

"Do you have any idea how horrible I've felt thinking I was a slut for wanting your attention? How guilty I've felt for not being a virgin? I may not know much, but I'm ashamed of what I do know. I shouldn't have any clue of how enjoyable a mon's touch can be, but I do. I was too embarrassed to say aught before because I didn't want to remind you of what I do know. But I'm angry at you."

Dominic swept Emelie into his arms, but she gritted her teeth when he carried her to a chair near the fireplace rather than to the bed. He settled into the seat and nestled her against his chest. She wasn't ready to be soothed by being in his embrace. She wanted things resolved.

"Em, ye seemed so broken and vulnerable when I met ye. I'd never felt such sympathy for someone in ma life. I did want to rescue ye and to fix everything. Ye looked as through the world had chewed ye up and spat ye out. I wanted to protect ye from that. I admit once I kenned yer situation, a small part of me did think offering ye a chance for marriage would redeem me, at least in ma own eyes. But more than aught, I wanted ye with me. I dinna ken why I felt that way. I just did. I just do," Dominic shrugged. "I dinna ken much aboot women and bairns. I dinna ken what's safe for a husband to do, so I thought it better nae to do aught. It's nae from lack of want. Ye were right that I should have talked to ye. I was too embarrassed by how strong ma desire is for ye. I dinna want ye to think that's all that matters to me. I dinna want ye to fear me or think I would force ye."

"Why would I ever think that? You would never, ever force me. You are not that type of mon. And I have to say, I resent you thinking I would ever think that aboot you."

"I dinna like ye being afraid to tell me aught. I thought ye kenned ye could trust me."

"Like you trust me?" Emelie snapped. She took a breath before continuing. "You wouldn't have told me how you feel if I hadn't confronted you tonight. You would have continued to decide for both of us until you spoke with Nora. Mayhap I would like to be part of that conversation. Mayhap I want to hear what she has to say."

"Ye're right."

Emelie sat up and looked at Dominic, unprepared for him to capitulate so easily. "Are we having our first fight?"

"I suppose." Dominic shrugged. He'd always given in to Colina or managed to avoid confrontation, since she claimed she grew faint or ill any time an argument loomed. He felt like a weak man as he realized that his backbone had disintegrated during his marriage. "Em, I didna trust ye enough to share how I was feeling. I decided for ye that ye needed shielding from me. I didna do it to hurt ye, but I did nonetheless."

"I know that wasn't your intention, Dom. I was angry with you before, but now I'm just frustrated by the situation. I don't think you'll agree to couple with me until you—*we*—speak to Nora."

"I'm nae trying to be stubborn. I genuinely fear that I might injure ye. I canna think of aught worse than that." Dominic tucked a platinum lock of hair behind Emelie's ear. He considered what she'd said earlier. "I dinna want ye to be ashamed of yer past. I dinna think ye want me to go through life with ma guilt as I do now, and ma sins were far worse than yers. I dinna think the worst of ye because ye arenae a virgin. I dinna hold it against ye that ye ken a mon and a woman can enjoy being together. That was never a reason for me to stay away."

"Then why—"

"I rather like the idea that ye ken what happens. I've only been with one virgin, and that wasna a wonderful experience that night, truth be told. Before that, I'd only been with experienced women. That I dinna frighten ye makes me even more eager. Ye are nae a slut because of what ye ken or what ye want. I loathe that I made ye feel that way by making ye think yer feelings are unrequited. They arenae. I want ye vera much, wife."

"Is there no compromise? What aboot that first morning here? It felt wonderful. And you can see I'm no worse for wear from you touching me."

"There are other things I can do to pleasure ye."

"I want to know what I can do for you," Emelie blurted. She figured they were being candid, so she wouldn't hold back.

"Ye dinna have to do aught. I dinna expect ye to. I want ye to ken that joining together isnae just for a mon's enjoyment."

"I know that. Or at least, you made me realize that. But I want to touch you, Dom. I want to share, not take. I know you want to give and not take, but that's not what it would be. Not if you let me be your partner in this." Emelie brushed back dark strands that brushed Dominic's eyelashes. It was her first wifely display of affection, and they both realized it. Emelie sank against Dominic as their lips fused together once more. Emelie slipped her fingers beneath the collar of Dominic's leine as his hand glided along the back of her thigh until he grasped her backside.

"Dear God, ye're perfect," Dominic whispered. He tightened his hold on Emelie and stood. She felt as though she floated until he laid her on the bed and followed her onto it. He supported himself on one arm as his other hand pulled her chemise to her waist. She reached for his leine, which billowed nearly to his knees, but he caught her fingers. "If there is naught between us, I dinna trust either of us to stop."

"I don't think that would be so horrible. Do you think I would lie to you?"

"Nae at all."

"Dom, I'll tell you if aught makes me uncomfortable or makes me nervous. But I don't think joining with you will harm me. My body aches with need. Why would it do that if it weren't meant to accept you?"

"Nora is to return tomorrow. Can we wait one more night until we can speak to her? I dinna ken who ye saw in Stirling, and I would feel better if she examined ye anyway. She delivered Brodie and me, and ma brother trusts Nora to care for Laurel."

Emelie cupped Dominic's face and nodded. She nudged him closer, wishing he would settle more of his weight onto her, but she knew he wouldn't. She gave his lips a peck. "I want you to know I appreciate

151

your concern. It annoys me, but I appreciate it." Emelie grinned, but she soon moaned as Dominic rocked his hips against her mons as his hand traveled over her waist until it cupped her breast. He was slow to add pressure, watching for any sign that Emelie didn't enjoy his touch. But she arched her back into his hand and covered it with her own. She squeezed, encouraging him to hold the globe tighter. Her hips undulated in a rhythm that matched how Dominic's cock continued to rub against her mound.

Dominic needed more, needed as much as he dared take. He wanted to see Emelie. He'd fantasized about her each time he bathed, imagining how it would feel to have her clinging to him as he thrust into her over and over. He doubted his imagination would do justice to what lay beneath her linen chemise. He inched it higher until he bared her belly. The creamy white expanse of her midriff was soft and smooth. He pushed away the thought of the babe growing within her as he uncovered her breasts. He was certain he would expire as his eyes strayed over her body, lingering on her breasts and the blonde curls at the juncture of her thighs.

Emelie pulled the chemise over her head, uncomfortable with it bunched beneath her chin. But she had a moment of fear when she realized there was nothing hiding her from Dominic's sight. She met his gaze, and the hunger she spied made her hips tilt toward his shaft, a silent invitation.

"Emelie, I want to devour ye. I dinna ken what to kiss or touch first. Ye've presented me with a feast, and I dinna ken what I should choose as the first course," Dominic mused. He pressed a kiss to the crook of her neck before shifting to lick her nipple. The damp skin soon puckered, making it easy for Dominic to pull it into his mouth. He was careful not to suckle, swirling his tongue over the dart. But

Emelie's mewl of frustration made him wonder if he should dare more. She answered his silent query when her hand cupped her breast, offering it more fully to him, as her other hand pressed lightly on his head. He opened his mouth to take as much of her breast as he could. He sucked until the nipple protruded enough for him to nip it with his teeth.

"Dom, I need you. What're you doing to me?" Emelie rasped. Her body's demands shocked her. She thought she'd been aroused and experienced desire with Henry, even if he had done little to fulfill those feelings. But the sensations Dominic created with his hands and his mouth made Emelie question if she'd ever experienced arousal, or if it had been mere curiosity before.

"I'm making yer body crave mine as much as I do yers."

"You have. Please don't stop. If you do, I truly fear I will die. I will either explode or shrivel up."

"We canna have that," Dominic growled beside her ear. His hand slid from her breast, where it had replaced his mouth as he nuzzled her neck. His fingers toyed with the sensitive bundle of nerves hidden within its hood.

"Please," Emelie whimpered. Dominic delved his fingers within her sheath, thrusting two in at first. When Emelie's legs parted wider, and she raised her hips and kept them off the mattress, he added a third. His thumb swirled in her dew before seeking her bud once more. He worked her sheath inside and out until her nails bit into his shoulders. He watched as Emelie's head tilted back, her eyes shut while her mouth formed a perfect O. He watched as she crested, but he wasn't through. He'd shown her how he could pleasure her with his hand, but he had far more he wanted to teach her. He eased down the bed until he hooked her knees over his shoulders. He pulled her hips to his mouth, but he paused at her look of confusion. He offered her a wolfish grin before he flicked his tongue against her button.

"I have lost time to make up for, sparrow. And I find our conversation has made me hungry. I crave the taste of honey, yer honey."

Emelie watched in amazement as Dominic's tongue laved her seam. His gaze locked with hers, and she was certain his expression taunted her. She pressed her mons to his lips, encouraging him to do something she'd only heard matrons at court whisper about. A deep moan poured forth as Dominic dipped his tongue into her entrance and swirled it within. His teeth grazed her bud before he sucked on it as he had her nipple. His stubble rubbed against her swollen flesh and the insides of her thighs. She was certain he would leave the skin red, and she found she liked the idea that he'd marked her as his. It would be a secret only they shared.

Emelie was unprepared for the tsunami of sensations that ripped through her as her climax crashed over her. It outshone her two previous ones and left her panting with her heart racing. She was certain Henry never could have made her body hum and sing as Dominic did. As she watched him, the strongest realization came over her. She'd been infatuated with the attention Henry paid her, and she'd thought she could gamble and win. But her emotions seemed frivolous compared to what swelled in her heart as she watched Dominic. She wouldn't deny how she enjoyed his touch, but it was far more than that. It was the way he touched her, the consideration he gave with each movement, always giving.

Dominic was lightheaded. He was starved for more, wanting to worship Emelie over and over, but he understood she wasn't used to such bed sport, and it was likely she would grow sore if he continued to tease her overly sensitive nerves. He wouldn't rob her of her pleasure and only leave her with pain. He nipped his way from her hip up to her breast, alternating swiping his tongue and catching her skin between his lips. When he hovered over her once again, he lowered himself for another kiss. He felt the difference. He was sure of it. There was a tenderness they shared that didn't diminish their passion, but it made it clear that what they shared in that chamber went far beyond the pleasures of the flesh. Something deeper, more substantial was growing between them.

Emelie poured every ounce of emotion she could muster into their kiss. She wanted him to understand what she wasn't ready to say. They'd shared more than enough of their private thoughts that night. She couldn't bring herself to divulge feelings she didn't even understand. But she desperately wanted him to know that their time together meant more than just a romp. She pressed his shoulder and tried to roll to her side. Dominic took her hint and rolled onto his back. His arm slid beneath her and pulled her onto him. Her leg slid between his, and his muscular thigh pressed against her mons. His hands grasped her backside, and together they moved Emelie over his thigh. Their kiss grew untamed as Emelie fisted his leine.

"Dom, oh God," Emelie breathed. His fingers bit into her bottom, and the tighter his grip, the more she needed. She buried her face in the crook of his neck to muffle her scream as yet another release ripped through her. She was left feeling wrung dry and breathless, but she wasn't ready to move. The hand that clutched his shirt slid down, searching for the hem. Her hand dove beneath the fabric until it brushed along his rod. Her fingertips grazed the satiny skin as they moved up and down. She slid one

155

over the tip, finding a dollop of moisture. She glanced down, taking in her first sight of a man's cock. As her hand wrapped around it, she realized Dominic hadn't exaggerated, and she wondered if his concern wasn't misplaced.

"Emelie," Dominic groaned. "Slide yer hand up and down." His eyes squeezed closed as he fought the urge to thrust into her hand and spill. Her tentative touch drove him to the brink.

"Is this what you like?"

Dominic peeked at Emelie, and if he hadn't seen the uncertainty in her gaze as she looked at his rod, he would have thought her a practiced courtesan. She hadn't realized how seductive her words were.

"Vera much," Dominic's voice rumbled.

"I like it when you talk like that," Emelie whispered.

"Like what, sparrow."

"Like a Highlander. It does something to me."

"And what might that be?" Dominic asked as he covered Emelie's hand and guided her. It took only a moment for her to catch on. She worked his length, growing braver as she alternated her grip and speed. Dominic tweaked her nipple as he grazed his teeth along her neck. "Does it make ye wish to feel me buried inside ye?"

"It does."

"One of these days, sparrow, I will show ye just what yer touch does to me. I will bury maself to the hilt and make yer body clench around me as I spill inside ye." Dominic thrust into Emelie's hand, and when she squeezed, he lost the battle to hang on. His cock pulsed as his seed spilled across Emelie's hand and his belly. She eased her hand away and dipped her finger into the viscous fluid. She held up the finger and looked at Dominic. She brought her finger toward her mouth, but she waited for Dominic.

"Do ye wish to ken how I taste, lass? Do ye wonder if I might taste as good to ye as ye obviously do to me?" Dominic jerked his chin, telling her to go ahead. Emelie dipped her finger into her mouth. She wasn't certain what to make of the taste at first, but she wasn't opposed to it. She licked her lips and pulled her teeth over her lower lip unconsciously. Dominic growled and pounced. His arm became a steel band around Emelie's waist as he hauled her across him. She straddled his hips as he sat up. Their bodies finally pressed together, and Dominic's cock rested between them. Dominic guided Emelie's hips, hinting at how they could move together once their bodies joined.

"I—" Emelie licked her lips again. Dominic shut his eyes against the erotic scene Emelie created every time she ran her tongue over her lips. "I've heard women talking. I know I can suck—" Emelie feared she would die of mortification, but she'd already said the hardest part. She plowed on. "—your manhood. But I don't know how."

Dominic made a choked sound as his eyes flew open. Once more, Emelie clearly didn't understand the power of her words as she continued to ride his hips. He stilled her movement, far too tempted, but he pressed her against him.

"Never feel obligated to do such a thing. I ken many women dinna care for it. I dinna expect it, and ye dinna need to fear that I will search for it elsewhere. I can only imagine what ye heard the women say at court. Aye, it can bring a mon to his knees, but we can all live without it. We arenae rutting beasts."

Emelie chuckled. "I did hear women say it was a mon's favorite, sometimes even more than a woman's —" Emelie lowered her voice "—quim."

"Aye. Ye enjoyed what I did, so it stands to reason a mon would enjoy a woman giving the same favor.

But I willna fault ye if ye dinna like it. And I can live without it." He had lived without it. Colina had refused the few times he hinted at it. But after discovering her with Graham, he suspected he was what she rejected, not the act. Dominic eased Emelie onto the bed, and they lay facing one another on their sides. Her contented sigh made him smile, and she wriggled closer when he encouraged her to shift toward him.

"Can you stop sounding like a Lowlander?"

Dominic guffawed. "You're a Lowlander." He switched his speech back to what his tutor had drilled into Brodie and him. It wasn't that often that either of them spoke with a brogue; usually it was when they were angry or flustered. Dominic knew Brodie abandoned his courtly speech during intimate moments with Laurel. She did the same.

Emelie playfully swatted at his chest. He caught her hand, kissed her fingertips, then guided it around his waist. "I know I am. I know what I sound like. I like the way you sound. It suits you."

"Suits me? And just how is that?" Dominic's piercing gaze held a sultry allure as he stressed each syllable.

"That." Emelie raised her eyebrows. "It suits that wolfish look you get."

"Wolfish look, lass. That's because I wish to devour ye. Mayhap I will stalk ye around this chamber morning, noon, and night. I'll capture ye and bring ye back to ma den, or rather ma bed, where I shall ravish ye."

"I wouldnae fight ye," Emelie grinned as she tried to sound like him. Dominic had never heard anything more endearing than Emelie attempting to sound like a Highlander.

"There's hope for ye yet, sparrow."

"Only if you promise that you won't be tame with me here, wolf."

"Wolf?"

"If I remind you of a sparrow, then you remind me of a wolf."

"I stand by ma hesitation to couple with ye, Em. Until I hear it from Nora that I dinna have to fear harming ye, I willna relent on that. Ridiculous as it seems to ye. But ye ken now there are other things we can do."

"Och, aye. I shall hold you to it." Emelie's saucy comment matched her expression. They dissolved into laughter before Dominic drew the covers over them. "Goodnight, wolf."

"Goodnight, sparrow."

They fell asleep wrapped in one another's arms, and they awoke the same way. Dominic didn't rush from the chamber. He reminded Emelie of what she'd discovered the night before. They were late to the morning meal, but neither cared about the knowing looks directed at them. They were too busy chatting about the coming day.

ELEVEN

"**D**amn it," Dominic muttered as he looked at the northern sky.

"What is it?" Emelie asked as they walked back to the keep from the village. They'd spent most of the afternoon visiting with clan members who still hadn't met Emelie. They were mostly the older members, and it amazed Dominic at how naturally Emelie charmed them, even the most cantankerous.

"There's an almighty storm brewing, and it looks like it's already dumping rain to the north." Dominic pointed to the thick, dark clouds in the distance.

"We have plenty of time to make it back inside."

"Aye. But that's the direction Nora would come from. I doubt she'll travel in a storm. She shouldn't travel in a storm," Dominic conceded. He looked down at Emelie and knew her disappointment matched his. They'd made tremendous strides the night before, and they were both eager to hear Nora's verdict. Emelie knew they hoped for the same thing, but even if they didn't hear what they wanted, she knew it would relieve them both to know one way or another.

They entered the keep together just as Laurel stumbled against a wall and bent over. Emelie and

Dominic ran to her side. They found her perspiring and pale. Dominic didn't hesitate. He scooped Laurel into his arms and charged toward the steps, bellowing, "Find Brodie."

Dominic could only imagine the state his brother would be in if no one sought him immediately. Emelie gathered her skirts to her knees and rushed up the stairs ahead of him. She threw open the door to the laird and lady's chamber and rushed to pull back the covers. Dominic eased Laurel onto the bed. He moved to stoke the fire while Emelie pulled off Laurel's boots. The woman had said nothing since Emelie and Dominic reached her side, and it terrified them.

"What happened?" Brodie demanded as he burst into the chamber.

"Wheesht, bear," Laurel whispered. "Ye're making ma head ring."

Emelie jumped out of the way, glad when Dominic pulled her back against him and out of Brodie's way as he stormed across the chamber. Emelie feared he would bully Laurel into speaking. It stunned her to see how gentle Brodie was as he lifted Laurel's hand into his and brushed hair from her perspiring brow.

"What do ye need, thistle? What's wrong?" Brodie asked in a hushed voice. He stroked his wife's damp hair as he watched her.

"Sleep. Naught is wrong with the bairn, so ye dinna need to fash. I just felt lightheaded and suddenly so tired. I fear I may be coming down with something."

"Nay."

"What do ye mean, nay?" Laurel opened one eye and scowled at her husband. "Ye canna just tell me I canna get sick."

"Because ye dinna listen anyway," Brodie scolded

161

before he kissed Laurel's forehead. He kicked off his boots and laid his sword across the foot of the bed. Emelie watched in amazement as Brodie climbed over Laurel without releasing her hand. He was agile and barely moved the bed as he settled beside her. She rolled toward her husband, and it was only a moment later before Emelie, Dominic, and Brodie realized Laurel had already fallen asleep.

"I'll ask Berta to send a tray up with a proper meal for you and some broth for Laurel," Emelie offered.

"Have her send up half a hog. Laurel willna want just broth," Brodie teased, but the words were hollow. It was obvious to Emelie and Dominic that Brodie was frightened.

"If you wish to sleep later, I'll stay awake in case she needs aught," Emelie said.

"That's kind of ye, lass. I still havenae apologized for the horrible things ye heard me say yer first morn here. I'm sorry. It was uncalled for. Ma brother annoyed me, and ye were an easy way to get back at him. It wasna right, and I am sorry." Brodie offered his apology to Emelie, then looked at Dominic. "I am sorry to ye too. Ye didna deserve ma doubt or suspicion. I've told ye before that I dinna blame ye for the past, and I meant it then, just as I mean it now. I shouldnae have been testy with ye, and I shouldnae have used yer wife like that."

Laurel stirred. "Aboot bluidy time," she muttered. "Now quiet, bear. Yer chest moves too much when ye speak. Just hold me."

"We'll be back later," Dominic said before he led Emelie to the door. They both looked back to find Brodie whispering to Laurel as he rubbed her back. His eyes were closed, but it was obvious he was still alert. Dominic and Emelie made their way back to the Great Hall. They found Aggie looking for Laurel, so they explained what happened.

"Should someone fetch Nora?" Emelie asked.

"Nae yet," Aggie said. "We'll see if we can get Lady Laurel to rights by tomorrow midday. If nae, then we'll see aboot sending someone out for the healer."

Emelie turned to look at Dominic, who nodded in agreement. "Aggie's right. It's going dark already. It'll be more dangerous for the rider, and there's no guarantee the mon would reach Nora tonight, anyway."

"Do you mind what I offered?" Emelie asked Dominic, wishing they were alone for a moment.

"Not at all. It was kind of you. I will stay up too, if you wish," Dominic said as he wrapped his arms around his wife. He longed to point out that Laurel wasn't the only pregnant woman who needed rest, but they had told no one yet, and Aggie was watching them.

"Ye should rest, ma lady. Ye and yer bairn need it, too," Aggie whispered. Emelie and Dominic turned stunned faces toward her. "I was there when yer mother was carrying ye and the laird. I've had three bairns of ma own. And I've seen countless other women with child. It doesnae take being a healer to notice that ye dinna care for the morning meal and stick with plain porridge. Ye canna stomach rich foods, but ye seem to be doing better. Ye dinna turn green anymore. Ye canna sit with yer gown laced tightly through the entire evening meal. And aye, I can tell ye the maid has already mentioned she isnae pulling yer laces as tight as she was a sennight ago."

"Aggie," Dominic warned.

"Haud yer wheesht. I willna tell anyone, but ye'd do well to share the good news before others realize it. I've sworn Ethel to silence after I heard her hinting at yer condition to another maid." Aggie took Emelie's hands, but not before she cast a motherly scowl at Dominic. "Ma felicitations, ma lady. We're all glad ye're part of our clan now, and everyone will be overjoyed to ken both the laird and his brother have bairns on the way."

"Thank you, Aggie," Emelie said, unsure how she felt knowing that others had already deduced her condition.

"Well done, lad. Ye didna waste any time this go around."

Dominic opened his mouth to chastise Aggie for the insensitive comment, but she'd already turned toward the kitchens. He looked down at Emelie, who watched him. "Em—"

"What does haud yer wheesht mean?" Emelie didn't want Dominic to make apologies for Aggie when she was certain the older women had intended no harm. She would rather forget Aggie referred to Colina and compared her to Dominic's first wife.

"It means to be quiet and not get worked up," Dominic answered.

"That is far better than all that you just said. I shall remember that."

"Em, she didn't mean aught by—"

"Haud yer wheesht, wolf," Emelie grinned and giggled. "Came in handy already."

Dominic glanced around them, then pressed Emelie backward into a dark passageway. When they were in the shadows, he lifted her off her feet and pressed his mouth to hers. She opened without hesitation, and they both shared a sense of relief that they'd worked past the invisible barrier that had kept them apart until the night before. While it disappointed them both that Nora wouldn't be able to examine Emelie that day, they both knew they would find other ways to be intimate.

"I'm glad we argued last night." Emelie was breathless when they pulled apart. Dominic sensed her smile, even if he couldn't see it.

"I am too. And I admire you for speaking up. I know that it wasn't easy. I won't let things get to where we have to argue for me to be forthcoming."

"Neither will I. Dom, we've learned a lot aboot each other in a short amount of time. But it stands to reason that we're still learning how to be married." Emelie cringed. She wasn't certain when she should refer to them as handfasted or married. She didn't know if they were interchangeable.

"Handfasted or married. Either works," Dominic said, reading her mind. "You're my wife either way. And you're right. We are learning. I will try not to be so highhanded in how I treat you. I'm your husband, not your father. You are my partner, and I don't want you to feel like your voice doesn't matter."

"Thank you. And I understand that there may be times when you can't always explain your reasoning or your decisions. But when it comes to what we do in private, I want to be open with you like I was last night. It was scary, but secrets got me into the mess I was in when you found me."

"I like knowing I can confide in you. I didn't realize how much I needed that until I told you the truth aboot how I feel." Dominic paused as he collected his thoughts. "Em, I will keep my promise that I will release you at any time with no grievances or grudges. But I'd like you—or rather, I hope you'll think aboot Kilchurn being your home from now on. That you will consider staying even after you have the bairn. I'm not asking for your answer right this minute. But I want you to know that I want you to stay."

"Why?" Emelie whispered.

"I think I'm wiser than I was four years ago. I won't pledge undying love within a matter of sennights. But because I think I'm more mature than I was then, I can also see the difference in the situations. I respect you, Em. I admire you, and not just because you're the most beautiful woman I've ever seen. I admire your resilience, and your kindness, and your bluidy endless patience with me."

As Emelie listened to Dominic, she realized his compliment about her appearance was more an observation than a trick to gain her trust and lower her resistance. That was what Henry had done. He'd showered her with compliments, and she'd lapped them up like a thirsty kitten.

"Dom, I've already started thinking of Kilchurn as my home. But I didn't want to think aboot aught beyond our year before last night because I wasn't sure I could spend a lifetime beside you if you didn't want me as I do you. I think we resolved that matter quite clearly last night. And this morning. And just now." Emelie giggled again.

"You don't know how that sound affects me. I will never grow tired of hearing you laugh. It's like a balm to my soul, sparrow."

"Then I shall endeavor to laugh often." Emelie stood on her toes and aimed to kiss Dominic's cheek. But in the dark, her lips landed against his throat. "And I shalln't always laugh at your expense. I promise."

"Cheeky," Dominic growled as he pinched her backside and lifted her up once again. They exchanged a smacking kiss before embracing. Emelie rested her head against Dominic's shoulder and closed her eyes. "I would hold you all day, sparrow."

"I was just thinking how much I wish you could. Must you always read my mind?"

"I don't read your mind. We just think a great deal alike."

"Mmm. I like that." Emelie grew quiet, and neither was in a rush to leave their secluded spot. It reminded them both of the alcoves they'd ducked into at court. But noise from the Great Hall told them people were gathering for the evening meal. They made their way to the dais and shared a trencher. They'd learned what each other preferred, and they'd begun serving one another. They didn't notice what a blissful couple they made, but others did. More eyes followed them than they realized, and not all liked what they saw.

Emelie and Dominic passed the night in Laurel and Brodie's chamber. Emelie held a cool compress to Laurel's forehead while Dominic sat silently by the fire. They convinced Brodie to sleep in spurts, arguing that he needed to be awake during the day, too. When Brodie was awake and insisted that he care for his wife, Emelie nestled against Dominic's chest as he held her. She dozed as she sat on his lap, but she knew he didn't sleep at all. He said someone had to stand watch over her, Brodie, and Laurel. Emelie wanted to argue, but Dominic was resolute.

Morning passed into afternoon, then into evening. Laurel woke for much of the daylight hours, but she was too fatigued to do anything more than watch the surrounding people. The weather had grown worse, and there were periodic reports of flooding in the village. Laurel refused Brodie's demands that someone fetch Nora. She didn't want to be responsible for Nora being injured if her horse spooked in the thunder or if the older woman caught the ague.

By day three of Laurel's illness and the foul weather, reports were steadily arriving of flooding in many of the outlying villages, and two deaths from people being washed away by swollen rivers. Brodie was torn between not wanting to leave Laurel's side and knowing he had a duty to ride out and help their clan. Emelie watched the intimidating warrior humbled by his fear for his wife's wellbeing. It didn't thrill Dominic to leave Emelie, but he insisted he would go on patrol and visit those who were suffering.

"Em, I don't want to leave you here alone, but I can't let Brodie go out there while Laurel is ill. Neither of us would ever forgive ourselves," Dominic said as they stood together in their chamber. He tossed three leines and three plaids into a saddlebag along with as many pairs of stockings as he had. Someone had brought his belongings from his old chamber, sparing him the onerous task. He hadn't asked questions when he returned to the chamber one afternoon and found his chests against the wall; he simply thanked Laurel.

"Wheesht," Emelie said with a lopsided grin. "Dinna fash. I'll be fine here. You're right. You are the one who needs to go, and Brodie needs to stay. No one else is ailing, so mayhap whatever is wrong with Laurel is a fluke, or mayhap her body is merely adjusting once again to having a bairn. If her babe comes out aught like Brodie, he'll be a colossus too. She may be taller than me, but she isn't that big. Poor woman is likely to give birth to a bairn the size of a three-moon-old."

"But I don't think you are going to rest if I'm not here to insist. You're trying to do everything Laurel does during the day, then serve as her nursemaid at night. I fear you will exhaust yourself, and then you will fall ill."

"I'll take care of myself, of us." Emelie placed

Dominic's hand over her belly. They'd whispered while Laurel and Brodie slept, and they'd finally begun talking about the babe with anticipation. They told one another stories about what they wanted to emulate and avoid from their own parents' experiences. It convinced Emelie that Dominic would be a wonderful father, and her excitement grew the more time they spent together.

With Laurel's illness, there had been no time to consider their missed opportunities for intimacy. A different, but just as necessary, type of intimacy bloomed between them. "I'm afraid for you, Dom. I'm scared for you being outside in this. I know you will have to sleep on the ground. I'm scared something will happen, and you will be one of the people washed away."

Dominic pulled Emelie into his embrace, and he felt her tremble. Looking at her, he saw her concern. But it wasn't until her body pressed against his that he understood her fear. He leaned back and cupped her jaw. "I am coming home to you, Em. To you and our bairn. Naught will keep me from that. I want it too much."

"I pray Mother Nature listens to you and doesn't have other plans."

"Wheesht," Dominic mumbled before kissing her. They walked to the main doors of the keep. Laurel had taught Emelie how to wear a plaid as an arisaid, so Dominic pulled the extra fabric up over Emelie's head and shoulders. She grasped the edges and clenched it beneath her chin. "Send word if you need me. The council knows which route we're taking."

"I will. Just please be careful, Dom."

"I will, sparrow. I'll be home and underfoot before you know it."

"I will hold you to that promise, wolf." With an

all-too-brief kiss goodbye, Emelie watched Dominic and half a dozen guardsmen ride out into the storm. She looked at the early afternoon sky. An onlooker could confuse it for the night. The clouds blocked out all but the sun's most persistent rays. Driving rain pelted the ground, creating puddles that reached mid-calf. Protected by the overhang above the door, Emelie watched until she could no longer see Dominic or the other men. Resigned to waiting, Emelie made her way inside and looked for Aggie. She would ensure everything was ready for the evening meal.

Brodie spent his mornings alone with Laurel but, with much regret, he dragged himself to his solar in the afternoons. He couldn't neglect all clan business, especially with his tánaiste away. Emelie kept Laurel company in the afternoons. She spent the first two nights after Dominic left in the laird and lady's chamber. But as Laurel improved, Emelie offered the couple their privacy. She found Brodie's hovering endearing, even if Laurel didn't. She supposed she would feel as Laurel did if Dominic pestered her like Brodie did Laurel. But it also made her miss Dominic more.

Emelie realized that while his protectiveness had inadvertently put a wedge between them in the beginning, once they'd had it out, she appreciated him even more. The small things he did while she tended to Laurel proved he didn't see Emelie as a duty. He genuinely cared. He'd held her when she slept and requested Berta send up foods he knew Emelie liked and that would keep her from growing hungry during the wee hours of the night. He'd ordered a bath for her in their chamber every night, reluctantly leaving her just before she stripped off her chemise. He only did so because he promised to take Emelie's place beside Laurel and Brodie while she bathed.

Emelie was eager for Dominic to return so that she might return the favor. She couldn't fathom how cold and miserable he must be since the rain refused to cease. She was determined to have a bath ordered the moment the men on the wall walk spotted Dominic's return. She would carry a tray laden with food to their chamber herself. In preparation, she asked Aggie for all the blankets she could spare. The woman had looked at her oddly but nodded. Aggie watched as Emelie spread them over the bed, one layer after another, then peeled them back. They laid at the foot of the bed, ready to pull them over the bed's occupant. Aggie smiled and nodded when Emelie caught the aging housekeeper watching her.

"Ye're good for the lad."

Emelie had no opportunity to respond or ask what Aggie meant. The woman scuttled off to some other task. Emelie did what she could around the keep, but she didn't dare work on the ledgers. She hadn't learned Laurel's system yet, and she didn't want to create a mess. But she helped mold more candles and took an inventory of the larder and suggested what they should bring up to the kitchens. She helped bake the morning bread and surprised many at how quickly she peeled vegetables.

Emelie laughed and explained that her mother made her top and tail green beans and peel vegetables as a punishment, and Emelie frequently found herself in trouble as a child. Of the three sisters, she was always the most precocious. When her belly bumped against the table as she reached across it for another bowl, it was a silent reminder of what trouble she'd gotten herself into this time. The change in her body was subtle and not yet noticeable with her clothes on, but she was certain she could see a small rounding to the bottom of her abdomen. She wondered if Dominic would notice.

"I swear to you, Laurel. I saw a pair of ducks, a pair of pigs, and a pair of goats walking together toward the river. One even asked me if I'd seen Noah," Emelie teased as she sat beside Laurel on the edge of the bed. It had been four days since Dominic rode out and a full sennight since Laurel nearly collapsed. She developed no symptoms other than extreme exhaustion. No one could explain the reason for her sudden illness other than to say it was one of the trials of carrying a babe.

"And has an ark sailed into the bay?" Laurel teased.

"It's due any day now," Emelie answered with false solemnity, but she burst into laughter, unable to keep a straight face.

"Speaking of things being due…" Laurel gave Emelie a pointed look.

"Aggie already figured it out, and so did Ethel, but Aggie swore her to secrecy. I don't think we can keep it to ourselves much longer. I need my gowns loosened more each day, and I can't get half of mine over my bust."

"I have naught to do but sew while I'm stuck in bed. Aggie can help me by pinning the gowns I can no longer wear either. Then I'll alter them for you. And before you argue, I need something to do. I can admit I'm not back to full fettle yet, but I also don't need to sleep as much. Sewing will keep me occupied and keep Brodie alive. The mon is wonderful, but I didn't nickname him 'bear' for naught. He can be as ornery as a bear with a burr in its paw."

"Or a thistle." Emelie winked. She'd heard the

couple's pet names for one another. It made her smile because it always made her think of how Dominic called her sparrow and how much she enjoyed calling him wolf.

"Aye, well…" Laurel shrugged.

"I'm going into the village soon to check on some crofts that the storms damaged. I know Brodie will tend to the structures, but I also know you would see to the people. I'm going to take bread, pickled vegetables, and cheese to those who will accept it."

"It may embarrass most because you're still new, but they aren't too prideful to accept generosity. They'll appreciate your kindness," Laurel explained. "But take at least three men with you."

"I know. Dom would be livid if I left here without at least three guards. And to be honest, with how dark it is all day, I feel better having them with me. I'm not scared of the dark, nor do I think danger lurks in every corner, but you and I lived at court long enough to know what can happen to a woman in dark corners."

"Aye. Wise lass." Laurel nodded, then pointed toward a chest. "Pick out the gowns you like, then call Aggie. We can get you fitted, then I'll sew while you're in the village. I can have something ready for you before the evening meal."

Emelie followed Laurel's instructions. It amazed her at how efficient Aggie and Laurel were, and in less than an hour, Laurel had four kirtles measured and pinned. Emelie gave her a brief hug before fetching her arisaid from her chamber and making her way to the guardroom.

"Lady Emelie, it isnae fit for mon nor beast," a guard greeted her.

"I agree, Alec. But I need to go into the village. Are there at least three men who can accompany me?"

"Aye, ma lady. Give me but a moment."

"Please send them round to the kitchens. I have some baskets I need help to carry."

"Will do, ma lady."

Emelie picked her way to the kitchens, and it wasn't long before Alec and three men joined her. They lifted the baskets as though they were empty, then surrounded Emelie as they made their way out to the village. It took Emelie nearly four hours to make her rounds. Each family offered her a dram of whisky or something to eat. She didn't want to be rude, but eventually she had to turn down the alcohol. Once she explained how much she'd already had, no one took offense. Most cheered her on for staying on her feet after so much liquor and being so petite. She figured she rose in many people's estimation since she could hold her whisky. As she stepped out of the last croft, bells tolled. She looked at Alec, who grinned.

"Yer husband is nearly home, ma lady."

"Bluidy hell!" Emelie laughed as four stunned faces turned to her. "I'm excited he's home. But I planned to have a bath and food waiting for him. At this rate, he'll be in the keep before me. Can you keep up?"

Emelie gathered her skirts into her hands and dashed toward the postern gate. She leaped over one puddle after another, finding the few spots that weren't miniature bogs. She ran across the bailey, not caring about the puddles as Dominic rode through the gates. She was within earshot of Dominic when a squealing piglet dashed in front of her, splattering mud across her skirts. She tried to veer away from the animal, but her shoe squelched full of mud and wouldn't pull free. She pitched forward, her hands going out to break her fall. But it was to no avail. She landed face down in the muck. As if to add insult to injury, the piglet pressed his snout to Emelie's face and grunted as if it were foraging for truffles.

"Emelie!" Dominic bellowed as he watched the horror unfold. He sprang from his horse, but he couldn't get to his wife before she landed in the mud. When she heard his roar, she pushed up enough to look at him. She rose to her knees, but a yapping dog ran toward the piglet and splattered mud into Emelie's face and knocked her backward. Dominic bolted across the bailey and swooped Emelie off the ground before another animal could injure her.

"You're home, and I'm the one who will need the bath," Emelie grumbled.

"What?"

"Naught. Oh, Dom. I'm so glad you're safe and home."

"I'm safe, but are you hurt? Why were you running?"

"I was fine until that blasted pig came out of nowhere. What's it doing out of the pen, anyway?"

"I dinna ken, ma lady. I am so sorry." A young boy ran up to the couple. His face was ruddy, and he was out of breath. "I ken I closed the gate to the pen. I just fed the lot of them. I turned to call Loki to ma side. He was digging at something, so I went to get him. Then I heard the squealing and saw ye fall, ma lady. Then ma dog knocked ye over. I didna mean for ye to get hurt."

"I'm not hurt. Only dirty. And I've seen you with the animals. I know you're very responsible. This must have been an accident." Emelie smiled down at the boy before Dominic nodded and turned toward the keep.

"But I ken I locked the gate," the boy insisted.

"I believe you. Mayhap the pigs knocked against the gate and loosened the lock," Emelie suggested.

The boy looked ready to disagree, but he thought better of it and nodded.

"Thank ye, ma lady." The boy bowed, then chased after his pig and his dog.

"What were you doing running in this weather?" Dominic asked.

"I wanted to get to the keep before you. I wanted to order a bath for you and have a tray of food ready. I wanted to greet you properly. Now I'm the one who's filthy and needs the bath. You don't look like you've been sleeping outside for four nights."

"The rain's been washing the mud off us faster than it can stick. Em, are you sure you're not hurt?"

"I'm fine. You can put me down."

"And give up the chance to hold you? Not a chance, sparrow." Dominic nuzzled Emelie's neck. "We'll have that bath together."

"Lad." An older woman approached them. Dominic groaned.

"Aye, Nora. This is my wife."

"Ye said ye wanted me to examine yer wife, but she looked hale as mountain goat a moment ago. And just as graceful until she met that piglet."

"Hello, Nora," Emelie smiled. "I know you haven't been home in days. I can wait until morning." At Dominic's groan, Emelie chuckled. "Mayhap my husband can't."

"Then let's have ye up to yer chamber. Get yerself cleaned up while I check on Lady Laurel." Nora tsked as she shooed them toward the doors. "Let's go, lad. Before yer wee wife catches her death."

Emelie tucked her face against Dominic's chest to hide her laughter. Nora was hardly bigger than her, but she issued orders to Dominic as though he was still a young boy like the one who tended the pigs. She sensed Dominic wanted to argue, but she knew he wouldn't dare. Emelie gathered her skirts to keep

176

the mud from dripping onto the Great Hall's floor. When they reached their chamber, Dominic kicked the door shut and lowered her to the floor. But she remained on her feet for only a moment before Dominic lifted her and guided her legs around his waist.

"How I've missed ye, sparrow. Ye made ma heart stop." Dominic captured Emelie's lips. She opened to him, moaning as her fingers tangled in his hair. He pressed her back to the door and rocked his cock against her mons. Their kiss grew wilder and hungrier with each heartbeat. When they were breathless, Dominic panted, "Bluidy good thing Nora is here. I dinna ken that I can keep ma resolve."

"I don't want you to. Let Nora tend to Laurel. I'm fine, Dom."

"I might have believed ye if I didna just see ye take a tumble."

"If I let you keep complaining, will you keep talking like that?"

"Like—are ye teasing me right now?"

"A little." Emelie held up her thumb and forefinger to show him a small amount. He nipped at her neck and used his teeth to tug at her earlobe.

"Let's get ye undressed and cleaned up enough for Nora. Then into a hot bath for ye."

"Will you scrub my back?"

"I'll scrub all of ye." Dominic put Emelie down and pulled her laces free. Mud caked them and made it harder to loosen than normal. As he worked to get her kirtle off, Emelie scrubbed soap and a wash linen over her face and neck. She scrubbed her hands once Dominic helped peel her gown over her hips. She finished rinsing off most of the mud when a knock sounded at the door.

Dominic looked to Emelie, and when she nodded, he opened the door. Nora bustled in, clucking as she prodded Emelie toward the bed. "Yer mon just said he wanted me to see ye. He wouldnae tell me why. I'm guessing ye're with child. Nay mon gets in such a tiswas unless he's fashing over his wife carrying their bairn."

"That's sounds like Dominic," Emelie grinned. She climbed onto the bed and watched Dominic look in every direction but toward the bed. She held out her hand to him. She watched as his face flushed, but he came to stand beside her and held her hand.

"How far along do ye think ye are, lass?"

"Mayhap nearly two or three moons. I dinna ken for sure." Emelie held her breath, but Nora didn't respond. She pushed Emelie's chemise to her waist and set to work pressing on Emelie's belly. She nodded several times before she raised the chemise high enough to glance at Emelie's breasts.

"I'd say two moons. Ye look well, ma lady. I dinna see any reason for yer husband to be so nervous."

Emelie realized that if Nora's estimation was correct, she'd gotten with child the second time she coupled with Henry. It would make the timing of her babe more reasonable.

"Nora," Dominic cleared his throat. "I wanted to ken…" Dominic glanced at Emelie, who he could tell was fighting not to laugh once again. "Ma wife is so tiny, and I'm, well, I'm nae. I'm scared I'll…"

"Wheesht, lad. Ye willna break yer bonnie wee bride. She's small, but she's healthy."

"So we can…" Dominic didn't know where to look.

"As entertaining as it would be to make ye keep squirming, I'll take pity on ye. Ye can bed yer wife. Have ye nae been?"

"Once I knew she was with child, I was nervous that I would—"

"Ye dinna think ye're going to poke the bairn, do

178

ye?" Nora interrupted. When Emelie choked, both women laughed. "Ye told him he couldnae, didna ye?"

"I did. But don't fault him. Dominic is a good husband. He takes wonderful care of me."

"I dinna doubt it. Listen to two words when he talks aboot ye, and it's obvious how much he loves ye." Nora patted Dominic on the arm. "Dinna keep the poor lass waiting. A good tupping will do ye both some good. Obviously, ye ken what works for ye. Ye already got her with child."

"Thank ye, Nora." Dominic guided the older woman toward the door.

"Seek me out if ye need aught, ma lady." Nora peered around Dominic's broad shoulder. "Give her some good loving before ye expire."

Nora left just as a train of servants arrived with the tub and steaming buckets of water. Dominic let them in once he noticed Emelie had the bed curtains pulled. Not having to look at his wife made some of his embarrassment settle. He couldn't believe Nora said he was in love with Emelie. He was certain he was well on the way, but he hadn't wanted someone else to declare his feelings for him. He didn't want to correct Nora or say anything about it to Emelie, but he knew she wouldn't forget.

When the door closed behind the last servant, Emelie pushed back the curtain and emerged without a stitch on. "You're overdressed, husband. The healer says I need a good loving to keep me healthy. I agree."

"Em," Dominic croaked as he watched Emelie saunter to the tub. She bent over and swirled her fingers in the water. He couldn't tear his eyes from her body. Her breasts swayed over the lip of the tub, and her lush behind made his palms itch to touch her. He ripped his clothes off and hopped around as he kicked off his boots and peeled down his stockings. Emelie stepped into the tub but waited until he followed her and settled before she eased into the water. She sat between his legs and leaned back. With a sigh from them both, Dominic's hands slid over Emelie's breasts.

"Do you have to meet with Brodie tonight?"

"I dinna care what he wants. I amnae leaving this chamber until at least two days from now. And neither are ye."

"Promise?"

"Och, aye, sparrow. I'm only opening the door to let food in."

"Then let's hurry and get clean." There was no rush, though, as they ran wash linens over each other's bodies, heightening their arousal. They scrubbed each other as Emelie straddled Dominic's hips. His eager cock slid along her seam. As the tip of his sword pressed into her sheath, Emelie grasped the rim of the tub behind Dominic's back. He met her gaze. When she nodded, he eased his sword further into her sheath until he was seated to the hilt. Neither moved, luxuriating in the feel of finally joining their bodies. It had been five weeks of unspent need and unsatisfied curiosity.

"Em."

"I know, Dom. This feels…"

"Sublime."

"Aye. I never imagined it could feel this good, and we aren't even doing aught."

"Yer body is doing plenty to mine. I never want to leave this chamber. I never want to let ye go."

"Then don't, wolf." Emelie flicked her tongue against Dominic's lips before sinking into the kiss. They moved together as the water lapped around their chests. But it wasn't long before the tub forced limitations, making it difficult for Dominic's massive frame to maneuver. With Emelie's arms and legs wrapped around him, holding her in place, he rose and quickly toweled them dry. They laughed as he walked to the bed with her still hanging on. He moved as if there was no extra weight attached to him. Emelie eased back onto the pillows as he lowered himself. "You won't squash me."

Dominic nodded as he pressed a fraction of his weight against Emelie. She pulled him closer as they moved together. It wasn't long before urgency made their movements less graceful as they thrust against one another. Emelie clawed at Dominic's back as her sheath spasmed around him.

"Dom!" Emelie screamed before moaning her release.

"Em!" Dominic howled as he thrust once more, the tight muscles of Emelie's core milking him. With shaking arms, Dominic rolled off Emelie but pulled her over his body. He fumbled around as he reached for the covers.

"Am I really your wife now?" Emelie asked softly.

"Ye've always been ma wife. Even before we met. Ye were meant to be ma wife, just as I was meant to be yer husband."

Emelie propped herself up as she rested her forearm on Dominic's chest. "Dom, I will never pretend to understand why the Lord guides us as he does. But He brought us together, and there is nowhere else I want to be but with you."

"Good because I amnae letting ye out of ma reach." Dominic kept his word. Throughout the night, they moved together. Each time Emelie shifted, Dominic followed. They woke nestled together and blissfully happy.

TWELVE

Emelie stretched as her belly rumbled. Calloused fingers tickled her belly as a bristly jaw rubbed against hers before nuzzling her neck. She rolled toward Dominic and eased beneath him as he came over her. Her legs fell open as he nestled between them. They'd coupled throughout the night, but it had sated neither of them yet. Emelie reached her hand between them, stroking Dominic's morning arousal. She'd woken to the feel of it pressing against her backside. She'd rocked her hips back and sighed when Dominic pulled her against him and thrust. Her stomach rumbling brought a moment of levity, but neither would deny a different type of hunger. Dominic's slid along her entrance and stoked the embers of desires that smoldered from the last time they joined, just before dawn.

Emelie guided Dominic's sword into her sheath, another sigh escaping. They relished the first moments of being one body. They moved with a synchronicity that surprised them both. They'd only truly been man and wife for one night, but intuition and attentiveness made their coupling natural and fulfilling. With each thrust, each moment they gazed into one another's eyes, Dominic and Emelie felt the bond growing between them.

Emelie knew she'd never imagined such a thing could happen—should happen—between a married couple. She suspected she never would have found it with Henry, and she wouldn't have been any the wiser to know what she would have missed. Dominic tried to keep Colina from his mind, and he usually succeeded when he was with Emelie. But as he made love to Emelie, he knew that his three-year marriage never held the genuine partnership that he was discovering with Emelie. As devoted as he'd been to Colina, as much as he'd enjoyed making love to her, he never once found in her what he already felt with Emelie.

Both Emelie and Dominic realized their pasts were slipping away. No longer did their experiences with other partners matter, nor did they form who they were or who they would be. It was their time together, the intimacy Dominic and Emelie shared with their bodies and their quiet conversations that were making them into the individuals they wanted to be. While they'd only spent a night making love, they'd spent weeks getting to know one another. They realized separately that they'd taken more time to get to know one another than they had the people they once planned to spend their lives with.

During Dominic's brief courtship with Colina, he'd hung on her every word. He'd showered her with compliments and been at her beck and call. He'd done everything he could to please her, enamored with her and stunned that a woman he believed was so beautiful welcomed his attention.

Emelie knew all along that she and Henry weren't well acquainted, but his effusive praise and quick promises led her to believe she would have years to get to know him better. She saw the blessing that they didn't marry, and she was grateful that she had an opportunity for a life with Dominic instead.

After they reached the edge of the cliff together and catapulted over it, they lay in one another's arms panting and smiling. They exchanged soft caresses and gentle kisses as they coasted back down to Earth. Dominic tucked Emelie beneath his chin as they faced each other. Her contented sigh felt as though the very breath she exhaled filled his heart. Someone knocking on the door shattered their peace.

"Go away," Dominic bellowed.

"What if something's wrong with Laurel?" Emelie whispered.

"Then whomever is there would call through the door." When the intruder knocked again, Dominic reached to the floor and grabbed his boot. He flung it against the door. "Unless someone is dying or something is burning down, don't come back."

"Dominic," Aggie's stern voice came through the door. "At least feed yer wife. She's bound to be half-starved."

As if on cue, Emelie's stomach rumbled again. She chuckled as Dominic rolled his eyes. He climbed from the bed and wrapped his plaid around his waist while Emelie pulled the covers up to her chin. Dominic yanked open the door and glowered at Aggie and the trembling maid who stood behind the formidable housekeeper. Dominic hadn't seen this expression of Aggie's since he was a child and tried to steal a pie, but only succeeded in knocking four of them to the floor. He stepped aside and ushered the two women in, which earned him a cluck of disgust from Aggie. The maid settled the tray on the table and scurried out of the chamber. Aggie wasn't so quick to leave.

"Ye can at least let the maids in with three meals a day. Berta insists I let ye have them. But mind ye,

Dom, it isnae for yer sake. Berta is partial to yer wife and doesnae want her wasting away. Neither do I, and Nora will have plenty to say since I ken she kens, too."

"One meal. She missed one meal," Dominic grumbled.

"I didn't want to go belowstairs, Aggie," Emelie intervened. They'd never talked about it, but Emelie would have told Dominic her preference was to remain closed away in their chamber. She believed they'd proven to one another what they wanted. "I missed my husband and didn't want to share him. I admit it."

"And I had lost time to make up for," Dominic quipped. Aggie's expressive face made it clear she knew how things had stood between the couple. Emelie and Dominic couldn't look at each other or her.

"And I suppose ye intend to spend the next sennight making up for it too."

"I'd planned to," Dominic said with his arms crossed.

"That didna intimidate me the first time ye tried it when ye grew taller than me, and it does naught to me now. I wiped yer arse and changed yer raggies," Aggie reminded Dominic. "It's the lass I worry aboot. Let her eat and sleep, or she'll wind up ailing like Lady Laurel."

"How is Lady Laurel?" Emelie asked, hoping to steer the conversation away from Aggie's amusing chastisement.

"Improving. She was up and aboot last night to greet ye and the other men, but ye werenae to be seen." Aggie grinned. "But we heard ye. That's how we kenned yer wife hadnae starved to death."

"One bluidy meal," Dominic grumbled again.

"Aggie, stop teasing my poor husband. We're glad

to hear Laurel is feeling better. If Dom promises to let the maids in with trays, will you tell everyone I am fine?" Emelie offered Aggie, then Dominic, an indulgent smile.

"Aye. Just making sure yer husband understands we like ye." Aggie cocked an eyebrow at Dominic, who shifted uncomfortably. He would speak to Aggie later about not comparing Emelie to Colina anymore. He hadn't realized until after Colina's death how many people disliked her for more than just being lazy. He learned she'd threatened and intimidated most of the maids, and she'd scared them too much for anyone to complain.

"Thank you, Aggie," Emelie said. "I'm certain Dom will grow hungry enough to let the maids in with trays. But in the meantime, he takes good care of me. He won't let me starve."

"Good care of ye," Aggie chuckled. "Be sure that he does. A woman in yer condition will find ye're hungry for more than just food." Aggie didn't wait for either Emelie or Dominic to say anything more. She closed the door behind her to Dominic's playful grumbles.

When the couple was alone again, Dominic carried the tray to the bed and sat beside Emelie. He poured cream in her porridge and handed it to her while she poured honey onto a bannock. Neither noticed the simple acts of domesticity as husband and wife prepared food they knew their partner preferred. After feasting on cheese and dried fruit to go along with the porridge and bannocks, Emelie leaned back against Dominic's chest as they sat against the headboard.

"Em, we don't have to leave our chamber today, but if you have duties you wish to see to, I won't keep you from them. I was only half-jesting that I would keep you here for two days."

"Can you make it a sennight?" Emelie asked as she ran her hand over Dominic's rippled belly. The grooves and peaks the muscles made fascinated her. Everything about his body was so different from hers. She understood why mothers kept virgins in the dark about the finer parts of the male anatomy. Henry seemed almost scrawny compared to what Emelie discovered lay beneath Dominic's clothes.

"Whatever you wish, wife," Dominic said as his fingers trailed along Emelie's back.

Emelie sighed. "Would that we could. I know you must meet with Brodie, and I wish to check on Laurel. I just find I'm not in a hurry for us to do either. But I don't want people to talk, especially aboot you."

"They already know you're not *her*."

"But didn't she start out as a doting and dutiful wife? I don't want them to think I'm trying to fool them, too."

"I understand that. But they also know we're newlyweds, and I've been away for several days." Dominic tilted Emelie's chin until he could look into her eyes. "We'll do whatever you wish, sparrow."

"What I wish and what I should do aren't the same. Mayhap this afternoon will be soon enough." Emelie wrapped her arm around Dominic's waist, and they sat together discussing what they needed to do before that evening. They dozed together for several hours before making love once more. They completed their ablutions and readied themselves to face the world by midafternoon. Just before they left their chamber, Emelie touched Dominic's forearm. "I enjoy talking to you."

"I enjoy our conversations too, Em. I know confronting me that night couldn't have been easy for you. But I'm glad that you feel comfortable doing so."

"I don't know that I would have ever been that direct with another mon. But I knew you would listen to me, and I didn't fear you growing angry." Emelie shrugged.

"We might not always like what the other has to say. It might make us angry with one another. But I will never hold it against you if you have something to say. I know most other men wouldn't agree. I've seen how Laurel and Brodie are together, and while they may bicker, I know their marriage is better for the openness they share. Laurel doesn't fear Brodie like my mother feared my father. It made my mother withdraw into a shell, and it created tension throughout the clan. It wasn't until my father died that my mother came back into her own and became the woman I remembered from early in my childhood. She was never my father's confidante, and I believe it hurt her until she was numb to everything. That's not what I want with my wife."

"Were you and Colina close?" Emelie bit her bottom lip, praying she hadn't overstepped. She knew Dominic disliked discussing her, but she didn't want to make the same mistakes Colina had. She didn't want her actions to remind him of her.

"We were in a way. I thought we were one another's confidants, but she only told me what she wanted me to know. And I know now that I told her far too much. When I look back on it, she complained a great deal, and I spent most of my time trying to placate her. I wanted to because I thought it was my duty to. And she seemed so frail, like she needed my protection."

Dominic found it was getting easier to think about his time with Colina. Her memory still angered him but having Emelie in his life made him understand the past was where it should remain. Emelie

188

brought him too much happiness to cling so tightly to his resentment.

"But as much as I try to avoid comparing you to her, I realize now that she never needed my protection. And what I offer to you is not the same. I don't wish to shield you from the world because I think you can't face it. I would shield you from those who might truly hurt you. I talked to her aboot clan matters when I had no one else to speak to. I actually didn't think she listened that closely. I talked to her aboot Brodie when he frustrated me. But never did we have such simple conversations as what we planned for the day or what we did. She had naught to contribute to a conversation like that since she did little but weave, sew, and nap. She took little interest in how I spent my days when I was away from her. And we never talked aboot the future, aboot having a family together."

"Didn't you wonder why she never got with child?" Emelie whispered.

"Aye, I did. But I didn't push the issue because it upset her. I promised her that since I didn't need an heir, I would be happy with our marriage, even if we never had weans."

"And now you will have another mon's child to care for. I doubt that's how you imagined you'd enter fatherhood. I wish it could be different, Dom. I wish—"

"Em, I already told you it doesn't bother me that it wasn't my seed that created this child. If you decide to stay and the Lord blesses us, we will conceive our other children. But a bairn comes into this world not knowing his mother or his father. It is the mon and woman who raise him who matter. This bairn is mine because I claim him or her. This bairn is mine because I will be there from the beginning. I wish to be a father more than I realized. I wish to be a father to your bairn and make the child mine." Dominic placed his hand over the tiny swell at the bottom of Emelie's abdomen. His touch was light, but Emelie felt the sincerity. She cupped his cheeks and stood on her toes, still needing him to bend forward before she could kiss him.

"There is no luckier woman than me. I won't bring it up again." They exited the chamber to begin what was left of the afternoon. In just the space of a day, they'd deepened their relationship by leaps and bounds. It wasn't just the words they spoke or the movement of their bodies. It was the knowledge that they wanted to build a future together, and it was a realization that they had both found a helpmate.

"I'm so relieved to see you up and aboot, Laurel," Emelie said as she embraced her sister-by-marriage and friend. "You gave us all a fright."

"I gave myself a fright," Laurel grinned. "I suspect this bairn will be large. Aggie told me something similar happened to Brodie and Dominic's mother when she carried each of them. Apparently, they were enormous bairns when they were born. Nora said they are still two of the largest bairns she's ever delivered."

"Do you think people will talk when my bairn isn't that big?" Emelie worried.

"I doubt it. Emelie, you know how you're built. People will worry for you and your bairn, but no one will question why a woman so small as you gives birth to a normal-sized bairn."

"I suppose it will be as good an explanation as any if the bairn comes sooner than people expect and is big."

"Aye. They'll think your body couldn't keep such

a big bairn any longer, and so it was time for you to deliver." Laurel wrapped her arm around Emelie's shoulder. "Does it worry you much?"

"Yes. Dominic swears he doesn't care that he didn't sire the bairn, and I believe him. I just fear what people will say to him and aboot us, aboot our child."

"I understand why you're worried, but you are so different from Colina. People knew it the moment you arrived. Yes, she pretended in the beginning, but people saw in her what Dominic was blind to. From what I've been told and even what I saw, she had no warmth for anyone but Dom. Had she fallen in the mud like you did, we would have had roast piglet for the evening meal, and the lad would be barred from tending the livestock. If Dom hadn't agreed, she would have gone behind his back."

"Do people think Dom is weak?" Emelie feared the answer.

"No. Not at all. Some blame him for Colina because of the lives lost at her hands. But they've known him his entire life. Apparently, he and Brodie used to find ways to get in between their parents when their father had a go at their mother. He never raised a hand to her, but he was unkind. Brodie would distract him while Dom went to cheer her up. He's been trying to find the best in people and please people since he was a lad. That's why it didn't surprise Brodie or me when you both explained the circumstances. He has a heart as vast as the Highlands. But it was Colina's downfall to underestimate him. He is a warrior through and through, and he is an exceptional leader. It's why Brodie trusts him when he must be away for long stretches. Dominic is far from weak."

"I know that. I don't need convincing of that. I just hate the idea that anyone thinks less of him."

"Protective of him already?"

"Very." Emelie didn't have to think of her answer. The single word was emphatic and would have held an element of warning if they weren't friends.

The women left the upstairs solar where they'd been chatting while Emelie tried on the gowns Laurel adjusted. It amazed Emelie how quickly Laurel altered the gowns, since she practically recreated them. Laurel confided in Emelie that she'd been a seamstress for years while at Stirling Castle. When her father cut off her allowance for not finding a husband, she'd had to resort to making her own income. She'd designed and made half the gowns women wore at court, and they were all none the wiser because she sold them to haberdashers in town.

The two women made their way out to the bailey to enjoy the first reprieve from the rain they'd had in a sennight. They made their way to the gardens, where they helped other women pull the weeds that sprouted from the deluge. They worked until the sun began to set. Standing and stretching their backs, Emelie glanced toward the flower garden. She spied a patch of primrose, a flower that thrives in cool, damp conditions. She appreciated its scent and often purchased primrose-scented soap when she lived at court.

"Laurel, may I cut some primrose? I'd like to use it to make some soap if that's all right."

"Of course you may. You don't have to ask, Emelie. This is your home. You know I don't stand on formality between us."

"Thank you. I won't be long. The light is growing dim. The last thing I need is to sever my finger trying to cut it in the dark." Emelie hurried toward the blooms, picking her way around puddles that lingered. She reached the patch and drew a knife from her belt. Her mother had been adamant that she and

Blythe learn to wield and carry a knife before they went to court. The sisters, much like Isabella had before them, carried a dirk in their belts beside their eating knives. Emelie had never needed it while a lady-in-waiting, but she'd been glad to have it more than once when she feared men she encountered in passageways, even when she wasn't alone.

Emelie squatted to cut a bunch of flowers, but she glanced over her shoulder when she sensed someone nearby. She looked around, but she could see no one. She waited to spy any movement, but nothing stirred. She turned back to her task but hurried. Just as she rose, she heard a crash and a distinct, angry buzz. Several apple trees lay between her and the gate. A hive of wasps swarmed from the ground where their home now laid.

Emelie looked around, but there was no other way out of the garden, and the angry colony was moving toward her. With a scream, she dashed toward marigolds, knowing they repelled wasps. But the swiftest flying insects were already attacking. Emelie fought the temptation to swat away the stinging bugs and kept running toward what she hoped would be a sanctuary. She felt the sharp pain on the outside of her shoulder, on her neck, her cheek, and her back. She dove into the patch of marigolds and did what she could to hide among the petals.

Without a large target, the wasps filled the air, but no longer attacked. Emelie huddled in pain until something crashed through the flower garden. Before she knew what was happening, powerful hands pulled her from the ground and swathed her in a thick plaid. She knew without looking that it was Dominic who carried her. He ran toward the gate and into the bailey. He didn't slow until he reached the steps to the keep.

"Open the bluidy door," Dominic bellowed to someone Emelie couldn't see. "Fetch Nora."

Dominic's heart pounded more from fear than exertion. He and Brodie ran into Laurel as they returned from surveying the storm's damage to the village. Laurel was in the middle of telling the men that Emelie went to cut flowers when they heard Emelie scream. Dominic hadn't waited, but he was forced to watch in horror as the stinging insects attacked Emelie. He couldn't understand why she was running further into the garden until he saw her dive into the marigolds. While he ran, he yanked the pin from his shoulder, dropping it somewhere in the garden. He drew the extra yards of fabric loose, never so grateful to be a large man than in that moment, knowing his plaid was longer than average.

"Dom," Emelie wheezed. "Can't breathe."

"No, Em. No. Nora will be here. Hang on, sparrow."

"Too hot. Too tight," Emelie gasped.

Dominic looked down and realized that between his hold on his wife and his plaid, he was nearly suffocating her. He fumbled and pulled the wool from her face, shocked to see the swelling on her cheek. He could see the stinger protruding from her downy flesh. When he reached their chamber, he kicked the door open, unable to reach the handle. It splintered from its frame, and he knew it would need repairing, but he cared not. He lowered Emelie to her feet and pulled at her laces. She stood trembling as he stripped her bare and began pulling stingers from her. When he got all that he could see, he carried her to the bed. Nora arrived just as Emelie whimpered and tried to roll onto her stomach.

"Vinegar, honey, and lavender," Nora commanded to anyone available. She rushed to Emelie's side and ran her withered hands over Emelie's back, barely touching her patient. Dominic paced as Nora found stingers he hadn't. Laurel arrived with the requested supplies but frowned when she couldn't shut the door completely. She glanced at Dominic but said nothing. Nora ordered over her shoulder, "Lad, fetch the basin and drying linens."

With the supplies she needed, Nora soaked the linens in vinegar and laid them across Emelie's back and shoulders. She dabbed the foul-smelling liquid on Emelie's face where the wasps stung her more than once by the time she and Dominic left the garden. With a moan, she reached out her hand. Laurel took it, but Emelie pulled away.

"Dom," Emelie whispered. He was across the room and kneeling beside the bed before Emelie could turn her head to look at him.

"Wheesht, sparrow. I'm nae going anywhere. I'm here."

"Did you get stung?"

Dominic had, but he would say nothing about it. He was too frightened for Emelie to draw any attention away from her. He glanced at Nora, relieved to see the woman moving efficiently but without haste.

"As long as she keeps breathing easily, Lady Emelie will be right as rain. But she'll be in pain for a while. The vinegar will take the burn away. Then I'll lather honey on the stings to help them heal. Lavender oil later tonight or in the morn will take away the last of the pain. But someone must stay with Lady Emelie to be sure she doesnae get worse."

No one had to explain what Nora meant. There would be nothing any of them could do if her breathing grew labored, and her throat swelled. Dominic accepted the chair Laurel offered. He wouldn't leave Emelie's side until he was certain she would recover. Emelie released Dominic's hand and reached toward his shoulder, but her arm was long enough.

"You did get stung. Nora, please tend to Dom. I'm fine," Emelie mumbled against the pillow.

"It's only a couple, Em. I dinna need tending. Let Nora work."

"Will you lie beside me?"

"Aught that ye want." Dominic moved around the bed and slipped onto it beside Emelie. He lay as close as he dared and placed her hand over his heart, covering her hand with both of his. He needed the contact as much as she did. Laurel left with no one noticing, and Nora changed the vinegar-soaked linens thrice before she scooped globs of honey and smeared it over Emelie's wounds. Emelie was asleep by the time Nora finished, her mind and body too exhausted to fight.

"Let me see yers," Nora whispered. Dominic sat up and pulled his leine off. He had a few on his chest from running into the swarm. He grunted with discomfort when Nora wiped them with vinegar. But her touch was gentle when she applied the honey. "She'll be all right, lad. It's bad, but she's breathing easy. Just stay with her. And before ye get yerself in a right fit, she and the bairn will be fine."

"Can ye say that with certainty?"

"Aye. Yer bride isnae the first woman carrying who's been stung. She is the first person I've seen stung that many times who hasnae shed a tear." Nora patted Dominic's shoulder and dropped a kiss on his forehead as she had countless times when he injured himself or was sick as a child. She'd been more like a grandmother than the village healer to both Brodie and him. "I'll leave ye. She's sleeping soundly, so she willna hear ye if ye wish to have a good cry. I willna tell anyone, and I dinna blame ye if ye do. Ye've both had a right nasty scare."

"Thank ye, Nora," Dominic croaked.

Nora tsked when she reached the door and shook

her head, but she pulled it closed as best she could when she left. Dominic rolled onto his side and stroked Emelie's hair while she slept. Silent tears fell as he looked at his wife. It had terrified him that he wouldn't reach Emelie in time, and they'd never had reason to talk about whether either of them had been stung before. He didn't know if she was one of those people who died from the stings. There were far more wounds than he'd found, and he wasn't convinced Nora was right, though he trusted the healer with his life and Emelie's. But as he lay there, he felt useless. Emelie slept, so he knew she wasn't in pain. However, he was certain she would be when she awoke, and there would be nothing he could do.

"Dom," Emelie mumbled as she opened one eye. "She said we would be all right. Stop whittling. Just stay with me. That's all I need from you."

"Whatever ye wish, sparrow."

"Kiss."

Dominic pressed a soft kiss to Emelie's lips before she drifted back to sleep. His mind ticked over as he remained awake. He wanted to know why the wasps attacked Emelie. As long as no one disturbed their hive, wasps normally left people alone. He knew Emelie wouldn't be foolish enough to tamper with the insects' home. He heard the evening meal belowstairs, and he allowed a maid in with a tray, but Emelie slept, and he wasn't interested in the food.

At some point, he fell asleep. He woke to Brodie shaking his shoulder. Dominic glanced at Emelie to make sure the sheet and blanket properly covered her. The sheet laid around her waist, but she remained on her belly. Dominic could see the swell of her breast from the side, but he knew his brother wouldn't look. He didn't want it to embarrass Emelie once she knew Brodie had visited.

"Someone cut down the hive," Brodie whispered.

"How do ye ken?" Dominic asked as they stood beside the window embrasure. He was bone-weary. Despite sleeping, he didn't feel rested. He'd woken several times to check on Emelie, who slept so soundly it scared Dominic even more.

"It was a clean cut, likely from a sword to keep whoever it was away from the hive. It wasna the weight that made it fall," Brodie explained, forgoing his refined speech as he watched his brother. The deep lines around Dominic's eyes and between his brows concerned him. He hadn't seen his brother in such a state since their mother was dying.

"Who would do that?" Dominic wondered.

"I dinna ken. As far as I've noticed, everyone likes Emelie. She's impressed them with how she helped while Laurel was ill, and they say she's friendly with everyone. Dom, they ken Emelie isnae like Colina. The clan is glad ye handfasted. The only gossip is good."

"But someone did this. Why?"

"All I can think is there's someone who doesnae feel like everyone else. I dinna ken if this person doesnae like Emelie, or they dinna approve of ye re-marrying."

"Ye said a sword. That makes sense, but that makes it a mon. There are few women who could lift any sword high enough to cut down the hive, nor run fast enough to get away while carrying a sword."

"Aye. That's what Laurel pointed out. She's asking discreet questions to see if she can learn who did this. Did any mon show Emelie attention while ye were gone? Anyone angry that she rebuffed them?"

"Nay. She would have told me. It would have made her uncomfortable."

Brodie looked at his sister-by-marriage and nodded. "I dinna think she'll ever keep secrets from ye unless she thinks it'll protect ye. Laurel says she's vera protective of ye. She doesnae like the idea that anyone might speak ill of ye, especially for bringing her here. Dom, I ken it hasnae been long, but I ken from ma own experience with Laurel. Ye're falling in love with one another. If she thinks ye or yer position among the clan is in danger, she'll say she wants to leave. Until we ken why this attack happened, ye canna let her entertain the idea for even a moment. Things have been quiet with the Lamonts and Mac-Dougalls, but I dinna put aught past them."

"I was thinking the same. I ken she's concerned aboot people comparing her to Colina. The few times anyone has, it's been to say how much they prefer Em to Colina. But could someone have sneaked inside the gates? How could they?"

"I dinna have an answer to that. But from now until we resolve this, we have to assume one of our enemies is lurking nearby."

"Do ye think the incident with the piglet wasna an accident?"

"Mayhap. Noel swears up and down that he fastened the latch, and I believe him. He said a meaty bone his dog found distracted his animal. The dog distracted him. It gave someone the time to nudge the piglet out, and the dog chased it."

"But why Emelie?"

"Because she's the tánaiste's wife. It makes me wonder if there was something genuinely wrong with Laurel. Are they attacking us through our women? It's nae secret how I feel aboot Laurel, and people are noticing ye and Emelie are falling in love. It willna be long before people realize the only way to bring either of us to our knees is through our wives."

"I dinna want to order Emelie to remain within the walls, especially since both accidents," Dominic scowled, "happened in the bailey."

"I dinna want to do that to Laurel either. She'll accept it because she'll understand, but it willna sit well with her if she canna go to the village. She'll feel guilty for nae seeing to our people."

"Emelie will feel the same. She enjoys going there. I dinna ken how she's gotten the auld coots to like her so much, but she has."

"I'll send extra patrols out to see if there's any sign that someone's crossed onto our land. I would go, but I'm nae comfortable leaving Laurel, despite how much I want to find the bastard. I ken ye feel the same way."

"I do. Brodie, ye're right. I am falling in love with Emelie. It doesnae feel aught like before. I dinna ken what it was last time. Mayhap puppy love or infatuation, but this is vera different. I dinna want to say it isnae sweet because it is. Mayhap I'm more mature than I was before, but there's a gravity that goes with ma feelings. It's nae just lighthearted."

"I canna say I was ever in love before I met Laurel, but I think ye are right that it is maturity. Age and experience have changed ye. Ye were still young when ye met Colina. Ye'd barely been tánaiste for a year, and she was the first lass to turn yer head for more than a tumble. Ye're a different mon than ye were six months ago. I hate that it came aboot because of such pain, but ye have a wisdom that ye didna have before." Brodie pulled Dominic in for a manly embrace that involved several thuds against each other's backs. "Ye'll always be ma baby brother, but there isnae a part of ye that I amnae proud of. I would have saved ye the heartache if I could. But I nae only love the mon ye are, I like all of ye."

"Thank ye, Brodie. I didna realize the rift that she put between us. I thought it was just being a married mon. But I dinna feel it anymore, and I'm glad for that."

"Me too."

The men pulled apart as Emelie stirred. Brodie left the chamber with haste, and Dominic returned to the bed. He brushed hair from Emelie's neck as she rolled over with a wince. She looked around, then struggled to sit up. Dominic helped her as she shifted to lean against him.

"Was that Brodie?"

"Aye. He came to tell me he thinks someone cut the hive on purpose."

"I'm not surprised. I didn't think aboot it once we came inside, but I thought someone was in the garden with me. I looked around but saw no one. It was only a moment after I turned back to the flowers that I heard the wasps."

"I dinna ken who would do this, but Brodie and I now think the incident with the piglet wasna an accident too."

"Do you think it's someone in the clan? A woman who isn't happy you remarried?"

"Nay. I swore I wouldnae remarry, so none set their sights on me."

"Dom, even more reason it might be a woman. If someone's been coveting you, and you said you wouldn't remarry but then did, that's enough to make jealousy into vengeance."

"Mayhap." Dominic could see the merit in Emelie's explanation. He'd seen plenty of men fight over jealousy, be it for a woman or something else. But it didn't sit right with him. "Brodie said it wasna the weight of the hive that made it fall, so if someone cut it, it was likely done by a sword. A dirk would have required the culprit to get too close. Since it was most likely a sword, whoever did it had to run away quickly. There arenae any women who could do that."

Emelie listened to Dominic and felt his explanation was more reasonable than hers. She'd seen more than one woman look appreciatively at her husband, but she had found no reason to think any of the women would act on it. "Do you think it's one of the clan's enemies? I don't want to think it's a Campbell."

"I dinna want to think that either. But truth be told, it could be a clan member or an enemy. Em, I dinna want to tell ye to nae go anywhere, but I am nervous aboot yer safety, especially since both incidents happened within our walls."

"Would it make ye feel better if I had a guard, even in the keep?"

"It would, but I dinna like it."

"I know. I'm not looking forward to a second shadow. But I know it would put both of our minds at ease. If it were just me, then I wouldn't be so quick to suggest it." Emelie and Dominic looked at her belly, and they both placed their hands over it.

"Vera well. I will assign men I trust implicitly, and only them. How're ye feeling?"

"Better than I expected. I ache all over, but I'm not in pain anymore."

"Would ye like me to rub in the lavender oil Nora left?" Dominic asked. Emelie waggled her eyebrows and grinned as she nodded. "I dinna ken that ye're up to that yet."

"We can find out." Emelie slipped from the bed, taking a couple gingerly steps before being sure she was steady on her feet. She retrieved the vial of oil and climbed back onto the bed. Dominic wasted no time stripping off his clothes, then rubbing the oil onto the wounds and several other places. He guided Emelie to straddle him, aware that pressing her against the mattress wasn't wise. He gripped her hips as she ground her mound against his pubis. Emelie leaned forward, and Dominic captured her breast in his mouth, suckling as Emelie rode him. Their mouths collided as they swallowed one another's screams as they climaxed together.

Emelie stretched out across Dominic, yawning. She relaxed as his hand held her backside and the other stroked her back. She nuzzled his neck and ran her fingers through his chestnut hair. "I think I like these moments after as much as I do the coupling, wolf."

"I agree, sparrow. The pleasure is divine and unlike aught I ever imagined. But ma heart is so full when I can just hold ye."

"I could lie here all day. Though your burr does something to me. I could go again right now."

Dominic adjusted their position and sat up. He eased Emelie onto his shaft, hard once more just from being near Emelie. Their movements were small and intense as they kissed throughout this round. The pace was languid as they reveled in the feel of being joined and pressed so close together. Emelie's head fell back as her fingernails bit into Dominic's shoulders. His fingers dug into the generous flesh of her backside. The waves of ecstasy rolled over them until they were both depleted. They curled up with Emelie against Dominic's side. They were soon asleep. Emelie slept throughout the day and well into the evening, and Dominic remained by her side, always within reach.

THIRTEEN

The next two moons passed without incident. Brodie and Dominic grew comfortable enough to go out on patrol but never together. The scouts Brodie sent discovered no evidence of strangers crossing into Campbell territory, and neither Laurel nor Emelie suffered any illnesses or accidents. At four months pregnant, there was no way to continue hiding Emelie's condition. They announced the impending birth to the clan, and it delighted the clan to know that both the laird and their tánaiste would have bairns soon. Laurel was approaching her confinement, and Emelie encouraged her to rest in the afternoons. Brodie hovered at first when Laurel began retiring to their chambers in the afternoons, terrified she would grow mysteriously ill again. Eventually, he used Laurel's afternoon naps as an excuse to spend time alone with his wife during the day. No one disturbed the couple.

When Dominic wasn't on patrol, he and Emelie continued to spend their afternoons together. They went for long walks along the river, and Dominic kept his promise to teach Emelie to swim. He cheered her on as she grew more confident, and it wasn't long until she was proficient and able to swim alongside Dominic. They finished each of Emelie's lessons with an erotic interlude in the sun-warmed water. They never left the walls without at least four guards, but the men kept their distance when the couple shed their clothes and slipped into the bay. They visited the village often, and Dominic took Emelie to view the crops as harvest time drew near. She impressed him with her knowledge and how she estimated how much food was growing, how long it would last, and how many people it would feed. She shrugged and reminded him she hadn't always been a lady-in-waiting. She may not be a chatelaine by title, but her mother trained her to be one since she was a young girl.

They walked arm-in-arm or holding hands whenever they ventured out together. Emelie knew Dominic was as attentive to their surroundings as he was to their conversations. They had one scare when a lone wolf emerged from a thicket, but the men easily scared it off. Emelie teased Dominic that he should be kinder to his relatives. He scooped her over his shoulder, swatted her backside, then took her to their chamber and reminded her of why she'd given him the nickname.

Their relationship grew stronger, and they enjoyed the time they spent together. But despite growing closer and it being obvious to all who surrounded them, neither confessed their feelings. There was an implicit understanding, but they also shared an apprehension that they might confuse enchantment and infatuation for love. Separately, Laurel and Brodie encouraged them to speak their feelings and to assure them that what they felt was genuine. Brodie and Laurel insisted Dominic and Emelie were the only ones who didn't see it.

Dominic didn't fail to see how differently the clan responded to Emelie. He pushed regret for his past marriage aside and enjoyed seeing how his people accepted his new wife. He realized one night while he was on patrol, as he lay beneath the stairs thinking about Emelie, that he no longer grieved the end of his first marriage. He didn't grieve the loss of what he thought he had, or the theft of his future that he once felt. Instead, he realized he was happier and more fulfilled than he'd ever been before. He thanked God frequently for placing him near the royal gardens just as Emelie entered them that day. He was certain it was divine intervention that brought them together.

Emelie hurried through her duties each day to ensure she did them in time to spend the afternoon with Dominic. The highlight of her day, besides when they retired and made love, was when they chatted about their morning and discussed what they would do the next day. They often lay in the grass and watched the clouds overhead. It was one such afternoon that Emelie lay on her back, and Dominic was on his stomach. He teased a buttercup against the underside of her chin. The weather was turning since it was mid-autumn, and there weren't as many flowers as there had been only a fortnight earlier. Emelie gasped and grabbed Dominic's hand. She placed it on her belly and turned wide eyes to him.

"I felt it!" Dominic exclaimed. A soft but clear jab pressed against the palm of his hand. He knew Emelie had felt flutters for a few sennights, but it was the first time he'd been able to feel it. When the tiny protrusion shifted, Dominic wrapped his arm around Emelie and drew her closer. He whispered, "Our bairn."

"Ours," Emelie smiled blissfully. "We still haven't settled on a name. I know we have time, and I don't want to tempt fate by referring to our bairn by name.

But I'm eager to pick. I'm rather partial to Dominic." Emelie winked.

"Two Doms? I don't know that the clan could manage. If our lad is aught like I was, I don't think the aulder members want a reminder."

"Were you really that much trouble?"

"Aye. Always. I was trying to keep up with Brodie before he left to foster. Then when he returned, I wanted to be a great warrior just like him. He never turned me away, either." Dominic laughed. "He didn't mind the hero worship."

"What if we named a lad Dominic, but he went by Nic instead?"

"Mayhap. And a lass named Emma?"

"Emma and Emelie? I don't know aboot that. It's normal to name a son for his father. I don't know aboot naming a daughter for her mother."

"I won't consider Nic if you won't consider Emma."

"Stubborn."

"Aye," Dominic chuckled as he nipped at Emelie's earlobe. They rolled, so Emelie rested on her side. Her belly now made it difficult to lie across Dominic for long. Her petite stature left little room for the bairn to grow but outward. Emelie moved to kiss Dominic but screamed as an arrow landed where she had just been lying.

Dominic was on his feet with his sword drawn in a heartbeat. He eased Emelie to her feet as the guards ran toward them. They surrounded Emelie, making her invisible to anyone outside their circle. The men scanned the meadow, and those facing the tree line peered among the trunks. Nothing moved, and no sound greeted them as they strained to hear.

"Alec," Dominic whispered.

"Aye." Alec broke away from the group. With his sword raised, he crept toward the trees. None of the men had targes with them, but they were all armed to the teeth. Dominic insisted they all wear as many dirks as they could fit when they left the keep with Emelie. It wasn't long before Alec returned. "I can see where he stood to take the shot, but there is nay other sign. Nay footprints, nay disturbed leaves. It's like a wraith came and went. I looked into the branches and didna even spot a squirrel."

"Stay in formation. We get Lady Emelie back to the keep, then I'm coming back to look for myself."

"Dom," Emelie protested.

"No," Dominic barked. Emelie remained silent as the men kept her in the middle. Alec and Garrett, another guardsman, walked backwards to protect Emelie from the rear. Dominic whistled, and the postern gate opened. The men didn't separate until they walked Emelie up the stairs to the keep. Brodie came running from the lists.

"What happened?" Brodie demanded.

"Someone shot at Emelie," Dominic said as he bustled Emelie inside. Laurel was in the Great Hall and caught sight of the trio and hurried toward them. She looked at her husband, but Brodie could only shrug. Dominic steered Emelie toward Brodie's solar. Brodie and Laurel followed, and Brodie locked the door once they were all inside.

"You don't know that it was at me. It could have just as easily struck you if we hadn't moved when we did," Emelie disagreed.

"Em," Dominic pulled Emelie onto his lap as he took a seat at the enormous wood table in the center of the chamber. "That arrow was fired as we moved. It landed next to you for a reason. I'm a far larger target than you. If they aimed it at me, it would have hit me. The only other reason to fire it was a warning. Either way, it shouldn't have been anywhere near you. I will find who did this, and they will pay."

Emelie nodded as she swallowed. She really didn't want Dominic to go anywhere near the woods, but she knew she wouldn't dissuade him. And she knew they had to discover whoever was a threat to her and the clan. "Will you promise to take a targe?"

"Yes, sparrow. I promise."

Emelie closed her eyes, but they burst open. She leaned against Dominic's chest and didn't notice she had a handful of his leine clasped in her fist until her fingers ached. She released it and tried to smooth the wrinkles. "I know I'm not a Highlander, but I did grow up near the border. Please be careful. I know what a mon looks like riddled with arrows. I can't stop picturing that being you every time I close my eyes."

"Wheesht, sparrow. I'll be careful. I won't go alone, and all the men I will go with will have targes. But I must go soon before whoever it is puts too much distance between us." Dominic looked at his brother and sister-by-marriage. "Stay with Em, please."

"We will," Laurel nodded as Emelie stood. She wrapped her arms around Emelie as best she could with their bellies in the way. Dominic and Brodie left the solar to talk in the passageway.

"I thought everything was fine. Naught's happened in over two moons," Dominic whispered.

"Aye. And we have heard no rumblings from the Lamonts. Now that David is dead, it seems they aren't so eager to keep the feud going as we feared. Without them, the MacDougalls are unlikely to strike. The MacArthurs know better than to cross the river. We left the few that did right after you returned from court as food for the animals. They have sent no one since."

"MacGregors?"

"That's my thought. With it now autumn, they

won't have a harvest, and they are likely fuming. Mayhap we send them grain and a few sheep and heads of cattle."

"Do you think they'd take a handout from the very clan that ran them off their land?"

Brodie shrugged. "They will if they have more sense than pride. The Bruce gave us the land."

"Aye." Neither Dominic nor Brodie needed to re-hash how their father and Brodie had led raids against the MacGregors that gained them land be-sides what the Bruce gifted them for loyalty. It was unlikely the MacGregors would ever forgive the Campbells, but the Campbells were an ever-growing clan that needed arable land for farming and space for crofts. Brodie would never feel guilty for pro-viding for his clan.

"Go, but be careful, Dom. Your wife will run me through if aught happens to you." Brodie grinned, only half-jesting. Dominic nodded and hurried out to the bailey. Men were already assembled, making his eyebrows shoot up.

"I told them what happened," Alec explained. "Garrett, Tim, and Davey have already set out. We waited to be sure ye settled Lady Emelie. We'll go with ye. Whoever did this to Lady Emelie and ye will pay."

Dominic looked at the steely gazes of the men awaiting his command. There was a personal ele-ment to their determination, and Dominic realized the men took the threat to Emelie seriously. They wanted to avenge her because she was important to the clan, not just because they had a duty as guards-men. Alec handed him his targe, and the men set off. They jogged across the meadow until they met up with the three warriors who set off ahead of them.

"We spread out, form a line, and sweep the tree line before pushing inward," Dominic commanded.

The men worked in silence, their footsteps making no sounds. They combed through the woods for two hours, but they found no signs of anyone entering or exiting from the far side. Dominic examined the only spot where someone disturbed the land. It was obvious that was where the shooter stood. Dominic saw what an unimpeded line of vision the culprit had, and he chastised himself for ever taking Emelie to a place where there was no cover for them but plenty for an attacker. The men headed back to the keep, and Dominic followed them into the barracks.

"I want the watch doubled on the wall tonight and tomorrow. Whoever tried to shoot my wife likely isn't done yet. Whether it was bad aim or a warning, someone intended to hurt Lady Emelie. Until I know who that is and they're dead, I don't want any stranger within a league of here without me or the laird knowing." Dominic met each man's eyes, ensuring they knew how serious he was about guarding his wife. When he had their agreement, he turned back to the keep. He watched Nora hurrying across the bailey, and his heart jumped.

"Nora," Dominic called out.

"Yer wife is fine. I heard what happened. It's Lady Laurel. She's in labor." Nora lumbered up the stairs, and Dominic rushed ahead to open the door. Emelie hurried toward him and threw her arms around him.

"I have to go upstairs, but I couldn't go until I knew you were hale. Did you find aught?"

"No. Is Brodie abovestairs with Laurel?"

"Aye. Her water broke in the solar, so he carried her to their chamber. She's been laboring all day but didn't tell anyone. Brodie is beside himself."

"Should I try to get him to come belowstairs?"

Emelie snorted. "Do you think you could? You're a strong mon, but I don't think you could carry a thrashing Brodie down the stairs without you both rolling and breaking your necks."

"I suppose not. I know I'll thrash him if he thinks to keep me from you when it's your turn."

Emelie's brow furrowed. "You'll stay with me when I labor?"

"Of course, I will," Dominic said indignantly, then reconsidered. "Unless you don't want me to."

"I'm quite sure I will. As long as you stay up near my head. I don't think I want you to see all that."

"I'll do whatever you want when the time comes, sparrow."

"I—" Emelie came closer than she ever had to declaring her feelings, but she caught herself. It wasn't the time nor the place where she wanted to share them. "I need to help Nora and Aggie. Berta will oversee everything for the evening meal."

"What do you need me to do?"

"Naught, wolf. At least for now. I suppose whatever Brodie would be doing." Emelie stretched to kiss Dominic. He lifted her off her feet and brought her to his eye level. "Thank you for protecting me today and for going out to search. I know it scared you, even if you won't admit it. But it scared me too, and not just for the bairn's sake. It scares me that the arrow came so close to you."

"I'll readily admit it. It terrified me. I can't stomach the idea of losing you or our bairn, Em." He brushed a quick kiss across her lips before putting her back on her feet. He watched Emelie dash toward the stairs, then climb them before disappearing into the dim passageway. He didn't know what to do with himself, so he went to Brodie's solar. He poured himself a healthy dram of whisky, swallowed it all, then poured himself another. He considered looking at the ledgers and seeing if he could get any work done for his brother, but the incident still rattled him too much, and he admitted to himself that he also worried about Laurel. He abandoned the downstairs solar for the upstairs one, where he paced and looked out the window embrasure for hours. When a shrill wail pierced the silence, Dominic breathed easier.

"It's a lad!" Emelie chirped as she hurried into the solar. She'd heard Dominic pacing hours earlier. She'd poked her nose into the chamber a few times to give him updates. Dominic opened his arms to her, and she flew into them. "You're an uncle."

"And you're an aunt. Again." Dominic knew Emelie's older sister Isabella already had children. He gazed into Emelie's sparkling blue-hazel eyes, and he knew he couldn't wait another moment. Emotion filled his voice and brought back his brogue. "Emelie, I love ye."

Emelie's mouth dropped open in surprise, then her face beamed with the most joyous smile he'd ever seen. "I love you, Dominic."

"Between feeling our bairn for the first time and hearing our nephew, I just canna keep that to maself anymore. And coming so close to losing ye, I regret nae telling ye sooner. I've loved ye since the beginning, Em. I was just too cautious to admit it."

"I feel exactly the same. I made a mistake once thinking my feelings were more than they were. I wanted to be certain this time. But I have been since the start." Emelie rubbed the tip of her nose against Dominic's before they shared the most tender kiss they ever had.

"I love ye, sparrow," Dominic whispered, relishing the sound of the words. He felt them to his very soul, and they carried more truth than they ever had before.

"I love you, wolf. Will you come meet your nephew? Laurel should be presentable by now."

"Our. The only thing I look forward to more is meeting our own bairn."

Emelie led Dominic into the chamber where Brodie sat on the bed with Laurel between his thighs. His brawny arms cradled his wife and their newborn son.

"I'm a da," Brodie whispered with reverence.

"And I'm an uncle," Dominic grinned. The happy family of five passed the rest of the evening together as they cooed over the new heir to Clan Campbell.

Laurel spent most of the next fortnight in her chamber with her newborn son, Broderick – most often called Rick – named for his father, Brodie. The bairn was as large as Nora had predicted, and Laurel's body needed the time to recuperate. Her son also seemed to be starving every hour. It left her little time to do anything but rest and nurse. Emelie took on Laurel's duties entirely, surprising many with the ease by which she did so. She was unassuming and hardworking, which won over anyone who was still skeptical of Dominic's bride. She set aside time to have the midday meal with Laurel and baby Rick. She still spent her afternoons with Dominic, but they rarely strayed beyond the village.

Most afternoons, Dominic kept Emelie company while she worked at Laurel's desk in the upstairs solar. She took responsibility for the household ledgers, and Dominic didn't have to try hard to convince Brodie to let him take over the clan ledgers, along with most of the correspondence. This gave Brodie time to spend with his wife and newborn.

"He shall spoil that bairn," Dominic whispered. They could hear Brodie singing to his son in the next chamber. "I shall take lessons from him over the next four moons."

"You both will be terrors with these bairns. Laurel and I shall end up the mean parents while you and Brodie have all the fun."

"Aye, sparrow." Dominic said as he pulled Emelie from her seat. His hands settled on her backside, enjoying that she'd filled out through her hips. Her breasts were no longer as sensitive, so he had free rein to fondle and suckle whenever they had privacy. Emelie arched her back in invitation. Dominic kissed the swells that pushed against her neckline, dipping his tongue into the deep cleavage. One hand continued to grasp her backside as the other kneaded her breast. "Are you nearly through?"

"I just finished. You've been very patient while I work. Shall I give you a reward?"

"If ye mean slipping off to our chamber for an hour or four, then I would vera much like a reward," Dominic purred as he waggled his eyebrows. He took Emelie's hand and led her toward the door, but a servant intercepted them before they could reach their chamber.

"Dom, this missive just arrived," a young maid said.

"Is the messenger belowstairs?"

"Nay. Garrett handed it to me and said to bring it up to the laird, but I found ye instead. He said the messenger didna wait for a reply and left as soon as he handed it over."

"Thank you, Mary." Dominic's intuition screamed for him to chase down the messenger. He turned to Emelie and handed the folded parchment to her as the maid scurried away. "I need to catch him before he goes too far."

"But you don't even know what the missive says. Mayhap there's no reason for a reply."

"Em, it's odd that he wouldn't try to give the missive to the laird or the tánaiste himself. He didn't stop for a drink or food either."

"At least read it. Know what it is it says before you go chasing after him." Emelie handed it back to him, and they returned to the solar. Dominic unfolded it and scanned the document. Without looking at Emelie, he refolded it and dropped it in his sporran. "Won't you even tell me what's in it?"

"Not right now. I need to go."

"Dom?" Emelie dashed to keep up with her husband's long stride. "Dom?"

"Stay here, Em."

Emelie tugged at his sleeve as they reached the stairs. She tried to place herself between them, but Dominic eased her away. She knew the steep stone stairs made him uneasy as her belly grew. She didn't fight him and moved aside, but she didn't release his sleeve.

"If this is something you can't discuss with me, fine. But please promise you'll be careful. You're scaring me."

"Wheesht, sparrow. All will be fine. I need to see to this. Then we'll meet with Brodie and Laurel. I'll tell you everything then. I promise. And I promise to be careful. You owe me that reward, and I intend to claim it." Dominic stooped and pulled Emelie in for a passionate kiss that made her toes curl, but at the same time frightened her even more. She feared that Dominic kissed her with such heat because he thought it might be the last one they would share. "I need you to promise me you will go to our chamber and lock the door. I'm going to send Alec and Davey to guard you."

Dominic had relieved the guardsmen of their duty to follow Emelie since there had been no incidents in weeks. But the hair rose on Emelie's arms when Dominic said he would send two men to stand outside their door. She nodded, knowing that whatever concerned him that much was urgent. She wanted him to hurry and catch the messenger, so he could hurry and return. He kissed her once more before he watched her walk to their chamber. When she closed the door behind her, he ran down the stairs, jumping from the fourth from the bottom.

He burst into the kitchens and found Aggie chatting with Berta as women worked on the evening meal. He tilted his head toward a storeroom and the women followed him. When they were tucked away, he kept his voice low. "Do not let Lady Emelie or Lady Laurel have aught to eat or drink. Even if ye prepare it."

"What's amiss, Dom?" Berta asked.

"I don't know yet. Just don't serve either lady aught until I'm back. If the laird asks why, tell him we received a missive and the messenger left without seeing him or me."

Berta and Aggie exchanged a look and nodded. Aggie spoke. "The laird is with Lady Laurel, should he remain with her until ye return?"

"Aye. Make sure that he does. Don't say aught if you don't have to because I don't know what's going on yet. I'm sending men to guard my wife."

"Be careful, Dom," Berta whispered. Dominic nodded before he opened the door to the storeroom and followed the women out. He sprinted towards the stables, calling out to a stable boy to saddle his horse. He bellowed the names of five men and ordered them to saddle their horses in turn. Dominic stormed into the barracks and looked around.

"Alec! Davey!"

The two men poked their heads out of their small chambers. They glanced at one another when they saw Dominic's expression and hurried toward their tánaiste. Davey peeked out the door. "What's happened?"

"The messenger? Did you see him?"

"Nay. I didna ken there was a messenger," Davey answered.

"Me neither," Alec chimed in.

"I want you both outside my chamber door until I return. Targes and swords drawn the entire time. Do not let anyone in that chamber with Lady Emelie unless it's Lady Laurel or the laird himself. No one. And absolutely under no circumstances is she to receive aught to eat or drink. Aggie and Berta already know."

"Aye, Dom."

"I don't know how long I will be away, but I expect to find you outside my chamber door. If you aren't there, I will kill you. If aught happens to my wife, I will kill you." Dominic narrowed his eyes, and the men saw a side of him they'd only seen on the battlefield. There was none of the competitiveness or jesting they were used to in the lists. They were looking at a warrior ready to fight.

"Ye have our word, Dom. We'll be waiting outside yer door when ye return," Alec swore. Dominic nodded and stopped by the armory to fetch his targe before he left the barracks. His horse was already moving toward the gate as he swung into the saddle. He set a grueling pace as he and the five warriors barreled south. The men didn't speak, but they exchanged confused glances. It took nearly an hour, but eventually they spied a lone rider in the distance. The horse moved at a canter, but the rider must have heard them because he nudged his horse into a gallop. Dominic prayed the Campbell horses would keep gaining on the messenger despite being lathered and winded.

"Stop or I will put an arrow through your neck,"

Dominic bellowed. He reached out and took a bow and arrow from the man who rode beside him. He placed his reins between his teeth and took aim.

"I would stop if I were ye," Garrett called out. "He will do it. He's a fine shot when he isnae moving, but he's astonishing on a horse."

The messenger looked back over his shoulder and noticed Dominic aimed for him. As the Campbell men approached, they recognized the rider's MacLaren plaid. Like most clans, the MacLarens were small compared to the Campbells. The only clan that rivaled them in size was the MacDonalds, and that was only because there were so many branches and septs.

"You delivered a message to Kilchurn." Dominic reined in, his words a statement, not a question.

"Aye," the man nodded.

"If it was from your laird, why didn't he sign it?"

"It wasna from ma laird," the stranger hedged.

"What's your name, MacLaren?" Dominic demanded.

"Ye ken ma clan, so ye ken ma name."

"At this point, ye're going to die if ye dinna answer ma questions, so ye can choose whether it's quick or agonizing," Dominic growled. He fought not to clench his fist around his horse's reins. He would only make the steed aware of his emotions, and he didn't want the animal sidling away. He was too furious to notice his brogue. "Answer me honestly, and there is a chance ye will ride away still sitting on yer horse, nay lying across it on yer belly. What's yer name?"

"Hammond MacLaren."

"Who gave ye this missive if it isnae from yer laird?" Dominic pressed.

"I dinna ken the mon. I was out hunting, and I came across a mon who needed a missive delivered.

He said foul weather delayed him, and he needed to return home. He paid me well, he did."

"What clan was he from?" Dominic struggled not to explode.

"I dinna ken," Hammond responded.

"His plaid. What clan was he from? I dinna believe ye dinna ken."

"He wasna wearing one," Hammond replied.

"Lowlander?" Dominic asked.

"Mayhap. He didna speak that much, and he kept his voice low. I couldnae tell for certain."

"And ye just go riding onto other clans' lands with nay idea of what ye carry or who ye carry it for?" Dominic scoffed.

"He paid me well enough. All I had to do was get the missive to the Campbells at Kilchurn. The mon didna say who was to receive it but a Campbell."

"A Campbell or the Campbell?" Dominic pressed.

"He didna say it had to be the laird. I ken ye arenae him. Ye're only the tánaiste, so I suppose it didna matter, did it?"

"Och, aye. It matters." Dominic raised the bow he still held. "Ma brother has a steadier temper than I do. Tell me aught more ye ken or saw aboot this mon. His hair color, his eyes, his size, his horse, his clothes."

"He was aboot ma size, dark hair, dark eyes, dark horse, and he wasna wearing a plaid," Hammond described.

"Breeks?" Dominic snapped.

"Aye."

"So he was a Lowlander," Garrett muttered. Dominic had already assumed as much, but he said nothing.

"Mayhap we will accompany ye home and let yer laird ken how helpful ye've been to both this stranger and to me," Dominic suggested. He watched the man's face pale.

"I truly dinna ken aught else. And I'd rather ye didna come back with me. I'm supposed to be hunting for the laird's saint's day. I dinna need him to ken I'm late returning because I took a half day's detour."

"Ye live only because I dinna want to bother digging ye a grave," Dominic sniffed. "Go."

Hammond MacLaren didn't need telling twice. He spurred his horse, continuing south. When he was beyond sight, Dominic signaled for the men to turn back toward home. They stopped five minutes later to let their horses drink from a stream and to let the beasts rest. Dominic stepped away from the men and pulled the missive out of his sporran. A shiver skimmed along his spine, and the hairs stood up on his arms all over again.

There will be a next time. And she won't survive.

The two sentences struck fear in his heart. There was no way to be certain the missive was a warning about Emelie, but he was certain it was. Other than the unexplained exhaustion Laurel suffered, she hadn't ailed at all, nor had she any unexpected accidents. There was still a chance something other than pregnancy had caused Laurel to take to her bed for a sennight, but there'd been the piglet, the hive, and the arrow. It seemed more likely that the invisible antagonist meant the threat for Emelie. As soon as the horses were ready, the men rode back to Kilchurn.

FOURTEEN

Dominic nodded to Alec and Davey, who stood with their targes together and their swords in hand, just as they promised. He approached his chamber and breathed easier. It didn't feel like he'd learned much, but he supposed knowing slightly more than nothing was somewhat helpful. He dismissed the two warriors and knocked on the door.

"Sparrow, it's me." Dominic heard something pulled away from the door before Emelie lifted the bar and unbolted the door. She opened it an inch, and Dominic spied a dirk in her hand. "Running me through, and I havenae even kissed ye," he jested weakly.

Emelie's nose twitched. Dominic hadn't been speaking in a burr before he left, but he was now. Something had upset him enough for him to not even notice. She tucked the knife back into her belt and opened the door wider. Dominic pushed it closed and lifted Emelie off her feet. The kiss was desperate as they clung to one another.

"I didn't expect you to be out for so long," Emelie murmured against Dominic's neck.

"It took an hour to catch up to the mon. I canna say I'm surprised he was in a hurry to get back to his own land. The messenger was a MacLaren." Dominic lowered Emelie to her feet, but he noticed her confusion. "They're to the south of us. At least another hour past where we caught up to him."

"Was it Laird MacLaren who sent the missive?"

"Nay. It's unsigned. Come. We need to tell Laurel and Brodie." The couple walked down the passageway, and Dominic knocked. When they were bade to enter, Dominic pulled the missive from his sporran. They found Brodie and Laurel sitting before the fire while Laurel nursed. Brodie and Dominic locked eyes. Brodie rose and distractedly offered Emelie the seat as he crossed the room. He took the missive from Dominic's outstretched hand. "I tracked a MacLaren halfway to their land. A Lowlander paid him to deliver this to us. He doesnae ken who the mon was, and he didna ask questions. All he could tell me was dark hair, dark eyes, dark horse, and breeks. Nay plaid."

"Brodie? Dom?" Laurel asked as she drew a blanket Emelie knitted around her son and her chest. Brodie handed the missive to Laurel, who gasped and looked at Emelie.

"Dominic, tell me what it says. You haven't let me see it, and now everyone but me knows what's in it." Emelie rose from her chair and took the missive from Laurel before either of the men could retrieve it. She glared at Dominic until she read it. Her brow furrowed as her hand trembled. "It's aboot me?"

"You don't ken that," Laurel blurted. "Aye, a Lowlander had it at some point. But we both spent years at court, and I didn't make many friends. I left not that long ago. It could just as easily be aboot me as it could be you."

"It says a next time. Naught's happened to you. Not that I would want it to. This has to be aboot me," Emelie argued. She turned an accusatory glare at Dominic. "You didn't tell me before you left. I thought this was something to do with the clan. I'm not a child. Do not hide things from me."

Emelie looked at Brodie and Laurel and shook her head. She thrust the missive back at Dominic and stormed out of the chamber as Dominic and Laurel called her name. She had enough sense to know that she couldn't leave the keep, even though she wanted fresh air. She wanted to be alone, but she knew Dominic was following her. She breezed past their chamber and went to the one place she was certain he wouldn't follow. Her hand was on the latch to his former chamber when a broad one covered hers.

"I'll give ye all the space ye need. I will leave ye alone for as long as ye want. But please, dinna go in there, Em. Please."

Emelie turned around and saw the distress in Dominic's eyes as easily as she heard it in his voice. She swallowed, then nodded, realizing she would have gone too far if she'd entered the chamber. She was angry, but she didn't want to hurt him. Despite her emotions, she still knew that Dominic tried to protect her. She held out her hand and led them to their chamber. Neither spoke until they went inside.

"I know you were in a hurry to catch the mon, but you could have told me, Dom. You raced out of here with barely a word other than you were having guards placed at the door. I didn't know if someone was aboot to attack the keep or if something happened in the village. You should have told me the threat was to me."

"I believe it is, but like Laurel said, it could be to her, too. I warned Aggie and Berta not to let ye or Laurel eat or drink aught. And if Brodie asked, they were to tell him he was to remain with Laurel until I returned."

"And he would have trusted you and done as you

224

asked, just like I did. But I'm your wife, and I was standing right there. You could have told me. You could have trusted *me*."

"I ken. But ma thoughts were racing. I kenned two things for certain. I needed ye safe and guarded, and I needed to catch the messenger. I wasna thinking beyond that. I'm sorry, Em."

Emelie's mouth thinned, but she nodded. She watched as Dominic ran his hands through his hair, making it stand on end. His gray eyes matched the storm clouds that had hung over the keep for a sennight. She could feel the tension in his body without touching him. It poured from him.

"Dominic?"

"Aye." Dominic met Emelie's gaze, and all he wanted to do was bundle his wife and the bairn she carried onto a horse and ride far away, to anywhere the unknown threat couldn't reach them. Emelie stepped toward him until the toes of their boots brushed. She placed her hands on his chest. She could feel his heart thudding. The pace was still racing, and she didn't know how he could breathe so smoothly.

"I think I'm more annoyed that you showed Brodie and Laurel before me. That hurt."

"I'm sorry. I didna really think aboot it. It seemed natural to hand the parchment to Brodie first. He's ma laird and ma brother. I canna say it should surprise me that Laurel would get it next, but aye, it should have been ye first."

"You're really shaken by this," Emelie mused as she soothed her hand over his chest. "I know you didn't want to scare me until you knew more, but not telling me aught just made my imagination run away. You still have your burr."

"Do I? I hadnae—hadn't—noticed."

"I like it. I don't like that you're upset, but I told

225

you, it does things to me." Emelie winked before she kissed Dominic's neck. They walked to the chairs placed near the empty hearth. Without either giving it any thought, Emelie sat on Dominic's lap. She rested against him as his hand rested on her belly. A sharp kick greeted his palm. Emelie chuckled as Dominic's hold tightened. "We're both fine. The bairn is just saying hello to his or her da."

"Ye're learning, lass." Dominic gave Emelie a wink of his own, pleased to hear her use the more informal, typical Highland address rather than "father." He rubbed his palm over her belly as they sat together. "What do ye wish to do?"

"You're asking my opinion?"

"Aye. As ye pointed out, this involves ye. I might disagree or suggest something else, but I would hear yer ideas and what ye want. I dinna want ye to be scared or think me too highhanded."

"I know you don't mean to be. And I appreciate that you want my opinion. I don't know what to suggest other than keeping the guards and me not leaving the keep."

"I hate that ye are being made a prisoner in yer own home. And I'm nae even comfortable with ye eating aught that's served."

"You think a servant would try to poison me?"

"I dinna ken what to think. I dinna want to believe they would, but I also ken someone slipped in and let the piglet out. I ken we never caught who fired the arrow or who cut down the hive. If it's the same person—or even worse, if it's more than one—they're vera sly. I willna put aught past them, including figuring out how to tamper with yer food."

"But we share a trencher at nearly every meal. I'm served from the same dishes and platters as everyone else. They would have to poison you and everyone else on the dais to get to me."

226

"I dinna ken how desperate they are. Mayhap they would do that just to get to ye."

"Dom, I can't stay here then. If me living among your people is going to endanger everyone, then I need to leave."

"'Yer people'? When did they become mine again and stopped being ours?"

"When someone targeted me and brought danger to the clan, it made me an outsider all over again. They can't leave, so I must."

"Ye will do nay such thing, Emelie. Ye will remain here if I have to chain ye to the bed." Dominic lightened his threat by offering her his wolfish grin. "And if I must make love to ye all day and all night to keep ye from trying to slip away, then that is the best post I've ever stood—or laid—or sat. Mayhap we can start right now." Dominic playfully pulled Emelie's skirts toward her knees, but a loud knock interrupted them.

"Go away," Emelie called before she leaned in for a kiss from Dominic.

"Emelie?" Laurel called. "I came to check on you."

"Damn," Emelie hissed as she wriggled off Dominic's lap. She hurried across the chamber, glancing down at her gown, glad that she did. She adjusted the neckline to hide the nipple peeking over the top. She pulled the door open and found Laurel appearing worried on the other side. "You shouldn't be walking around yet."

"I'm fine. I wanted to make sure you are. Where's—" Laurel snapped her mouth shut as she noticed Dominic looking put out in the chair by the fire. Emelie glanced back at her husband and snickered. "You made up. That didn't take long."

"No quicker than you make up with Brodie," Dominic mused. He rose from the chair and came to stand behind Emelie. He cupped her shoulders and kissed the top of her head. Calmer than he had been since they received the missive, he said, "We should go back with you so we can all talk."

"Aye. But in the solar. Rick is sleeping," Laurel answered. She went to fetch Brodie and then met Emelie and Dominic in the upstairs solar. Laurel took Emelie's hand. "Before you even suggest it, and I know you will because I would, too—because I *did* —you're not going anywhere, Emelie."

"Neither of you are," Brodie decreed. He crossed his arms and leaned back in his chair. Laurel had the temerity to laugh. She looked back at Emelie.

"Since we don't know for sure that the threat is just aimed at you, I told Brodie that I should go to one of our nearby keeps but not let anyone know where I've gone. If he hadn't been holding Rick, he would have screamed down the roof," Laurel explained.

"And I already told Dom that I didn't want Emelie going anywhere when we had the wasp incident. It's not safe for either of you to go anywhere. Dom and I can best protect you here, with our largest contingent of warriors in our most secure keep."

"And if they harm others because I stay? I'm not convinced this is aboot Laurel." Emelie said.

"And I'm not convinced it isn't. This could still be aboot the Lamonts and MacDougalls. Or it could be Liam Oliphant. He was involved in the wagers. It could even be Laird Gunn. Either of them could hold a grudge against Brodie and me," Laurel reasoned.

It hadn't thrilled everyone at court to see Laurel snag Brodie's attention. Several men wagered Brodie would only marry Laurel to win the bet that he could tame the Shrew of Stirling. A handful of them went much further to win. Nelson and Matthew Mac-Dougall lost their lives for it. But Liam Oliphant had once been Nelson's confidant and instigator of the bets. He avoided the battle outside the bailey wall where Matthew and Nelson met their ends, so he was still alive to cause more trouble. Laird Gunn also played a role in trying to keep Laurel and Brodie apart. He'd returned to his home along the north-eastern coast, but Laurel wouldn't rule him out.

"Laurel's right. It could be aboot her," Brodie chimed in. "There are more people and more reasons to see Laurel harmed than for anyone to attack you. Mayhap whoever they sent before confused you for Laurel in the garden or even in the bailey. Your hair isn't similar, but it's clear you're a lady too. If the person orchestrating this said the lady had unique hair, it could be either of you. Mayhap someone didn't want Laurel to give birth to my heir. That could be any number of people, including every MacGregor drawing breath."

Emelie nodded, but nothing Laurel or Brodie said made her feel any better. If they directed the attacks at her, then she had a legitimate reason to fear for her life. But she also quailed at the idea that an assailant might confuse her for Laurel, or that anyone would seek to harm her friend. In the time since she arrived at Kilchurn, she and Laurel had grown even closer than they'd been at court. They were nearly as close as Emelie was to Blythe, and far closer than Laurel had ever been to any of her sisters.

"What do we do?" Emelie asked the still-unanswered question. "If they directed this at Laurel, then Rick is in danger too. Mayhap whoever this is doesn't know Laurel has already given birth. But if they do, then they might go after your bairn, too."

"Beyond assigning guards to you both, for now

there isn't much more. I will assign more patrols near our southern borders, and I'll set patrols ten leagues from the keep. If anyone approaches the keep, they will meet our warriors first," Brodie decided aloud.

"Can we eat?" Emelie looked at Dominic.

"Aye. But you both eat only what the servants bring everyone else first. You don't drink from your own chalices, and we all stick with water or watered ale," Dominic stated. The bells tolled for the evening meal as Dominic finished speaking. Laurel and Brodie retired to their chamber where Laurel laid down, exhausted from her brief time out of bed and on her feet. They would dine together in their chamber that night. Dominic accompanied Emelie belowstairs.

"You sound like a Lowlander again," Emelie whispered. "It's vera disappointing." She winked and patted her husband's backside just before they reached the dais. They took their places at the high table, and Emelie looked at the senior warriors seated around them. The men were all combat hardened, but they were kind and welcoming to her. She turned toward Dominic as he whispered to Aggie. When he was through, he kept his voice low as he explained his conversation.

"Berta is to oversee the dishes that come to the high table, and Aggie will serve them herself."

"That'll draw more attention. Aggie is our housekeeper, not a maid or serving lass."

"Aye, but she also makes a fuss over you already. She and Berta will say they don't think you've been eating properly and want to put some meat on your bones." Dominic leaned so far over that he flicked his tongue against the back of Emelie's earlobe. His gravelly voice rumbled in her ear as he exaggerated his words. "And I wouldnae mind if it all went to that lush backside of yers."

"If I eat more than I do now, I'll be as broad as the side of the stables."

"Then eat up. I won't complain if there's more of you to hold when I make love to you or when you sit in my lap. I might not let go at all."

"You're a tease, Dom," Emelie giggled.

"We'll see who's jesting tonight when I show you just how much I enjoy your lovely charms." Dominic's hand inched up Emelie's skirts until his fingers dipped between her thighs. Emelie struggled not to squirm. She licked her lips and pulled her teeth along her lower lip, knowing how Dominic's body would react. She slid her hand under his plaid and up his thigh until the back of her hand touched his steely length. She cocked an eyebrow before she withdrew her hand. Dominic groaned and squeezed her thigh. "I won't forget that."

"Good."

Neither could say more because Aggie arrived with the first dish. She moved along the table, serving the senior clansmen before reaching Dominic and Emelie. The men, many of whom sat on the clan council, watched Aggie in confusion. She should have served Dominic and Emelie first from dishes reserved for the laird's family. But Dominic wished for everyone to see that Emelie ate from the same platters as the clan council, so unless the covert menace intended to poison the clan's senior leadership, food wouldn't be the right approach. Dominic prayed it would work because he didn't know of anything else to do short of a food taster.

Emelie sipped the watered ale Aggie brought and nibbled on a heel of bread as she watched the men eat. When none keeled over or dropped dead in their trencher, she grew confident enough to eat her own portions. With gowns properly fitted from Laurel, she could sit for the entire evening meal, and her appetite from their journey had returned. Dominic encouraged her to eat, but he also silently signaled that he would taste each item before her. Emelie felt guilty for the thought, but she would have much rather the other men at the table be ill or succumb rather than Dominic if the food were poisoned. But the meal progressed without incident.

The next three sennights dragged for Emelie. The men Dominic assigned to guard her were polite and diligent, but she couldn't imagine it thrilled them to play nursemaid and follow her around. Dominic spent less time in the lists so that he could serve as her guard for most of the day. The time spent with him was the only blessing in the whole mess. She'd caught glares from the council members when they realized, one by one, they were unofficial taste testers. She worked in the gardens, but she was finding it more and more difficult to kneel and then stand up. The other women helped her, but it only made them comment more about how small she was, how large her belly was, and the giant she was bound to give birth to since they believed she carried Dominic's child. Laurel eased back into her routine and took back many of her chatelaine duties, which only left Emelie with more time to fill and nowhere to go.

Dominic knew Emelie was growing frustrated with her isolation, and he regretted that he still felt it was necessary. He accompanied her into the village two afternoons, but he spent the entire time on edge. His hand didn't leave the hilts of the dirks tucked in his belt. He reached back several times to touch the sword in its scabbard on his back, as though he would ensure it was still there. He knew Emelie picked up on his discomfiture because she spent nearly as much time watching him as she did looking at the people they visited.

When Dominic offered to take her for a third afternoon, she declined. He felt guilty, knowing she did so for his sake. He tried to make it up to her by taking her to their chamber and reading to her throughout the afternoon. It had only taken ten minutes before she was sound asleep next to him as they reclined on their bed. After that, he suggested she nap every afternoon, but she claimed she'd only been tired because he kept them up most of the night. He'd had the decency to look abashed for a moment, but then he gloated and waggled his eyebrows. Emelie giggled and shook her head.

FIFTEEN

Emelie and Laurel sat together in the upstairs solar as Laurel went over the week's accounts and Emelie held a sleeping Rick. She gazed at the infant boy's cherubic face and wondered what her child would look like. Laurel's son was the spitting image of his father. There could be no doubting the lad's paternity. It made Emelie uneasy to think that her child might look more like Henry than her. She feared what people would say if the child didn't look like her, and it was impossible for the child to look like Dominic.

"I already told you. We'll say the bairn looks like your mother or father. No one here knows them," Laurel said, reading Emelie's mind. She laid down her quill and smiled. "Don't worry until there is a reason to. People will just be excited that there's another bairn. They won't be talking aboot how he or she looks."

"Just like they aren't all talking aboot how much Rick looks like Brodie?"

"Och, well, I suspect every child I bear will look like their father. I think the mon willed it."

"I think it would be nice if your children had your strawberry-blonde hair," Emelie mused.

234

"Not so easy to blend into a crowd with it," Laurel grinned. Emelie picked up a lock of her own white-blonde hair and gave Laurel a pointed look. "Mayhap your children will have your hair. We'll be able to tell who's who when they're off playing."

Emelie swallowed as she nodded. She'd been thinking incessantly about the future, and the more she dwelled on the lingering threat, the more resolute she became that she would need to leave Kilchurn and the Campbells. Her heart felt like it was pinched in a vise whenever she considered leaving Dominic and repudiating the handfast. He was adamant that she didn't leave Kilchurn, but she also knew he would honor his promise to release her if she wished. It was the last thing she wanted, but it felt like the ethical choice.

Waiting another four months seemed unrealistic. But as strongly as Emelie's mind pulled her away from Dominic, the more she feared the consequences to her child if people considered the babe a bastard. He or she would live with that stigma for the rest of their life, and it would make it difficult for the child to marry and have a family of their own. It would be far worse if she had a son, since men would never let him forget as he trained to become a warrior. She didn't know if a son would find a place among her father's warriors. The potential rejection hurt as much as the thought of leaving Dominic.

Rather than respond to Laurel's last comment, she cooed at Rick, who gurgled in his sleep. As if not to be outdone, her bairn rolled within her belly. She'd felt rhythmic hiccups on most days. It reassured Emelie that all was fine within her womb. Dominic often rubbed her belly in wonderment, and as she thought about that now, she wasn't certain she could take that from him. Never had he made her worry that he wasn't as committed to being a father

235

as he swore. She didn't want to imagine the heart-break she would cause him if she left, and she wasn't certain she could bear her own. It only left her con-flicted and drained.

"Do you think we can venture to the gardens for a walk?" Emelie asked as Rick's eyes fluttered open. "After you feed him, of course." Emelie grinned as Laurel playfully sighed and rolled her eyes.

"I never imagined a bairn could eat so much. He'll be swinging a sword before he can walk if he keeps growing as he is."

"It just means you're a wonderful mother."

"It means I'll never fit back into any of my clothes, since I have to eat nearly as much as him to keep up," Laurel chuckled. "But aye. I think we can go for a walk if our guards come. Naught has hap-pened in sennights. Mayhap something has drawn our nemesis away. Mayhap the men will relent and call off our guards."

Brodie insisted Laurel have two guards, and he ordered two more for Rick's personal detail. Emelie supposed she was luckier than Laurel, who had what felt like a small army trailing behind her. Both women felt safer, if a bit stifled, by the contingent. Neither dared complain to their husband because they could see the toll the men's frustration and worry was taking on them.

"Not bluidy likely, but we can ask." Emelie's mouth twisted, and she didn't appear hopeful. Laurel chuckled again.

"Just ask him at the right time."

"Och, aye. When he's nearly asleep. I tried your timing before. It led to another round, so I'm not complaining. But it did naught to convince him. He distracted me, not the other way around." Emilie grinned ruefully. She rose and handed Rick to Lau-rel, who nursed the famished bairn before they left the solar. The six men milled around the passageway, waiting for the two ladies. The women's shoulders slumped in unison, feeling guilty for the men's unfortunate assignment.

"Ma ladies, we dinna mind. We would rather keep ye safe," Garrett said, reading their body language. "It's a point of pride that the laird and Dominic chose us. I can say with truth that the other men are jealous that the laird and Dominic trust us with yer safety."

Laurel and Emelie smiled and thanked the men, but Garrett's words didn't convince Emelie. Three men led the way down the stairs as the other three followed behind the ladies. Laurel carried a plaid with her, and once they were in the garden, Emelie spread it on the ground. The late-autumn sun lacked the strength of a couple of months earlier, but it was pleasant as the women chatted together. Rick was once more asleep, swaddled in the blanket Emelie knitted. He lay between the women and blew bubbles in his sleep.

The women passed an hour in the garden until their husbands came in search of them. Dominic helped Emelie to her feet, but his eyes swept the garden and rested for a moment on each guard. Brodie picked up Rick after helping Laurel to stand. When Laurel bent to pick up the blanket, Brodie muttered, "Leave it."

Emelie and Laurel looked at their husbands and understood something had happened. They walked with the men to Brodie's solar, and he locked the door. Both husbands appeared shaken as they led their wives to chairs before the fireplace where a toasty blaze warmed them from the light autumn chill in the chamber.

"Our men captured an intruder approaching by raft on the river. We suspect he was meeting someone

237

coming from Loch Awe. He kept looking toward the bay," Dominic explained.

"Who is he?" Emelie asked.

"We don't know yet," Dominic answered. "He's wearing breeks. We need you to see him. We need to know if you recognize him."

Emelie and Laurel exchanged a brief glance, nodded, and rose. Brodie took Laurel's hand and wrapped his arm around her and Rick. "It doesn't have to be right this moment. He's in the dungeon now, so he's not going anywhere. We want to place you somewhere where you can see his face, but he won't see you. Dominic will take you while I stay with Rick."

"Can't Aggie stay with him?" Laurel asked.

Brodie shook his head. "No one but the four of us is to mind our son, Laurie."

"You don't even trust Aggie? She practically raised you," Laurel said in disbelief.

"Laurie, she's much aulder now. If someone tried to take Rick from her, she wouldn't be able to fight or run like she once did. I trust her when there is no threat. It's not a slight against her," Brodie explained. Laurel nodded, but she held Rick tighter, making the babe flail his arm in protest. But he never woke. Emelie marveled at how the child only ate and slept. She wondered if all newborns were the same.

"Mayhap only I should go," Emelie suggested. "We would know the same people most likely."

Laurel shook her head. "I was at court much longer than you were. There are plenty of people I met and saw years before you arrived. I don't want to miss the chance to discover who this is."

Brodie lifted Rick from Laurel's arms and held him up so Laurel could kiss the bairn's forehead. Dominic ushered the women to the door, and two of Laurel's guards stepped inside to wait with Brodie.

They heard the door lock behind them. Dominic led Emelie and Laurel to a second-floor arrow slit in the tower. It overlooked the exterior entrance to the dungeons.

"Wait here. Don't stand directly in front of the slit. Position yourselves so you can see out, but no one can see you." Dominic pressed a brief kiss to Emelie's lips, then spun on his heels. Emelie watched as Dominic's plaid swished against the back of his thighs. She could see his calves flex beneath his stockings and over the top of his boots. He set his shoulders back, and she knew the broad expanse of his chest would make even seasoned warriors think twice before engaging him. Standing beside Brodie, Dominic's size didn't seem unusual. But Emelie had seen him with the other guardsman. While he wasn't the tallest among the Campbells, he was one of the most powerful looking men she'd ever seen. He'd never used his size to intimidate her, so it took her aback whenever she thought of him in a fight.

They didn't have long before they watched Dominic drag a man through the doorway and into the bailey. He was wet and dirty, but it shocked Emelie to see he had no injuries. She realized no one had beaten the man, so Laurel and Emelie could examine his features without distortion. Emelie squinted as she studied the prisoner. There was something familiar about the man, but she couldn't pull forth a memory.

"Do you recognize him?" Emelie whispered.

"No. Do you?" Laurel responded.

"I think so. I'm certain he isn't a Dunbar. I doubt he's one of our neighbors because we're on good terms with them. An Englishman wouldn't travel this far into Scotland just for a border lord's daughter. I must have seen him at court," Emelie reasoned.

"Do you think it was after I left?"

"Mayhap. I have this feeling that I've seen him before, but no memory is coming to me. I don't know. He looks like most Lowlanders. Mayhap I'm confusing him for someone else." Emelie jerked her chin toward the arrow slit. "The mon will get suspicious being outside and naught happening. We need to let Dom know we don't recognize him." Emelie turned to Garrett and waved him over. "Tell Dom we don't know who he is."

Garrett nodded and hurried away. It was only a minute or two later that he whispered in Dominic's ear. As soon as Garrett stepped away, Dominic's fist plowed into the man's cheek. Rather than let him fall backwards, Dominic grabbed the head of dark curls and jabbed another punch at the prisoner's nose, followed immediately with an upper cut to the stranger's jaw. He released the man, but only long enough to wrap his hand around the prisoner's throat. Emelie could tell Dominic spoke, but she was too far away to hear anything. A punch to the gut made the man double over. Dominic pushed him toward the dungeon door and disappeared behind him. Emelie had never seen Dominic fight, but it surprised her that Dominic let the man live. She supposed more would happen in the dungeon, more that her husband didn't want her to witness.

"Let's go back to Brodie's solar," Laurel whispered. The ladies arrived just as Dominic knocked on the door. One of the two guards admitted them, then both slipped out. "We don't know who he is, Brodie."

"Did he see you, Laurie? Did he know you were watching?" Brodie asked as he stroked Laurel's cheek.

"He didn't," Dominic interjected. "I watched his eyes. They never strayed in our wives' direction."

"Did you learn aught from him?" Emelie asked. "We saw you say something to him."

"He works for someone. He had another missive. When I opened it and showed it to him, I could tell he wasn't pretending. He doesn't know how to read. I made sure of it when I pressed my dirk against his throat." Dominic frowned. He hadn't enjoyed beating the man, knowing Emelie could see. But he was unconvinced the man worked alone. He suspected someone within their walls was part of the scheme. He needed anyone conspiring with the prisoner to see Dominic would show no mercy. He didn't relish sharing that detail. "I don't think he was meeting a stranger at Loch Awe. I think he was meeting a Campbell."

"What?" Brodie roared.

"Shh," Laurel hissed.

"Sorry." Brodie hushed. He turned to Dominic. "Why do you think that?"

"Besides none of our sentries spying strangers in the loch or bay, he kept looking around the bailey and up at the wall. I watched his left eye twitch when he looked at the wall walk. I believe he recognized someone up there. But I couldn't tell who he spied because of the distance. It could have been several men. I know who to question though."

"Who do you think it was?" Brodie asked.

Dominic grimaced. "You won't like it, Brodie. It was—"

"Who?" Brodie demanded. Dominic scowled, annoyed that his brother interrupted.

"Wallace and Walter were up there."

"I will kill him," Brodie fumed. "I guarantee it involves the fucking bastard. Nay playing stupid this time. He willna live to see sunset."

Emelie looked back and forth between Brodie and Dominic, then at Laurel. She leaned over and explained, "When we were traveling here, Wallace was one of two men Brodie assigned to guard me while we stopped at an inn. Brodie went to get a horse—Graham's horse—reshod. Wallace said he was only following Michael's lead when they took me into the market crowd and conveniently lost me. Men forced me onto a ferry and away from Brodie. Michael is dead, and you know what happened to Graham. Wallace lived to tell the tale because he played dumb. It looks suspicious now."

"And I'll have Walter's head if I find out he covered for his maggoty nephew. Stay here," Brodie barked at Laurel.

"Bear, wait," Laurel spoke softly as she stepped in front of Brodie. "What did the missive say? Naught happened to us. Mayhap he recognized Wallace and Walter from accompanying you to court. Don't go lopping off any heads yet."

Dominic pulled the missive from his sporran and handed it to Emelie. Her smile tugged at the corner of her mouth before it turned down into a frown as she opened the parchment.

Her days are nearly over. Every time you think it's done, it isn't. It's not done until she's dead, and so is her bairn.

Emelie's hand shook as she handed the missive to Laurel, who gasped as she read it. Dominic pulled Emelie into his embrace, and she clung to him. Laurel did the same with Brodie.

"I swear, Laurie. We will keep you both safe. We have the would-be assassin this time. Whoever sent this willna ken if his mon died before or after he got to ye."

"Aye, he will," Laurel argued. She lapsed into her own brogue. "He'll ken the moment we have a market day, and people pour in. It willna be a secret that Emelie and I are still alive. Even if ye hide us, people will still talk. It isnae over."

"Dom, can I speak to you alone?" Emelie whispered. Dominic looked down at her earnest expression and nodded. He glanced at Laurel and Brodie, but they focused on one another. Dominic led Emelie to their chamber, neither talking, since they didn't trust the walls not to have ears. As soon as the door closed, Emelie spun around. "I can't stay."

"And where do ye think ye're traipsing off to?" Dominic's voice was ominously low, but Emelie didn't miss that there were now three upset Highlanders involved in the situation.

"I don't know. But I can't stay here. We don't know if this is aboot me or Laurel. Until we do, we're both in danger. What if someone mistakes us for the other? We'll both wind up dead, and so will our bairns. Laurel's right. Even if you hide us in the keep, people will still talk. If we're apart, then we can figure out who the target is faster."

"And possibly get ye killed just traveling. Ye are too far along to ride a horse, Emelie. I willna hear of it. A wagon is a bluidy huge target and will be too slow. Nay. Ye stay. Once we resolve this, if ye wish to leave, I willna break ma promise." Dominic fought to keep calm when he feared he would be ill. The threat to Emelie and her wish to leave made his head ring like a blacksmith's anvil.

"If we resolve this, Dom, I have no reason to leave. I don't want to leave *you*. But I can't stop thinking this is the right decision."

"Canna stop." Dominic's eyes narrowed. "Just how long have ye been crafting this idea, sparrow?"

"Since the arrow in the meadow," Emelie confessed. "I'm scared, wolf. I'm scared for you, for our bairn, for this clan, for me. I don't know what else to suggest. Staying here isn't hiding me well enough if this is even aboot me. We don't know if the cause of

243

this is purposely being cagey, or if they don't know there are two bairns involved."

"I ken ye're scared, but where do I take ye? South to yer family and toward every Lowlander in Scotland? North in late autumn, where we could be snowed in if winter comes early? Do I take men from the garrison who we need to protect the keep, Laurel, and Rick? Do I take ye to another one of our keeps and bring danger to people who dinna have the resources to defend themselves as we do here? Ye canna leave, Em. Nay until we ken who this is aboot."

"Then ask your prisoner again. Demand the men on the wall speak."

"We dinna consider going anywhere without thinking this through, Em. I still believe ye are safer here than out on the road."

"I don't disagree with you," Emelie said. "But staying may not be a choice much longer."

Dominic studied Emelie, making his heart race with apprehension. "Promise me ye willna take this into yer own hands. Promise, Emelie, or I willna let ye out of this chamber until ye die of auld age. I will break ma promise to release ye if ye dinna promise me right now."

"Do you really think I would take off without you?"

"Aye. I think ye're growing desperate enough to do just that."

"You really believe I'm that stupid."

"Dinna pretend to be insulted. Stupidity and desperation arenae the same, but sometimes desperation makes people do unreasonable things. I dinna think ye're stupid in the slightest. I think ye're canny enough to figure out how to slip out. But ye ken I will come after ye. What happens if I canna get to ye soon enough?"

"Then we're at an impasse." Emelie crossed her arms and inhaled a deep breath. Her lips pursed to keep from saying more.

"We are nae. We are coming to an agreement to consider as many choices as we can think of, then we will pick the best one. And that may be staying here. Promise me, Emelie." Dominic's fingers bit into Emelie's upper arms as he grasped them. She suspected he wanted to shake her, but he wouldn't. The punishing hold spoke of his fear though, and she knew she was adding to it. She leaned against him, and he released her arms immediately. He wrapped himself around her. "I'm terrified, Emelie. Please dinna decide aught without me."

"I promise," Emelie conceded. She could hear the raw anguish in Dominic's voice, and she realized that not only was he scared, he also felt guilty. He feared what she did: that she brought danger to the clan. But he also believed he brought yet another wife to his people who caused trouble, even if this wasn't Emelie's fault. She understood he was grasping at any means to fix the problem. "Dom, I'm tired. Can we lie down for a while? Will you stay until I fall asleep?"

"I'm nae leaving yer side." Dominic pulled the laces free from Emelie's gown and lifted it over her head. Pushing it down over her belly and hips was no longer an option. He stripped off his boots and plaid as Emelie climbed into bed in her stockings and chemise. He drew her closer once he tucked them under the covers. He knew she suggested the nap to give him time to think, comfort her, and to ease his own fears. He knew she understood all he wanted to do was hold her, to feel that she was safe with him.

"Dominic, no matter what happens, I love you. That won't change, whether I stay or I go."

245

"I willna break ma promise like I said. I shouldnae have threatened that."

"I promise not to leave on my own. I'm not bothered by what you said. I understand. But I need you to stop thinking this is your fault. Whoever is doing this brought danger to our clan. It wasn't you." Emelie's voice dropped, and Dominic struggled to hear her. "I don't want you to regret bringing me here."

"Emelie, ye are ma wife. I love ye, and I do nae regret handfasting with ye. I havenae once, and I willna. Emelie, I want ye to marry me. A priest, the kirk, and vows nay one can break."

"I want to marry you too. My answer is yes. Without reservation, yes. But I'm scared this isn't the right time for that."

"Some people—especially Lowlanders who dinna understand our traditions—will claim it isnae a proper marriage. And in a sense, they arenae wrong. If ye're ma wife before God and the law, whoever this is, may nae be so quick to act anymore." Dominic tipped Emelie's chin until their gazes met. "But dinna for a moment think that is the only reason I wish to marry ye. Trouble or nae, I want to spend the rest of ma life with ye, Em; I want to build a family with ye, and I want to grow auld with ye. I want to share ma life with only ye. I have since the vera beginning. I would have married ye from the start. I offered the handfast because I realized marrying a stranger might be too much for ye to accept."

"It was, but only because of the situation I was in. I wanted to marry you, too. I still do. And not for the protection you've given me. I want to marry you because I can't imagine spending a lifetime without talking to you, seeing you, holding you. I don't want any other mon to be the father of any of my children. I love you." Emelie paused as a new thought came to mind. "Do we have to post the banns still?"

"Aye. Even with a handfast, we must."

"It'll force this person's hand. Either they come forward to stop us, if this is aboot me, or they'll get more desperate to keep us from marrying."

"I'm nae eager to tempt fate, Em. I dinna want to make them act in haste. It only makes it more dangerous for ye."

"The only other option, besides me leaving, is waiting indefinitely. Do you want that?"

"I dinna want any of this." Dominic considered their choices, which seemed as limited as Emelie said. "We post the banns. If aught happens, then we ken it's aboot us. If that's the case, we'll sail down Loch Awe. Brodie and I have a winter hunting cabin. Nae many people ken where it is. We can go there if we canna stay here."

Emelie nodded, glad they finally had a possible resolution. She tucked herself back under Dominic's chin. When he spoke again, she fought to listen. The rumble of his chest made her sleepy.

"I'm hesitant to take ye because it willna be vera comfortable for ye. It's meant for a handful of men who only need a place to lay their head at night while they spend the day hunting. There arenae any beds, nae even cots. We just use bedrolls."

"If it's safe and with you, then I don't need aught more."

"Mayhap, but ye'll wish for a lot more," Dominic muttered.

"Aye, privacy to make love to you. But I suspect that will be in short supply."

"Mayhap we can practice how quiet ye can be." Dominic guided Emelie to roll away from him before hiking up her chemise and his leine. He drew Emelie's top leg over his and ran his fingers over her mons, rubbing her pearl as her body prepared to accept his. "I would bury maself in ye and never leave."

"That would be quite the sight in the lists."

"That isnae the sword I wish to wield. And a lively bed partner like ye willna let me run to fat." Dominic nibbled where Emelie's shoulder and neck met as she reached behind her to stroke him.

"Dinna keep me waiting, wolf," Emelie teased as she pressed her hips back. Dominic entered her in a single thrust, eliciting a moan from Emelie. He grunted as he surged into her over and over. "I thought we were practicing how to be quiet."

"Another time. I intend to make ye moan until ye climax. Then I would hear ye scream ma name. Let the whole bluidy keep ken I'm yers."

"I think they already know that. I don't think there is anyone in doubt. We're worse than rabbits."

"Bunnies are cute," Dominic said before squeezing her nipple. Emelie's nails dug into his thigh as she rocked her hips to meet his. "The only problem with this position is I canna enjoy yer breasts as much. I would have them while they're still mine to play with."

Dominic eased away from Emelie's sheath. She rolled on top of him, but between her short body and her rounded belly, it was awkward as his cock returned to her core. Dominic sat up, bracing Emelie's back and head in one hand as she leaned away. He pulled her chemise down her arms before he laved her nipple until it tightened into a dart, then grazed his teeth over it. When he felt Emelie shiver, and her core tightened around his shaft, he drew her breast into his mouth. He sucked as his cock pulsed within her. Still supporting her weight with one arm, his hands guided her hips as she ground her mons against him. It wasn't long before Emelie's gasps turned to deep, throaty moans.

"More," Emelie panted. Always careful not to press his weight onto her, Dominic turned them again. He drew her to the edge of the bed as he stood and ripped his leine over his head. He rocked his hips as he leaned forward, resting his weight on his forearms. Their kisses were unrelenting and hungry. "More, wolf."

"Whatever ye wish, sparrow. I will hear ma name on yer lips." Dominic wasn't as forceful as he had been before Emelie's condition became obvious, but he ensured she received what she wanted. Her fingernails ran over his chest and abdomen, her touch inflaming him.

"Wolf!" Emelie screamed with one of the strongest climaxes Dominic had ever wrung from her. He thrust thrice more before his bollocks tightened, and his cock pulsed. He felt his seed shoot from him.

"Sparrow!" Dominic bellowed as an echo to Emelie's cry. He suspected that he and Emelie would easily rival the number of children he expected Brodie and Laurel would have. But that thought brought fear back to him as he worried about keeping Emelie alive long enough to have their first child, let alone thinking about the dangers of childbirth.

Dominic climbed back onto the bed, and they rolled to their sides and shared light kisses until Emelie dozed off. But a sharp rap on the door made her eyes spring open. Dominic glared at the closed portal. "Can our chamber nae be the one place we can come where we willna always be disturbed?"

SIXTEEN

Dominic donned his leine once more and waited for Emelie to put her chemise to rights. She pulled a Campbell plaid around her shoulders as she kneeled on the bed. The wool blanket engulfed her, leaving only her head visible. He crossed the chamber and unlocked the door to find Brodie on the other side, frowning.

"Dinna give me that look. Ye were nay better before Laurel gave birth, and ye are already back to being nay better. Ye're fooling nay one when ye retire with yer bonnie wife every afternoon. Rick is sleeping, but Laurel isnae," Dominic glowered.

"Do ye wish to ken what I learned from Wallace or nae?" Brodie hissed. Dominic looked back at Emelie, who listened attentively. Brodie whispered, "Ye dinna want her seeing him. Laurel has a sturdy stomach, but I worry even she will be ill if she sees how I left him."

"Aye. Let me dress. Where is he?"

"Dungeon. He's next door to our guest," Brodie explained. He shut the door to let Dominic dress and speak to Emelie.

"Lock the door while I'm gone, Em. I'm going

down to the dungeon with Brodie. He spoke to Wallace."

"I'm guessing he did far more than just talk if he doesn't want me to know."

"He has. He willna let Laurel see him, either. I dinna ken that he will survive whatever Brodie doled out." Dominic pulled Emelie into his arms.

"Dom, your heart is racing. I can feel it pounding."

"Em, Brodie was too calm for this to be aboot Laurel," Dominic stated.

"Oh." Emelie couldn't think of anything else to say.

"If ye're in agreement, I will speak to Father Lonergan aboot posting the banns."

"The sooner the better," Emelie agreed.

"Get dressed. Put what ye need in a satchel. Depending on what Wallace says, we may sail tonight. We may nae wait to see if aught happens from announcing our intentions." Dominic kissed Emelie before stepping away to pleat and wrap his plaid. Emelie marveled at the process and hoped one day she would be proficient and could help fold the even pleats. "Ye make it mighty hard to leave."

"I ken I make it mighty hard," Emelie jested. Dominic caught her in his arms and gave her bottom a playful tap.

"Be ready to go once the sun sets, Em. I dinna like the idea of leaving, but I've finally accepted that it might be necessary. I love ye, sparrow."

"I love you, wolf. I'll be ready."

Dominic gave Emelie a peck on her nose, then joined Brodie in the passageway. "Ye should ken Emelie's agreed to marry me. When we're through with Wallace, I will speak to Father Lonergan aboot posting the banns." Dominic stopped and pressed his hand against Brodie's chest to make him halt as well.

"Tell me now what Wallace is likely to tell me. Dinna let it be a surprise. Depending on what he's said, I may take Emelie to the hunting cabin."

Brodie nodded as he studied his younger brother. He'd witnessed the changes in his brother since Emelie arrived, and he believed his brother was better for it. No longer was he a lovesick pup following around a woman he was infatuated with. The man who stood before Brodie was the same fierce warrior he'd known since the first time Dominic rode into battle beside him. But now he also saw the level-headed, shrewd man he'd prayed Dominic would become. His devotion to Emelie only made him wiser and more mature, and Brodie was proud of him.

"Wallace doesnae ken who is behind all of this. The mon we have has been feeding Wallace information aboot Emelie, but from what I can tell none of it is true. This invisible enemy's made Wallace believe Emelie is a threat to the clan and needs chasing away or killing. The mon is more gullible than any I have ever met. I believe he's a wee dimwitted."

"It's only aboot Emelie then," Dominic surmised. Brodie nodded before they made their way down to the dungeon. Dominic peeked through the metal bars at the man they captured, but he continued to the next cell, where he found Wallace chained to the wall. His arms were stretched above him, and his head lolled from side to side. He was in a worse condition than the prisoner next door. Brodie had beaten Wallace within an inch of his life. Dominic glanced at his brother.

"He let me think Laurie was the target for too long," Brodie shrugged.

Dominic spotted a bucket of stale water. He tossed it at Wallace, reviving him enough for the chained man to lift his head. Dominic grabbed a fistful of Wallace's hair and pulled his head up, but he kept his hold light. He slapped Wallace's cheeks until the man's vision cleared, and Dominic believed he would get true, understandable answers to his questions.

"I'm certain the laird has asked ye many questions already, but I would hear it maself." Dominic also wanted to be certain that Wallace's answers matched whatever he told Brodie. "Who's the mon next door?"

"Maxwell," Wallace grunted.

"He's a Maxwell, or that's his Christian name?"

"Christian name," Wallace choked, then spat a wad of blood between Dominic and Brodie. "I didna ask his surname, and he doesnae wear a plaid."

"How much did he pay ye?" Dominic asked.

"Nae nearly enough for all this," Wallace grumbled.

"Ye had to ken this would be yer fate," Dominic pointed out.

"I'm doing the clan a favor. Ye brought a whore into our midst. Again."

"I dinna need to talk to ye. I can just go by what ma brother tells me. If ye wish to die with some honor left, then dinna speak aboot ma wife like that."

"She is a whore. She was tupping some mon at court. Do ye even ken if that bairn is yers?"

Dominic's gut clenched as his chest swelled with rage. Wallace was far too close to the truth. "Who have ye been blathering such nonsense to?"

"Ye dinna claim they're nae lies."

"They're too ridiculous to believe," Dominic countered. "Who have ye been talking to?"

"Walter, ma parents."

"Anyone outside yer family?"

"Nay. The mon swore he'd kill me if I told anyone. He doesnae trust me that much."

"Rightfully so if ye told yer family. I suppose ye dinna care if he kills them, too," Brodie mused.

"He doesnae ken who ma family is, Laird."

"Ye daft bugger. If he kenned ye're more gullible than a blind sheep, then he kens plenty aboot ye," Dominic snarled. "What did he tell ye to do?"

"I was to chase Lady Emelie away, so he could get her while she traveled. I cut down the hive. She nearly saw me."

Dominic's free hand clenched, but his willpower was stronger than the temptation. If anyone beat Wallace anymore, he wouldn't be able to think or speak. "Did ye shoot the arrow?"

"Nay. That was him."

"He couldnae read the missive he carried. Who sent him?"

"Dinna ken. Same mon who gave the missive to the MacLaren, I figure. A Lowlander. Mayhap the mon isnae pleased ye're buggering his woman now," Wallace sneered.

"Ye are undoubtedly going to die. Decide how painful it will be. Tell me everything ye ken, and I will slit yer throat mercifully. Make me ask ye questions, and I will cut off yer fingers for each one. Pray I get what I want before I saw off yer twig and berries."

Wallace looked at Dominic, then shifted his gaze to Brodie, who rocked back on his heels with his arms crossed. After the punishment Brodie rained down on him, he knew the laird wouldn't suggest mercy. He was likely to give Dominic his own dirk. He knew he wasn't long for this world, so he decided he preferred the less-agonizing option.

"Like I said already, he told me Lady Emelie was a blight on our clan for her whoring ways. He said everyone at court kens aboot it, and that she would dishonor the Campbells just like Lady Colina did.

He said even the king bedded her often. He didna tell me who sent him, but they had paid him well enough to pay me. He kenned he couldnae get inside the walls, and Lady Emelie rarely leaves the keep these days. I think it's the king. I think she's bearing his royal bastard, and he doesnae want her telling anyone. She's cuckolding ye, Dom."

"The king has at least five bastards strewn across Scotland. Those are the ones he acknowledges," Dominic pointed out.

"The mon said his employer's married now, so it's different if he had any more. Mayhap it's the queen. Mayhap she's put out that her husband was fucking her lady-in-waiting."

Dominic's fist slammed into Wallace's already-broken nose. "Watch how ye speak, or I will make yer death slow."

"I'm going to die anyway," Wallace taunted. "What does it matter how?"

"It'll matter when I drag ye out to the bailey and make yer mother watch," Dominic warned.

"Ye wouldnae dare," Wallace challenged. Dominic whistled, and a guard appeared with a rattling set of rusty keys.

"Shall we test yer claim?" Dominic asked as he took the keys. He unlocked the manacles and caught Wallace as he slumped forward.

"Wait!" Wallace wheezed. "Dinna make her see. She's auld, and her heart isnae vera strong. It'll kill her."

"And yer shame willna?" Brodie asked. "Ye should have considered that moons ago when yer uncle warned ye aboot being part of the plot against Lady Campbell."

"When is the next attack?" Dominic demanded.

"I dinna ken. I was to tell Alec and Davey that ye assigned me to guard her. Now that ye have me and

255

him, I dinna ken what comes next. King Robert or Queen Elizabeth willna be satisfied until she's nay longer a Campbell. I dinna ken what happens after that."

Dominic flipped a blade from his wrist bracer and ran it across Wallace's throat. He and Brodie jumped away to avoid the splatter, and Wallace fell to the ground, already dead.

"I feel for his parents, but I dinna regret beating the maggot, and I wouldnae have stopped ye from doing worse," Brodie said as he clapped Dominic on the back. He pulled Dominic close, so his voice wouldn't echo in the cell. "We both ken he's been told lies. I dinna think anyone he told would believe such aboot Emelie. The woman is utterly in love with ye, and everyone's seen it for moons."

"That's now. What if they think she was different before she arrived here?"

"Then make sure nay one questions when ye handfasted and get to Father Lonergan sharpish. See if ye can convince him to marry ye without the banns."

"He kens of the attacks, and he will bury Wallace. He'll say this is enough proof someone is contesting our marriage already. He'll say it's as good as posting the banns and having someone speak up."

"Nay." Brodie shook his head. "He's fond of Emelie. Mayhap he already kens. Mayhap she's confessed to him." He shrugged as Dominic wiped his blade on Wallace's back. They left the dungeon without a backwards glance.

"I need to ask Emelie aboot Father Lonergan before I say aught to him."

"Are ye going to take her to the cabin?"

"I dinna think there is any other choice now. This isnae over even with this Maxwell mon locked up and Wallace dead. What if there is someone else in the clan? The best I can hope for is the priest marrying us today, and we can be off tonight." Dominic pushed hair that stuck to his brow away from his eyes.

"When ye tell Emelie what Wallace said, she'll ken what I'm certain ye already guessed."

"Aye. Pringle."

"Most likely."

"I canna keep it from her, and I willna. But it is going to upset her badly." Dominic glanced toward the keep.

"I'm tempted to send Laurel and Rick with ye. We dinna ken if it is Pringle. If it is, we dinna ken if he's even thought how far along Emelie must be. I dinna want him just giving orders to nab, or worse kill, the woman with a bairn."

"I'll take Laurel and Rick if ye wish, but I dinna think it's wise to keep them together any longer. They're more likely to both get killed. Whoever this is willna care who they strike first, and they willna leave anyone to tell the tale. Can ye get word to Monty and Donnan?"

"I dinna ken we have that much time, but I will. I'll ask them to come. It'll appear like they've come for Rick's christening. Laurel may refuse to go to Balnagown, and I dinna blame her, but her brother can take her to one of our more remote keeps. I trust him and his second." Brodie hadn't revealed even to Dominic why he trusted Donnan as much as he did Monty. It was a secret he and Laurel would likely take to the grave. Donnan and Monty were best friends as children, and their relationship grew into much more over the years. Donnan considered Laurel his sister as much as Monty did. The men would do anything to protect her and Rick.

Dominic stopped at the well in the bailey's center and pulled a full bucket over the stone enclosure. He dunked his head in before scrubbing his hands. He wiped as much blood and grime from his hands and face as he could before dumping the bucket toward the stables. The brothers entered the keep, each seeking his wife.

⁂

"Is that what Wallace believes, or what he was told?" The story Dominic recounted to Emelie stunned her.

"It's what he believes. I dinna ken if he's told anyone other than his parents and uncle. Brodie doesnae think anyone will believe him," Dominic assured her.

"I doubt the bairn will be born with russet hair, so hopefully, that will put paid to any rumors. All King Robert's bastards bear a resemblance to him," Emelie noted with a sigh. "Can we see Father Lonergan now?"

"We can. We can ask him to marry us today and argue our handfast is grounds to skip the banns. Em?"

"Yes?" Emelie's brow furrowed when she noticed his hesitation.

"I dinna like asking ye something so personal, but have ye told Father Lonergan aught in confession that would make him believe these incidents are someone's way to protest our marriage?"

"You wish to know what I've confessed?"

"Nae really. I told ye, I dinna like asking. Ye dinna need to tell me aught, but it would prepare me in case the priest argues. Dinna tell me the details of what ye've said, but please tell me enough for me to be ready."

"I haven't confessed aught to any priest aboot this. I confessed in Stirling after the first time Henry and I coupled. But I didn't after the second time. I couldn't bring myself to say I'd been such a fool twice. I have said naught to our priest here. I confessed to you, and I've done as much in my prayers. God knows my contrition, and I think we're all suffering my penance."

"Vera well. Let's see our priest aboot getting married, sparrow." Dominic offered Emelie his hand as they left their chamber. "Nudge me if you hear my brogue. Father Lonergan will know something is amiss if he hears it. He drilled Brodie and me for years not to sound what he called 'common' when we went to court. His didactic pontifications stuck with us. We learned it was easier to sound like Lowlanders than deal with him."

"He's the one who ruined your accent?" Emelie asked, aghast. "I should like to have a few words with him aboot that. Don't people think you sound pretentious?"

"I think most are used to it. He corrected us so often as children that I think people grew to prefer hearing our courtly speech than hearing Father Lonergan chastising us. Usually at the end of a switch."

"He beat you? A priest beat you?"

"No, but he threatened us. As lads, we believed him. When we were auld enough to know he would never make good on it, we were auld enough to know we shouldn't anger a mon of God."

"I'm telling you right now, Dominic. He is not changing our child's accent. If he or she sounds like you and not me, then I will have no one interfering. I like your brogue, and I wish you would speak normally. It comes out when you're upset, so I know it's what your mind is trying to tell your mouth is right."

"Aye. I ken. I ken I think with a burr. If only ye could hear ma thoughts when they're of ye," Dominic teased as he squeezed Emelie's bottom before they reached the kirk's door. They slipped inside the clan's chapel and found the priest in prayer in the front pew. The white-haired, white-bearded man turned toward them, not expecting anyone to interrupt.

"Dominic, Lady Emelie," Father Lonergan greeted them.

"Father, Lady Emelie and I would like to marry. We wish for our relationship to be binding until we meet again in Heaven," Dominic announced without preamble.

"And Laird Campbell agrees?"

"Aye. He knows we're here with you," Dominic explained.

"Then we can post the banns this Sunday," the priest beamed.

"We're hoping we can forego the banns. It's obvious Lady Emelie is with child, and we handfasted moons ago."

"Church doctrine says," Father Lonergan started.

"Father," Emelie spoke up. "I don't think church doctrine knows that much aboot handfasting. Since it's a trial marriage, anyone could speak up during the year to give reason a couple shouldn't marry for good. We handfasted over five moons ago. That must be equivalent to at least twenty sennights of posting the banns."

"My lady, I don't know how our laird and our tánaiste came to find such brilliant women, but I am certainly relieved you are on our side."

Emelie wasn't convinced the priest was that thrilled to have two intelligent women helping to lead the clan, but she accepted the compliment at face value and smiled. Whether or not he liked her reasoning, all they needed was for him to agree to it.

"Can we marry at sunset today?" Dominic interjected.

"Why such a rush?" Father Lonergan looked between the two. "Lady Emelie has a few months before her confinement. And the bairn will bear your name, even if you're only handfasted. You don't want the banns posted, and now you tell me you want to marry today."

"We've wanted to marry since the beginning," Dominic explained, leaving out the part that they hadn't shared those sentiments with one another until that day. "We handfasted because we didn't want to wait to post the banns in Stirling. We've been content with a handfast, and I wanted Lady Emelie to get acquainted with life in the Highlands. But we wish to marry and don't want to waste any more time." It took no effort to offer Emelie a genuine smile as he wrapped his arm around her shoulders. She turned toward him and wrapped both arms around his waist. She didn't notice her long blink or her deep sigh as she enjoyed the comfort she always found in Dominic's embrace.

"Och. There's no point in denying the pair of you. It's obvious you're a love match and have been since the day you rode in here. Truth be told, I'm surprised it's taken you this long to come to me."

"Then we can marry this eve?" Emelie asked, wanting to hear it from the priest.

"Aye. This eve. Tell the laird and lady. The clan will want to witness this, so you may as well tell poor Berta to plan a feast."

"We don't need a feast this eve," Emelie disagreed. "That is far too brief notice for Berta. We can feast tomorrow eve, or whenever Berta can have one ready. We won't be any less married tomorrow eve than we will be this eve."

"Clever, my lady," Father Lonergan nodded. The indulgent tone rankled with Emelie, and she felt Dominic tense. But he hadn't refused them, and that was all that mattered. They sought Brodie and

Laurel to share the good news. They spent the few hours remaining before sunset preparing the bride and groom. Laurel presented Emelie with another gown she'd worn to a feast a few months earlier. She'd started working on it when Brodie mentioned the couple might marry that night. Emelie marveled at how quickly Laurel worked, and she was deeply touched that Laurel had gifted her such a beautiful gown.

As the sun sank toward the western horizon, Brodie escorted Emelie down the steps and through the bailey as clan members gathered on both sides of their path. Women offered Emelie late-blooming heather and lavender, while men bowed their heads. Emelie nearly missed a step when she caught sight of Dominic standing at the base of the kirk's steps. He was freshly bathed and wore his best plaid. The brooch he'd dropped that day in the garden when the wasps attacked shone on his shoulder. He'd polished the hilt of his sword and every dagger Emelie could see. She'd helped her husband undress enough times to know there were several more where only she would find them. The thought made a grin tug at the corner of her mouth.

"You can stop that right now, lass. We all know the lascivious thoughts you have aboot one another. Ogling your husband just proves it," Brodie teased.

"And where are you looking but at your wife's breasts," Emelie mused with a giggle.

"My brother seems to be intent upon that part of you," Brodie pointed out.

"Never," Emelie scoffed quietly. "I'm just short. He has to look down to see me."

"Och, such clishmaclaver, lass. We'll make a right Highlander of ye yet." Brodie kissed Emelie's cheek and released her arm as they came to stand beside Dominic. Laurel waited to Emelie's left, and

Brodie joined her, lifting Rick from her arms. The ceremony was brief. It surprised Emelie how quickly they exchanged their vows, and Father Lonergan pronounced them married. The laird's family and those of the clan council moved inside for the wedding Mass while the clan dispersed. They would gather for the evening meal in the Great Hall in an hour.

"I can't tell you how happy I am, Em," Dominic whispered as the Mass ended. The priest announced them as man and wife, and the couple took no time to seal it with a kiss. Dominic lifted Emelie off her feet, just as he did so often when they kissed. Despite Emelie's belly between them, Dominic's long arms easily wrapped around her and kept her close. Father Lonergan cleared his throat, but no one would rush either of them. Emelie cupped Dominic's cheeks as she returned his kiss with equal tenderness and fervor.

"You can devour your bride after the evening meal," Father Lonergan grumbled. After one more long kiss, Dominic adjusted Emelie and cradled her in his arms as he carried her back to the keep.

"We will celebrate with the clan," Dominic said. "I won't rob you of that, sparrow. But when the meal ends, we will make our way to a birlinn. Garrett, Alec, Davey, and Tim will travel with us as your personal guards. I have four more men coming to sail the birlinn back. We can't have any sign that we're near the cabin."

"I'm ready. I needed little, so I packed my satchel with ease. Does the cabin sit on the water?" Emelie wondered. Dominic hesitated before he shook his head.

"It's too far to walk, and we can't take a wagon with us. Em, you'll ride in front of me on my horse." Dominic still hadn't resolved himself to making

Emelie mount a horse, but it was the only means to get them to the cabin.

"I'll be all right. Will we need to canter?"

"No." Dominic's answer was emphatic. "I don't want us moving faster than a walk. You can sleep in the birlinn while we're underway because it will take us a couple hours to get to the cabin."

"But it would only take half that time if the horses could canter," Emelie surmised.

"Whether or not it would doesn't matter. We're not going faster than a walk, Em."

"I'm not arguing, Dom. Just making an observation. I won't pretend like I know how to lead this expedition better than you. And I won't lie that riding makes me nervous. I don't even know how I'll mount the beast."

"The same way you mount me," Dominic whispered. "One leg on each side with a firm grip."

"Dom," Emelie hissed. "Do you ever stop thinking aboot coupling?"

"Not since I met you," Dominic said unrepentantly. "And you're no better."

"I know I'm not," Emelie giggled. "I think I will say the excitement exhausted me and then retire when the music starts. Don't dally. I'd like to consummate our marriage before we sail away."

"Yes, my lady. I would never deny you that right." Dominic squeezed Emelie's thigh before wrapping his arm around her shoulders. It was an unconventional wedding evening, but nothing about their relationship had been traditional. It suited them both, and they were excited to have married finally, even with a threat looming over them. They shared one dance before Emelie begged off. No one questioned the pregnant woman, and many pushed Dominic to follow her, reminding him that a husband had a duty to care for his wife. A few bawdy comments floated above the cheers, but Emelie and Dominic didn't care. They retired to their chamber, passing the next three hours ensuring no one would doubt they'd made their marriage binding.

An hour after the Great Hall grew quiet, Dominic and Emelie met Brodie and Laurel in the upstairs solar. Keeping their voices low, the laird and lady wished the newlyweds well a second time over. Then Dominic and Emelie made their way through the postern gate and down the path to the bay where they boarded a birlinn. Nothing stirred, not even the night air. The eeriness made a shiver zip along Emelie's spine, and when she chanced a glance at Dominic, she knew he felt the same. Once they pushed them away from the coast, the breeze filled the sails. When Kilchurn was out of sight, the men dipped their oars into the water and propelled them southwest toward their hideout.

SEVENTEEN

Dominic hoisted Emelie onto his horse before he climbed on behind her. He wrapped his arms around her and encouraged her to lean back. She didn't hesitate and was soon asleep again. She'd fallen fast asleep as she sat beside Dominic in the boat's hull. Her plaid covered her hair, which shone in the moonlight. Petite as she was, no one outside the boat could see her, but she was a target now that she rode with Dominic. He looked down frequently to ensure she was warm enough and that her hair remained covered. There would be no confusing her for anyone other than her sisters, and they were nowhere near Campbell territory.

The wind picked up an hour after the party mounted their steeds. It gusted around them and made it difficult for the horses to plod along the path. They wouldn't have been able to move faster than a walk if they wanted. But the wind also disguised the surrounding sounds, and that set Dominic's nerves on edge. He struggled to hear any of nature's sounds beyond the whistle of the wind. He tried to discern if there were any manmade noises coming from someone who wasn't part of their group. The more he strained, the less he seemed to hear. However, his senses told him something was amiss.

"We pull off the road," Dominic ordered. He roused Emelie with a gentle shake. "Sparrow, we're going to stop for a moment. Stay mounted."

"What's wrong?" Emelie murmured.

"I don't know. Probably naught, but I want the men in the rear to check. I just have an unsettled feeling. The moon and stars are keeping the path visible, but the wind is making it hard to tell what surrounds us." Dominic climbed down but kept a hold of the horse's bridle. He gave his orders and watched as three men backtracked, while the others spread out to surround him and Emelie. It relieved him that he'd told the men sailing the birlinn back to remain with the party until they reached the cabin. Now he had men to scout and men to protect Emelie.

It was only a matter of minutes before a tree crashed to the ground ahead of them. The noise made his horse shift, but Dominic had trained the beast for battle, so little spooked him. Dominic's head whipped in the tree's direction as men appeared. He knew before he saw them that it was no accident. Their unknown assailants felled the tree to block their way. He moved to mount, when his three scouts raced back toward them with mounted warriors chasing them. The strangers launched their attack without hesitation, the two groups closing in on the Campbells.

"Em, can ye ride alone?" Dominic asked Emelie.

"Yes. But where do I go?" Emelie wondered.

"Through the trees until ye can get past them. Dinna stop until ye reach the end of the woods. Veer to the left, and ye'll find a rock formation. Hide among the standing stones," Dominic explained. "Go."

"What aboot you? There's too many," Emelie worried.

"Dinna fash, sparrow. I'll be there right behind ye," Dominic encouraged. Emelie didn't believe him. It terrified her that this might be the last time she would see her husband alive. "Ye have the extra dirks I gave ye. Dinna hesitate to use them like yer father showed ye. If in doubt and ye canna get away, fight first, ask questions later."

"I love you, wolf."

"Nearly as much as I love ye, sparrow. Now go." Dominic slapped his horse's rump when he was certain Emelie had a firm hold of the reins. He trusted his steed as much as he did any man in his clan's army. The beast had kept him alive countless times, and he prayed the destrier would do the same for Emelie. He angled himself to combat an attack from his left as he watched Emelie disappear into the trees to his right.

Emelie clung to the reins and leaned forward, protecting her belly from the branches that tried to pull her plaid from her shoulders. She tucked her arms in as best she could, hoping to make a smaller target and to keep anyone from aiming at her babe. As desperately as she wanted to, she didn't look back for Dominic. She remained focused, weaving through the trees. She moved further into the woods as she approached the opposing force that cut down the tree to block their way. When she was certain she was past them, she moved closer to the road. It was nearly pitch black in most parts of the woods, and it was virtually impossible to see. She trusted Dominic's horse had superior night vision to hers.

When Emelie feared testing her theory any longer, she moved to the side of the road. She peeked over her shoulder, but saw no one. She steered the horse back onto the road but regretted it the moment she did so. Without the surrounding trees to buffer the sound, she realized she was much closer to the fight than she thought. She tugged the right rein to guide the horse back into the trees, but the animal screamed and stomped. Emelie looked down and found an arrow protruding from its hindquarter. Before she could think what to do, two men raced toward her on foot. Their swords raised toward her, Emelie tried to turn Dominic's horse. But the battle-trained animal reared, ready to attack the approaching men with his hooves.

Emelie didn't expect the horse to bring its front hooves up and paw the air. Her center of gravity wasn't what she was used to now that she was pregnant. She felt herself flying backwards as she gripped the horse's flanks with her thighs and clung to the reins. Tugging back on them only made the horse rear more. With another scream, she tumbled from the horse. She landed hard on her back, and a searing pain burned through her side and lower back. She tried to suck in air, but her lungs wouldn't cooperate. As she lay on the ground gasping, she felt her kirtle grow wet.

"No," Emelie whimpered as air finally filled her lungs. "No." She wrapped her arms around her belly and tried to roll to her side, but the pain stole the little breath she'd caught.

"Emelie!" Dominic roared. She couldn't move to see how close he was. Pain ripped through her belly, making her want to curl into a ball. But she still couldn't move to her side without being in even more agony.

"Dom," Emelie cried, but little sound left her mouth. She squeezed her eyes shut as something leaped over her and crashed to the ground. She

269

peeked out of one eye and found Dominic near her feet. He'd jumped over her and launched himself at a man drawing close to her. She clenched her eyes closed once more, but not before she saw Dominic drive what appeared like a small boulder into the man's head. He pushed himself to his feet in time to swing his sword and cut down the second man who'd attempted to attack Emelie. The man fell onto his back with Dominic's sword still buried in him.

"Emelie!" Dominic fell to his knees beside her. "Where are ye hurt?"

"Everywhere," Emelie sobbed. "I'm going to lose the bairn. My gown is all wet, and it's too soon. Dom." The last word was wrenched from the depths of her soul.

Dominic lifted Emelie into his arms, feeling where her gown was soaked in the back. He looked down, but he could see little in the dark. His men fought with a tenacity he hadn't seen before as they worked together to defeat the men who attacked from behind before they pushed their way through the forward attackers. He'd heard Emelie's screams. He'd prepared to find her dead. Rage unlike anything he'd dreamed a human could possess overcame him. He launched himself at the first man within reach, crushing his head with a rock in one swing. He ran the other man through, turning toward Emelie before he even fully withdrew his sword.

"Hold on, Em." Dominic didn't know what to do. He understood Emelie was right, that it was too soon for the bairn to be born and survive, so he doubted he could do anything for their child. But he would do everything he could to keep Emelie alive. His mind raced as he tried to decide what would be better: take her to the cabin, which was closer than Kilchurn, or risk the journey back to Kilchurn, knowing Nora would tend to Emelie. He could only accept the choice that gave Emelie the greatest chance of surviving.

"Your horse," Emelie whispered. Dominic looked down at his wife, but her eyes were closed. He glanced at his steed and spotted the arrow shaft sticking out of its rump. It wasn't the first time someone had shot the animal. Dominic felt guilty knowing it likely wasn't the last. But he wasn't sure he could ride the beast, and he was certain he and Emelie couldn't ride the mount together. Emelie was far lighter than him, but he feared she'd topple from the horse if he didn't hold her.

"Cut two poles from the tree," Dominic ordered as he jutted his chin toward the trunk that laid across the road. "Sturdy enough to bear Lady Emelie's weight. I need yer spare plaids."

The Campbells understood Dominic's intentions and set to work cutting the wood needed to create a stretcher with their battle axes. The men worked efficiently and placed the plaids in overlapping layers between the two poles. Dominic eased Emelie onto the makeshift stretcher and tied the plaids around her. He had to take his chances with his own horse, since it would only slow them down further if he shared a mount with another warrior. All the horses were sturdy, but so were the men. It would be a hefty burden for any mount. He ordered Alec to bear the opposite end of the stretcher across his horse's back. They tied it to their saddles and to their waists with the rope they always traveled with. His father taught Brodie and him to always have rope when they went into the mountains. The brothers had adopted the habit of always having lengths with them and demanded their men do the same. The habit had come in handy countless times, just as it did now.

"Dom?" Emelie gasped. Dominic brushed hair from her face and neck as they began a slow trek back to the birlinn. "It hurts, but naught is happening. I don't know what to do."

"Neither do I, Em. We're going back to Kilchurn and Nora," Dominic responded.

"I don't think our bairn will live that long. The pain is—" Emelie moaned as the stretcher jostled. "I can barely breathe."

"Stay with me, sparrow. I need ye," Dominic whispered as Emelie's eyes drifted closed. His heart lurched as he feared he was watching his wife die.

"I'm alive, wolf," Emelie whispered. "Just hurts so much."

Emelie struggled to stay awake, passing in and out of consciousness. Dominic supposed it was a small mercy that she wasn't awake for the bumpy ride back to the birlinn or the swells that crashed against the hull. When they arrived at Kilchurn's dock, Alec bolted from the boat to find Nora, and Garrett raced to the keep to rouse Aggie, Laurel, and Brodie. Davey and Tim helped Dominic carry the stretcher into the keep and up the stairs to Dominic's chamber.

"Dom?" Emelie whispered.

"We're home, Em. Nora and Laurel will be here in a moment. Ye'll be all right."

"Still hurts, but still naught's happened. I don't understand. My gown is even wetter than before, but the bairn isn't moving. I don't know if my body can get him out." Emelie felt the panic rising in her chest as she thought about the child she was certain no longer lived within her. She feared she would die trying to give birth, or that she would die from not being able to give birth. "I need to hold your hand."

"We're almost to our chamber, sparrow. As soon as ye're off the stretcher, I'm nae letting go," Dominic promised. Davey helped Dominic ease Emelie onto the bed while Tim lit the fire and candles. The three men steeled themselves against the sight of Emelie on the bed. With plenty of light to illuminate the room, it was clear blood soaked Emelie's gown. The men looked at Dominic before grabbing the stretcher and leaving the couple to a few moments of privacy.

"What happened?" Nora demanded as she stormed into the chamber. "Bluidy hell."

Dominic stared at Nora before reaching for Emelie, horrified that Nora's reaction would only make Emelie feel worse.

"Get her out of her gown and let me see her wound," Nora barked at Dominic as Laurel and Brodie arrived. When they spied Emelie, Laurel pushed past Brodie and Dominic. She pulled a dirk from her pocket and began ripping Emelie's kirtle down the middle. Nora glanced at the men. "Dinna stand there. Get me hot water, linens, and get Aggie in here."

Brodie spun around, happy to leave the chamber while his wife undressed his sister-by-marriage. He went in search of Aggie. Dominic bellowed to a maid to fetch the water before he went in search of more linens.

"Nora," Emelie croaked.

"Aye, lass. I shall get ye all mended."

"The bairn is dead. You can't mend that."

"What makes ye think that?" Nora paused to look at Emelie.

"Dom's horse threw me. I felt my waters. It soaked my gown. The bairn hasn't moved." Emelie fought to get every sentence out.

"Lass, I dinna think ye're waters broke. It doesnae look or smell right to be the birthing fluids. It's blood ye felt, but it doesnae soak all yer skirts. The bairn's probably been a bit rattled aboot and is trying to stay in one place. Mayhap he's even sleeping until all this upset is over."

"Nora, don't lie to me," Emelie warned.

"Ma lady, I dinna lie. If I thought ye or yer bairn were dying, I would tell ye so. I'd tell ye to say yer last goodbyes to yer kin." Nora looked at Laurel. "Help me get this gown off her. I need to find where the bleeding is from."

Laurel helped Nora ease the mangled gown from Emelie's arms. "Nora, over here. Look." Laurel pointed to a long cut in the fabric. She slid her fingers along Emelie's ribs until Emelie screamed, and Laurel's fingers came away bloody. "Emelie, did someone stab you?"

"No." Emelie looked between Laurel and Nora in confusion. "Dom's horse reared when two men approached. He was ready to fight, but I couldn't keep my seat. I fell off. When I hit the ground, all I felt was the worst pain I've ever experienced, and I couldn't catch my breath. Everything got tight, but it hurt more when I tried to roll on my side."

"This sheath is empty," Laurel said as she held up the belt that had kept Emelie's arisaid in place. "Did you have a dirk in here?"

"Yes. It must have fallen out when the horse threw me."

"Let us have a look," Nora said as she bustled around the side of the bed. With a touch gentler than Emelie expected, Nora shifted Emelie and looked at where the ripped material had been. "Och, a blade's sliced ye deep."

"I'm telling you, no one came close enough."

"Emelie, where did you wear your knife on your belt?" Laurel asked.

"It was over my right hip, but I pushed it aside when I had to ride alone. I was leaning over the horse to protect my belly and to stay on."

"Did you push it around to your back?" Laurel asked. She watched Emelie and realized that the injured woman's mind wasn't working as quickly as it normally did. "Em, where was the blade when you were falling?"

"Right here." Emelie reached back and screamed. Her fingers accidentally pressed against her wound. Dominic burst through the door, splintering the wood and knocking it from one of its hinges.

"What happened?" Dominic demanded.

"We think it was Emelie's blade that sliced her when she fell," Laurel explained. She took Emelie's hand and squeezed gently as she looked down at her friend. "You said you pushed it around you to get it out of the way. You're certain no one else did it. It must have stabbed you when you landed."

"Aye. It would have gushed a stream at first," Nora spoke up as she prepared a basin with steaming water and various medicinal leaves and petals. "But ye're a wee heavier than ye used to be. The weight of the bairn pressing ye into the stretcher likely saved ye from bleeding to death. It didna staunch all the blood, but it slowed it. I kenned it wasna birthing waters that soaked yer gown."

"But I still havenae felt the bairn," Emelie shuddered. Dominic dropped the linens he carried and climbed on the bed beside Emelie. Her eyes drifted closed as Dominic settled beside her. "No shoes on the bed. Disgusting."

"Aught ye want, *mo chridhe, mo ghaol.*" Dominic yanked his boots off with one tug on each.

"You know I don't speak Gaelic," Emelie whispered, suddenly overwhelmed with fatigue now that Dominic lay beside her, and she felt safe again.

"My heart, my love," Dominic murmured against her ear. He watched Nora and Laurel, not understanding what was happening. He tried to work through Laurel's explanation. He hadn't seen a dirk where Emelie lay on the ground, but it could have been there in the dark. He'd only felt the wet gown. He hadn't thought to examine it or her arisaid. He pointed to Emelie's plaid that he'd pulled off when he moved her to the bed. "Let me see."

Dominic shifted to hold it up, and there was a clean cut through the wool. Laurel held up the piece of Emelie's gown that had a matching slit. He always kept his dirks sharp enough to kill, and one had almost stolen his wife and child's lives. Nora moved beside Laurel, as Laurel and Dominic eased Emelie onto her side. Her eyes flew open as she buried her face against Dominic's chest to muffle her scream. Her fingers bit into his arms, but he accepted the pain if it helped Emelie relieve some of hers. Nora cleaned the wound before she went back to her medicinals basket.

"I need to stitch the wound. It's vera deep. It doesnae look infected, but I canna be certain it willna become so. I got all the fibers out and cleaned it as best I could. I'll pack it with yarrow," Nora explained. "Ma lady, have ye had a wound stitched before?"

Emelie shook her head as she clung to Dominic. His hand pressed the back of her head, holding her closer, knowing she was about to endure even more pain. He wasn't certain how much more his tiny wife's body could manage. He didn't dare ask about the babe, and at the moment, he only cared that Emelie lived. He knew they would feel different soon enough, but he couldn't think beyond keeping her alive.

Dominic thought Emelie passed out when Nora began stitching. She didn't move or make a sound. But when he looked down, he noticed her eyes were open, and she clenched her jaw. She'd dived deep into herself and found resolve that was seeing her through the excruciating pain. When Nora finished, Emelie's eyes drifted closed, but he was certain she wasn't asleep.

"Lady Laurel, place a pillow beneath Lady Emelie's shoulder and another beneath her arse. I need to roll her back to examine her belly, but I dinna want any pressure on her wound. It'll bleed again if it's pressed on." Laurel rushed to follow Nora's instructions. Dominic watched Emelie as the women adjusted her, and her eyes opened. Her gaze appeared sightless, and she made no sounds as Nora and Laurel positioned her. When Nora pressed against her belly, she didn't look to see what Nora was doing. Dominic turned panicked eyes toward Laurel.

"She's in shock, Dom. She's reached the point where she can't handle any more right now. Let her rest," Laurel whispered.

Dominic nodded as he returned his gaze to Emelie. He kissed her forehead, but she didn't react. He gathered his courage and turned his head to watch Nora. He'd seen the same determined look on the old woman's face throughout his life. The last time he'd seen it was when she struggled to find a cure for his mother. No one knew at the time that Colina was poisoning her. Nora had tried everything she knew to save Dominic's mother. He wasn't certain whether he appreciated seeing the same expression now. He reached out his hand and laid it on Emelie's belly.

Nora poked and prodded in several places before she pressed heavily just below Emelie's breasts. Dominic felt the quick succession of angry kicks and punches. Emelie turned glassy eyes toward him as she tried to focus. When she finally registered the sensations, her hands covered Dominic's, and she burst into tears.

"Yer bairn is alive and kicking, just as her da will tell ye. I'd say it's a lass with a temper like that." Nora smiled. Emelie's mind flashed to the wheat from all those months ago. She wouldn't correct Nora. She was too ecstatic to feel the babe kick to care what the babe's gender was. "Ye're going to be on bedrest likely for the rest of yer time, ma lady. It'll take several sennights for yer wound to heal. I canna see inside ye to ken what damage might have been done to yer bairn's little home. If ye dinna bleed between yer legs and yer waters dinna break, ye should be all right if ye stay abed."

"Whatever you say, Nora. I'll do whatever you tell me," Emelie swore.

"A wee piece of bad news for ye both." Dominic grasped Emelie's hand, and she gripped it with a strength that surprised Dominic. "Ye canna be pawing at one another until Lady Emelie's wound heals, and I can take out the stitches. After that, her condition will limit what ye can do. I'm afraid yer past fears have come true, Dom. But that doesnae mean ye canna still enjoy one another."

"That is the least of ma concerns," Dominic muttered. He freed his hand from Emelie's and cupped her cheek. "Ma only concern is ma wife and bairn are alive. I have years ahead of me to chase ma wife around this chamber."

"Who says I won't be chasing you?" Emelie whispered.

"Ye willna because I'll never run from ye, only to ye. For the rest of our lives, Em. I love ye."

"I love you, wolf. I never feel safer or happier than when I'm with you." Emelie brushed a thick curl back from Dominic's brow. "Will you hold me while I sleep? Now that I know our bairn is safe, and

I'm not in so much pain, all I want is to sleep for a month of Sundays."

"That isnae a bad idea. Let me get some willow bark tea into ye, ma lady. Then ye and Dom can sleep off tonight's trials," Nora said. She puttered around the chamber as she steeped the tea and helped Emelie drink it. She patted Emelie's shoulder and dropped a maternal kiss on the young woman's head. Laurel bent over and embraced Emelie, careful not to disturb the position she was in since she was finally comfortable. When Dominic and Emelie were alone, she pulled Dominic in for a passionate kiss. He adjusted the blankets, but when he leaned forward to kiss Emelie again, he discovered her light snores.

EIGHTEEN

It was a sennight before Emelie could leave her bed to perform the most basic tasks such as take a sponge bath and use the chamber pot. Nora checked on her twice a day, pleased with how her wound was healing. It defied reason, but Emelie never developed a fever, despite how long her wound went untended. She had little appetite, but she forced herself to eat for her babe's sake. Dominic and Laurel took turns keeping Emelie company in the mornings, and Dominic continued to dedicate his afternoons to his wife. She slept most of the time, so he completed correspondence Brodie assigned him. He took all his meals with her and only left the chamber when Emelie shooed him away when his duties as tánaiste demanded his attention.

After a fortnight, Emelie wanted nothing more than to leave her chamber. She'd convinced Laurel and Dominic that she didn't need around the clock monitoring, appreciating the solitude while no one hovered. But she wanted fresh air and sunshine. She wanted to see something besides the four walls that closed her in. Nora refused to let Emelie walk as far as the bailey, and she was adamant that Emelie not stand over five minutes at a time. Dominic resolved the battle by ordering a manservant to take Emelie's chair from the dais to the edge of the garden. He carried Emelie outside and helped her get comfortable with a blanket wrapped around her. The autumn air had a brisk chill to it, hinting at winter.

"MacLeod approaching from the south!" A guardsman called from the battlements. Emelie looked at Dominic, but he appeared as puzzled as she. They watched a man ride into the bailey and look around. When he spied Emelie and Dominic, he hurried toward them.

"Micheil," Emelie greeted him. "What's happened to Blythe?"

Emelie assumed the only reason a MacLeod from Assynt, which lay to the northwest, would detour to Kilchurn was to bring a message. Emelie intuited that it involved her sister. She knew Micheil and Blythe were acquaintances, so it stood to reason that he would bring a message on his way home.

"Lady Blythe is hale. She bid me deliver this missive," Micheil explained as he looked at Emelie, surprised to see her in a chair outside and so pregnant. Blythe informed him that Emelie handfasted and left court, but she'd neglected to mention her sister had left pregnant. Micheil kept his thoughts to himself as he bowed to Emelie and handed her a folded parchment.

"Does she expect a response?" Emelie asked as she broke the seal.

"I don't know. I can't travel back to court. My father expects me home within a fortnight," Micheil answered. Emelie glanced at the visitor, certain she heard regret in his voice. Something flashed in his eyes, but it left too soon for Emelie to decipher it. She turned her attention to the missive, the salutation already raising an alarm in her mind.

Emmy,

HP tore through court, searching for you about a moon after you left. He received your missive and demanded to know where you were. I don't think it was because he misses you. The king informed HP that you handfasted with Dominic and went to Kilchurn. He was gone for ages, so I thought he returned home.

But he came to back to Stirling yesterday, which would be nearly a sennight from when you're reading this. He backed me into a corner and threatened you, me, and your bairn. It was Micheil who spotted us and came to my rescue. I've never seen a man so enraged.

I digress. I fear it is Dominic who reads this and not you, sister. I don't think he told anyone but the king why he searched for you. I don't think he wants anyone to ask questions about your wellbeing or a bairn's if he's done something to you, or at least tried. I only know any of this because the king summoned me to the Privy Council chamber when HP claimed he hadn't been allowed to see you. The king suggested I might have useful knowledge to help HP gain entry to Kilchurn, but I think he wished to warn me that HP still searches.

I don't want to believe you're gone, Emmy. I'm certain I would feel it in my bones if you were. But if it's Dominic who's reading this, you must know that HP is after my sister. One way or another, aught that happens is his fault.

Emmy, if you're reading this, you aren't safe. The king appeared shocked that HP went in search of you, but he did naught in front of me that leads me to think he will intervene. I regret to say it, but I don't think the king cares what happens to you or your bairn. I believe he's passed that responsibility to me.

Send a response if you can, be it yours or Dominic's.

I miss you terribly, Emmy, and I fear for you. Dominic, protect my sister if she lives.

Devotedly your sister,

Blythe

Emelie read the letter twice. It was on rare occasions that Blythe addressed Emelie by the pet name

Isa gave her when they were all young. The last time Blythe called her Emmy was just before she left Stirling, and it had been years before that. Her hand shook as she passed the missive to Dominic. She looked at Micheil, who watched her. His expression gave nothing away, but she knew he was aware of some of the missive's contents since he'd found Henry intimidating Blythe.

"Did he touch her?" Emelie kept her voice low, careful not to name names.

"Nay. He would have strangled her had I not rounded the corner from the lists when I did. It was the middle of the day, but he backed her into a corner. It was pure coincidence that I was there, but I will be forever grateful that I was," Micheil explained.

"Were they arguing?" Emelie pressed.

"They must have been, but he was only threatening Lady Blythe when I arrived. I told him that if he wished to kill someone by strangulation, he should know it's a slow death. He didn't appreciate me demonstrating on his throat. He'd best hope he's sired an heir off his wife because he may not after my boot met his cods."

"Blythe's safe? Is he still there?" Emelie demanded.

"He left just before I did." Micheil shifted his gaze to Dominic. "I followed him toward here. He and his men camped about fifteen leagues from here to the southeast. I passed him two days ago."

Emelie shifted her attention to Dominic, and her gut clenched. She'd seen her husband's fierce appearance before, but the look he possessed as he listened to Micheil was unlike anything she'd imagined. Gone was the doting husband and eager father-to-be. Gone was the calm, trained warrior. She read vengeance in Dominic's expression, and she feared he wouldn't cease pursuing Henry even if it killed him. She made to rise from her chair, but Dominic's gaze swung to her. It softened, but his command was clear.

"Sit," Dominic growled. Micheil shifted toward Emelie, but she waved her hand at him.

"The missive is upsetting, to say the least. And I'm to be on bedrest right now. I begged Dom to bring me outside. He's worried for me, not angry at me," Emelie explained. "Dom, I think we need to go inside."

Dominic nodded before he eased Emelie into his arms as though he feared she would break. She sagged against his chest, terror still making her heart pound. She was apprehensive for her babe, Dominic, Blythe, and herself. She needed Brodie and Laurel to talk sense into Dominic before he dumped her in their chamber and raced off.

"Bring the chair. You're coming inside, anyway. Brodie needs to know." Dominic's terse words made Micheil scowl, but he nodded and brought the chair with him as he followed the couple into the keep. Micheil moved toward the dais as Dominic strode to the stairs. Brodie poked his nose out from his solar, but Dominic maintained his course. He would not shut Emelie into their chamber and make decisions for her.

"Brodie!" Emelie called out. "Stop him from doing something foolish."

"Emelie," Dominic warned.

"No. You are not locking me away in our chamber, then hying off to get revenge. You'll get yourself killed."

"I'm not racing off anywhere. You need to rest."

"Don't tell me what I need, Dominic. I'm not the one acting like an impetuous child. What I need is for my husband to live. If you take me up those stairs, you'd best be taking me to the solar. I will crawl if I have to, but you are not sticking me in our chamber."

Dominic couldn't miss the resolve on Emelie's face, and he didn't doubt she would crawl if she had to. He switched directions and walked toward Brodie's solar. Brodie recognized Micheil, who trailed behind.

"MacLeod, what brings you here?"

"I brought a missive from Lady Blythe," Micheil answered.

"I will have our housekeeper bring you food and drink. Laurel will see to a chamber if you wish to spend the night."

"He's coming with us. I have questions he will answer," Dominic cut in. Emelie prayed Micheil had answers because she wasn't certain Dominic's temper could withstand any more frustration.

"Should I get Laurie?" Brodie asked as he looked at the couple now standing before him.

"Yes," Emelie responded.

"I'm already here," Laurel said from behind Micheil. "I heard we had a guest. Welcome, Micheil."

"Lady Campbell, you look well. That's a healthy lad you have." Micheil waggled his eyebrows at Rick, who kicked his legs and grabbed a hank of Laurel's hair in response. She had him fastened to her back with a plaid tied around them. The two couples and Micheil retreated to Brodie's solar. Dominic thrust the now-crumpled missive at his brother. Laurel stood beside her husband as they read it together. Matching looks of shock turned toward Emelie and Dominic.

"Laurie," Brodie warned.

"What?" Laurel snapped, her eyes narrowing at her husband.

"You're a wee avenging angel when your loved

ones are in danger. You're also a mama now. You're staying with Emelie. She needs you more," Brodie whispered, but the others heard him.

"Bring Henry back here," Laurel muttered.

"On a skewer," Brodie offered.

"No one is going anywhere until Micheil tells us aught he saw of Henry's men and camp," Emelie declared. Micheil stepped forward, wanting the conversation over so he could be on his way.

"He's traveling with only a half-dozen men. He knows his way here with ease. It makes me think he's already spent time near or on your land. He camped near a thicket that someone would only find if they scouted a hiding place. We camped upwind of them, but my men and I sneaked as close as we dared. I don't know if they sensed someone followed them, but they were all vigilant."

"Why involve yourself?" Brodie asked, suspicion lacing his tone.

"Because Henry threatened Lady Blythe. I trust him not at all," Micheil replied.

"Bluidy hell," Emelie muttered. She looked at Dominic. "Do you remember the night we were dancing, and I wanted to leave because I recognized a Pringle coming toward us? That's the man you have in the dungeon. I recognize him now."

"I remember. I hadn't seen his face at court," Dominic stated. He looked at Brodie. "We left no one alive on the road. That means Henry had more men at some point. He could have watched the entire bluidy melee, then run back to court. Five days each way. That matches with when Blythe wrote the missive to Emelie and the time it took Micheil to ride here."

"Blythe wrote that Henry claimed he wasn't allowed to see me. Does he think I died during the attack? Why would he come back again?" Emelie wondered. "Did Blythe tell you aught more?"

"No, my lady. I don't know why Henry searches for you. That's not my business," Micheil hedged.

"What happened after you got Blythe away from him?" Emelie pressed.

"Naught. I ensured she was safe and escorted her to the queen's solar, where she was headed before Henry accosted her," Micheil stated. Emelie sensed far more happened, but she suspected it had nothing to do with her or her situation. It was something between Micheil and her sister.

"Is there aught else you can tell us about Henry's camp or that you've seen?" Dominic inquired.

"He was in a hurry to get here. He pushed his horses hard some days, but it only exhausted them sooner. He didn't get here any faster than he would have, had he not nearly ridden them into the ground." Micheil glanced at Dominic before looking at Emelie. "When Henry arrived at court this last time, I believe he sought your sister before he even sought his chamber. I know King Robert summoned Lady Blythe to meet with him while Henry was in the Privy Council chamber, too. The anger I saw in Henry when I found him with Lady Blythe didn't match the jovial mon he pretended to be when he wasn't cornering her. He was the mon I saw with Lady Blythe when he rode out of Stirling."

"If he threatened Blythe, it could have been to ensure she told no one that he might be to blame once word reached court that I was dead," Emelie reasoned. "Or he knew before he reached Stirling that I was still alive, and he threatened Blythe because he thought she knew something he didn't."

"I doubt we will solve this riddle until we have him," Dominic said as he absentmindedly stroked Emelie's hair from where he stood behind her chair.

He watched her rub her belly, uncertain if she did so to assure herself that all would be fine or if knowing her babe was well calmed her. She turned to look back at him.

"What're you going to do?" Emelie asked.

"I know which thicket Micheil described. He may or may not still be there. I won't assume he only has six men. He may have men he was meeting there or somewhere closer to here. Obviously, they tracked us once we were off the birlinn." Dominic looked at Brodie and Laurel. "Who else knew we left that night? There were men ahead of us on the road, and we saw no one sailing behind us. I didn't think of this sooner, but someone knew where we were going and told Henry or his men."

"Only the men who sailed with you," Brodie answered.

"I told no one," Laurel added. "That means one of them got word to Henry."

"I'm taking you to our chamber, Em. Laurel, will you come and stay with Emelie, please?" Laurel nodded, but Emelie opened her mouth to argue. Dominic lowered his voice, thick with emotion. "I ken ye want to ken what's happening. I will never leave here without telling ye that I'm going. But ye have been out of bed too long. I can see shadows forming under yer eyes. Ye need to rest. Yer mind is willing, but yer body isnae able. Brodie and I must see to the men. We need to ken who betrayed us." Dominic leaned farther forward until he whispered in Emelie's ear. "I dinna need Micheil hearing this. We need to ken if our men's involvement has aught to do with Graham wanting to be laird, or if this is just aboot ye."

Emelie nodded, not having considered that there might be a bigger issue at hand. If this was connected to Graham and Colina's plot, then they weren't the only treasonous members of the clan. It was a far greater matter than any of them may have known. While Graham was no longer alive to assume the lairdship, there might be clan members embittered by that or who supported Graham's claim that Brodie shouldn't be laird.

With her concession, Dominic scooped her into his arms. While Dominic and Emelie headed to the stairs, Laurel offered to arrange for a guest chamber for Micheil, but he declined. It was clear he didn't want to linger and get further involved in the Campbells' affairs than he already was. Emelie bid him farewell as Dominic carried her abovestairs.

Once Emelie settled into bed, she felt the remnants of her energy drain away. Dominic had been right that she needed rest. She'd known it before he said anything, but she had wanted to miss none of the conversation. Too many things were whirling around her, beyond her control. She didn't want to be left in the dark.

"Em, I likely won't leave until morn. This won't be a quick conversation to discover who's been spying for Henry. Obviously, Wallace wasn't the only one involved. I suspect Wallace and whoever this other person is didn't know they were both working for Henry. I also need to visit our prisoner."

"I don't think I can stay awake much longer," Emelie said just before she yawned.

"Rest, *mo chridhe*. When I return, we can sup together, then decide on middle names for our bairn. Nic is growing on me."

"I don't like Emma any more than I did before." Emelie yawned again, but she decided that she would tell Dominic about the ancient prediction that said they were having a son. Emelie shifted further under the covers as her eyes slid shut. She was asleep before Laurel arrived and didn't hear Dominic leave.

Dominic and Brodie had an unsuccessful visit with the imprisoned Pringle. The man knew no more than he'd already told them. Henry sent him to recruit someone in the Campbell clan to try to scare Emelie away. When Dominic confronted him about a second man, he shrugged and said he figured Henry arranged for more than one spy in case the Campbells captured one of his men.

Dominic met the men who sailed with him, the four men he'd brought to sail the boat and return it to Kilchurn, plus the men he'd tasked months ago to be Emelie's personal guards. They met in confidence in Brodie's solar, where Dominic told them he and Emelie were leaving again. This time they would sail to Fraoch Eilean, a small island in Loch Awe that had a Campbell keep on it. It would take less than a half an hour to reach it.

Dominic and Brodie stood together at the parapet and looked out to the land on the other side of the postern gate. It was gloaming, and just enough light remained for them to see. Tucked in the shadows, they were unnoticeable to anyone who didn't stand within a few feet. They watched as the postern gate swung open, and a man stepped through. Dominic was certain he would be ill. He watched Alec, a man he'd trusted his entire life, look around. Alec moved into the retaining wall's shadow and leaned back. From their position, the brothers could still see him. Dominic's fists burned as he clenched them.

Just as Dominic was about to run down the steps and confront Alec, another man approached from the right. Whoever it was wore a plaid and had likely come from the front gate. As the unidentified man passed Alec, the latter knocked the former to the ground. Alec straddled the man's chest, pinning his arms to the ground.

"Ye would betray him after everything he's done for ye." Alec's accusation floated up to the parapet. "He trusted ye. Lady Emelie gave yer family clothes and food when yer croft practically caved in after the storms. Ye repay her by helping a mon nearly kill her."

"She's a whore!"

Dominic recognized the man's voice as one of the birlinn's crew. It belonged to Stanley, one of the men he'd sparred with the day he arrived with Emelie. He'd broken Stanley's nose for insulting Emelie, but that was many months ago. Dominic thought Stanley now held a different opinion about Emelie. He was also a skilled sailor, so Dominic had assigned him to the mission. While he hadn't liked him since they were children, he'd believed he could trust the man's honor. Dominic breathed easier to know the traitor wasn't Alec, Garrett, Davey, or Tim. He believed he could still entrust Emelie's life with them.

"Call her that again," Alec warned. "And ye willna live long enough for Dominic to mete out justice. Ye have nay right to make such accusations. And even if the shite ye were shoveled were true, who the bluidy hell cares? The laird has a son now. Who cares what Lady Emelie did or didna do before she married Dom? It's nay one's business but their own. Ye ken ye willna survive this. Was it worth the coin? Was it worth the shame ye'll bring yer family? Ye will die a traitor's death. Why?"

"Graham was the auld laird's first son, the one he wanted. He should have led us," Stanley argued.

"Ye would side with a bastard taking his place as

laird, but ye would have a woman harmed for supposedly carrying one." Disgust resonated in Alec's voice. "Who is this mon?"

"I dinna ken his name. I dinna care. I ken to look for a mon with light wavy hair and green eyes," Stanley spat without thinking. He'd just let slip a valuable piece of information.

Alec rose to his feet and pulled Stanley with him. Stanley tried to break free. "I will kill ye if ye keep me from delivering ma message," Stanley warned as he drew a dirk.

"And I will kill ye if ye move even a hair," Dominic called down as he raised the bow he'd propped beside him as they waited. He had an arrow nocked and pointed at Stanley. "Ye've never kenned when to keep yer mouth shut. Now ye're going to put yer blathering to use."

Dominic and Brodie wound their way down to the ground as Alec dragged Stanley through the postern gate and shoved him at Dominic, who gave the bow to Brodie and drew his sword. Stanley kneeled before Dominic, a mutinous glare directed at the tánaiste.

"Kill me like ye did Wallace. He kenned the truth too. Yer wife is a whore!" Stanley bellowed the last sentence, drawing attention from the few people who milled around the bailey before the evening meal. Shocked whispers echoed against the retaining wall.

"I'll kill the maggot for ye, Dom," Anthony, the blacksmith, offered as he stepped away from his forge.

"Beat him," came a woman's voice.

"He brought another whore into our clan," Stanley argued.

"Ye traitor," Anthony spat. He stood with his massive forearms crossed. "I will gladly lay yer throat across ma anvil and lop off yer head. I have a new sword to test. Then I will craft the finest iron pike for Dom to stick yer head on."

"I'm nae the traitor. Dom is. He keeps bringing these bitches into our clan," Stanley seethed.

"Even if she were that vile word ye called her," Berta said as she joined the crowd, having heard the commotion in the kitchens. "What business is it of yers to judge her? We all ken how ye carry on at the alehouse. Ye're the biggest whore of them all, and yer wife, bless her, is stuck with yer ugly heid. Dinna think we dinna ken ye have two bastards of yer own."

"I'm a mon," Stanley protested. His words garnered mocking laughter.

"This clan approves of Lady Emelie and loves her. It's clear what she's done for Dom," Berta asserted. "She will make a fine mama, and Dom couldnae be more excited to be a da."

"Her bastard's father thinks differently," Stanley spat.

Berta wielded the rolling pin she'd been carrying. "Speak another lie, and I will clobber ye. Ye are a vile liar."

"I'm nae lying," Stanley whined.

"Ye are a fool. And I dinna believe for a moment that bairn isnae Dominic's. They canna keep their hands off one another. It's nay surprise she wound up with child in a flash. It wouldnae make sense if she hadnae," Alec reasoned.

"But you did betray us," Dominic interjected, schooling his temper and his accent. "You told someone outside our clan where Lady Emelie and I were going. You were aboot to do the same tonight. Except there is no trip, and we now know who the traitor is."

"Why would someone want to get rid of the whore if there wasna a reason, a secret needing keeping? Something they dinna want anyone to ken," Stanley demanded.

That made some in the crowd pause as they considered the question. It was Alec who laid doubt to rest. "I heard a mon was courting Lady Emelie, but she picked Dom because she loves him. The mon must nae have accepted the rejection. What he canna have, he doesnae want Dom to have either. Jealous as an auld hag. That's all. Ye would repeat his lies because ye have nay sense. He spews them because he's whinging like a wean. He doesnae even want to get his hands dirty. He paid ye and Wallace to do the deed. He had men attack us, but there was nay lordling Lowlander dead on the road. Shut yer gob and hang from the gallows as the traitor ye are. I'll raise the first pole to build them."

"By your own admission, you are a traitor to Clan Campbell," Brodie pronounced. "You will spend the night in the oubliette. You will not bid your family goodbye. You will die by hanging at sunrise. May God have mercy on you because I won't." Brodie nodded to Alec. The guard dragged Stanley to his feet as Garrett and Davey pushed through the gathered crowd. They took Stanley from Alec and led him to the trap door in the ground beside the dungeon entrance. With a scream, Stanley landed inside the pit, forgotten until the next day.

"He must have planned to meet whomever this is nearby," Alec whispered to Brodie and Dominic. "He was going on foot toward the river."

"Aye. You're the same height and hair color as him. Do you think you could pass for him and learn where our enemy is?" Dominic asked.

"I can. I will tell them what ye told us. Ye set off at dawn to Fraoch Eilean. We can watch from the battlements to see if anyone sails down the river and through the bay," Alec reasoned.

"We end this one way or another tomorrow. I won't have my wife live another day in fear," Dominic pronounced. He and Brodie watched Alec slip out of the postern gate before retiring to Brodie's solar to wait.

NINETEEN

Emelie's eyes fluttered open to the sound of Dominic and Laurel whispering, then the door closing. She tried to roll toward the door, momentarily forgetting about her stitches. She groaned as Dominic came to sit on the side of the bed.

"Did you sleep, sparrow?" Dominic asked as he brushed hair back from Emelie's rosy cheeks, warm from her nap.

"Like the dead." Emelie smiled. "What happened? It's dark. You were gone for hours."

"Brodie and I talked for a while in his solar. We knew a man who traveled with us must be a traitor because there were men waiting for us on the road to the hunting cabin, and ones who chased us. I gathered the men and told them you and I were sailing at dawn to Fraoch Eilean, a keep on a wee island about half an hour down the loch. Brodie and I stood at the parapet over the postern gate. We watched Alec slip out."

"No!" Emelie exclaimed as she attempted to push up on her elbow.

"Wheesht, sparrow. Dinna fash. I feared the same, but Alec was waiting for Stanley. He stopped him as

Stanley came around the side of the keep. *He* was the one slipping away to tell Henry our plans. Henry or his mon. Alec stopped him, and Brodie and I heard them talking. I threatened to shoot Stanley. He made the same claims as Wallace, but he made them in the bailey." Dominic watched the color leach from Emelie's face. He cupped her cheek and kissed her. "Alec, Anthony, and Berta all denounced him. They said his claims were rubbish. I don't know yet if it involves anyone else, but Stanley would have sided with Graham if there'd ever been a fight for the lairdship."

"But what if people believe him after they've had time to puzzle through everything?"

Dominic grinned before kissing Emelie again. He swiped his tongue along her lips, and she opened to him. He plied her tongue with his, and she sucked on it. Dominic drew back with a groan. "Alec pointed out that we can't keep our hands off one another. He said people would have questioned why you didn't get with child rather than people questioning why you are with child. I tend to agree with him." Dominic grinned shamelessly. "Berta warned Stanley that she would beat him with her rolling pin if he didn't cease his prattle. And she may have called him a mon-whore since he has two bastards of his own, and the entire clan knows he hasn't been faithful to his wife."

"Disgusting pig," Emelie grumbled before she forced a smile. "I don't enjoy worrying that anyone will believe him."

"I don't either. But as Brodie and Laurel tried to tell us, everyone could see we were in love before either of us recognized it or admitted it. Only the men Henry paid are questioning you. Our bairn is ours, no matter what. What married couple doesn't have secrets only they share? I don't doubt there are things

Brodie and Laurel know that they'll never tell another soul."

"I believe you," Emelie conceded. "What will you do now that you have Stanley?"

"He, Brodie, and I have already had a more private conversation. We know he was meeting someone, but he didn't know the mon's name. He said the mon has light, wavy hair and green eyes."

"That's not Henry; his eyes are brown. That's his brother, Simon," Emelie closed her eyes and tucked her chin as she inhaled. "He always scared me. There's something aboot him that isn't right. Henry said I was silly when I shied away from Simon the few times I met him, but he put me on edge. He and Henry's other brothers, Oliver and Harrold, are overindulged. Becoming their sister-by-marriage was the only hesitation I had when I believed Henry was courting me. He swore his father was sending them to their own keeps, and Henry would one day lead from their clan seat at Hoppringle. He claimed his brothers wouldn't be around often. Now I'm certain that was yet another lie. It wouldn't surprise me if Oliver and Harrold are with them too."

"Alec went to scout and meet Simon. He'll use the dark to help him hide that he's not Stanley. We'll know more in a couple hours. Once we know how many men Henry has, we can decide, but for now, Brodie and I intend to lead the Pringles to Fraoch Eilean. Brodie's already sent men to warn the people there. The fight will be there, far from you, Laurel, and Rick."

"What if he doesn't believe Alec? What if he discovers Alec isn't Stanley?"

"Alec will tell them he's Stanley's aulder brother. He came because Brodie happened to post Stanley on guard duty and couldn't shirk it without drawing attention," Dominic reassured her.

"And if they won't sail after you?"

"We know their camp is nearby if Stanley planned to walk. Alec will tell us once he finds it. Or if he meets Simon along the riverbank, he'll work the conversation to give Simon an estimation of how long it would take Henry and his men to get to the island. Whether they come to us, or we go to them, they aren't leaving Campbell territory." Dominic's tone convinced Emelie that Henry, his brothers, and their men would be in graves or carrion by midday. "Berta will send a tray up soon. Are you hungry?"

"Yes. I don't think you can call me sparrow anymore. I'm not the size of one, and I don't eat like one." Emelie grinned as her belly rumbled as if on cue.

"You will always be smaller than me and eat less than me. You will always be my sparrow. And if you're up to it, I know just what I'm having for dessert."

"And will you be baying at the moon if you don't?"

"I am your wolf," Dominic said before answering the knock at the door. It surprised the couple to find Aggie and Berta on the other side of the portal.

"Ma lady, we hoped we might talk to ye." Berta eyed Dominic. "Alone."

Dominic filched a chunk of bread from the tray Berta carried and stepped into the passageway while Emelie watched the two older women. Her curiosity mingled with dread. Aggie handed her a plate with cheese and dried fruit.

"Ma lady, Dominic likely told ye what Stanley said in the bailey," Aggie began. "A few eyebrows rose when we realized ye arrived here already carrying. But ma lady, Berta and I want ye to ken that nay one has ever thought the bairn is anyone's but Dominic's. At first, we wondered if ye'd been indiscreet

299

and that's why ye handfasted. We didna ken ye were a love match from the start. We thought mayhap ye'd had to marry because of the bairn."

"But it took less than a sennight to realize ye adore each other," Berta chimed in. "Nay one wanted to speak out of turn, but we kenned ye thought Dom grieved his first wife. We wanted to ring his neck for nae setting ye straight, but it warmed our hearts, it did, to see how much ye worried for him. Dom is different from before."

"Aye. He isnae trying to keep the peace when he worries aboot ye. He genuinely wants to be a good da, and he dotes on ye because he loves ye. We all kenned it was infatuation the last time. She manipulated him into thinking it was love, but it was infatuation tangled up with duty, made dirty by deceit," Aggie said. Emelie saw the pain in the woman's eyes, and she knew Aggie had never spoken out against Colina, but it was clear she wished she could have.

"He wouldnae have listened to anyone even if we tried," Berta said. She confirmed Emelie's suspicions. "I think he kens how different things are this time around. I think he appreciates ye even more for it. Anyhow, we dinna want ye thinking we're talking out of turn. But we also want ye to ken the clan isnae blind. We understood Colina long before Dom ever did. We understand ye too, ma lady. Whenever ye conceived yer bairn doesnae matter a wit to any of us. Ye and Dom love one another and love yer bairn. Nay one will say otherwise without looking like the village eejit."

"I hope ye dinna, but ye may hear what Stanley said repeated. We came here to make sure ye ken people might gossip. But when they talk aboot that, it willna be because they believe the lies aboot ye. They'll be talking aboot how outlandish the notion is and what a traitor Stanley is," Berta explained.

"Was," Aggie corrected. "He'll hang at dawn."

"Like Graham?" Emelie muttered.

"Aye, just like that traitorous dung pile," Aggie agreed with emphasis.

"We'll leave ye to yer meal with Dominic, ma lady. Dinna fash aboot aught. The clan loves ye as much as we do Lady Laurel. Ye're kin now," Aggie said as she squeezed Emelie's hand. She dropped a kiss on Emelie's forehead and stepped aside for Berta to do the same. They walked to the door and grinned at Dominic.

"In ye scoot, mon. Yer food will be cold," Berta chided playfully. Once the women left, Dominic carried the tray to their bed, and they sat together as they did for every meal they shared in their chamber.

"You don't need to wonder or worry. Aggie and Berta came to assure me that no one believes what Stanley accused me of. They admitted people thought we handfasted because you got me with child, and we had to. But they said it matters to no one when our bairn was conceived because it's clear we love each other and our bairn."

"We do," Dominic agreed. "I'm glad they came up to speak with you. Do you feel better for it?"

"I do." Emelie would tell Dominic if he asked for more details, but she chose not to volunteer what the women told her about Colina. She better understood why Aggie had compared her to Colina in the beginning. She'd always known Aggie meant no harm by her words, but now everything made more sense. The couple continued their meal, chatting about baby names.

"Dom, it's a lad," Emelie confessed, apprehensive about his reaction to her declaration.

"Nora swears it's a lass," Dominic countered.

"I've kenned since the beginning that it's a lad, Dom. I was too scared to tell you at first, and then I worried it would still disappoint you to know your first child is a son."

"We talked aboot this a long time ago, Em. I thought you understood I don't care if I didn't sire this child, lad or lass. Regardless of whether he inherits a castle or a croft, if this bairn is a lad, he's still mine and my heir."

"I know, and I believe you. I just still worried you might feel differently once you knew."

"I don't," Dominic said with such certainty that Emelie didn't doubt him. "How can you know?"

"The midwife in Stirling gave me a bunch of wheat and a bunch of barley. The ancients said that if a woman pishes on them, and the wheat blooms, then she's having a lad. If the barley blooms, she's having a lass. Either way, if aught blooms, she's with child. The wheat was the one to change."

"That makes this easer. I'll agree to Nic, but you realize his name will rhyme with his cousin's. Nic and Rick. Sounds like endless trouble already," Dominic chuckled.

"Sounds more like, like father, like son," Emelie giggled. "And I'm convinced you will make me the ogre parent who insists on rules while you have all the fun spoiling them."

"Most likely," Dominic guffawed with a wink. As they finished their meal, Emelie put the plates and dishes back on the tray, and Dominic moved it to the table.

"When will you set off?" Emelie asked.

"Alec should be back any time now. I'll meet with Brodie and him, then we'll leave a couple hours before sunrise."

"I pray Alec is safe. No matter what, do not trust completely aught you hear from Henry or his brothers."

"I suspect one or two of them will stay behind,

since they will undoubtedly question whether our scheme is a ruse. Brodie and I are prepared for that. If need be, Brodie will remain here in case they don't follow or they split their forces."

"Do you think there is anyone else involved? You already discovered two traitors. Are there others who supported Graham in secret?"

"Likely. Colina didn't limit her affairs to Graham. She bedded other men I trusted. I never learned who, but I suspect Wallace and Stanley were on that list."

"Oh, Dom," Emelie groaned.

"It's fine, Em. It doesn't bother me as it once did. I no longer care what she did or who she did. All I care aboot is my life with you. She deserves no more of my feelings. Not hate, not love, not regret." Dominic slid under the covers beside Emelie. "There is no room in my heart or my mind when that space belongs to your and our family. I can't say I'll never think of her. It's obvious she isn't yet completely in the past. But I find there is naught but ambivalence now. It's as though I think and speak of an acquaintance, not a woman I married."

Emelie nodded, uncertain how to react to Dominic's confession. Part of her was glad to hear it, and another part of her remained uncomfortable. It relieved her when Dominic blew out the candle beside the bed and drew her closer.

"Wake me when you go to speak to Alec. I don't want to wake alone and panic," Emelie said.

"Do you wish to be part of the conversation?"

"If you'll let me," Emelie replied.

"This isn't aboot allowing you to do aught. You have a right to know if you wish. If you prefer to not know, or to sleep and hear from me later, then I won't disturb you. If you want to discuss this with Brodie, Alec, and me, then I want you to come."

"Don't forget Laurel. You know she won't miss this."

"True. Then I'll wake you when Alec returns. I won't leave the keep without you knowing."

Emelie nodded as she settled against Dominic. It felt like only a moment later that Brodie summoned Dominic to the upstairs solar. He carried Emelie and settled her on his lap as Laurel and Brodie entered with Alec behind them. The conversation carried on for nearly an hour as Alec recounted what he learned. The Pringles weren't interested in sailing anywhere else. He relayed that there were closer to two score men now, and they intended to infiltrate the castle before Emelie and Dominic supposedly planned to leave. They expected Alec to let them in.

"Emelie, Laurel, and Rick will come here," Brodie decided. "We'll have three men inside here, and three posted outside. Alec will let the Pringles in, just like he promised. No one makes a move until they're all within the walls. Then we seal the postern gate and leave none of them alive."

"We need to bring the villagers inside the keep," Laurel spoke up.

"Aye. We can't risk the Pringles attacking the village as a distraction," Brodie agreed.

"Won't they notice they deserted the village? The men head to the fields at sunrise, so people are already moving around their crofts before then," Emelie pointed out.

"Then we bring them in, and we send a handful of men to the crofts. They can move around and sound like the villagers, but they can fight if the Pringles attack," Dominic reasoned.

With a plan in place, there was little for anyone to do but try to catch a few more hours of sleep, but Brodie would speak to his men first. Emelie feared she couldn't, but as always happened when she nestled against Dominic, she was asleep within minutes.

"Sparrow," Dominic murmured as he shook Emelie's shoulder to rouse her just before dawn. "It's time for you and Laurel to go in the solar with Rick."

Emelie's eyes snapped open as reality came rushing back. She gazed at Dominic and realized this was the first time she would watch her husband ride off to battle. But she wouldn't actually watch because she would be locked away in an abovestairs chamber, and the battle would take place in their bailey, only yards below where she hid. She would have to trust all went well. She wanted to cling to him and keep him in their bed, but she never would. She would be stoic and send him off with a kiss. She would never tell anyone how her heart ached at the idea that he might not return. She accepted his help out of bed and dressed quickly. It seemed only moments later Dominic carried her into the solar and eased her into a chair by the fireplace.

"Will you be comfortable here? Mayhap Laurel and Rick should come to our chamber. I don't like the idea that you'll be sitting for hours. That's what I'll do." Dominic talked more to himself than he did Emelie. His mind could focus on little more than how to keep Emelie safe and comfortable. He scooped her back into his arms, not hearing her protests. He tucked her back into bed, even as she insisted that she would be fine in the solar. She didn't want to inconvenience Laurel, even if Dominic were correct that it would be safer to remain in bed. "I'll let Laurel and Brodie know that you're sheltering in here. They'll understand, and Laurel will likely appreciate having a bed to lay Rick on when he naps."

"Thank you, Dom." As Dominic's eyes met Emelie's, he knew she was thanking him for far more than thinking about her comfort that morning.

"There's naught I wouldn't do for you and our family, sparrow." Dominic pressed a kiss to her lips, but it was over far too soon. He ducked out of the chamber to find his brother and sister-by-marriage, and to summon the guards to their new post. Laurel arrived with her infant son, who slept soundly bound to Laurel's chest with a length of plaid. She stood whispering with Brodie when he arrived with Dominic. It wasn't the first time Laurel said goodbye to Brodie before battle, but Emelie intuited it hadn't grown any easier with experience. She doubted it would ever get easier for her.

"Wolf, I know you can't promise to come home to me, but promise me you will do everything you can. You don't have to win this war alone," Emelie beseeched.

"Brodie and I will do what we've done since I was auld enough to ride out with him. We will fight back-to-back, guarding one another. We have the advantage that this is our home. There's isn't a spot that we don't know as well as our own hand. I am coming back up here to you. And I am going to hold you tonight and make love to you. I'm going to do that every night for a long time to come," Dominic pledged. Emelie could only nod, the lump in her throat too large to speak. "I need you to promise that no matter what, you do not open that door to anyone but Brodie or me. It doesn't matter what you hear in the passageway. Short of the keep being on fire, you remain here with your guards. There is no safer place for you."

"I promise," Emelie whispered as she rose to her knees on the bed. She wrapped her arms around Dominic's neck, resting her head on his chest as she'd done so many times since they met in the garden. Just as his presence calmed her the day her world fell apart, so did he give her strength now. Their kiss was poignant, a promise of more to come, but there was a note of farewell. "I love you, wolf."

"Nearly as much as I love you, sparrow."

"Don't jest. I love you with everything I am, everything I have. I need you to know that," Emelie insisted.

"I do. You fill my heart and my mind. I am going to protect you, Em. I'm going to end this today. God has ordained our family, and no mon will put it asunder." With a final embrace and kiss, Dominic walked to the door and waited for Brodie. The brothers left the chamber, walking shoulder to shoulder to the bailey.

TWENTY

"Stay beside me, little brother," Brodie instructed. It was the same thing he'd always said before he and Dominic rode or marched into battle. Brodie had fought back-to-back many times with Graham when he was alive. But he'd fought at Dominic's back just as many.

"Keep up, auld mon," Dominic jested, his habitual reply. "Your wife will take my bollocks if aught happens to you."

The last battle the brothers fought together had taken place just beyond the barmekin wall. It had been brief and fierce, but the Campbells won the day. However, Dominic would regret to his last breath that he prioritized Colina over his duty to his clan and Brodie. He'd ridden off the battlefield to reassure Colina he survived. It had put what he once feared was an irreparable rift between him and Brodie. He glanced at his brother.

"I won't leave until it's done," Dominic promised.

"I ken, Dom. It's nae the same," Brodie said, his voice laden with emotion. "Dinna fash. I trust ye as I always have." Brodie wrapped his hand around the back of Dominic's head and brought their foreheads together.

"I love ye, brother," Dominic whispered, just as emotional as Brodie. They'd always made time to tell one another that before battle. Their mother had insisted, despite how their father had scoffed and mocked them.

"I love ye," Brodie replied. The men gathered their targes from the armory, moving now in silence as the sky lightened and the hour moved toward dawn. Brodie had met with his captains after their conversation with Alec ended and Dominic returned Emelie to bed. Dominic learned Brodie and Laurel remained discussing the plan for a while before Laurel retired to bed. He'd shared further details he devised with much input from Laurel. She was the greatest strategist any of them knew, and her plan had won them the last battle.

Dominic strained to make out the men on the wall walk. He recognized Alec, who stood looking out toward the river. He was to watch for the signal Simon told him the Pringles would use as the sun rose, but the stars remained. When it came, Alec was to slip down to the postern gate. His movement would be the alert to the Campbells. The clan warriors were tucked away in the shadows of the outbuildings and the keep. Dominic knew the villagers had arrived while he was settling Emelie. They were hidden in storerooms inside the keep and below ground in the storage buildings. As much as he wished to go up to the battlements to check the village, they could not afford anyone recognizing him. It would ruin their ruse.

The minutes dragged as everyone waited, alert and tense. Dominic could still see Alec from where Dominic waited at the corner of the keep, Brodie to Dominic's left. They would lead the offensive against the unsuspecting Pringles. When Dominic and Brodie emerged from the shadows, their warriors would attack. Their goal was to take the Pringles off guard. Dominic closed his eyes and said a hurried prayer. When he opened them, Alec was no longer in his spot on the wall walk. Dominic's gaze jumped to the stairs, finding Alec rushing down them. While Dominic was certain Alec couldn't see him or Brodie, the senior warrior nodded in their direction.

The guard beside the postern gate sprawled on the ground, pretending to be knocked unconscious. He would seal the postern gate behind the last Pringle and join the fight from the rear, alongside men who hid behind barrels now placed near the retaining wall. Alec glanced around once more, then eased the portal open. A man fitting Simon's description stepped inside the bailey, his gaze sweeping across his surroundings. In the otherwise silent night, Alec's voice carried bits and pieces of what he told Simon.

"They rode west this morn. They're taking the birlinn when they are across from the island. They didna want ye seeing them go by boat again," Alec explained, just as he'd been instructed. "Be quick, lest the men above sound the alarm before ye are all inside."

Alec backed away with haste, not trusting Simon to leave him alive after his supposed treachery. Simon nodded before pushing the gate open wider. Three more men stepped through, and Dominic was certain he looked at all four Pringle brothers: Henry, Simon, Harrold, and Oliver. He wondered for a moment what their father believed his sons were off doing with all four away from Hoppringle. He wondered if Laird Pringle sanctioned Henry's attempts to get Emelie to leave Kilchurn. He would fight his way to Henry, everyone knowing he reserved the right to end their nemesis's life and to exact justice for his wife.

Brodie nudged his arm as the last Pringle entered. They watched the guardsman in repose ease to his feet and slide along the wall to lock the hatch. With the front and rear gates sealed, the Pringles were now caught in the Campbells' net. The Campbells waited patiently as the Pringles crept forward, spreading out toward the barracks and the keep. When Henry was nearly to Dominic, the latter stepped out of the shadows.

"Ye've got bollocks. I'll give ye that, since ye have nay sense," Dominic greeted Henry.

"And you have a whore for a wife, heathen," Henry smirked.

"Yet ye sneak into a Highlander's home and think to leave here alive. Like I said, ye have nay sense." Dominic stressed his brogue, rolling his letters and deepening his voice. He would posture and distract just long enough for the other Pringles to move within easy reach of his men. It only took a moment. Henry opened his mouth to retort, but Dominic released a piercing birdcall. Henry twisted to see who Dominic whistled to and froze with shock as Campbells poured out of every shadow and building in the bailey. "How do ye nae ken we're one of the largest clans in the Highlands? Daft sod."

Dominic ran toward Henry, his sword raised and ready to engage. Brodie burst from the shadows, maneuvering himself to protect Dominic's back as two Pringle brothers swerved to come fight beside Henry. Two Campbell warriors approached, but Dominic shook his head. They turned to find other opponents. The imminent fight was too personal to Dominic to let anyone else join him, and he didn't trust Henry not to reveal Emelie's secret when he undoubtedly would want to taunt Dominic. Launching an offense, Dominic and Brodie angled themselves to take on the three Lowlanders.

"She spread her legs without me even asking. Wet for me before I could even stuff her with my cock," Henry jeered. Dominic said nothing. "She begged like a two-pence whore."

Dominic feinted to the left but brought his sword down and slashed across Henry's legs. Henry wobbled before his legs buckled, blood gushing from the deep laceration. Dominic's grin held only malice. "I will bring ye to yer knees."

Dominic didn't wait for Henry's response. He thrust his sword into Henry's groin, eliciting a howl of pain. "Ye should have kept yer wee stick in yer breeks. Can ye imagine her surprise when she learned it should last longer than a sneeze?"

Henry struggled to his feet. "She wasn't worth wasting more time than it took to spill."

"Then why come after her? Why try to get her to leave here?"

"Because my useless cu—wife," Henry caught himself, sensing more vulgarity would cut his life short with no more chance to fight. "Is barren. The bitch has never bled. That bairn is mine. If it's a son, he's my heir. I will have what is mine."

Dominic was in no mood to banter now that he knew why Henry pursued Emelie. While Henry's wounds weren't fatal, they left him unable to further defend himself. Dominic thrust his sword toward Henry's throat, stopping just as the tip pricked Henry's skin. "Ye erred coming after ma wife. Ye wanted naught to do with her until ye feared she would tell yer secret, until ye needed *ma* child. Ye should have remained in the Lowlands with yer wife, and we could have all lived happily, none the wiser of one another. But ye couldnae do that. Ye couldnae leave well enough alone and found some other woman to carry yer bastard heir. This may be the best gift I ever give ma wife." Dominic thrust his sword into Henry's throat until it poked through.

"No!" Harrold Pringle bellowed. Brodie had kept the two brothers at bay, but the third brother raced toward Dominic. While all the Pringle brothers were experienced men, used to fighting along the Scottish-English border, they were unprepared for the size and agility of a Highlander. Harrold's fury overcame him, making him careless and impulsive. He lunged toward Dominic as the tánaiste withdrew his sword. Brodie bumped Dominic aside, only for Dominic to step behind and around Brodie, effectively switching positions. Brodie cleaved Harrold's head from his neck, his enormous claymore more powerful than the thinner sword the Lowlander carried. Simon panicked from witnessing both of his brothers die. He searched for a way to escape, but there was none. Dominic prowled toward him until Simon's back banged into a wall.

"Mayhap I should leave ye and the other one alive so ye can run home to yer da and tell how yer brothers led ye into a battle ye could never win. But I dinna trust either of ye to tell the truth. And since I dinna need ye telling tales that'll bring more enemies to ma door, I think I shall silence ye." Dominic rained down one blow after another as Simon struggled to defend himself. The man put up the most skilled fight of the four, but it wasn't enough to overcome Dominic's determination. Despite his anger and his desire to rush back to Emelie, he moved methodically as he wore his opponent down.

"Dom!" Brodie yelled, and Dominic knew his brother wanted him to cease toying with the man. Brodie had just slain Oliver, leaving Simon the only son left from Laird Pringle's brood.

"Vera well." With a final thrust, Dominic skewered Simon through the heart. The man looked down in shock as the blade vibrated in his chest. His eyes grew dim, and his body sagged. Dominic withdrew his blade, allowing the body to crumple to the ground.

"Yer faithless leaders are dead," Brodie announced, his voice ringing against the walls and over the ongoing battle. "Lay down yer swords, and yer fate is ma dungeon. Continue to fight, and ye will die." Neither Brodie nor Dominic expected many to accept a life sentence in a dungeon, but a handful dropped their weapons. Surprise distracted the other Pringles, allowing the Campbells to end the battle in victory.

"Do ye still wish for the dungeon, or would ye now prefer death?" Dominic called out. There would be no honor in begging for death rather than languishing in a dungeon cell, but it offered a merciful reprieve from starving to death or dying of disease in a dungeon. The Campbells watched as each man who'd laid down his weapons made their necks and throats clear targets. Brodie nodded to his men, and they dispatched the last of the Pringles. None resisted. The battle had been vicious but brief, and there were few Campbell casualties. It surprised and relieved Dominic that none of the dead were Campbells.

"Nay one entered the keep, Laird," Alec said as he jogged toward Brodie and Dominic. "We can manage here, and Nora will be along soon. See to Lady Laurel and Lady Emelie." Dominic and Brodie appreciated the offer, but they remained until Nora had a triage in place, and Aggie and Berta were ordering maids to bring boiling water and linens to the Great Hall. The men staggered or helped move the wounded to tables where Nora could work with light and less dirt.

"I'm ready to kiss ma wife and hold ma son," Brodie said after Nora tended to a short but deep gash on Brodie's sword arm. Dominic hadn't felt Henry catch his ribs with a glancing blow, but the wound required stitching and bandaging, just like Brodie's. The men climbed the stairs and nodded to the guards posted outside Dominic's door. He rapped on the wood.

"Em, Laurel. Brodie and I are here. Ye can let us in." The men heard shuffling within the chamber before the door swung open, and Laurel launched herself into Brodie's arms. Dominic squeezed past, his eyes on Emelie as she reclined in bed, propped up by several pillows. With an absentminded wave and nod to Davey, Garrett, and Tim, Dominic sank onto the bed beside Emelie and pulled her into his arms.

"It's over, sparrow," Dominic whispered. "He canna threaten us anymore."

"You're safe," Emelie said, not caring at that moment what happened to Henry or the outcome of the battle. She clung to Dominic as tears she didn't feel careened down her cheeks. She heard Laurel and Brodie moving around the chamber, but she didn't even notice Brodie picking Rick up from the bed, where he lay cooing beside her. All she wanted was to get closer to Dominic. She wanted nothing between them, nothing to keep them apart. She and Dominic looked at the door as it closed behind their relatives. Alone at last, their kiss burned hotter than the sun. Relief burst into a conflagration of need. Need to hold, to touch, to hear.

"I'm here, Em," Dominic reassured her as she ran her hands over him. He pressed her against him, grateful that no one breached the keep and that Emelie's condition hadn't worsened from the agitation he was sure she experienced. He didn't know enough about pregnant women to know if being upset could bring the babe too soon. All he wanted was to wrap Emelie in a cocoon that would protect her from any risk or harm.

"I will say prayers of thanksgiving all day, every day, for at least a fortnight," Emelie babbled, but she leaned back as a more pressing thought permeated her relief. "Did he say why?"

Dominic hesitated before he nodded. "He wanted our bairn, or at least he wanted a son. Alice is barren. Since they havenae been married that long, I'd say it was a secret she withheld. He needed an heir, so he was prepared to take the child from ye."

Emelie's visage mottled with rage. She clenched her jaw as she forced herself to breathe. "His soul—whatever's left of it—will rot in hell. I hope it was sheer agony as he died. The hell he would have taken our child from us."

"I never would have let him, Em," Dominic whispered as he stroked her back and felt her shuddering sigh. It took several minutes, but Emelie finally relaxed. The haze of rage fading, leaving just a burning anger. She soothed herself by running her hands over Dominic. When she caught the bandage against the side of her hand, and Dominic winced, she demanded he take his leine off. Her eyes widened with horror as she noticed the blood spotting the bandage. She turned an accusatory look to Dominic.

"I didna set out to get injured," Dominic said, a boyish lopsided grin tugging at his mouth.

"I didn't think you had. You could have told me to be careful. I didn't mean to press against it," Emelie responded.

"And miss out on ye touching me? Nae bluidy likely. I took ma leine off. Now ye can touch me even more," Dominic purred, his wolfish grin making Emelie's belly flutter. She was certain it wasn't the babe.

"Take a bath first, then we shall see what I can do." Emelie cocked an eyebrow as she raised her hands, staggered with palms facing one another. She twisted her wrists and waggled her eyebrow. Dominic pounced, but he remained ever careful not to press Emelie too hard. But she had none of the same reservations. She pulled Dominic down with her. She pushed hair away from his ear and whispered. "I'm going to watch you bathe, enjoying every single moment, so don't rush. Then I'm going to touch all your favorite places before my mouth winds up in *my* favorite place."

Without a word, Dominic pushed of the bed and crossed the chamber, flinging open the door. "Bring a tub and water up here as soon as someone can!"

"I can survive waiting, Dom," Emelie teased. "The women have other things to do before they get to your bath water."

"But I canna," Dominic huffed playfully as he came back to the edge of the bed. He looked down at himself, and his lip curled in disgust. "I'm filthy, and good God do I reek."

"But you're here, and that's all that matters to me. Though I won't turn away the bath when it arrives."

"Now that ye can get yer back wet, I would suggest sharing a bath. But I dinna think ye want anywhere near the sludge I shall turn the water into."

"And I couldn't watch you if I'm sitting in front of you." Emelie shot him a lascivious grin before she drew her teeth over her bottom lip. Dominic growled as he launched himself at her again, but he eased her down on the bed. He kissed her cheeks, her eyelids, her lips, her neck, and her jaw.

"Emelie, I love ye. I will always fight for ye. I am a better mon than I was before I met ye. Ye've made me learn a great deal aboot maself, nae all of which

I've always liked. But I needed to see it. I want to be a husband ye can always rely on and trust. I canna promise that I will always be able to put ye and our bairns ahead of duty, but ye will always come first in ma heart."

"Dominic, you've been exactly the mon I've needed through all of this. My protector, my friend, my confidant, my lover. Our lives together might have started as a solution to our own problems, but all I can see down the road is a life built with you. I knew people married for love, but until I married you, I didn't understand what that meant. I might never have known what I was missing if I'd married someone else. But I will be grateful to my last breath that you stumbled upon me in that garden and took an enormous risk with me. I love you more fiercely than I could have imagined."

Someone knocking at the door interrupted their heartfelt moment, but they both sighed when they discovered servants waited with the tub and buckets. Dominic wasted no time diving into the tub and scrubbing himself clean. Emelie teased, pointing out spots he missed that required him to twist and turn as his muscles flexed to avoid getting his stitches wet. He came to stand beside her, and she kneeled as she helped dry him. Dominic was clear when he refused the servants when they returned to get the tub. He would have no more interruptions. He climbed into bed, helping Emelie remove her clothes and turn to her side. Her hands explored his body, feather-soft touches combined with more demanding kisses.

When her hand brushed his rod, they both moaned. She wrapped her hand around his length, stroking him. Dominic's mouth sought her breast, his tongue flicking her nipple over and over as Emelie arched toward him. He drew her into his mouth, swirling his tongue over the puckered flesh before suckling. Emelie's grip tightened as she continued to fist him, but she was determined to do all that she promised. While it was somewhat awkward, she positioned herself between Dominic's legs while he propped himself up with pillows. The most erotic sights he'd ever seen were when his wife's mouth pleasured him, though he thought watching her ride him and watching his cock slide into her from behind were top contenders for the designation.

Emelie bent over Dominic, her tongue sweeping the broad head of his cock before flicking the tip. She slid her tongue down the length, cupping and rolling his bollocks as she went. She tantalized and teased, moving in no hurry until Dominic shifted, restless and eager. Her mouth consumed his length until it pressed against the back of her throat. Reminding herself to relax and breathe through her nose, she worked his rod until she felt him twitch and his bollocks contracted. She withdrew her mouth and stroked him until his seed splattered her chest. She swiped a finger through the viscous cream and licked it clean.

Dominic reached between Emelie's legs, finding her pearl. Careful not to press within her entrance, he worked the aroused nerves until Emelie rocked against his hand. Her fingers dug into his shoulders, as she tried to keep her balance when her eyes drifted shut. While they hadn't coupled since Emelie's injuries, they'd fondled and pleasured one another over and over. Despite their limitations, neither was dissatisfied with the situation. It had only made them more creative.

"Dom," Emelie panted. "Nora came to see me today to make certain I fared well through all of this upset. I know we weren't supposed to let anyone in, but it was Nora. We talked quietly, so the men couldn't hear. I asked her—" Emelie swallowed as she tried to concentrate on her words, but it was a struggle as her body hurtled toward release. "—if we could couple again. She still isn't convinced we should. But she suggested we—" Emelie moaned as her core tightened. She abandoned trying to speak as pleasure crashed over her and swept her away in ecstasy. Her mouth sought Dominic's, suddenly starving for his kiss. While they'd both found release, neither was sated.

"What did she suggest?" Dominic asked.

"She was rather blunt." Emelie blushed but pushed on since she'd brought it up. "She made it clear that my hand and my mouth aren't the only places you could be, even if you can't be in my quim." Emelie prayed Dominic understood her meaning. The shocked look on his face told her he did.

"Nora suggested yer arse?" Dominic guffawed. "She's been a widow for years, but I remember she was a wild one when I was a wean. It shouldnae surprise me."

"You're not disgusted that I brought it up?"

"I wouldnae have because I didna want to insult ye or make ye fear I expected it," Dominic shrugged. Emelie's eyes narrowed.

"It doesn't sound like such a foreign idea to you." Emelie tried not to sound accusatory, but she suspected she failed.

"Em, I'm several years aulder than ye. Even if I hadnae been married before—and nay to that," Dominic said pointedly. He would end her curiosity about Colina without mentioning the woman's name. "I was with other women before. I never wanted to sire a bastard, and I dinna trust whores nae to spread something."

"So it's something only whores do?" Emelie asked, utterly humiliated that she brought it up, and annoyed Nora would mention it.

"I didna say that. I said I already kenned it was an option. And aye, I ken from experience. But I have never thought of ye as a whore. Ye are a woman I'm attracted to beyond reason, but ye're also nae in a position to couple with me right now. I've thought aboot having ye just aboot everywhere and in every way, but this wasna something I would suggest. And coupling will never be more important than yer health and wellbeing, sparrow. Never," Dominic insisted before he kissed her cheek. "If ye wish to explore, then I will because I wish to pleasure ye and to share all intimacies with ye. But I will think nay less of ye if we do or if we dinna."

"Can it be pleasurable for us both? I can only imagine it being good for the mon. I don't mind that," Emelie rushed to add. "I want to be intimate with you the way we were before. I want us to join not just to climax, but to be one. That sounds ridiculously naive." Emelie shook her head, embarrassed by what sounded lame to her own ears.

"It is neither ridiculous nor naive. I miss being one with ye, but I still feel connected to ye in other ways. Em, we can go slowly. If ye dinna like it or it scares ye, we stop immediately." Dominic's final words weren't offered as a compromise or platitude so much as a command. Emelie nodded and looked at a vial of oil that sat on her bedside table.

"Nora said the oil would help," Emelie whispered. Dominic followed her gaze and realized she was right. He hadn't considered such an aid before because the women in his past were far more experienced than he'd been as a curious, callow man. He'd never worried about them as he did Emelie.

"Do ye wish to try now, or do ye need to rest? It's

been a long morning for ye." Dominic realized he might be pushing Emelie too much. They'd been awake for hours, and normally Emelie would be napping after so much activity.

"I think I shall sleep soundly after this." Emelie winked and nudged Dominic to get the vial. Moving slowly, Dominic positioned Emelie onto her hands and knees. Their height difference and her belly necessitated the position. He readied his body and hers with the oil before he pressed against her rosebud.

"Relax, *mo ghaol*. I will go slowly. I can only imagine how odd it will feel at first. Tell me immediately if ye wish me to stop."

"I will."

Emelie pressed her hips back as the tip of Dominic's cock eased into her rear passage. She flinched and gripped the bedding, blowing air out through her nose. She told herself to relax as Dominic waited for her. She nodded, and he pulled back on her hips, gradually allowing her body to take more of him. His hand slid around to her mons, his fingers slipping through the dew between her legs. With his fingers damp, he sought her pearl once more. He rocked his hips as he worked her nub. His other hand sought her breast, kneading it before tugging and pinching her nipple.

"Dom," Emelie moaned. Dominic froze, not knowing what to make of the sound. "I didn't believe I would enjoy it, but holy mother and all the saints. Or rather the devil and all the demons."

"Do ye want me to keep going?" Dominic needed to hear her say it because he would never forgive himself if he misunderstood.

"Och, aye," Emelie mumbled, the first hints of a genuine Highland brogue slipping into her speech. She wiggled her hips, making Dominic groan and grasp them.

"Dinna do that, sparrow. Ye push me to the edge of control. Ma body wants to fuck ye, while ma heart wants to make love to ye. And ma mind is telling me I'm a wretched husband for bedding ma pregnant wife when ye're on bedrest."

"I like your body. Your heart is already in the right place. And your mind can haud its wheesht." Emelie wiggled her hips again, turning Dominic's chuckle into a groan. He pressed slightly deeper, then rocked his hips as his hands continued to work Emelie's body. It wasn't long before they both catapulted into their climax, their bodies trembling together as they spasmed. Dominic eased away from Emelie, helping her trembling body behind the screen to give her a moment of privacy. When she was through, she sagged against him still breathless. "I can only imagine what that'll be like when I'm not with child. Jesus and all the angels, I had no idea."

"Ye didna mind it?" Dominic whispered as he carried her to bed and arranged them against the pillow.

"Didna mind it?" Emelie repeated. "It felt like the next few months would be interminable with no way for us to couple. I admit I worried it might put distance between us. Now I don't worry. Unless Nora tells us otherwise, this is the only way we can couple. I can't promise I'll always be up to it, but I'm relieved to know we can."

"Did you worry that distance would be the width from here to me in another woman's bed?"

"A little, at times. But I trust you, Dom. I only feel that way when I'm feeling sorry for myself. I know coupling isn't more important to you than being a good husband," Emelie assured him.

"Em, one of the intimacies I like best with ye is talking as we do. I'm glad ye ken ye can tell me aught. I ken I can do the same."

323

"You've put me at ease since the very beginning. I trusted you before it even made sense to, but I just knew I could. I might be uncomfortable or uneasy aboot telling you something, or even afraid it might disappoint or hurt you. But I'm never afraid of the actual telling part," Emelie explained. She leaned against Dominic as his arm slid beneath her neck. She nestled closer to him. "There must be things you should be doing right now instead of coddling your wife."

"The married men are doing just what I am." Dominic tried to stifle his laugh and ended up coughing. "Mayhap nae exactly what I was doing, but they are with their families, too. There will be work to do this afternoon and tomorrow, but right now families are celebrating their warriors' homecomings. Nay one will fault us. Brodie is likely with Laurel right now. And I am certain they were doing just aboot the same thing as us. He practically pushed me down the bluidy stairs in his hurry to get past me. I canna believe he remembered this is our chamber, nae his. I half expected him to pound the door down rather than let me knock. I dinna ken—and dinna want to ken—how Laurel came up with calling him bear, but it fits. He's beastly."

Emelie smirked as she tickled Dominic's ribs. "He isn't the only wild beast who resides under this roof. How did you not hurt yourself further during all our rambunctiousness?" Emelie rested her hand near his wound.

"It smarts, but Nora put plenty of salve on it, and I wasna turning down the opportunity to make love to ye." Dominic kissed Emelie's lips and sighed. "Now rest, sparrow. Ye've worn me out. I need a nap."

"I've worn you out?" Emelie giggled and burrowed further against Dominic's side. They were asleep within minutes. Dominic dragged himself from the chamber that afternoon when duty demanded it, but he hurried back to Emelie's side to share the evening meal and their bed with her.

TWENTY-ONE

I t had been three-and-a-half moons since her fall
from Dominic's horse, and Nora had finally
agreed a fortnight earlier that she could walk on her
own and leave her chamber. Emelie suspected Nora
relented because she knew Emelie wouldn't last
long on her feet anyway. She no longer walked but
waddled around the keep. Everything felt squashed,
but Nora told her that was a sign her time would
come soon. She prayed the midwife and healer was
right.

It had also been three moons since the battle
against the Pringles in the bailey. Brodie sent word to
King Robert, informing him of Henry's stalking of
Emelie and the Pringles' attempted invasion. Dominic had been livid when the Bruce insisted he appear before the monarch in Stirling. He took himself
for a long ride lest he tear through the keep, throwing
things. He refused to leave Emelie, and there was no
way he would consider her traveling with him. He
returned calmer but just as resolved. Had the Campbells not been so influential, both during the Wars of
Independence and now during peacetime, Brodie
wouldn't have let Dominic refuse. But King Robert
still relied heavily on the Campbells to support his

claim to the throne and to govern a large segment of the Highlands.

It was Emelie who crafted the response to King Robert's demand, tactfully explaining that Dominic could not leave Emelie when her pregnancy remained such a risk. He would attend court once he was certain Emelie and their child were well enough for him to be away. Emelie eloquently pointed out that the outcome wouldn't change just because Dominic wouldn't stand before the king for another four moons.

There'd been grumbles from some of the other clans about the Campbells living with impunity from everything, but a missive from Blythe explained that once people learned of Henry's lack of honor—his *attempt* to seduce Emelie with lies, then stalking her in a jealous rage over Dominic marrying her—gossip ceased. Blythe noted that while people bemoaned the Campbells' long reach, no one pitied anyone foolish enough to test the powerful clan.

As Emelie now stood in her chamber, she pressed against her aching lower back, then rubbed her hand over her belly, still amazed that it could stretch so far. She'd been uncomfortable all day, starting the previous night. She felt unsettled and irritable, though she couldn't pinpoint a reason. She paced the width of her chamber, unwilling to get into bed since she didn't have to, but not wanting to risk the stairs alone. She conceded that she couldn't see well enough to manage them on her own. Her short stature made her belly more pronounced and harder to see around. As she walked, restless and bored, the baby seemed to drop until she was certain he wished to slide out. She stopped walking when tightness in her belly stole her breath. Just as she straightened and was able to breathe easier, a gush between her legs had her staring at a puddle.

Emelie froze until another contraction brought her back to the present, snapping her out of her stupor as she looked at her soaked gown. Wincing and waddling, she cradled her belly as she went to the second-floor landing. She searched for her husband but didn't see him.

"Wolf!" Emelie called out. She was in such great pain that she didn't consider what she called Dominic. People turned to look at her. "Can someone fetch my husband, pleeee—" Emelie gripped the railing in front of her. She watched as people scurried in different directions, understanding why her need was pressing.

"Wolf!" Emelie screamed this time, the pain growing exponentially worse with each contraction.

"I hear you, Em. I'm coming." Dominic's voice floated up to her as he came into the Great Hall from Brodie's solar. He looked around but didn't see Emelie.

"Now!" Emelie screeched. Dominic spun around and spotted her leaning over the railing. He sprinted up the stairs, moving faster than he ever had before.

"Where the devil is Nora?" He bellowed just before he swept Emelie into his arms. He kicked the door open, slamming it against the wall.

"You know, the carpenters are going to stop fixing our door if you keep kicking it off its hinges," Emelie pointed out before her face contorted in pain. "I remember Laurel being in pain, but why didn't she tell me how bad it is?"

"I did," Laurel said as she rushed in. "But no woman believes it until she feels it. God bless us all that it's women who give birth. We'd have died off eons ago if men were left to procreate. It bluidy hurts." Laurel had already pushed Dominic out of the way as she efficiently stripped Emelie of her gown and stockings. Now she pushed Dominic back toward his wife, ordering him to help her onto the bed. She ducked out of the chamber but soon returned with drying linens and sheets. Nora arrived, breathless, moments later.

"Aboot time, ma lady. I dinna ken how ye kept this giant in ye for so long," Nora mused. Emelie shot a panicked glance at Dominic. Her fear that people would question her when her babe wasn't as large as Rick still plagued her. Laurel was already carrying again, and people were guessing that her second bairn would be even bigger than her first. All the women subscribed to the wives' tale that each babe was larger than the last. Emelie couldn't imagine giving birth to anything larger than what she feared she would deliver soon.

Dominic kicked off his boots and eased Emelie forward, catching her just as a contraction made her grasp his hand in a grip that he was certain would crush half his bones. He slipped onto the bed behind her, bracing her against him. Nora examined Emelie and tsked.

"How long have ye been in labor, ma lady?"

"I don't know," Emelie gasped.

"Ye're crowning already. It must have been several hours. When did the pains start?"

"When my waters broke." Emelie looked dolefully at Laurel, who'd swiped up the puddle. "I'm sorry aboot that."

"Were ye restless and edgy?" Nora persisted, ignoring Emelie's comment to Laurel.

"Yes. Since last night. I've felt unsettled."

"Then ye must have started laboring earlier this morn and didna ken," Nora surmised. "This one's determined to be here soon. I think yer bairn is even more eager to meet ye than ye are to meet her."

Emelie squeezed Dominic's knee, neither correcting Nora about the baby's sex. Sweat broke out on Emelie's brow as contraction after contraction ripped through her until they were one on top of another. She panted, "I need to push."

"Then listen to yer body, ma lady," Nora instructed. With four strong pushes and nearly breaking both of Dominic's hands, a squalling baby boy entered the world. Emelie reached for her son, unsure she had the strength to hold him but needing to nonetheless. Dominic's powerful arms braced hers, his touch so gentle that it belied the giant's strength.

"Nic," Emelie whispered. "Do you know how much your da and I love you?"

"He will, every day for his entire life," Dominic whispered. "You amaze me, sparrow."

"I would have given up after the first push if you weren't holding me," Emelie confessed as she positioned Nic at her breast.

"Nic?" Laurel asked. The couple had kept their choice to themselves, superstitious that telling too many people would bring Emelie's already precarious pregnancy more bad luck.

"For Dominic," Emelie explained.

"Would ye look at that downy white hair," Nora crooned. "He's the spitting image of ye, ma lady." Everyone looked at the nursing babe, and it was true. The head of hair was the same white-blond as Emelie's, and the babe's features distinctly favored Emelie.

"Then he's perfect," Dominic whispered. Emelie sighed and closed her eyes as Nora and Laurel bustled around the chamber. Dominic gladly held his newborn son while the women helped Emelie bathe and changed the bedding.

"Can ye manage six more sennights, lad?" Nora asked Dominic as she came to stand before him. She grinned at the babe, then Dominic. "There's nay reason to fear like before. With how easily this birth went, she will be right as rain and likely expecting before we pass another two moons."

"You have to learn to keep up, little brother," Brodie said as he entered the chamber with Rick. The little boy bounced and clapped as though he agreed with his father.

"I doubt that will be a problem," Emelie grinned. "I'm aboot as patient as Laurel was."

"Aye, well. I can't complain," Laurel said as she rubbed the small bump just barely showing beneath her kirtle. With an embrace for Emelie and Dominic, Laurel shooed everyone from the chamber, leaving the new family of three to marvel at one another.

"Wolf, are you happy?" Emelie asked.

"More than I deserve to be," Dominic responded. "My wife and my son are in my arms. You're both safe, and we're living in peace these days. I have more than any mon can ask for. I love you, sparrow."

"Nearly as much as I love you, wolf," Emelie countered. She nestled against her husband as their son slept in their arms. They sat in silence as they marveled at the life they were building together as a family. It hadn't started out as either expected, but it was better than they could have wished.

EPILOGUE

E melie gritted her teeth as she lifted her skirts
and leaped from one tiny patch of mud to another, avoiding the ankle-deep puddles. She made
her way to the lists, scanning the men for the white-
blond and chestnut heads of hair she sought. Even
more frustrated than she had been moments ago, she
whistled the call Dominic had taught her more than
two decades ago. It was the one she was to use to
identify herself and let Dominic know where she was
if they were ever separated while riding or traveling.

Dominic pushed Nic away with his targe, barely
keeping his ear attached when Nic swung his sword
as Emelie's whistle caused a distraction. Dominic
tilted his head toward Emelie, and father and son
jogged over, mud splashing around their ankles.

"Get your brothers, too," Emelie commanded
Nic. "I would blister their ears along with yours."

"What's wrong, sparrow?" Dominic asked as he
leaned forward to kiss Emelie, but she stepped back.

"Oh, no. You're in the shite, right next to your
brood of sons. Always the bluidy fun parent."

Emelie and Dominic watched their six sons walk
toward them. They could tell the young men were
teasing one another until they spotted their mother's

expression. They'd seen it enough times to all go pale and approach with more caution. Emelie knew the boys' cousins were elbowing one another and watching, but Laurel and Brodie's five sons would hear from Laurel any moment.

"Dominic, Nic, Fergus, Stephen, Tavish, Cormac, and Charles." Emelie rattled off her husband's and sons' names. They all knew they were about to face their doom, since the only name she shortened was her oldest son's, and he never went by Dominic. She glared at them and cocked an eyebrow. She watched them shift nervously before she crossed her arms. The men looked at one another. Then she tapped her toes, making a squelching sound in the mud.

"We didna mean to," Nic spoke up.

"Mama, it was a complete accident, we swear," Tavish swore. Emelie kept her eyebrow raised, surprised it hadn't stuck that way after years of motherly expressions. She tilted her head to the side as she looked at her husband.

"Dinna look at me," Dominic raised his hands in defense.

"I still don't hear a confession or an apology," Emelie pointed out. She watched all seven men, all of whom towered over her and weighed at least twice as much as her, squirm. She pursed her lips to keep from laughing.

"Mama, it was dark when we came in last eve," Stephen began. "And ye ken it's been raining for days. Ye even told us ye thought ye saw Noah and his ark."

"And? You can't tell, but my hair is turning gray waiting for you," Emelie prodded.

"And we were so tired from sleeping in the rain and mud," Cormac chimed in. "But we thought we rinsed all the mud off."

"But did you?" Emelie pressed as she watched her sons, three with her white-blond hair, and three with Dominic's darker locks.

"Mama, we realized we hadnae. That's why we tried to clean it up," Fergus asserted.

"And you just happened to use my absolute best linens to wipe the mud from your boots and what you trailed through the buttery. And why did you need to stop there?"

"It was so cold, Mama. We thought to have a little ale to warm up," Charles reasoned.

"And I can guess whose idea that was." Emelie swung her accusatory glare at her husband. "At least you've stopped giving them whisky."

"The whisky puts hair on their chests," Dominic guffawed. But at Emelie's pointed look, he pressed his hands against his own chest, as if to cover the smooth skin beneath his leine.

"So my best linens," Emelie said bringing them back around. "How did you end up with them?"

"That was me," Nic admitted. "We didna want to leave a mess, so I told them I would fetch drying linens to clean up after ourselves. But like Stephen said, it was dark."

"And which of your cousins went with you as you foraged for linens?" Emelie demanded. Six heads turned back to Laurel and Brodie's sons, Rick, Monty, Aidan, Craig, and Donnan. The cousins shuffled forward toward their irritated aunt, but collectively they spun on their heels and bolted across the lists when they heard Laurel calling. "You're lucky I'm the nice one."

"Some days," Stephen muttered.

"Och, not today," Emelie snapped. "Since it's taken me a score of years to make the linens you *accidentally* ruined, you shall set things to rights. It's a good thing you've all learned to sew wounds. You shall put those skills to use. Come with me."

"Mama," six voices protested.

"Dinna Mama me," Emelie snapped. After a score and five years of marriage and living in the Highlands, a burr slid into Emelie's tone when she was most exasperated. She found there was no better way to get her point across. "You were drunk off your arses. Nic, you've known where the daily linens are kept since you were a wean. Even sloshed, you had to have known you were in the wrong cupboard. Now be glad it's only linens you'll be replacing. Your cousins were the ones that got into the food for tonight's feast. Who do you think will be helping in the kitchens? At least you can practice your stitching in private. Your cousins will be up to their elbows in flour with every bonnie lass laughing at them. Now scoot!"

Six chagrined men bent over to kiss Emelie's cheek as they trudged past. She and Dominic watched the youths ranging in age from six-and-ten to five-and-twenty elbow one another and bicker as they headed into the keep, stopping first by the barracks to wash mud from their arms and legs. When they reached the keep's doors, Nic gave orders to the others, and soon they all stripped off their muddy boots and stockings, entering the castle barefoot.

"Don't think you're off the hook, wolf," Emelie said as she turned toward Dominic.

"I wouldnae dream of it, sparrow." Dominic lifted Emelie to eye level, just as he had nearly every day of their marriage, his arms resting beneath her backside. He pressed a kiss to her lips that rivaled even the most passionate they'd shared when they were falling in love. Over two decades of marriage hadn't dimmed the fire between them. "Shall this wolf take ye back to his den?"

"Aye. There's a pile of mending waiting for you," Emelie teased.

"I'll put something to rights, Em, but it willna be yer sheets." Dominic nuzzled behind her ear.

"Those were my very best linens your sons used," Emelie scolded.

"Ma sons? They're only mine when they've done something wrong. The rest of the time they're yer wee perfect angels," Dominic grumbled before tickling Emelie's ribs. "This wolf shall make a meal of his sparrow."

Emelie wiggled out of Dominic arms until he put her on the ground. She reached around and pinched his backside before lifting her skirts above her ankles and dashing back to the keep. She knew she wouldn't get there first, but they both enjoyed the chase. Dominic scooped her around the waist and swung her over his shoulder as her peals of laughter filled the bailey. The clan had long since given up on Emelie and Dominic, and Laurel and Brodie, knowing the two irrepressible couples were still as deeply in love and deeply in lust as they were when they each arrived at Kilchurn.

Dominic bounded up the stairs and opened their chamber door. The battered portal creaked on its hinges, having suffered Dominic's impatience each time Emelie went into labor. It wasn't long before they lay together, tangled in the bedcovers, their arms and legs entwined. The wolf and the sparrow. An unlikely pair, but a couple that couldn't be more in love. A love that grew with each changing season, each challenge, and each joy. Unbridled passion burned between them, just as it had the first time they kissed in the alcove in Stirling Castle, and just as it had the first time they made love in the bed they still shared.

"I'm a lucky mon to be married to ma best

friend, sparrow," Dominic whispered as they rested together, sated after making love.

"I didn't know men and women could even be friends before I met you. Now I can't imagine ever being closer to someone than I am with you."

"I love you," Emelie and Dominic said in unison. Laughing, they tried again. "Nearly as much I love you."

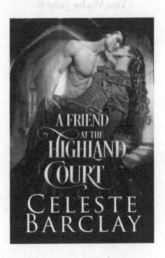

Preorder Now for July 6

Alexander Armstrong, heir to the Clan Armstrong lairdship, took for granted his strength and size until that strength was taken from him. Injured during a skirmish with another Lowland clan, Alex finds himself struggling to wield his sword. His once handsome face is now marred by a vicious scar. Forced to attend court as his father's representative, Alex's anger and bitterness threaten to chase away the one woman who's loved him most of her life.

Lady Caitlyn Kennedy usually finds the bright side of everything. Friends with Alex since childhood, when he fostered with her clan, Caitlyn attempts to lure Alex back from the brink of self-destruction. But their once budding romance seems destined to fail. Alex recognizes he's losing the woman he's loved since he was a boy by pushing away the one person who can heal his unseen wounds.

Can these friends-turned-enemies turn into lovers?

Preorder Now And Have It Waiting For You When You Wake July 6

THANK YOU FOR READING A HARLOT AT THE HIGHLAND COURT

Celeste Barclay, a nom de plume, lives near the Southern California coast with her husband and sons. Growing up in the Midwest, Celeste enjoyed spending as much time in and on the water as she could. Now she lives near the beach. She's an avid swimmer, a hopeful future surfer, and a former rower. When she's not writing, she's being a wife and mom.

Subscribe to Celeste's bimonthly newsletter to receive exclusive insider perks.
Subscribe Now
Have you chatted with Celeste's hunky heroes? Are you new to Celeste's books or want insider exclusives before anyone else? Subscribe for free to chat with the men of Celeste's *The Highland Ladies* series.
Chat Now

www.celestebarclay.com

Join the fun and get exclusive insider giveaways, sneak peeks, and new release announcements in <u>Celeste Barclay's Facebook Ladies of Yore Group</u>

THE HIGHLAND LADIES

A Spinster at the Highland Court

BOOK 1 SNEAK PEEK

Elizabeth Fraser looked around the royal chapel within Stirling Castle. The ornate candlestick holders on the altar glistened and reflected the light from the ones in the wall sconces as the priest intoned the holy prayers of the Advent season. Elizabeth kept her head bowed as though in prayer, but her green eyes swept the congregation. She watched the other ladies-in-waiting, many of whom were doing the same thing. She caught the eye of Allyson Elliott. Elizabeth raised one eyebrow as Allyson's lips twitched. Both women had been there enough times to accept they'd be kneeling for at least the next hour as the Latin service carried on. Elizabeth understood the Mass thanks to her cousin Deirdre Fraser, or rather now Deirdre Sinclair. Elizabeth's mind flashed to the recent struggle her cousin faced as she reunited with her husband Magnus after a seven-year separation. Her aunt and uncle's choice to keep Deirdre hidden from her husband simply because they didn't think the Sinclairs were an advantageous enough match, and the resulting scandal, still humiliated the other Fraser clan members at court. She admired Deirdre's husband Magnus's pledge to remain faithful despite not knowing if he'd ever see Deirdre again.

Elizabeth suddenly snapped her attention; while everyone else intoned the twelfth—or was it thirteenth—amen of the Mass, the hairs on the back of her neck stood up. She had the strongest feeling that someone was watching her. Her eyes scanned to her right, where her parents sat further down the pew. Her mother and father had their heads bowed and eyes closed. While she was convinced her mother was in devout prayer, she wondered if her father had fallen asleep during the Mass. Again. With nothing seeming out of the ordinary and no one visibly paying attention to her, her eyes swung to the left. She took in the king and queen as they kneeled together at their prie-dieu. The queen's lips moved as she recited the liturgy in silence. The king was as still as a statue. Years of leading warriors showed, both in his stature and his ability to control his body into absolute stillness. Elizabeth peered past the royal couple and found herself looking into the astute hazel eyes of Edward Bruce, Lord of Badenoch and Lochaber. His gaze gave her the sense that he peered into her thoughts, as though he were assessing her. She tried to keep her face neutral as heat surged up her neck. She prayed her face didn't redden as much as her neck must have, but at a twenty-one, she still hadn't mastered how to control her blushing. Her nape burned like it was on fire. She canted her head slightly before looking up at the crucifix hanging over the altar. She closed her eyes and tried to invoke the image of the Lord that usually centered her when her mind wandered during Mass.

Elizabeth sensed Edward's gaze remained on her. She didn't understand how she was so sure that he was looking at her. She didn't have any special gifts of perception or sight, but her intuition screamed that he was still looking.

THE CLAN SINCLAIR

His Highland Lass **BOOK 1 SNEAK PEEK**

She entered the great hall like a strong spring storm in the northern most Highlands. Tristan Mackay felt like he had been blown hither and yon. As the storm settled, she left him with the sweet scents of heather and lavender wafting towards him as she approached. She was not a classic beauty, tall and willowy like the women at court. Her face and form were not what legends were made of. But she held a unique appeal unlike any he had seen before. He could not take his eyes off of her long chestnut hair that had strands of fire and burnt copper running through them. Unlike the waves or curls he was used to, her hair was unusually straight and fine. It looked like a waterfall cascading down her back. While she was not tall, neither was she short. She had a figure that was meant for a man to grasp and hold onto, whether from the front or from behind. She had an aura of confidence and charm, but not arrogance or conceit like many good looking women he had met. She did not seem to know her own appeal. He could tell that she was many things, but one thing she was not was his.

His Bonnie Highland Temptation **BOOK 2**
His Highland Prize **BOOK 3**
His Highland Pledge **BOOK 4**
His Highland Surprise **BOOK 5**
Their Highland Beginning **BOOK 6**

PIRATES OF THE ISLES

The Blond Devil of the Sea **BOOK 1 SNEAK PEEK**

Caragh lifted her torch into the air as she made her way down the precarious Cornish cliffside. She made out the hulking shape of a ship, but the dead of night made it impossible to see who was there. She and the fishermen of Bedruthan Steps weren't expecting any shipments that night. But her younger brother Eddie, who stood watch at the entrance to their hiding place, had spotted the ship and signaled up to the village watchman, who alerted Caragh.

As her boot slid along the dirt and sand, she cursed having to carry the torch and wished she could have sunlight to guide her. She knew these cliffs well, and it was for that reason it was better that she moved slowly than stop moving once and for all. Caragh feared the light from her torch would carry out to the boat. Despite her efforts to keep the flame small, the solitary light would be a beacon.

When Caragh came to the final twist in the path before the sand, she snuffed out her torch and started to run to the cave where the main source of the village's income lay in hiding. She heard movement along the trail above her head and knew the local fishermen would soon join her on the beach. These men, both young and old, were strong from days spent pulling in the full trawling nets and hoisting the larger catches onto their boats. However, these men weren't well-trained swordsmen, and the fear of pirate raids was ever-present. Caragh feared that was who the villagers would face that night.

The Dark Heart of the Sea **BOOK 2**

The Red Drifter of the Sea **BOOK3**

The Scarlet Blade of the Sea **BOOK 4**

Leif **BOOK 1 SNEAK PEEK**

Leif looked around his chambers within his father's longhouse and breathed a sigh of relief. He noticed the large fur rugs spread throughout the chamber. His two favorites placed strategically before the fire and the bedside he preferred. He looked at his shield that hung on the wall near the door in a symbolic position but waiting at the ready. The chests that held his clothes and some of his finer acquisitions from voyages near and far sat beside his bed and along the far wall. And in the center was his most favorite possession. His oversized bed was one of the few that could accommodate his long and broad frame. He shook his head at his longing to climb under the pile of furs and on the stuffed mattress that beckoned him. He took in the chair placed before the fire where he longed to sit now with a cup of warm mead. It had been two months since he slept in his own bed, and he looked forward to nothing more than pulling the furs over his head and sleeping until he could no longer ignore his hunger. Alas, he would not be crawling into his bed again for several more hours. A feast awaited him to celebrate his and his crew's return from their latest expedition to explore the isle of Britannia. He bathed and wore fresh clothes, so he had no excuse for lingering other than a bone weariness that set in during the last storm at sea. He was eager to spend time at home no matter how much he loved sailing. Their last expedition had been profitable with several raids of monasteries that yielded jewels and both silver and gold, but he was ready for respite.

Leif left his chambers and knocked on the door next to his. He heard movement on the other side, but it was only moments before his sister, Freya, opened her door.

"That armband suits you well. It compliments your

muscles," Leif smirked and dodged a strike from one of those muscular arms.

"At least one of us inherited our father's prowess. Such a shame it wasn't you."